CHRISTMAS WISHES

Sue Moorcroft writes contemporary fiction of life and love. *A Summer to Remember* won the Goldsboro Books Contemporary Romantic Novel Award. *The Little Village Christmas* and *A Christmas Gift* were *Sunday Times* bestsellers and *The Christmas Promise* went to #1 in the Kindle chart. She also writes short stories, serials, articles, columns, courses and writing 'how to'.

An army child, Sue was born in Germany then lived in Cyprus, Malta and the UK and still loves to travel. Her other loves include writing (the best job in the world), reading, watching Formula 1 on TV and hanging out with friends, dancing, yoga, wine and chocolate.

If you're interested in being part of #TeamSueMoorcroft you can find more information at www.suemoorcroft.com/street-team. If you prefer to sign up to receive news of Sue and her books, go to www.suemoorcroft.com and click on 'Newsletter'. You can follow @SueMoorcroft on Twitter, @SueMoorcroftAuthor on Instagram, or Facebook.com/sue.moorcroft.3 and Facebook.com/SueMoorcroftAuthor.

By the same author:

The Christmas Promise
Just For the Holidays
The Little Village Christmas
One Summer in Italy
A Christmas Gift
A Summer to Remember
Let it Snow
Summer on a Sunny Island

Christmas Wishes

Sue Moorcroft

Published by AVON
A division of HarperCollins*Publishers* Ltd
1 London Bridge Street
London SE1 9GF

www.harpercollins.co.uk

A Paperback Original 2020
2

First published in Great Britain by
HarperCollins*Publishers* 2020

Copyright © Sue Moorcroft 2020
Emojis © Shutterstock

Sue Moorcroft asserts the moral right to
be identified as the author of this work.

A catalogue copy of this book is
available from the British Library.

ISBN: 978-0-00-839299-4

This novel is entirely a work of fiction.
The names, characters and incidents portrayed in it are
the work of the author's imagination. Any resemblance to
actual persons, living or dead, events or localities is
entirely coincidental.

Typeset in Sabon LT Std by Palimpsest Book Production Limited,
Falkirk, Stirlingshire

Printed and bound in UK by CPI Group (UK) Ltd, Croydon CR0 4YY

All rights reserved. No part of this publication may be
reproduced, stored in a retrieval system, or transmitted,
in any form or by any means, electronic, mechanical,
photocopying, recording or otherwise, without the prior
permission of the publishers.

MIX
Paper from
responsible sources

FSC
www.fsc.org

FSC® C007454

This book is produced from independently certified FSC™ paper
to ensure responsible forest management.

For more information visit: www.harpercollins.co.uk/green

Acknowledgements

When I pondered settings for this wintry book my friend Pia Fenton, who is also author Christina Courtenay, suggested that one of them be Sweden. As well as masterminding the research trip she was my tour guide, historian, translator and host. Thank you *so* much, Pia! She lined up her friends and relatives to help and the only thing I had to do was organise a hotel in Stockholm for three days. I booked the wrong one.

I'm also enormously grateful to:

Pia's mother, Birgitta Tapper, who hosted me in her lovely home in Småland, provided delicious Swedish food and taught me about ice hockey. She took us to see Swedish Hockey League team HV71 play in Jönköping, a wonderful evening that left me in awe of the lightning-quick, skilful sport and its players.

Lars and Chicki Jonsson provided delicious fika (coffee and cake break) while they talked about teenage ice hockey. They, Pia and Gunbritt Lager shared their memories of growing up in Sweden.

Anthony Tapper and Malikah Semakula welcomed me

into their apartment in Östermalm and generously answered a hundred questions about Östermalm Man and Stockholm life.

Carol Dahlén-Fräjdin, Victor, Lisa and Johan Fräjdin gave me a delicious lunch and kindly illuminated the Swedish education system in interesting and relatable detail.

Nat and Eugene Powell offered entertaining and valuable insight into moving to Sweden and learning Swedish.

Anna Rambëck gave us a lovely evening chatting about Stockholm in the Ice Bar and then over Swedish meatballs.

Back in the UK, my niece Véronique Moorcroft, who you might know under her pen names of Ella Allbright and Nikki Moore, provided essential HR information and advice.

Nurses David and Julia Roberts shared their knowledge of the recovery timeline of an elderly lady with a broken arm.

Anne Dicks helped me with rural retail outlets and their signage.

Andrea Crellin never seems to mind me turning an evening out into a research trip and answered questions on primary schools in England.

Helen Cook responded to my Facebook plea for insight into fostering and social workers. Facebook and Twitter friends were also helpful on the likes and dislikes of eight-year-old girls, VW camper vans and campsites at Christmas.

As with all my recent books, my brother Trevor Moorcroft undertook significant amounts of early research on most subjects that arise in *Christmas Wishes*. He also heroically reread all my Middledip books to create spreadsheets of characters and places and in which novels they appear. We call these The Middledip Bibles. (If you'd like to know more about Middledip, go to www.suemoorcroft. com>Writing>Middledip Books and Map.)

Mark West was a first reader of *Christmas Wishes* and made helpful suggestions in his ever-entertaining style. My thanks to him and also to the other members of Team Sue Moorcroft, not only for their fabulous support but for suggesting character and place names.

Rosemarie Jarvis told me an anecdote that sparked off *Christmas Wishes*.

The Peterborough Pirates were a real ice hockey team. I hope they'll forgive me for giving them a fictitious coach and an equally fictitious junior team.

In the run-up to publication of *Christmas Wishes* my publisher Avon (HarperCollins) was awarded Imprint of the Year at the British Book Awards and I won the Goldsboro Books Contemporary Romantic Novel Award. A winning team! Every day I appreciate what we achieve together.

Without the expertise and support of my wonderful agent Juliet Pickering and all at Blake Friedmann Literary Agency my career would not and could not be what it is. They are awesome.

Most of all thank *you*. Thank you for reading my books, posting lovely reviews, sending nice messages on social media and turning up at events. Being an author is the best job ever.

To my brother
Trevor Moorcroft
for creating The Middledip Bibles
and undertaking much of my research.

Chapter One

'How is Rob's stupid sister?' The voice was deep with the slightest Swedish accent.

Hannah, who'd been gazing at towering boxes of new stock, swung around to see a tall, angular man standing in the middle of her shop, Hannah Anna Butik. His black coat was speckled white from the sleety afternoon that was Stockholm in wintry October, hood tossed back, dark blond hair messy and his eyes denim blue.

She stared. 'Nico?' Then he smiled and doubt fled. 'Nico Pettersson!' Their teen years in Cambridgeshire might be nearly two decades ago but that lopsided smile and his amusement at her and Rob referring to each other affectionately as 'bonkers brother' and 'stupid sister' hadn't changed. Unsure whether to offer him a handshake or a hug, she settled for a beaming smile. 'Wow, this is a nice surprise. Fancy you walking in!'

Safe from the steely chill outdoors, Nico unbuttoned his coat and pulled off his scarf. 'You're the only girl I've known called Hannah Anna. What's the English term for those words?'

'Palindrome.' She rolled her eyes. 'Wacky Mum – and Dad indulging her. I was used as an example in English lessons but at least it's cute and memorable. Hannah Anna Goodbody. Who can forget it?'

He grinned. 'I remember your family well. They were great to me.'

'You were Rob's best mate,' she said. How exotic the boy from Sweden had been, hanging out with her older brother and the Middledip village kids. Educated at an international school, Nico's English had been good even when he'd arrived at fourteen. His dad, Lars Pettersson, had come to coach the Peterborough Pirates ice hockey team and for four years Nico had been the shining light of the Peterborough Plunderers, the junior team of which Rob was already a member. Then an athletic scholarship at Minnesota State University had called Nico to America. Hannah, who skated well enough to help out with children's lessons, had missed seeing him fly around the rink, skates shaving the ice into glistening plumes as he checked, whirled and turned with unconscious grace. Four years his junior, she'd been old enough to wonder whether she was developing a crush on him just when he'd vanished from her life. She'd known he'd later left the US a year early and returned to Sweden to complete his degree. Then he and Rob had lost touch.

Now his gaze roved around the shelves and racks packed with colourful scarves, glossy belts and chic leather bags for the quality gift market. 'Get you, rocking a luxury accessories shop in the Old Town. I'm impressed.'

'Personal luxury goods go down well here so I'm doing OK,' she answered. It was barely OK, but with Christmas trading around the corner she was optimistic. Her boyfriend Albin, a fund manager, was doing much more than OK so it was his name on the lease. It had saved messing around with guarantors, especially as she wasn't a Swedish national, but lately she'd wondered if she should have found another way. Their relationship was so weird now. It was as if someone had switched the fun and affection off. Alarmed and confused, she kept trying to talk but Albin pleaded work hassles and put her off. Though she was thirty and he was only thirty-two he'd developed a habit of talking down to her about his job being 'high octane' and stressful. It made her reluctant to pursue the issue but the worry bee buzzed constantly in her bonnet.

Nico's blue eyes smiled. 'Strange you should end up in my homeland. *Så du talar svenska nu?*'

She laughed and answered his question as to whether she spoke Swedish, '*Ja, jag klarar mig.*' *Yes, I manage.* 'I came to work for IKEA originally but I'd had a shop in England and I soon went back to wanting my own name above the door.' But though her words were light, she was absorbing an unpleasant fact.

Nico was not the golden boy she remembered.

He was so gaunt his cheekbones almost broke through his skin and stubble carpeted a fleshless jaw. His battered sweatshirt bore a stain like a map of a country and his jeans were grubby. The workman's boots on his feet could have been dragged from a skip, his fingernails were black and his hair long grown out from any style.

What had happened to the shining teen who'd drawn everyone to his exotic light? Boys had wanted to be him and females had followed his tall, lean athlete's body as if attached by rope.

'What are you doing these days?' she asked. Then, realising that if he'd fallen on hard times he might not want to answer such a direct question, hastily interrupted

3

herself. 'Do you have plans? I'll be putting out new stock this evening so I'm closing now to grab a burger first. Why don't you join me so we can catch up?' She bustled past to switch the sign on the door from 'open' to 'closed' – *öppet* to *stängt*. He smelled of soil and vegetation and she recoiled, not from him but from the horrible thought that he might be sleeping rough. That would be awful in this sleet. She shivered. This would be her third Swedish winter and in Albin's apartment on the desirable thoroughfare of Nybrogatan she'd accumulated a closet full of coats, hats, scarves, walking boots, snow boots and a stack of thermal base layers.

What were Nico's winter resources?

Feeling as if her smile was becoming forced, she strode back behind the counter. 'I can tell you how Rob's getting on and . . . stuff.' She tailed off. If Nico was struggling to get by in Stockholm it might not be tactful to tell him how super-happily Rob was living in Cambridgeshire with gorgeous fiancée Leesa. Still, getting a meal inside him felt important and a fast-food eat-and-run between old friends would be more natural than taking him to the swanky apartment in Östermalm owned by Albin's mother's company as a tax efficiency.

'I'm not exactly tidy,' he pointed out, frowning down at denim that was ripped and not in a trendy way. He refastened his coat as if becoming freshly conscious of his appearance.

Hannah hated to think of him vanishing hungry and hollow-faced into the glacial early evening darkness. 'Aw, c'mon.' She dimmed the lights to closed-for-business levels then tucked her arm through his. 'I hate eating alone. All I do is check Instagram or answer emails. It'll be lovely to chat.'

After a moment when she thought he'd refuse, he muttered, 'All right,' and let her pull him out of the shop to hunch into his coat, hands jammed in pockets, while she locked up.

The sleet stung Hannah's face, though she knew the late October chill was nothing compared to the snow and ice the coming winter would bring. She pulled up her hood as she set off along Köpmangatan before Nico could change his mind, chattering as they crossed Stortorget, the cobbled square where the Christmas market would soon set up. The tall, ornate buildings painted sage, apricot and ochre reminded her of the pictures on the old Quality Street tin her grandmother kept in her kitchen. Or maybe a row of pepperpots with their swooping, curling rooflines.

She said, 'I'm building up business at this shop. My assistant Julia's off this weekend but she speaks German as well as Swedish and English so we have much of the tourist market covered. She was a find.' Albin had told her that – probably because he'd been the one to find her. Julia, pronounced Yule-ee-ah with emphasis on the Yule, was a beautiful, serene Swede, more patient than Albin when it came to correcting errors in Hannah's Swedish.

They made their way downhill through cobbled streets between tall, narrow buildings, illuminated shop windows displaying glowing amber jewellery, burnished copper, souvenir elks or '*tomte*', the pointy-hatted gnomes reputed to live beneath Swedish houses. Hannah talking and Nico listening, they passed gracious cafés and restaurants with blackboards offering '*fika*' – afternoon tea – and tempting meals, all places Hannah dismissed in view of Nico's expressed discomfort about his appearance.

A frosty breeze snapped at them as they turned onto Gamla Stan's main street, Västerlånggatan, still busy with shoppers and tourists bundled up in coats. When they reached Burger Town's red frontage. Hannah undid her coat as they stepped into its brightly lit interior of chattering people enjoying a fast-food fix. 'I'm having halloumi bites with fries, coffee and a brownie. What about you?'

Nico shuffled awkwardly and glanced at the illuminated menu above the counter. 'Just coffee.'

He looked so uneasy that Hannah's neck prickled. 'No food?' She added encouragingly, 'It's my treat.'

He looked at her as if she were speaking Martian. 'No food,' he agreed. Then, tautly, 'Thank you.'

'Right, OK.' She felt her cheeks heat. She was doing this all wrong. Nico obviously suspected that she was trying to do him a favour and his pride had kicked in. Damn. She wanted to help, not hurt. 'Why don't you grab a table while I queue?'

He nodded, then headed for a booth, pulling off his coat.

Hannah ordered far more food than she needed: a large meal, a side of Town Wings and two cinnamon buns. Gathering ketchup and mayo she joined Nico. Even scruffy and underfed he still garnered second glances, she noticed as she put down the tray of food. Two nearby women were obviously discussing him like schoolgirls.

She sat down, hoping she wasn't disappointing his admirers too much, dragged off her coat and started on the first wrapper. 'They made a mistake and gave me a large meal instead of medium. And the buns are two for the price of one so I thought I might as well get one for you. If you don't want it now you can take it with you.' Aware of rushing the fibs out she dipped a fry in ketchup and popped it into her mouth. It was hot and burned the back of her tongue, making her voice hoarse as she pushed the pack invitingly across the table. 'Want some? No point it going to waste.'

Slowly, Nico took a fry and ate it. Then he removed the lid from his coffee and sipped.

It was Hannah's turn to feel uncomfortable. When Nico had turned up at Hannah Anna Butik he'd appeared, apart from the skin-and-bones look, happy to see her. Now he was frowning and giving the food dirty looks, discouraging her from nudging him again to eat. She thought about asking after his family, particularly Lars, who she'd known quite well. But people in trouble often isolated themselves from loved ones.

Then, interrupting her thoughts, Nico slapped down his coffee, propped his folded arms on the table and leaned close, his voice low and rapid. 'I'm sure you mean well, Hannah, but trying to force-feed someone doesn't work. Rob's obviously told you my situation. I'm surprised and disappointed that he'd betray a confidence but I suppose he's got his head full of wedding plans.'

Hannah had to chew and swallow before she could answer. 'Your situation?' she asked evasively, before adding truthfully, 'I didn't know you'd been in touch with Rob.'

He sighed in the exaggerated manner of those who know they're dealing with prevarication and leaned closer still. The outdoorsy smell of him wasn't unpleasant. 'If you need it spelling out, yes, my marriage ending did trigger my eating disorder. But I'm fine. I'm a normal weight and functioning perfectly well.'

It was so far from what she'd expected that Hannah gaped, her voice squeaking. 'Eating disorder? I thought you might be homeless.' Then realising that she'd blurted her thoughts, stuttered, 'Well, m-maybe not homeless but—'

'Homeless?' He looked thunderstruck, his blue eyes ablaze. 'Why on earth would you think that?'

Hannah fidgeted with a halloumi bite. What should she say? *You look a half-starved mess?*

He shook the tension from his shoulders with an obvious effort. 'I'm not homeless. I'm a key account director for the London branch of a Swedish company, SLS. We're in sports memorabilia and promotions. Winter sports is our core business but we're gradually expanding our reach. I live in Islington in London with my daughter Josie, work in Holborn and travel to Sweden once or twice a month.'

Then he glanced down at himself and his expression lightened. He even laughed. 'Ah, the clothes! It's an SLS community initiative. We facilitate kids' activity days and because I had to be here for meetings on Friday and Monday I stayed the weekend and participated. Today we took a busload of children to Skytteholmsparken. I was with the eight- to ten-year-olds at the outdoor gym and woodland trails. I've been crawling under trees pretending to be a lion.' The angry grooves around his eyes relaxed into laughter lines.

'I *see*,' Hannah breathed, overdoing the sigh of relief. Though it was fantastic to know he wasn't sleeping in dumpsters, no way in the world was he a normal weight for a man of his height. She'd say at least twenty-five pounds under. Maybe thirty. Hannah didn't know much about eating disorders but she doubted she should jump in and tell him he looked gaunt. Instead, she tried to make sense of the rest of his speech. 'You've been speaking to Rob?'

He picked up his coffee and leaned back in the booth, lifting his voice over the chatter of the burger bar. 'I signed up for our old school's Facebook group and there he was. We've had a couple of long phone conversations too.'

'Oh. I haven't been on the Bettsbrough Comp group for months, with devoting so much energy to Hannah Anna Butik.' And wondering what on earth was happening with Albin. 'He didn't tell me.'

He let his gaze drop, picking at a white paper napkin. 'He thought it would be fun for me to surprise you. When I said I'd be in Stockholm, he said why not call in?'

Hannah's attention shifted. 'Call in? Skytteholmsparken's outside the city. It must be a half-hour drive from the shop.' She'd been a few times on summer Sundays with Albin and seen children swarming over the climbing frames and outdoor gym or splashing in the pool.

He shrugged. 'I guess Rob thought I wouldn't be too far away. He probably doesn't know Stockholm well.'

'He was once surprised to learn Stockholm's a cluster of islands,' she acknowledged slowly. 'Though he agreed there were a lot of bridges and water.' She eyed Nico who was flexing the plastic lid from his coffee and not meeting her gaze. 'So you didn't just call in because you saw a shop called Hannah Anna's and thought it must be something to do with me. Rob sent you.' She frowned. 'You might as well tell me why because I'll only call him to ask if you don't.'

Nico sighed, abandoning the lid and wiping his hands. He gave her a half-smile. 'He miiight have expressed a small worry that you're coming to his wedding on your own and wanted to know if you were OK.'

'So he sent you to *check up on me*?' Hannah's appetite for her fast-cooling meal vanished. 'I'm an independent woman and I'm fine on my own. They just want their top table balanced by me bringing a plus-one!' She used indignation to mask her reluctance to talk to Nico about Albin. Who would want to admit that the boyfriend she'd been living with for almost two years had snubbed the invitation, saying English weddings were unbearably twee and Middledip was the arse-end of nowhere? She'd snapped back that in that case she didn't want him there, looking down his nose at her friendly lot. Albin's comfortably off family had shipped him off to Sigtuna boarding school when he was a kid and considered 'close' interchangeable with 'overfamiliar'.

Not wanting Albin's hoity-toity attitude to hurt her wonderfully warm family in the exciting, loved-up run-up to Rob and Leesa's wedding she'd told them he couldn't get away from work. Now Nico had apparently been dispatched to evaluate her well-being. He hadn't mentioned Albin's existence so did that mean Rob hadn't told him, wanting an unbiased, fresh eye on Hannah?

Shrugging, Nico picked up his coffee, sat back and changed the subject, telling Hannah about his eight-year-old daughter Josie. 'She lives with me but she's with her mum Loren this weekend, using FaceTime on her tablet to catch me up on her doings. She's a little chatterbox.' His voice was soft and warm.

Hannah's heart suffered a pang at his obvious love for his daughter. 'I'm sure you make a lovely dad.' In return, she told him about her own baby – the shop. 'I'm gearing up for the gift-buying period. We haven't had Halloween yet so it's too early for festive decorations but I'm increasing my stock for the eager beavers who come into Stockholm on October weekends to start their Christmas shopping.'

'You don't mind giving up your Saturday evening to sorting stock?' Nico had finished his coffee but wasn't rushing to leave.

'I don't mind if long hours bring me success. I want to expand, maybe into larger premises or a more commercial spot in Västerlånggatan or Österlånggatan.' When she'd taken the shop the agent had insisted tourists loved wandering the narrow side streets like Köpmangatan. He hadn't yet been proved wrong but Hannah intended to ensure lots of Swedish kronor through her till in the bumper Christmas trading season and wasn't leaving it to chance. Even if Albin hadn't been elk shooting in Värmland this weekend she wouldn't have minded working this evening. Her shop made her happy and hunting made her feel ill. She continued, 'Tomorrow, I'll come in early to create new displays before I open at eleven for the Sunday shoppers. Gamla Stan—' she used the Swedish for 'Old Town' '—is open seven days a week.'

'Then I'd better let you get on with your work.' His eyes were very blue in the overhead lights as he reached for his coat. 'I'll walk you back to the shop.'

'I'll be fine thanks,' she answered, though touched by his thoughtfulness. Nico had always been one of those who opened doors for others.

He looked as if he might argue as they stepped back into a chilly Västerlånggatan where most of the shops were getting ready for seven o'clock closing but his phone began to ring. He pulled it out and smiled. 'It's Josie.'

Though sorry at the evening ending so abruptly, she smiled. 'I'll head back to the shop. Goodnight! Great to see you again.'

Then she slipped away as he took his call. She pulled up the hood of her parka against the sleet stinging her face like a swarm of tiny insects, hurrying along the clean cobbled streets in the golden glow of lamps on the corners of elegant, steeply roofed buildings painted cream and gold, catching glimpses of the soaring green German Church tower. As she crossed Stortorget she saw a team had moved in to string lights across from the peach-toned splendour of the stock exchange building that now housed the Swedish Academy and Nobel Museum and Library.

She wasn't the only one looking forward to Christmas!

Before long she was entering Köpmangatan, pausing between an art gallery and an antique shop to unlock the glass door of Hannah Anna Butik. She stepped inside, happy to spend the evening amongst the mixed smells of leather, silk and cardboard boxes.

In fact, for her, you could bottle the scent and sell it as perfume.

Chapter Two

On Sunday morning, Hannah stared at her new stock. The displays she was stripping hadn't been up to her usual standard. Maybe her creative energy had been dulled by boyfriend woes.

She was trying to think with the kind of breathtaking imagination of form and style that would compel people into the shop when Nico Pettersson tapped on the door. '*Hej, hej*,' she greeted him in surprise as she let him in, standing back so he could enter and close the door, making the '*stängt*' sign swing.

He looked a hundred per cent better today. His coat was brushed, his hair washed and combed, he'd shaved and his jeans and boots were clean. 'I could maybe double your takings,' he said without preamble, checking out the bags and belts ready for new displays.

She laughed. 'How? Doubling the prices? Magic wand?'

'Better. Magic visual merchandising power.' He winked, then gazed beyond her to the half-dismantled displays that looked as if a bear had blundered through them. 'You need visual appeal and style. Unanimity. Dynamic use of colour.'

Half-amused and half-annoyed, Hannah planted her hands on her hips. 'Sorry . . . does my shop look in need of a consultation?'

He ceased assessing the stands and sent her a rueful grin. 'I didn't mean to be presumptuous. I woke up and realised that, yesterday, though you didn't understand why I looked as if I lived in a cobweb and we hadn't met for eighteen years, you tried to help. To make up for being ungracious and defensive, I'd like to help you in return.' His piercing blue eyes looked as if they were silently urging her to accept.

It was impossible to look away. 'How?'

He returned his gaze to the interior. 'My first job was in a department store chain as an assistant account manager. My training took me through various departments and I worked with an outstanding merchandiser – what people call a window dresser. We saw each other for a while. She was stellar, like she was personally in charge of the rainbow. I used to go in on my days off to learn about texture and bold form from her and I was nearly tempted into a career change. Let me loose on your stock. People will be drawn in, I promise.'

Conscious of the jumble of scarves, handbags and belts, she protested, 'You're seeing it at its worst.' But she desperately wanted the shop's first Christmas to be a success and getting the place sorted before eleven was a big job. Even without Albin-issues on her mind she sometimes felt dissatisfied with the look of Hannah Anna Butik. She knew she could display stock well but was she ever magical? The kind of 'magical' that would open purses and wallets?

Nico nudged a box of wallets with his toe. 'If you don't

like it when I've finished, you can tell me what you want instead and I'll redo it. What are you leading with? Something with a good margin?'

'Åberg leather.' She dragged the Åberg box forward. 'They provide a display schematic—'

He took the goods, ignoring the schematic, then produced a palm-sized speaker from his coat pocket. 'I brought music.' He tapped his phone and an Imagine Dragons track leaped into the air. He hung up his coat and started pacing.

'What are you doing?' she asked.

'Looking at the space.'

Apparently surplus to requirements and feeling like a cat who'd had her fur stroked the wrong way, Hannah packed the pastels and delicate materials of summer into the stock room beside her office – where 'office' meant 'cramped room with a table and a corner for tea making'.

As she trekked back and forth, Nico stood at various points on the shop floor and stared hard, his head marking time as Imagine Dragons gave way to Yungblud. He frowned at the coils of belts and rivers of scarves then went outside and, regardless of the ice-edged wind whirling his hair into his eyes, stared at the window space.

Finally, he collected the display stands, racks and hooks in the centre of the shop. This left two shelves on each long wall, one interrupted by the window. He glanced at Hannah. 'Do you have a clean duster?' When she'd provided one, he methodically wiped down the shelves and displays. Hannah made coffee and Nico detached hooks from a counter stand and fixed them at precise intervals onto the wall shelving. Then he started placing handbags on the shelves.

'Placing' was an inadequate word. Each handbag was

wiped or brushed then positioned precisely on the diagonal. Starting with the largest and going smoothly down to the smallest he progressed through black, blues, greens, tans, browns, bronzes, reds, golds, yellows and lastly creams and whites. On the shorter shelving either side of the window he did something similar with clutches, evening bags and purses.

Scarves next, one per hook, each knotted in exactly the same way and dangling the same distance from the floor, the colour segue mirroring that of the handbags. The belts received a similar treatment on the shelves of purses.

The Åberg leather goods scored a stand to themselves near the door. Each bag, purse, belt, wallet, diary, notebook, organiser, pen case, blotter, wash bag, tech case, card case, flask and passport cover had arrived in this season's colours of burgundy and lime along with classic blacks and tans. He arranged them in tiers, stacks, fans and groups. Hannah hoped Åberg didn't send mystery shoppers to check whether she'd followed the schematic because Nico's arrangement was awesome.

Evidently it pleased him too because he paused to play air guitar along to the music – Fall Out Boy now. It was a quirky moment that made Hannah laugh. Nico grinned and turned to creating monochrome counter displays and a colour wheel of hats.

Lastly, he worked on the window, adjusting the lights, creating a swooping design of silk scarves and a contrastingly geometric design of bags. 'Halloween decorations?' he queried, sipping a second cup of coffee because he'd let the first one go cold.

'I haven't got them yet,' she confessed. 'Julia will be in tomorrow. It'll free me up to find something.'

He didn't look impressed. 'The Swedish like Halloween.

Get full value out of it before you dress the shop for Christmas.'

Suitably chastised, she watched him contrive flying bats from black silk scarves, suspending them from the ceiling with clear thread. 'I don't remember you being this creative.'

'Late developer.' His smile flashed and she realised how much he'd relaxed. It couldn't put flesh on his bones but it softened the hollows of his face.

While Hannah vacuumed the carpet and cleaned glass, Nico created artful cobwebs with parcel string that took on an ethereal shimmer under the window display lights.

He climbed out of the window, cast a last look at each stand and shelf, then turned to Hannah. 'OK?'

'I think the word "awesome" was invented for this,' she said frankly. She admired the meticulously positioned merchandise, the clever use of colours and hues, and shook her head. 'I can't thank you enough. My shop looks so high-end I can't believe it.' She glanced at her watch. 'And just in time to open.'

'I enjoyed myself,' he said quietly. He switched off the music, picked up the mini speaker and pulled on his coat. 'See you at Rob and Leesa's wedding.'

Though thrown by such sudden departure preparations, Hannah's attention was grabbed by his final words. 'You're going to the wedding?'

He opened the door, turning the sign to *öppet*. 'Rob's been kind enough to invite Josie and me. Sell well.' Then he was gone into the bright, freezing morning, his hair flowing like gold in the winter sun, leaving her still calling her thanks.

Customers began to trickle into the shop as soon as Nico left.

17

A couple told Hannah they'd never seen her shop before – she didn't tell them it had been there for ten months – and one telephoned friends to abandon Västerlånggatan for the hidden gem of Hannah Anna Butik. Between ringing up sales she hurried to replace sold items with others of sizes and colours to maintain Nico's magic.

She wished she'd taken his phone number so she could text: *Clever clogs! Things are flying off the shelves* before trade slowed to its more usual pace. But the tide of customers never dried up. Her takings didn't actually double, she saw when she finally took a reading from the till at the Sunday closing hour of five p.m., but this had been her best Sunday's trading since Hannah Anna Butik opened its doors. Sales were up sixty-six per cent on the Sunday before.

Sixty-six per cent!

Her heart soared. Whether from early Christmas shopping, a cruise liner disgorging shopping-hungry passengers or Nico's magical merchandising, sales were *up*. 'Keep this up and you'll be in Västerlånggatan in a year,' she told herself.

The shop bell pinged and she glanced up, formulating the Swedish to say she was sorry but she was about to close. Instead, she laughed. Framed in the doorway was Nico, orange pumpkins beneath each arm.

'Finishing touches,' he said, toeing the door closed. One pumpkin he placed carefully in the corner of the window display and the other atop the hat stand, all the time nodding along to her ravings about the astonishing day's trading. 'Yeah,' he said, as if he'd expected nothing less. 'Are you hungry?'

Hannah paused. Was this a trick question, bearing in mind what had happened the evening before?

18

'I know a nice little place,' he went on.

As he kept his gaze on the pumpkin, Hannah couldn't gauge whether her reaction was important or not. She glanced out at the now-dark afternoon and thought of the apartment, empty until Albin arrived home late tonight, no doubt to plummet into bed, exhausted. 'I could eat,' she answered lightly, beginning her closing-up routine. Nico, evidently feeling at home after a morning working at the shop, replenished a few shelf spaces she hadn't got to.

Then they fastened their coats and Nico led the way across the cobbles of Stortorget, which were just beginning to sparkle with frost, heading downhill, crossing Västerlånggatan, passing closed shops with heavy knits and wooden clogs in their windows, taking an alley so tiny they had to walk in single file to reach the broader street of Stora Nygatan. He stopped outside a dark green frontage, the glass lettered in gold with the restaurant's name: Hörnan – the Corner. Inside, stairs plunged steeply to a cellar bistro with a vaulted brick ceiling. Candles in bottles stood on red gingham cloths and the smell of coffee enveloped Hannah and Nico as they took a table by a panelled wall.

Hannah was curious. Nico had brought her to a restaurant. Yesterday, in Burger Town, he'd eaten one French fry.

Perhaps guessing her thoughts, once they were both seated he began to speak. 'You brought me up short yesterday with your reaction to my appearance. Scruffy clothes couldn't be enough alone to prompt your reaction so I presume I look thin to you?'

Although her heart put in a heavy beat at the challenge in his voice she didn't see lying would be a useful response. 'Thin's the right word,' she said gravely. 'In fact, too thin.'

His eyes flickered. Maybe he'd been hoping for another answer but he answered honestly. 'I weighed myself in the hotel gym. I'm ten kilos under the minimum healthy weight for my height.'

A quick mental conversion told Hannah ten kilos was about twenty-two pounds. 'Sounds about right,' she said cautiously.

His brows lowered. 'I've had a word with myself. My daughter needs me healthy so I'm going to pay more attention to my eating habits. And I'm going to try not to look as if I woke up in a ditch.' He lifted a hand, as if to stop Hannah commenting. 'To come clean, burger bars sometimes make me uncomfortable. That's the food I was discouraged from eating when I was playing hockey, so I craved it. I ate it. Then I . . . got rid of it. It was a difficult time, changing countries and school systems. Mum wouldn't come to the UK with Dad's job so my parents split up and my brother Mattias stayed in Sweden with Mum. I'd always spent more time with Dad because I played hockey but I missed them horribly. I guess I was eating to comfort myself then purging to control my weight.' Absently, he picked up a pale green menu. 'Last night, I attached the wrong reason to you wanting me to eat. Burgers and buns sent me back in my mind to those bad old days. I expect I was withdrawn.'

Mortification dried her throat. 'I'm sorry,' she began.

Nico's eyes flashed. 'Don't be! You made me see myself before I became downright unhealthy. I need to thank you.'

She waved this away. 'I don't remember your dad insisting Rob follow a particularly strict diet when he was playing hockey. He didn't eat loads of chips or ice cream but he'd have some.'

Lines formed on Nico's face. 'Dad was my dad but also my ice hockey coach. I wanted to please him twice over. He wasn't pushy or strict – that's not the Swedish way. But he got in the habit of holding me up as an example of athletic build and low body fat. When he discovered I was purging, he was horrified. We went to counselling together and I stopped. That my habit was relatively recent helped a lot.' He sighed. 'But then I compensated by cutting out entire food groups, like carbs and fats. I underate. After more counselling I learned that I wasn't gaining power by controlling my food because *it* was controlling *me*. I had to learn strategies and use tools to eat in a balanced way.'

'But it slips sometimes?' she guessed. She only had to look at him to know that.

He nodded, blond hair gleaming in the candlelight. 'Under stress I return to an unhealthy relationship with food. The last three years have been . . . hard. Ending a marriage is crappy and my ex, Loren, resisted.'

He flicked his hair from his eyes. 'My relationship with food's complex. When I come to a point where I can admit that it's become tricky again I make bargains with myself. The current one is I'll eat if I can eat healthily – like at this restaurant, where there are plenty of good choices. That way, the trigger goes away some.'

Hannah's cheeks and ears burned. 'I'm sorry I took you to Burger Town. I didn't even ask what you preferred to eat.'

He made an impatient gesture. 'My eating is my responsibility. I should be able to face the occasional burger without turning into a grouch but I'd had a bad day.' His eyes shadowed. 'I'd FaceTimed Josie earlier at her mum's. When I told her I'd be spending the day with other people's

21

children at Skytteholmsparken she began to sob that she missed me. I wanted to jump on a plane and go to her but I couldn't. People here were depending on me and it's Loren's weekend to have Josie and, although it's difficult sometimes, I have to let them have their own relationship. I got a bit unglued. When I'm upset . . .' He batted the air with his hand as if shoving something away. 'Anyway, I've talked to Josie since and she was cheerful.'

Hannah listened. Nico was tense but so controlled that it was hard to align him in her mind with the laughing, vivacious, hard-playing teenage star of the Peterborough Plunderers. She remembered how people used to stop to watch him, his grace and unthinking control as he swooped, raced, turned, reversed and traversed. Hannah had never attained anywhere near such mastery of the ice.

Yet all the time, under that vital, athletic persona, had lain a love-hate relationship with food.

A waiter in a green waistcoat arrived to take their order. Nico chose a plate, which included salmon, herring, prawns, eggs, cheese, butter and bread, along with a small glass of wine. Hannah chose roast beef with dill potatoes and a large glass of wine. She walked between Gamla Stan and Östermalm so didn't have to worry about drink-driving. She didn't run a car herself, although she could borrow Albin's Porsche whenever he wasn't using it. She rarely did, in case she scratched its sleek silver perfection.

'It sounds as if you have a wonderful relationship with Josie,' Hannah said, when the waiter had departed.

His face softened. 'She's cute, funny and a walking question mark. Blonde, blue-eyed, pretty.'

'A mini Nico?' Hannah joked. Their wine arrived and she paused to sip the rich red liquid.

The corners of his eyes crinkled. 'Hair and eyes, maybe. Her mother's pretty so maybe she got that from her.'

Hannah wondered whether to tell him that although he needed to fill out and should smile more, he, too, was eye-catching. She chose something safer. 'I'll bet Josie's into sports.'

'She's into unicorns and princesses,' he corrected drily. 'But that's fine. I'm not a pushy dad.'

'But she's a daddy's girl?' Hannah hazarded.

There was water on the table and he poured them each a glass. 'Maybe. We were both determined that she should stay with me when Loren and I split.' He hesitated. 'Josie now has a little sister, Maria, born after the split. Loren suffered severe postnatal depression after both her pregnancies. Josie feels secure with me. I can afford a nanny and my younger cousin Emelie is at uni in London so she lives with us and helps out too. Between us, we give Josie a good, loving home.'

'That's wonderful,' Hannah answered. 'Don't you have a new partner?' Then she flushed in case it sounded like she was making a play.

'No. Life's hard enough,' he joked. Then, sobering: 'Neither has Loren. I suppose that's partly why she hasn't completely accepted the divorce. Although . . .' He tailed off, fidgeting. He took a breath. 'I'm going to tell you because hiding things is a bad habit and not unassociated with eating problems. Loren got pregnant with Maria by another man while we were married. I couldn't take that. I admitted love was gone and the time had come to end things. I was full of doubts but I had to accept she was no longer the person I'd been crazy about. I had to make myself hurt her. The actual ending was difficult in a thousand ways. We had a child. Loren was accustomed to me

23

making her happy and wasn't convinced I couldn't . . . adapt. If I'd offered the option of continuing together and me accepting Maria as my own, she'd have taken it.'

Shock rippled through Hannah. 'That must have been tough,' she said sympathetically.

He slid lower in his chair as if the burden of the memories was weighing on him. 'She was drinking a lot so she probably didn't even mean it to happen. She wasn't sleeping with me so there was no question that Maria was mine.' Their food arrived courtesy of the waiter in the green waistcoat who whirled away with a genial, '*Varsågoda, hoppas det smakar!*' *Here you are. Hope it tastes good.* Nico thanked him but stared at his fish and seafood as if not seeing it.

Hannah picked up her cutlery. 'How has Josie coped?' Her first bite of beef smeared with fragrant dill sauce was perfection.

Just when she thought he wasn't going to eat he picked up a fork. 'Surprisingly well. It helps that Josie adores Maria, who's two. Whenever Josie comes home from Loren's she has new photos or videos of Maria to show me.' He pushed his food around and then took a small mouthful of salmon.

Hannah gave him time to eat some more before continuing the conversation. 'Do you mind?'

'Seeing photos of Maria? Of course not – she's my daughter's sister. None of the mess our relationship became was their fault, poor kids. Maria calls me "Mydad" because Josie says, "I'm going home with my dad now" and Maria thinks it's my name. Mydad. Kinda poignant because I'm not. Loren tried to get Maria to call me Nico but she soon reverted to Mydad. She's a little cutie.' He took a sip of wine, his strong throat moving. 'It was Josie's eighth

24

birthday last month and Maria was the first person on her party list. Loren came too. We're very civilised.' There was a trace of regret in the final sentence. Hannah suspected there was a lot going on under his controlled exterior.

He changed the subject. 'How do you like living in Sweden? I remember the hilarious results of trying to teach you and Rob Swedish when we were kids, yet here you are speaking it.' He rearranged his food again then ate a prawn.

'It's proved more useful than the French I used to sigh over,' she agreed lightly, surprised he retained such a clear memory of her. Somehow, her having easy recall of him was more understandable. Everyone had known Nico Pettersson, the athletic foreigner. Girls had befriended Hannah to get information about him because he'd been so tight with Rob. 'How's your dad?' she asked. 'Do you remember him telling people they could call him "Lasse" and them pronouncing it "Lassie"?'

He laughed. He'd eaten nearly half his meal now and was looking more comfortable. 'People named Lars are often called Lasse by friends. He was never sure whether being called "Lassie" made him a girl or a dog but encouraged people back to saying Lars.' He paused to sip wine. 'He's fine. He's living in Nässjö, in the Småland region in the south of Sweden, close to Lake Vättern. My brother Mattias lives in nearby Huskvarna with his girlfriend. Mum lives on the edges of Älgäng, a smaller town. Dad only coaches hockey at community level now – a retirement job. Mattias is an assistant curator at Husqvarna Museum. The Husqvarna factory has a varied history, producing anything from weapons to sewing machines, motorcycles and lawn mowers.'

'Do you see your family much?' She'd slowed her own eating, wary of laying down her cutlery in case he'd immediately do the same. The bistro was busy with people dining after the shops closed and before hitting a bar. Every time the door clanged at the top of the stairs a breath of cold air reminded them of winter lurking.

He nodded and looked down at his plate. To Hannah it appeared as if he were taking part in a silent argument with the food. He took another small forkful. 'I see Mum and Dad several times a year but I usually go to them rather than them coming to Stockholm on the train from Jönköping. Mattias a little less. I'll take Josie home for St Lucia's Day in December. She loves to make saffron buns and gingerbread – *saffransbullar* and *pepparkakor* – with my mum. She yearns to be Lucia and wear candles in her hair.'

Hannah had been in Sweden long enough to know about Lucia processions, the symbolic bringing of light into the short Swedish winter days by St Lucia of Syracuse. 'Maybe she could start as a handmaiden and work up?'

The lines of his face softened. 'The choosing of Lucia, the handmaidens and the star boys will have taken place months ago. It's a lovely time and we treat it like Christmas with our Swedish family. It's best for Josie to be in England for Christmas so she can see her mum too.' He moved the conversation back to Hannah. 'So you like being your own boss?'

'Definitely.' Finally finished, she laid down her knife and fork. 'This is my second venture. First time, I had a T-shirt printing business in a place called Creative Lanes down by the river in Bettsbrough. Do you remember The Embankment?'

He nodded. 'On the road out of Bettsbrough towards Middledip.'

'Creative Lanes is a group of off-high-street businesses. It was hard to make the T-shirt business pay – though I have the perfect surname and called it "Goodbodies" – so I took the job of assistant manager of the Lanes too. My then boyfriend, Luke, shared the unit, selling repurposed stuff like clocks made into paperweights and forks made into bracelets. When we split up he was obnoxious, trumping up complaints against me in my assistant manager role until I gave up the tenancy to him and joined IKEA for a complete change. It was so vast compared to Goodbodies. I learned a lot in sales, then customer support and customer relations. I came to Sweden with them. I had to learn Swedish but so many people speaking English helped.'

Nico had eaten most of his meal. He shoved the plate away as if showing it who was boss and Hannah bit back an impulse to compliment him on nearly clearing his plate. She went on, 'I love Stockholm but I hankered after my own business again.' She spread her hands. 'And here I am.'

Now his ordeal by food was over, he pushed his chair back so he could cross his long legs. 'Happy? I can tell Rob that, at least?'

'He knows I love Hannah Anna Butik,' she returned, once again keeping to herself the fact that her relationship with Albin was circling the drain. Rob would get big-brotherly with Albin and he deserved to enjoy the pre-wedding buzz without trying to fight her battles, even if she'd let him.

Nico nodded and signalled to the waiter so they could order coffee. 'How's your grandmother, Nan Heather? I remember how everyone in Middledip knew her.'

Hannah smiled at the thought of Nan, her small body

and huge smile, twinkling eyes magnified through her glasses beneath a curly cap of silver hair. The way her voice creaked. 'Because she fostered so many kids. The foster kids called her Aunt Heather originally but when Rob and I came along, calling her Nan, it segued somehow into Nan Heather.'

'She can't still be fostering?' Nico's eyes were half-shut as if he'd drunk a lot more than one modest glass of wine. It gave him a slightly dangerous air.

Hannah shook the thought away. Next she'd be developing a thing for him. Maybe it was just that he was raw, pulsing with life compared to Albin's glossy urbanity. 'She's just had her ninetieth birthday! Mum was born when Nan was thirty. Nan had been married since she was twenty and thought she wouldn't have any kids so had been fostering for years when Mum came along. Mum grew up with loads of kids around but not a sibling of her own.'

'Ninety!' Nico smiled. 'Good on her.' Their coffee arrived and his was strong and dark. The fragrance rose up around them.

'She lives alone and, apart from Dad doing her garden and Mum getting her a weekly food order, lives completely independently. Mum and Dad have recently retired. Dad's been doing up an old camper van – the proper old VW kind – for years and after the wedding they're setting off across Europe in it. I thought they'd wait for summer but they want the winter-wonderland experience in Switzerland and Austria. Nan says they should stay away for Christmas if they want because she'll find plenty to do in the village. She has a partner, Brett, though they don't live together. He's only eighty so he's a toy boy.'

'Won't you go to the UK for Christmas?' Nico's eyebrows rose.

'The shop's only shut on Christmas Eve and Christmas Day, like most Swedish shops. I can't expect Julia to cover for me so I can swan off and, anyway, it's Hannah Anna Butik's first festive season. I'll miss the Middledip festivities but being a business owner means sacrifices.' And Albin had said he wasn't going to England this Christmas anyway. Last year, he'd allowed himself to be persuaded but had sat on the fringe of every gathering and watched as if mystified. It had dimmed Hannah's enjoyment of the family fun.

She was wondering whether she and Albin would even be together this Christmas when Nico glanced at his watch and gave an exclamation. 'I'm afraid I'll have to wind this up. I promised Josie I'd FaceTime her before bed. With the time difference, I'll get back to my hotel room in time if I go now.' He gestured to the server for the bill and refused point-blank to let Hannah pay her share.

'But I owe you for helping me to a great day's trading,' she protested.

He waved her words away as he paid by card. 'It was my idea.' He pulled on his coat.

She followed suit. 'Well, thank you. I'll have to buy you a drink at the wedding.'

Politely, he gestured her ahead of him up the stairs. 'I'm looking forward to seeing your family again. Josie and I are staying at the hotel where the wedding's taking place.'

'Port Manor? We're staying there for the night of the wedding, too. It's extravagant when Middledip's two miles away but it's so comfortable to have your own room and not be hanging about for taxis in the early hours.' She felt a big smile take charge of her face at the thought of Rob's wedding bringing her family together. She loved Sweden but she loved going home, too.

He smiled as they stepped out into the dark evening. 'Sorry to rush.' He gave her a quick, friendly hug and set off at a jog, throwing 'See you soon,' back over his shoulder.

After watching him vanish around a corner, Hannah pulled a jaunty blue knitted hat from her coat pocket. She'd worn her hair up at work but she took the clasp out now and enjoyed the end-of-day feeling of her scalp relaxing before she crammed the hat on. Her breath clouded the frosty air and she headed out of Gamla Stan and over the bridge, the pavements looking as if they'd been sprinkled with diamond dust. Below, the black water reflected a million lights, as if the winter night stars had fallen in.

She set off briskly, the wind grabbing at her hair, hands and feet soon half-numb with the cold, past department stores and parks, black waterways and old buildings, to the broad thoroughfare that was Nybrogatan. At the five-storey honey-coloured apartment block near the metro station she keyed in the door code and, eschewing the lift with its metal concertina door, ran upstairs to the first floor and let herself in. Albin wasn't yet home, which was as she'd expected, and his lair of white leather and black granite felt emptily echoey. She wanted to introduce rich, vibrant fabrics to soften the monochrome minimalism but Albin refused to hear of it. It was his family's apartment so his preference prevailed. They'd actually argued about bathroom towels recently.

Hannah felt as if she was looking down the wrong end of a telescope at the whirlwind romance they'd once shared. In the past few months he'd become distant, even cold. No longer was he the Albin who'd been fascinated by her down-to-earth ordinariness, laughing at her jokes,

30

hungering for her body, sexting during the working day, and who had so wanted to make her happy that he'd made her business possible by signing the lease. She remembered the day; the way she'd thanked him and he'd whispered, 'It will keep you in Sweden.'

Rob had once asked her whether she'd fallen more for Albin's lifestyle than the man himself. She'd denied it hotly. She'd have found him attractive without the swanky apartment with use of the gorgeous courtyard where they ate in summer, the restaurant on every corner, the wherewithal to grocery shop at ICA Esplanaden. Hannah might be ambitious but that was about her own achievements. It wasn't about snaffling a wealthy man. Suits and haircuts were just suits and haircuts, even the expensive kind.

Now she was having to acknowledge that maybe Rob had seen something she'd been unable to see because the painful truth was that Albin had lost interest in her. She could parade around naked without distracting him from a text conversation. It smarted, but it was high time, in Hannah's opinion, to face the situation. And part of that was that she wasn't heartbroken. It had only been infatuation all along.

After kicking her boots into the hall cupboard she made steaming hot chocolate and went to luxuriate for half an hour in the main bathroom, which had a spa bath and the ruby red towels she'd hung in here in defiance of the apartment's colour scheme, making Albin snap, 'I'll only accept it because I prefer the en suite shower room so don't have to look at them.'

She closed her eyes while the hot water roiled about her body. It was like being pummelled by a boxer wearing soft fluffy gloves. She didn't envy Albin creeping through damp forests to destroy beautiful animals. At least he never insisted she join him on his blokey hunting trips.

Her mind wandered to Nico: first the scruffy, haggard Nico and then the cleaned-up, shaven version who'd paced her shop, observing it through narrowed eyes before changing everything. Her stock had looked so beautiful, so stylish. Mary Poppins would have been proud of the transformation.

Funny, but meeting a Swede in Sweden was making her think vividly of England, of Nico hanging out at their house in Middledip, smiling and good mannered enough to charm Hannah's parents and grandmother, treating Hannah as a special – if younger – friend, much to the envy of the older girls who hung around the rink.

When Hannah finally emerged from the swirling bath-water she slid into a robe and opened her laptop to FaceTime her parents, Mo and Jeremy Goodbody.

When Mo appeared on the screen she beamed all over her round, good-natured face, as delighted to hear from her as if Hannah hadn't contacted them for months. 'Can't wait for you to come home for the wedding, Han! Port Manor Hotel's doing Rob and Leesa proud. You'll be here for the rehearsal on Thursday evening won't you?'

'You know I will.' Hannah laughed. Wedding arrangements had been underway for more than a year. Leesa's dress was a secret from the groom. The shiny bridesmaids' outfits were hanging in bags in the home of Leesa's parents. Hannah's was a delicate colour of creamy peach. The gown of Jemima, Leesa's sister, was a shade darker as if to let everyone know she bore the exalted title of maid of honour. Mo had been prepared to battle on Hannah's behalf over the perceived implication that the sister of the bride was more important than the sister of the groom but Hannah had firmly restrained her. Maybe peachy-cream was more Jemima's colour than creamy-peach.

The other bridesmaids were Jemima's daughters Saffi and Raya and Leesa's best friend Amanda Louise Meller. Hannah knew little about her except she always insisted on being called the full 'Amanda Louise'. Leesa had whispered to Hannah that her friends called her 'Meller-drama' when she wasn't there to hear.

The bridesmaids' 'dresses' were actually jumpsuits, Hannah had been dismayed to discover. OK, it was dramatic and different but jumpsuits made going to the loo a pain. It had been Amanda Louise's idea. Maybe she had the bladder of a horse. She certainly drank because when they'd had the final fitting at the bridal shop she'd put away three glasses of champagne followed by a bottle of wine over lunch.

From Hannah's laptop screen, Jeremy's eyes twinkled beneath his receding fringe as he made his first contribution to the conversation. 'The camper van's ready! Can't wait to start our travels after the do. And did you know Rob's invited Nico Pettersson to the wedding? You remember him, don't you?'

Hannah nodded. 'I was about to say – he called at the shop this weekend because he's in Stockholm on business.' She described Nico revamping Hannah Anna Butik, rather than mentioning that Rob had sent Nico to check up on her. Mo's default setting was to worry about Hannah and it would fuel that if she realised Rob was worried too. Probably nobody in the family believed Albin couldn't make the wedding because of work but were pretending to accept it out of respect for Hannah's feelings . . . and they, and the aunts, uncles, cousins and old friends would enjoy it better without him. Hannah added,

'Apparently Nico and his daughter Josie are booked into Port Manor.'

'Rob didn't tell me Nico would stay at the hotel itself.' Mo sounded aggrieved at the oversight. 'Did he tell you, Jeremy?'

Hannah's dad shook his head. 'Don't think so.' Jeremy frequently made non-committal responses such as 'don't think so' or 'not that I remember' in the face of his spouse's forceful commentary on life. He was a dear, delightful dad and Mo holding so many opinions probably saved him the bother of forming his own.

'Nico's split up, hasn't he?' Mo demanded.

Although Hannah knew full well her mum meant Nico was divorced, the phrase made her visualise him in pieces. Metaphorically he had been, if his wife becoming pregnant by another man had triggered the eating problems that had winnowed the flesh from his cheeks and turned his neck and hands to cords and bones. 'I think it happened two or three years ago. His ex has another daughter,' she answered. Then she thought maybe Nico wouldn't appreciate being part of Mo's avid interest in the lives of others. 'I'll send you photos of what Nico did to the shop.' She paused to WhatsApp the pictures from her phone.

'Ooh, lovely,' Hannah's mum breathed when the colourful images popped up on her own phone moments later. 'Rob said Nico works in promo. I'd have expected him to be doing something to do with ice hockey. Some hockey players in America are millionaires.'

'I didn't even ask him about ice hockey.' And neither had he volunteered any information, Hannah realised, which was a far cry from when he'd lived and breathed the sport. She shrugged. 'I suppose making it as a pro player's mega competitive.' She changed the subject. 'Is

Nan OK? I rang her early in the week and I thought she was quiet.'

Mo gave a gusty sigh. 'She and Brett have fallen out. She says she "doesn't want to go into it" but she's obviously unhappy.'

'No!' Hannah breathed. 'I thought they were a fixture.' Hannah barely remembered her grandfather, who'd died when she was small.

'Something's changed,' Mo confirmed sadly. 'I thought he'd be here for her while we were away so it's bad news all round.'

They said goodnight a few minutes later and Hannah got ready for bed worrying about her indomitable little grandmother. She knew Nan wouldn't want her parents to miss their trip of a lifetime but couldn't somehow imagine her mum staying away for the weeks and months currently planned if Nan didn't have Brett's company and support.

By the time Albin finally arrived home it was past ten and she was more than half-asleep in their six-foot bed. He padded into the bedroom, flicked back his curtains of dark hair, kissed her temple and whispered, 'Don't wake up, I'm going to have a drink and unwind in front of the TV. I don't have to be in until eleven tomorrow.' She made a drowsy noise of agreement.

They'd developed a habit of creating a buffer zone after he'd been hunting because Hannah loathed it. She didn't see his contention that 'elk would take over the country if they weren't hunted' made bloodlust less distasteful or less alien to his otherwise citified, sophisticated lifestyle. As a result, he hadn't introduced her to a single one of his hunting buddies and kept his gun in a friend's gun safe.

But, with a sinking feeling, Hannah knew that wasn't the reason he didn't shower and get into bed with her.

She turned over and smothered a sigh. Their breathless, dizzy dance was over and their relationship was moving to the slowing rhythm of the last waltz.

Chapter Three

Back home in London on Tuesday morning, Nico ran eight kilometres on the treadmill in his bedroom then jumped into the shower, still breathing hard. He was tight for time and performed his hamstring stretches at the same time as soaping up.

Emelie, his younger cousin who lived with him while 'doing uni' would be getting Josie up and dressed. Nico would then enjoy breakfast with his daughter before Tilly, the nanny, arrived at seven-thirty and Nico zipped off to work. He loved Josie as fiercely as any parent had loved any child, ever, but he had to earn money. A Josie-centric mini-economy of home and household depended on it.

His new boss at SLS, Anders, had not so far shown himself to be overly sympathetic to Nico's situation as a lone parent. Or sympathetic to any staff member's needs outside devoting themselves to SLS.

He hadn't minded spending the two-hour flight home from Stockholm last night typing emails ready to send on landing, along with a text to Rob Goodbody. *Saw Hannah. Seems OK. Afraid she realised you'd sent me but no explosion ensued. Call me if you want to chat more.* Once home, he'd been too tired to do much more than fall into bed but now Hannah's clumsy but well-meaning attempt to feed him revolved in his head. After towelling off, he forced himself to stand naked before the bathroom mirror.

Shit. He *was* thin. Unhealthily so. He was saved from puniness by his exercise habit but his cheekbones jutted, his jawbone was a blade and he could count every rib. Angry with himself he shaved, dressed in a white shirt and charcoal trousers then went online and booked a haircut at Trimsters Male Grooming at two. He could use the lunch hour he didn't usually take.

He paused. Stared at his reflection again. He'd get his hair cut *and* eat. If he got stern with himself he could eat sensible food three times a day and he should do, for Josie's sake. He knew this. He knew about structuring his diet and pacing food intake, writing down what he ate so as not to kid himself about calories required for healthy weight. He needed to accept that Loren was not going to be an easy ex and find ways to live with life's stresses other than undereating.

Inside, he acknowledged that he'd called his parents lately, instead of FaceTiming. Yeah. He'd known he looked skinny and they'd freak.

He jogged downstairs and made himself a bowl of granola. Black coffee only breakfasts would now be out because they were a bad example to Josie. He sighed. No: they were out because he needed to be healthier. Then he heard Josie coming down the stairs, chattering to Emelie about it nearly being Halloween. He checked his phone calendar. October thirty-first was Saturday and *Trick or treating* was scheduled from six p.m. with two of her friends and their mums. The mums were dressing up too, apparently, but Nico planned to simply wear dark clothes and carry the haul of sweets the kids accrued. He was used to being in the background especially when, like in this situation, he was the lone male. The mums sometimes tried to include him in the conversation but he was always too conscious of them making an effort to find subjects he'd be interested in to feel comfortable with that. A couple had hit on him and he wasn't comfortable with that either. Imagine starting something with one of Josie's friends' mothers and then it ending and affecting Josie's friendships.

He didn't enjoy Halloween and taking kids door-to-door to ask for sweets. The Swedish *Allhelgonadagen*, All Saints Day, was more his thing, the opportunity to remember those who'd passed and the earthly feel of welcoming winter. Josie would have been aghast at missing out, however, and she hadn't settled at school this term so wanting to be with school friends should be viewed as a positive.

Just as he was wondering whether Josie minded that it was always he who was her supervising parent at Halloween and other red-letter days, she bounced into the room. 'Dad! Tilly's taking me to buy new face paints because I'm going to be a witch on Saturday.'

He smiled at her excitement, swung her up and kissed both her petal-soft cheeks. Emelie had brushed her fair hair into a ponytail and she was wearing a half-term outfit of pink fluffy jumper with jeans. 'That's exciting.' He hadn't actually taken a spoonful of his granola yet but he got up and made Josie's Weetabix with raisins, knowing exactly how much milk she liked.

Emelie joined him at the fridge, reaching for Josie's apple juice. 'I'll get that. You eat.' Emelie gesticulated towards his breakfast, which probably meant she'd noticed he wasn't eating properly too and wanted to capitalise on him actually having prepared food for himself. Her hair hung in a thick plait over one shoulder. She had a serene smile, a sunny nature and what Nico privately thought was a fairly undemanding lecture schedule, so living with them worked brilliantly. The exchange of accommodation for acting as a part-time au pair greatly reduced her student debt and enormously helped Nico's childcare problems.

Tilly wasn't a live-in nanny, though she did stay over in the fourth bedroom occasionally if Emelie couldn't cover Nico's trips to Sweden. In the last year she'd begun a side business as a gardener and now spent Josie's school hours mowing lawns and trimming hedges. He wondered if she earned more money from gardening because her attitude to nannying had certainly slipped. She'd become almost offhand sometimes, which was a shame because ensuring Josie had himself, Emelie or Tilly whenever she wasn't at school or at her mum's was a constant challenge for Nico, demanding adaptability and flexibility from all concerned, except Loren.

Loren wasn't one of life's copers. If he asked her to keep Josie even an extra couple of hours she'd respond with anxiety and maybe a hand clapped over her eyes in a 'I can't take any more!' gesture. She'd needed time off work with stress recently and sometimes went back on plans for a weekend with Josie, saying she wasn't feeling up to it. He worried 'not feeling up to it' translated to her old behaviour kicking in. She'd made a big effort with her drinking when pregnant with Maria – partly because she'd realised alcohol had led to the hook-up responsible and partly because she'd hoped Nico would relent and they could stay together. Loren's withdrawals troubled him but at least she seemed to look after Josie OK when she did have her. He kept in close touch to ensure it, though he worried that it was making both Josie and Loren cling to him.

He tried not to judge Loren's limitations. Stress had his body turning on itself by ruthlessly suppressing the desire to eat, after all. But, understanding as he tried to be, his ex-wife's issues left him with extra on his plate . . . figuratively speaking. He toyed with the analogy that the more he had on his plate emotionally the less he sat down to a plate of actual food. He couldn't immediately see a way to reduce what was on the emotional plate so it was up to him to increase portions on the real one.

He took up his spoon. 'Am I allowed to say you'll make a great witch?' he asked his daughter gravely. 'Or would that be rude?'

Josie clambered onto the chair next to his, giggles bursting from her like musical bubbles on the air. 'Witches are cool, Daddy. Tilly's going to buy me a long black cloak, too. And a little broomstick.'

He smiled to see her sparkling eyes. 'Fantastic. After trick or treating on Saturday I'm taking you to Mum's and she'll be able to see you as a witch too.'

'Am I staying overnight?' Josie frowned as if trying to remember.

'That's the plan,' he agreed. Loren owned a flat a ten-minute walk away. Maria's father played no part in Maria's life other than to pay minimal child support but Loren had inherited from her grandparents in time to buy a place for her and Maria. Just as well, as Nico was stretched enough meeting an Islington mortgage originally based on the earning power of two. The cost of a nanny, even if not full-time, was crippling, and the household bills were like boulders on his shoulders.

'Can I come home, instead?' Josie asked, tiny lines still puckering the space between her soft eyebrows.

Nico hesitated, trying to sense what was behind the question. Checking whether Nico wanted her around? Prodding boundaries? Did she not want to visit her mother? It wouldn't be the first time and while he hoped it came from a wish to be in two places at one time his radar always beeped in case there was more to it. 'Don't you want to go?' He made it a casual question, hoping for a genuine reaction.

'Yeah, if Maria will still be up,' Josie said, after a moment. Having tested the Weetabix had reached perfect sogginess, she scooped the first spoonful.

'I don't know Maria's bedtime.' Nico crunched granola, reflecting that Josie was a better example to him than he was to her, eating-wise.

She wrinkled her small brow. 'I think it depends on how Mummy's feeling. Maria always wants to share my room.'

'Do you like that?' Nico knew that Maria was a good sleeper and eater because, during civilised conversations as Nico picked Josie up or dropped her off, Loren would droop and sigh and murmur, 'It's a good job Maria's an easy child or I don't know what I'd do.'

He'd murmur, 'Yes, good job.' What was the point of observing acidly that her choices had put her in her current situation of bringing up Maria alone and being glad to let him have the major responsibility for Josie?

He was glad too. He'd have been miserable to only see Josie at weekends and for a holiday. Single parenthood was a hundred times better than that, even if holding down his demanding job and ensuring Josie was happy left him feeling as if his treadmill was set to its maximum and he could only just keep up.

'I don't have to go to school today, do I?' Josie said suddenly, through her Weetabix.

'No, it's half-term. Back on Monday.' Nico took another mouthful of granola, though he wanted to put down his spoon when he saw the apprehension that pinched Josie's face. Till this year, Josie had loved Barrack Road Primary School, a couple of streets away. Having lapped up pre-school work books she'd had a head start on reading and writing, had made friends readily and come home babbling about the games they played.

This year school meant anxiety and isolation.

Another school, St Kits, had been suffering falling rolls and then the ageing school building had developed problems at about the time the head teacher wanted to retire. A decision had been made to erect temporary buildings in the grounds of Barrack Road and amalgamate the two schools, meaning two classes to each year group. Josie, unfortunately, had been chosen to balance numbers in a class of mainly St Kits children who'd already formed their friendship groups and, transplanted, clung to them.

She didn't care for her new teacher, Mrs Calcashaw – also late of St Kits. Her objections were vague: Calcashaw was a funny name or Mrs Calcashaw's shoe had a crack in it. Josie yearned to be allocated to the other class, taught by Mrs Symonds.

Now she sighed. 'I suppose I have to go back next week, don't I?' Her eyes shone with tears.

Hardly able to bear even this tiny sadness, Nico wanted to scoop her up and declare that she didn't. He wouldn't go to work, he wouldn't travel on to Surrey for a meeting about a new ice rink and snow dome and how sports teams could be encouraged to make it their home turf. He'd stay at home with Josie and fend off any dragons trying to bring her grief.

But that wasn't pragmatic. 'Hey,' he murmured softly, rubbing a back that felt so small and vulnerable that he could distinguish every bump of her backbone. 'Tell me what's making you sad, sweetheart.'

Josie sniffed. 'Don't know.'

'You can tell me anything.' Nico reached out and picked her out of her chair. He should be heading for work but he wasn't leaving Josie like this. His twanging heartstrings would yank him back like elastic.

In slow motion, Josie's face crumpled. Her eyes scrunched shut and her mouth stretched wide as words tumbled out. 'Jessica doesn't want to be my friend any more. She says everyone in Mrs Calcashaw's class is dirty and stupid. She told Sadiq and Ira not to be my friends either. And I won't have anyone to play with at playtime after half-term,' she wailed.

'Oh, baby.' Nico rocked his slender daughter, his heart clenching in rhythm with her sobs, aware of Emelie giving a soft *ohhhhh* of sympathy. 'That's not a nice thing to happen, is it? But you know that Jessica, Sadiq and Ira aren't your only friends. Who's coming trick or treating on Saturday?'

Josie sniffed. 'Steph'nie and Martha. If Jessica doesn't stop them.' A shudder ran through her.

'I don't think she will and if Stephanie and Martha are your friends to go trick or treating with then they're your friends to play with at playtime too.' Nico decided to contact the school when it reopened to reiterate his concerns and wished kids came with a manual, giving parents a shot at doing and saying the right thing. 'Sometimes when children are difficult it's because they're upset about something quite different. It makes them cross and they say things they don't mean.'

Josie met this in silence. Nico didn't blame her. His words hadn't given her anything helpful and positive to go on. He cast about for something more constructive. 'I think Jessica, Sadiq, Ira, Stephanie and Martha are in Mrs Symonds's class, aren't they? Who do you like in Mrs Calcashaw's class?'

'No one.'

He debated whether to call her on such a sweeping statement but going through the names of every child he remembered and have her deny liking them or telling him loftily they were *all* in Mrs Symonds's class wouldn't help. He changed direction. 'Tell me what's your favourite thing to do at school and who you do it with.'

Josie released herself from his embrace and slid from his knee. 'Home time with you,' she sniffed, neatly converting his different approach into a blind alley. 'I'm going to the toilet.'

She trailed out of the kitchen, shoulders sagging. Nico stared after her. The negativity about school was worrying enough but why had she hit on him fetching her from school as her favourite thing? He rarely did it. Mid-afternoon, when school finished, he was usually in his company's offices in Holborn, visiting clients at their premises elsewhere in the country or in Stockholm for meetings.

He passed his hand over his face. If his life depended on it he couldn't face the rest of his bowl of granola. It felt as if eating it would betray his daughter, though that made no sense or logic. His little girl was unhappy and was getting unhappier.

Emelie blew out a breath, a frown on her young forehead. 'I took her to the indoor gym yesterday and Jessica was there. Josie was quiet last night and kept asking when you'd be home but I just thought she was missing you. I'll bet Jessica had been mean to her but Josie kept it to herself.'

'Yeah.' He flicked open his phone calendar. He didn't actually have a meeting until eleven. 'You get off to uni, Emelie. I'll stick around for a few minutes.' Quickly he texted his assistant, Katya.

Delayed by an issue with Josie. Will be in by 9.30 a.m. Please explain to anyone who needs to know. Thanks.

Katya was a star. She'd tell his team and recently arrived CEO Anders. He shoved his phone away, readied briefcase, jacket and coat then went upstairs to await Josie emerging from the bathroom so he could spend half an hour with her before battling the tube.

Emelie, who'd been bustling around downstairs, shouted, 'Goodbye!'

Then Tilly arrived and shouted, 'Hello!'

'Just spending a few minutes with Josie,' Nico called back.

Finally, Josie emerged, eyes pink. Nico eased her into his embrace and they sat on the landing listening to the sounds Tilly made in the kitchen.

'It was cold in Stockholm,' he said. 'It's only five weeks until we travel to Småland for Lucia.' St Lucia's Day was on the thirteenth of December . . . term time. Observing the abortive efforts of other parents to get term-time absences authorised Nico had simply decided to lie and say Josie had had a stomach bug. If she mentioned her trip at school and they challenged him, he'd admit the crime and pay the fine. It was probably a reprehensible attitude but it would get the job done. 'Farmor and Farfar can't wait to see you,' he added. They'd always used the Swedish for her Swedish grandmother and grandfather. 'And Mattias and Felicia.'

'Mm,' Josie answered unenthusiastically.

'And in a couple of weeks we're going to spend a weekend in a hotel, you and me, aren't we? We're going to a wedding.'

Josie perked up. 'Your friend Rob is marrying Leesa, isn't he? Will she have a dress like a princess?'

'We'll have to wait and see.' His tension slackened at her smile. 'I think you'll like Rob and Leesa. I used to know Rob's sister Hannah too and I met her in Stockholm at the weekend. She'll be at the wedding.' He had a sudden flash of schooldays at Bettsbrough Comp when bringing a girl's name into conversation was referred to as 'mentionitis' and was meant to mean you liked her.

'I'm going to have a new dress. We're going on Saturday to buy it, before trick or treating, aren't we?' Josie snuggled up to Nico on the mushroom-coloured carpet, relaxing as they talked of good things.

'That's right.' He kissed the top of her head. Would his heart get through his daughter's childhood in one piece?

He remained for another ten minutes, cuddling, chatting, comforting, until he could take Josie down to Tilly and belatedly hurry off to work.

At lunchtime, when he'd returned from getting his hair cut, he received a reply from Rob: *Thanks for checking on Hannah. Glad she's OK. See you at the wedding.*

Nico replied: *Sure.* Then he dived into meeting notes, eating a salad from the cafeteria.

His business week proved exhausting. Meeting chased meeting. A UK ice-hockey team client came to him with doom-and-gloom prophecies over a sponsor going bust. Two members of Nico's SLS team, Ellie and Jack, were found out in an affair and Ellie's husband worked for an SLS client. The husband screamed at Ellie and she turned up at work red-eyed. Jack stormed over to the client's premises in Borough and screamed back at the husband. It absorbed a lot of Nico and HR's time. After Josie went to bed each evening he caught up on emails, writing tenders or reading contracts and then fell into bed and struggled to switch off his brain.

Throughout it all, he ate conscientiously three times a day. Sometimes it wasn't as much as planned, but he ate. Emelie had checked out his haircut and given it the seal of approval with: ''Bout time,' and a thumbs up. He was meeting all his goals.

Now, Saturday, he refused to so much as glance at his inbox.

Today was for Josie. He'd take her to Brent Cross in search of a pretty dress for Rob's wedding and later they'd meet with Stephanie, Martha and their mummies and spend two hours begging at strangers' doors for tooth-rotting sugary crap – his interpretation, not Josie's. To her, trick or treating meant excitement and an excuse to gorge on treats not normally encouraged. Afterwards, he'd deliver her to Loren.

On Sunday, while Josie was with her mum and little sister, he'd treat himself to a long, long outdoor run. He'd go to Hampstead Heath and clear his lungs of fumes and over-breathed suburban air. Maybe then he'd get his emails and reports up to date before he picked Josie up ready for school on Monday.

School on Monday. *School on Monday*. SCHOOL ON MONDAY.

He didn't know if it loomed in Josie's mind but it did in his.

By mid-afternoon, Josie was the proud possessor of a cobalt blue dress studded with silver beads for Rob's wedding and was excited about jumping into a witch costume and acquiring a green face and a wart on the end of her nose, courtesy of Emelie's face-painting skills. Then they called for Josie's friends to go trick or treating. Nico strolled behind with the mummies, listening as they discussed balancing a career and parenthood, as if he didn't face that challenge. Josie, Stephanie and Martha gabbled and giggled, losing pointy hats and tripping over broomsticks as they trod garden paths at houses with pumpkins outside and knocked on doors, calling, 'Trick or treeeeee-eat.' He hoped fervently that renewing her links with Stephanie and Martha would reassure Josie that Jessica's defection wasn't the end of her world.

Finally, they said their goodbyes and, after going home to stash Josie's share of the tooth-rotting sugary crap and pick up her overnight bag, set out for Loren's soulless modern flat. It was eight-thirty when they climbed the stairs and rapped on the door. Josie, her face paint smeared, had already moved her focus from Halloween. 'Are we going to a fireworks display soon? And when will the Christmas lights go up in Oxford Street?' She knocked again, banging the letterbox with both hands.

Nico consulted his phone. 'Fireworks display on Saturday the seventh.' He was making a note to find out about the lights when Loren finally answered the door.

Josie gasped, 'What's the matter, Mummy?' and Nico looked up sharply. Loren, framed by the doorway, looked spaced out. Her short hair a dull brown bush, mascara crescents stained the skin below unfocused eyes. Maria could be heard wailing from another room.

'Oh.' Loren made an attempt to rearrange her narrow features into a smile. 'Is it that time? Love your witch costume, sweet pea.'

Nico, suspecting Loren had entirely forgotten Josie was supposed to be sleeping over, rested a reassuring hand on Josie's shoulder, noting the sudden tension beneath his fingers. 'She looks fantastic, doesn't she? Told you Mum would be impressed, Josie.'

Josie drew closer to Nico, her voice high and unhappy. 'Why's Maria crying?'

Loren twitched round as if only just hearing the heart-broken sobs. 'I've put her to bed but she keeps getting up. She has to learn to go to bed, doesn't she?' She forced a smile. Josie took a couple of tentative steps towards her and lifted her arms.

Then she stopped and wrinkled her nose. 'You smell funny again.'

All Nico's red flags flew up. Without waiting for an invitation, he stepped inside the flat and closed the door. It brought him close enough to his ex-wife to catch a strong whiff of stale alcohol. And maybe vomit. What the hell?

Instantly, he prioritised protecting Josie, whether or not that meant making decisions that weren't his to make. 'It's OK, Josie,' he said reassuringly, popping her overnight bag just inside the door. 'Maria's probably crying because she can hear your voice and wants to see you. How about you go and play with her while I talk to Mum?'

Josie gazed at him for several moments but Maria was still crying long, exhausted, heartrending wails, the hope-less kind of sobbing that had been going for a long time unanswered. 'All right,' she said. But she didn't move.

'It's OK,' he repeated. 'I'll be here.'

Finally, she headed down the hallway.

Touching Loren's elbow, he ushered her into the lounge and pushed the door to, taking in her pasty skin and crumpled clothes. On the table stood an empty red wine bottle and a glass, also empty. A drying patch on the sofa could only be the vomit he'd detected earlier. His stomach churned.

'Are you drunk?' he asked neutrally, staring into her dilated pupils.

'No!' Loren said too loudly. She lowered her voice. 'I was . . . winding down. I had a headache. I'm not sleeping well.' Then she put her hand over her eyes in the familiar gesture. 'OK. I might be tipsy. It's hard being a single parent.'

Nico bit both lips to prevent himself from snapping, 'You don't have to tell me!' Instead, he said, 'I'm sorry you're finding it difficult. Go and shower. You'll feel brighter and then we can talk.'

After a moment when it seemed she might refuse, Loren nodded shakily and headed into the square hall from which other doors led. He headed off to find Josie, following the exhausted *hurrrrr, hurrrr* of a child who's been crying so long she doesn't know how to stop.

Softly entering the bedroom he knew Josie used on visits, he found his daughter kneeling on the floor, her little half-sister clinging to her like a bear cub halfway up a tree. The room smelled.

Josie looked up, witch hat sitting drunkenly on her head. Tears tracked through her green face paint. 'Maria's weed herself,' she said in outrage. 'She never wees herself, even though she's little. And she's not in her pyjamas so she can't have been put to bed.' Her candid blue eyes

51

gazed at him and Nico could see she was drawing the same conclusions he was.

Loren had lied.

Maria had been left in her room unsupervised for so long she'd been unable to hold on for the toilet.

The two-year-old gazed at him through swollen eyes but remained trembling in her big sister's embrace.

Nico saw Maria regularly. She was a sunny, likeable child with blonde hair that curled at the ends. Josie loved her with a passion and Nico had begun by refusing to blame her for Loren's betrayal and, over time, had come to realise he genuinely didn't harbour rancour towards her.

Now, anger and alarm boiling up at the distress of an innocent toddler, Nico assumed a reassuring don't-worry-daddy-always-knows-what-to-do facade. 'We'll give Maria a quick bath and find her clean pyjamas, shall we? How about you show me where the bathroom is?' Loren's room he already knew to be en suite and he could hear her shower running. Then he thought of how a child might feel after being shut away to cry and reprioritised. 'Actually, you get the bath running while I pop into the kitchen.'

Leaving the two girls heading hand in hand for the bathroom he raced into the kitchen and located a plastic beaker, orange juice and two biscuits. He'd have preferred to make Maria a sandwich but couldn't find bread or much to put in it. When Maria saw the beaker she ran to him. 'Juice, p'ease!' Snatching the beaker, she gulped down the whole lot, breathing heavily through her nose.

Nico's anger and concern grew but he kept his voice gentle. 'More?' Maria nodded emphatically as she grabbed a biscuit and took a big bite. Nico fetched another drink, leaving Josie to keep an eye on the filling bath.

Then he checked the bathwater temperature while the girls threw off their clothes, Josie's heaped costume looking like the witch who melted in *The Wizard of Oz*. Maria, having eaten both biscuits and drunk most of the second lot of juice, scrambled over the bath side looking more cheerful, Nico automatically hovering his hands to catch her if she slipped. For several minutes he sat on the floor while they played, chatting to them, smiling as Maria yodelled, 'Yozee, Yozee, watch!' then clapped handfuls of suds to spatter the room. Her little girl laughter burst into the air. Then she beamed at him. 'Mydad, watch!' She repeated the trick.

'Yay,' he said softly, knowing all she needed was a smiling face and a response.

After several minutes, Loren appeared silently at the bathroom door. Asking Josie to wash off her green face paint and help Maria wash too, he backed up until he and Loren were standing in the hallway, able to see the sisters laughing together but out of earshot. 'Better?' he asked her quietly.

She nodded. Wet hair was combed back from her forehead, her skin pasty, so unlike the smart, sexy woman he'd married that it wrenched at his heart.

'You'd forgotten Josie was coming,' he murmured, feeling a statement was less likely to meet with a flat denial than a question.

Loren nodded again.

'And you were drunk. Maria had been ignored for hours. She was wet, hungry, thirsty and in distress.'

A sorrowful sound escaped Loren. 'I'm having a bit of trouble,' she acknowledged. 'I-I'm . . .' She took another deep breath. 'I shouldn't drink with my happy pills but I thought one wouldn't hurt. I didn't think it would make me sleep like that. I'll make sure not to do it again.'

'Maria's had two biscuits. Is there anything else for her to eat?' he asked.

Loren nodded, went away and then returned with two more biscuits.

Without comment he went back into the bathroom. 'OK, you two. Let's get you dried. Josie, you can get back into the T-shirt and leggings you had on under your witch's dress. There's a fleece in your bag. Maybe Mum could find Maria's clean pyjamas?'

Silently, Loren went into Maria's room and returned with a matching set, lemon yellow with a sun on the front.

When both girls were dressed he said, 'Josie, if you read to Maria in her room for a minute while she eats the biscuits, I'll talk to Mum in the lounge.'

Mutely, Loren followed him. Each avoided the soiled sofa and took a chair. Loren's eyes flicked over the empty wine bottle.

Nico's heart chugged like a train. 'I hardly know where to begin. Maria was properly distressed.'

Loren clasped her forehead. 'I know I've been stupid. I didn't mean that to happen. I put her down for a nap and just slept. That's all.'

'I don't think that's all, Lor,' he said gently, using his old name for her, the one from happier days. 'The wine bottle's empty. You'd puked on the sofa. You looked and smelled as if you hadn't washed for days and so did Maria. Josie's been odd about coming to visit you so I'd begun to worry you were drinking again. I wish I'd come right out and asked you.' He hesitated. 'I suppose it would have been futile because you've always hidden the extent of your drinking.' At least Josie hadn't suffered as Maria had, though thinking as if one child was more important than another made him feel guilty. 'I'm not buying this being a one-off. I presume the weekends you said you couldn't have Josie you were drinking? You've always seemed fairly together when I've dropped her off so I guess sometimes you've been able to make the effort. Otherwise, I wouldn't have left her here.'

He wasn't leaving Josie here tonight, either, but he didn't see any point in saying it just yet. 'What about Maria, Lor? You weren't looking after her today.'

Loren's hand slipped off her forehead and over her eyes. Tears began to leak down her cheeks.

Nico watched, trying to decide what to do. At length, he got up and went to the kitchen and fetched her a glass of water and the kitchen roll. Before sitting down again he took a peek in at the girls to see Maria once again clinging to Josie while Josie read aloud from a brightly coloured book. When he got back to the lounge Loren was blowing her nose.

He patted her arm. Her tear-ravaged face looked as if ten years had passed since she'd been his wife, not less than three. Apart from her period of postnatal depression she'd always looked after herself, had her hair cut and coloured, splashed out on clothes, make-up and shoes and generally lived up to her income from selling apartments in upscale retirement villages. Now she looked a pallid, broken wreck and he was getting a new and unpleasant perspective on the consequences of him ending their marriage. He'd provided security. He'd looked after her.

Softly, gently, he said, 'Lor, I think you need help.'

She nodded, keeping her gaze on the piece of kitchen roll in her hands as she searched for a dry spot.

'Maria mustn't suffer.'

She shook her head, managing a watery smile. 'You're a good man, Nico. Most men would have refused to have anything to do with Maria.'

'Josie loves her and Maria can't help what happened,' he said. 'She's a sweet little girl and I can't clear off home and risk her being left alone to cry for hours. She deserves healthy meals and drinks when she wants them. To have access to the toilet.'

Looking guilty and contrite, Loren nodded. 'How long can you take her for?'

Shock slashed through him. 'What?'

Loren looked confused. 'You said you couldn't leave her here, didn't you? Maybe a week or so's all I need to get my head straight—'

'Take Maria and look after her?' he demanded, to be clear.

'Oh, that wasn't what you meant.' Loren began to cry again. 'I know it's not fair. Her father doesn't want anything to do with her other than minimal financial support and Mum's stressed because Dad's having his triple heart bypass on Monday. I thought . . . well, you've got Tilly.'

'I know,' he said, helplessly. 'But—'

'Just a week,' she begged. 'Or I'll have to see about her going into care—'

'NO!' cried Josie, bursting into the room. 'No, Daddy, don't let her! I know what care is. It's in Jacqueline Wilson books about Tracy Beaker. Maria would be with strangers and I wouldn't see her.' Then she threw herself into Nico's arms, sobs roaring from the back of her throat.

Holding her warm, slight frame tight, Nico hunted for the right thing to say about a system he only had the vaguest knowledge of – except that, yes, it certainly meant

Maria going to strangers, if no one else could step in. And if his ex-in-laws had issues of their own then nobody sprang to his mind. Then he became aware of Maria standing just inside the door, gazing at the scene as if from the outside, fidgeting. Although there was no way she could understand what was happening her eyes were fixed on him. She gave him a tentative smile, round cheeks lifting and tiny teeth gleaming white.

He realised he couldn't turn his back and leave this innocent toddler to the neglect Loren appeared capable of, nor to the ministrations of a care system he'd never experienced. Although he knew social workers must do their best to keep children in communication with whatever family they had, he had a nightmare vision of her vanishing like a mountaineer into a crevasse.

'OK. For a couple of days until we see how you are,' he heard himself say.

Chapter Four

Nico wasn't happy about leaving Loren alone but he drew the line at inviting her back to what had once been their home. 'Should you ask a friend over?' he suggested, instead. It had been a while since he'd known much about her friends. After Josie had been born she'd withdrawn to a place where he couldn't reach her and even conversational questions hadn't been received well.

Her smile wobbled. 'I think it would be better to have an early night.' She didn't say 'sleep it off', probably because of the presence of Josie who was drying her eyes and gazing up at Nico as if he'd saved the world.

That might be the way children saw parents but, as Loren and Josie packed Maria's clothes and toys, he felt more at sea than in charge. What had he let himself in for? Loren had calmed now, softly murmuring, 'This is good of you. I'll be fine when I've had a break to get my head together.' Nico wished he shared her confidence. After what he'd witnessed tonight, things getting so bad that Loren had failed to hide her undesirable behaviour, he couldn't imagine when or if he'd be able to leave Josie with Loren overnight again and that thought led logically to uncomfortable conclusions about Maria's vulnerability. He might find himself in the position of telling social services that Maria was at risk.

Once all was ready, they said goodbye to Loren, who managed watery smiles. With a feeling of unreality Nico pushed the buggy bearing a toddler in pyjamas and a big coat through the chilly October streets, bags hooked over the handles. Josie hadn't needed a buggy for five years so he felt stiff and clumsy as he negotiated kerbs. Maria sang to herself for a couple of minutes then, no doubt exhausted, plummeted into the sudden sleep of the very young.

Josie kept glancing silently, uncertainly at Nico.

He wasn't happy with the situation but they were in it so it was up to him to make it work. 'So, this is a surprise.' He made his voice encouraging and calm and not as if the logistics of what came next were frying his brain. He had less than twenty-four hours in which to arrange childcare for a two-year-old. 'Shall we make up the pull-out bed in your room for Maria?' A mattress on wheels slid out from beneath the pink frame of Josie's bed. It was meant for the occasional school friend sleeping over but it would suit a toddler.

Josie nodded, managing a quick, watery smile. 'And if she wakes up in the night I'll cuddle her until she goes back to sleep.'

She was so quick with the response that Nico suspected, with a flash of anger, that it must already be a familiar situation. He toyed with saying something to remove the responsibility but decided that if Maria cried he'd hear her and would naturally intervene.

Once Nico had manoeuvred the buggy through their front door, wondering if the space had narrowed since he'd last tried it, he left Maria slumbering peacefully while he made up the pull-out bed. Josie alternated between excited assistance, shrill uneasiness and getting in his way. The ability to ease a slumbering toddler out of a coat and slide her into bed didn't seem to have deserted him and soon Maria lay looking tiny in the bed, fair hair curling over the pillow, eyelashes thick enough to cast their own shade on her cheeks. Nico wondered with detachment whether the curls came from her father. All he knew about him was that he had had a fling with a married woman and ignored his own kid.

That it had ended his marriage Nico had minded especially for Josie. He remembered the feelings of loss and grief when his own parents had parted, even though, at fourteen, he'd been better equipped to cope.

Purely for himself, the end of the relationship had, along with the sorrow, brought some relief. No more pretending he didn't mind living a sterile existence in which he could hardly remember what a woman's touch felt like. No more putting up with. No more being embarrassed by.

'I'll get in my 'jamas then turn out the big light and leave the lamp. Maria doesn't like full dark,' Josie whispered, suddenly older than her years as she pulled her pyjamas and dressing gown off the hook on the door.

Nico gave her a hug. 'I'll make us hot chocolate.' It would be too much to expect Josie to go straight to sleep, though it was past her usual bedtime. He was pouring the hot milk onto the drinking chocolate when she reappeared, her purple fleece dressing gown dotted with crescent moons.

She pasted on a bright smile and began to chatter. But the words wavered on her lips and suddenly she was crying instead. He shoved the milk further onto the worktop and caught her against him, holding her tightly, murmuring, 'It's OK, sweetheart. It's OK,' even though he knew a drunken mum and a neglected baby sister couldn't be an OK thing for an eight-year-old to see.

All he could do was cuddle up on the sofa and talk about what had happened, learning in dribs and drabs, shrugs and mutters, that Mummy had 'smelled funny' and Loren had seen her 'taking a long nap on the sofa' before. 'Two times me and Maria got up in the morning and Mum was asleep on the sofa.'

He stroked her hair, cold inside as he acknowledged that Loren must have waited until the girls had gone to bed then drunk herself insensible. 'Maybe Mum hasn't been feeling well. I'll talk to her about trying not to upset you or Maria in future.'

''K.' Josie buried her face in her mug of chocolate and he felt grieved for her jumble of emotions and loyalties. It was nearly ten by the time she'd unwound enough to go to bed, tiptoeing around Maria, though the toddler slept as if no more than a dragon's roar would wake her. Nico left her listening to a Roald Dahl audiobook and returned downstairs, tidying the kitchen and lounge with automatic movements, one eye on the clock. When Josie had been in bed for fifteen minutes without coming down he decided she was sufficiently settled for him to call Loren's parents in Reading.

Vivvi and Redfern occasionally had Josie to stay or took her out for a day. To Nico they were polite but chilly. It was as if, he mused as he listened to the ringtone, he'd been the one to let down Loren. Maybe he had. Maybe another man could have supported her through her post-natal depression better or stopped the drinking.

'Hi,' he said, when his ex-mother-in-law answered, her

voice surprised and apprehensive at the unscheduled call. He decided to jump straight in. 'Sorry to call so late. I have to discuss something with you and I had to wait for Josie to go to bed.'

'Oh?' Vivvi replied, sounding mistrustful. 'Is Josie OK?' When Josie had stayed with him instead of leaving with Loren, she'd been openly unconvinced that a father could look after a child as well as – or better than – a mother.

He began the story, speaking unemotionally and trying to be factual and objective, neither sensationalising nor trivialising but hoping to put over the unsettling reality.

At first, Vivvi was inclined to be defensive, as if he'd called her to tell tales.

Gently, he broke into her splutterings. 'I've talked to Josie and there have been elements of this behaviour before today. I had to leave Loren alone and bring Maria home with me. I've called you because I think you need to know those things.'

His words were met with several seconds of silence. Then Vivvi gave an exasperated groan. 'I suppose I'll have to drive over to see Loren tomorrow. But Red's having a triple bypass op on Monday, so I can't stay.'

'Loren mentioned that. I hope everything will go well.' Nico felt a band above his eyes as if he were wearing a too-tight hat. 'Will you pick Maria up at the same time?'

Vivvi gave a strangled exclamation, a cross between dismay and incredulity. 'How can I look after a two-year-old when Red's in intensive care? I'll have my hands full, especially once he's home from hospital.'

'Right.' Nico had asked the question more as a reminder that the toddler wasn't his responsibility than in expectation of her taking responsibility but the band around his head tightened.

'Look, Redfern's already in bed and I'm shattered.' Vivvi's tone indicated she didn't need additional worries. 'I'll ring Loren now. Thanks for letting me know.' She hesitated then added ungraciously, 'I accept it's awkward for you with Maria but it'll be short term. And you do have a nanny.'

Nico was left with a dead phone in his hand and a flame of anger in his chest. Term began on Monday and Tilly didn't work for him while Josie was at school. Any change to that would cost him a fortune. He wished Loren wasn't an only child. A handy sibling to give Maria a little holiday from Loren would be welcome right now.

He went upstairs and peeped through Josie's half-open bedroom door. Both girls were out for the count looking very much like sisters – lips parted, fair eyebrows half-lifted as if asking questions as they slept.

He jogged back downstairs, sloshed whisky into a crystal tumbler and threw himself into his favourite chair, swinging his feet onto the footstool before taking out his phone to text Tilly. *I have an issue I'd REALLY appreciate your help with from Monday. Can I call you tomorrow? When would be good?* He wouldn't call without notice on her off-duty hours. Tilly might not look like a typical party animal with untrendy hair and a dislike of make-up but, according to her, she packed a lot into her weekends.

It was late before he went to bed and then he slept fitfully, surfacing from dreams about Josie under some nameless threat or Maria vanishing from his temporary care. Even Loren flitted into his dreams long enough to jerk him awake with a heavily beating heart. Murky water might have flowed beneath their bridge but he cared what happened to her. Had leaving her alone been irresponsible?

But bringing her here had felt impossible. He closed his eyes and willed his body to relax.

A few hours later he jerked awake to hear Josie and Maria giggling. The events of yesterday rushed back at him. The clock told him it was before seven. After checking the girls were OK he watched them navigate the stairs together – Josie running lightly and Maria going down backwards on hands and feet. Nico made a fast circuit of the house to check for hazards. After putting bleach out of reach and the knife block in a high cupboard he saw the girls were watching TV. 'I'm going to run on the treadmill,' he said. 'Will you be OK with Maria, Josie?'

Josie nodded without looking round so he headed for the treadmill in his bedroom, leaving the doors open and the music off so he could listen for problems over the thumping of his feet on the rolling road.

When he'd run eight kilometres he went down to look in on the girls again, now playing with small chunky dolls that must belong to Maria while the TV still blared. Josie glanced up. 'Are we having eggs for breakfast?'

Nico took a look into the kitchen, seeing almost-empty cereal bowls and splashes of milk that suggested Josie had helped them both to sustenance already. He winked at her. 'Cereal isn't breakfast?'

'No,' she said with certainty, shaking her head so that her hair danced. 'Cereal's a snack.'

'Eggs, Mydad,' echoed Maria in her tiny-girl coo as if trying to encourage him to get cooking. Her hazel eyes were on him, one foot hidden by her pyjamas. She wrinkled her nose and lifted her top lip like a tiny horse whinnying.

He enjoyed seeing the sisters playing together. He supposed Loren was right and a lot of men would look at Maria and see 'problem!' flashing over her head but he

64

saw a toddler who deserved being looked after. Right this second, he seemed to be the person with that responsibility. 'Eggs first and shower later? Or shower first and—'

'Eggs first!' Josie leaped to her feet.

'Eggs!' Maria clambered to hers.

Nico got Josie to help Maria onto a bar stool as he had no high chair. She drank diluted orange juice from a plastic beaker, eyes swivelling between Josie and Nico.

He made scrambled eggs. Josie liked her toast so lightly done that it was little more than hot bread so he did the same for Maria and she ate it contentedly. He sat down with them at the breakfast bar and slowly ate one slice of toast with scrambled egg himself. The undemanding company of the two girls soothed the tight sensation of being under pressure.

A text arrived from Vivvi. *Spoke to Loren last night. She seems in a state. I'll visit her today. Will contact you when I know more.*

As he might as well be on good terms with his ex-mother-in-law if possible, he thanked her.

It was while he was supervising the girls dressing – Maria looking on trustingly while Josie selected her day's clothes from what Loren had sent with her – that Rob rang, his cheerful, booming voice full of bonhomie. 'So you think my stupid sister's OK?'

Drained in comparison, Nico settled himself on the bedroom floor, watching Josie try to coax pink ribbed tights up Maria's chubby legs while Maria pulled at the eyelashes of a doll. 'She seemed OK to me. Absorbed in her shop.' He thought about Hannah and the satisfaction he'd gained from merchandising her shop. And, if he was honest, the glow it gave him to see the pleasure in her eyes as she'd gazed at his handiwork. He tucked the phone beneath an ear so he could swizzle the foot of Maria's tights so the heel wasn't on top. He decided not to say anything to Rob about exactly how much time he'd spent with Hannah. If Rob's concern was, as Hannah said, that she had no plus-one for the wedding, it might heighten those worries if he got the idea Hannah had exhibited no plans for her weekend apart from work. Neither did he feel like explaining that his gaunt appearance had made Hannah suspect he was living on the streets. It wasn't shame he felt exactly but—

OK, it was shame. Or, at least, a need to hide the details, even from Rob, who knew about his issue.

'How are the wedding plans going?' he asked.

'All good!' Rob boomed. 'Honeymoon plans even better. Your family room at the Port Manor Hotel will be waiting for you from three p.m. on Friday thirteenth November. Check out by noon on Sunday the fifteenth.'

'Right.' Nico felt his heart give a slither of apprehension but he ignored it. Today was the first of November so he had a whole two weeks. *Something* would have happened to relieve him of Maria by then.

Tights finally in place, Josie threaded her little sister into a purple dress with a white fluffy rabbit on the front. Maria turned to him, pointing to the bunny. 'Look, Mydad.'

'Rabbit,' he said, automatically. And then, because the weird situation hit him with breathtaking force, he found himself jumping up and crossing the landing to his own room so he wouldn't be overheard, pouring out to Rob what had happened last night.

Rob gave a low whistle. 'She's seriously staying with you? Are you, like . . . sure? I mean, Maria—'

Nico rolled his shoulders to release tension. 'What else could I have done?' It wasn't an empty question; he was curious as to whether there was something he was missing, some door marked 'way out' that he was overlooking.

'Loren's family,' Rob suggested.

'I'm hoping, but Loren's dad's having heart surgery tomorrow so her mum has her hands full. Loren's an only child. I can't think of a handy aunt or cousin who'd step in.' Nico glanced in the mirror, rubbing his stubbly jaw and deciding tomorrow would be soon enough to shave.

'Loren's friends?' Rob tried again.

'No idea who they are,' Nico answered tiredly. 'If I'm not prepared to have Maria for a couple of days then the choice is: leaving her with a woman who's not looking after her or notifying social services.'

'Holy shit.' Rob sounded stunned.

'Yep.' When the conversation had ended with Rob wishing him good luck, Nico saw he'd received a text from Tilly. *Will phone you about noon.*

Great, thanks, he returned, and, to show appreciation, *You're a star.* Then he stepped onto the landing in time to see Emelie, who stayed at her boyfriend's place a lot at weekends, yawning her way up the stairs, flaxen ponytail dishevelled and mascara smudged.

'*God morgon.*' She smiled with sleepy eyes. Then she drew level with Josie's room and stopped when Maria said loudly, 'Yes! My dolly want beckfast.' Emelie craned around the door then switched her grey gaze to Nico. 'Maria's here?' she whispered.

Resignedly, Nico recounted the story again, adding, 'Talking to Vivvi, I was reminded that years ago she was head of a team selling time-shares. When they got you into a room they made you feel you were in the wrong if you wanted to get out. She doesn't let consideration for others get in the way of her goals.'

'Wow,' she whispered. 'But what about you? How are you feeling?'

'Blindsided,' he admitted.

She gave him a hug. Her hair smelled of coffee. 'You need someone on your side. I was going to crash but I'll stay up and help with the girls.'

He tugged her ponytail. Some students who'd fallen into free board and lodging while at uni would soon forget there was anything expected of them in return. Emelie, however, never failed to do her bit. 'Grab a few hours,' he suggested in a low voice. 'They're playing nicely at the moment. I'd like you fresh for if I need reinforcements.'

Emelie giggled then crept off to her room, obviously intent on flying under the radar of young persons who might demand her attention.

The girls played together all morning. After showering, Nico caught up on laundry and household stuff, interrupted by requests to rearrange things in Josie's room or approve snacks. Maria was so enraptured by having her sister to play with that she didn't ask for Loren once. She was a model houseguest except for her tendency to squeal at a pitch only dolphins could hear.

Tilly, as arranged, called at lunchtime. Nico was at the kitchen breakfast bar in front of his laptop. He recounted the Maria story yet again, though terming Loren merely 'unwell'. 'So I'm wondering whether you could come to me full-time this week to look after Maria. It'll mean extra money, of course.' He was erring on the side of caution in making arrangements for the entire week but there was no sense assuming Loren would have sorted herself out in a day or so, no matter how much he hoped that would be the case.

To his dismay, Tilly sounded astonished. 'I have gardening jobs booked in every day this week till two-thirty because Josie's back at school.'

'Every day?' Nico hadn't expected Tilly to leap at the chance but he thought she'd be a little more flexible.

Dubiously, Tilly amended, 'I suppose I can cover any day it rains heavily, so I can't garden.'

'Right.' Nico clicked on the weather app at the side of his laptop screen. Bloody England first week in November but not a drop of rain was forecast all week. 'Not even just Monday?' he pressed, in case he could coax her into a concession. Then, when Tilly just mumbled an apology: 'Right. I'll see you in the morning for the school run as usual. Can you look after Maria with Josie for three hours after school for an extra two pounds an hour? You'll be here with Josie anyway.'

Tilly said, 'OK,' but didn't sound enthusiastic.

'They play well together,' he said encouragingly, before ending the call and dropping his phone on the counter.

Bollocks. Damn, blast and bugger. He'd been relying on Tilly but it had been hopelessly optimistic, he saw now. Since Tilly began her side hustle she reacted less well to being asked to do extra hours and he suspected that she'd one day drop being a nanny and stick to gardens. Still, he was angry with himself for not acknowledging her gardening work as important before asking her to shove a week's worth of it back.

He turned to his electronic diary, being ruthless about what meetings he could put off to the following week, trying to remember how much you could get done working from home with a two-year-old running around and realising that without Josie to play with during school hours Maria might turn fretful and miss her mum.

He checked the Josie rota and saw that as well as getting Josie up in the mornings Emelie was currently down to take over from Tilly on Tuesday and Thursday at six because he had meetings likely to run late. Maybe he could ask whether she'd be able to pitch in a little more. From the corner of his eye he saw a Facebook notification pop up. *Hannah Anna Goodbody has sent you a friend request.* She was right that it was an eye-catching name. He remembered, when they were teens, Rob simultaneously liking 'Goodbody' for himself but not jokes about the name and his little sister.

He grinned faintly, feeling cheered by the echoes of days at the rink, the hiss of skates on ice, his dad Lars putting the team through endless skills training, Hannah bringing cookies with her mum, or taking youngsters out on the ice while Lars had the team clustered around the whiteboard talking about match play. Visiting Hannah and Rob's village of stone or brick cottages, chattering at their dinner table, laughing, hanging out 'over the fields', as the kids called the areas outside leafy Middledip. There had been a nearby private estate that had proved an irresistible draw. He remembered being chased out of a posh gazebo by estate staff and over a bridge onto the public footpaths, laughing, breathless, pulling a panting Hannah along because her legs were shorter, climbing the fence into the primary school grounds to escape.

It had been nearly Christmas then, too. Snorting with laughter, they'd hidden amongst the families queuing to go into the school Christmas concert. He'd loved Christmas in the village: the traditional bits like carol singers gathering at The Cross, muffled in coats and scarves; the over-the-top stuff like competing neighbours smothering their cottages with twinkling fairy lights. His first experience of kisses beneath the mistletoe had been at the teen party at the village hall.

He shook himself out of Memory Lane, Middledip, and accepted the friend request. Then, because there was no one to see him cyber stalking, looked over Hannah's profile page for the past few weeks, seeing it full of pictures of Hannah Anna Butik, of Stockholm and one of Hannah with a man with dark hair and a remote expression. Nico regarded him critically, automatically categorising him as 'Östermalm Man' with a cashmere sweater tied around his shoulders. He decided from their distant body language that he was nobody special in Hannah's life.

He followed a link to the business page of Hannah Anna Butik and 'liked' it. Then, seeing a picture of his own displays, typed: *Awesome! What genius dressed your shop? Must be the best in Gamla Stan.* ☺

Then, reluctantly, he returned to the problem of the day and called his boss, Anders, and explained the situation yet again. There was no way he'd change his plans for St Lucia's Day and his Swedish early Christmas so he suggested bringing forward the week of annual leave presently reserved for February's spring half-term, speaking English because Anders had this thing about speaking English while he was in the UK and Swedish when he was in Sweden. Anders enjoyed pointless boundaries.

'*This* week? From *tomorrow*?' clarified Anders, sounding as astonished as if Nico had requested permission to become a Christmas elf.

Nico kept his voice neutral. 'Yes. Sorry. At least I'm not due in Stockholm. I can work with Katya to rearrange my diary. I should be able to find time while I'm off to work on tenders and contracts. My team can telephone me whenever they want.'

'And this upheaval is for your ex-wife's child?' Anders demanded.

'That's right. But I wouldn't ask to take short-notice annual leave if it could be avoided. She's a child,' he added grimly, when Anders remained silent. 'If I can get—' He bit back 'get rid of her'. 'If I can make other arrangements for her then I will, obviously, but it's not looking good at the moment.'

'I understand,' Anders said, though he didn't sound as if he did. 'I'll leave it to you to talk to HR.'

Nico thanked him and thought that if he was ever asked for a favour by someone in as tight a spot as he was he'd be more generous than Tilly or Anders.

He considered texting Tilly to say he wouldn't want her at all this week as he'd been forced to take time off but thought better of it. Loren used to complain he gave off a distinct 'my job's more important than your job' vibe and maybe he'd been guilty of that with Tilly. Good nannies your child liked were hard to find and Nico planned to keep Tilly until Josie began senior school.

A small voice behind him said, 'Where's Mummy?'

Nico swung around on his stool. Maria stood in the doorway, her head tilted and her tights drooping. He smiled reassuringly. 'Mummy's having a rest, which means you can play with Josie.'

She didn't look upset or worried but merely nodded. 'Yozee wee.' A toilet flushed, as if to confirm her observation.

He glanced at his watch. 'Shall we have lunch? Josie likes chicken sandwiches. Do you?'

Maria nodded, silky hair bobbing. 'With catch up.'

'Red ketchup?' He opened a cupboard. 'Like this?' He produced a squeezy bottle of Heinz, Josie's favourite.

72

'Yes!' Maria broached a bar stool and automatically Nico helped her up, wishing either she had a high chair or he had a lower table. Still, she'd only be here a couple of days.

'Catch up,' she reminded him.

'OK.' He laughed, entertained by her single-mindedness. 'Let me make the sandwiches first.'

Josie thundered downstairs, ponytail flying, and soon the three of them were eating companionably.

Maria proved herself an unnaturally amenable child. Throughout the rest of the day she went about her business without crying for Loren though asked a couple more times, 'Where Mummy?'

Josie answered matter-of-factly, 'Mummy's at home and you're staying with me and my dad.'

Maria wrinkled her nose at Nico and said, 'Mydad.'

It was late on Sunday afternoon when Nico's ex-mother-in-law Vivvi turned up. The girls were playing upstairs and Nico, spotting Vivvi's car, opened the door before she could ring the bell. 'Come in,' he suggested. 'If we keep it down we can talk before the girls know you're here.'

Vivvi followed him into the kitchen, face pale, creases around her eyes. She refused refreshment and didn't sit down. 'I've been with Loren,' she whispered, blinking rapidly. 'It's much worse than I'd feared. She was out cold when I got there at ten this morning. I gave her a talking-to and she's confessed to misusing prescription meds. Barbiturates. They mix badly with alcohol.'

Nico's heart turned to lead. 'I had no idea,' he murmured, wondering if 'a talking-to' ever solved a substance abuse problem.

'No chance of an emergency appointment with her GP on a Sunday,' Vivvi went on, shoving back her silver-streaked

73

hair wearily. 'She talked to a helpline but wouldn't tell me what they said. She made promises about cutting out these bloody pills but says I'm not to push her too hard to do things she's not ready to do.'

Nico blew out his cheeks. 'Hmm.' It sounded like Loren-speak for 'I don't want to be held accountable.'

'Well.' Vivvi made an ungainly hand-waving, shrugging motion as if shaking off responsibility. 'I must go home. It's Red's triple heart bypass tomorrow. The problem arteries aren't easily accessible and he'll go into intensive care. I'll take Loren home with me. I hadn't bargained for it but at least I've taken time off to look after Redfern. We'll have to try and make the best of things.'

Heart in his boots, Nico managed to murmur, 'I hope Red does well after his op.'

Vivvi zipped her coat. 'Thanks. It means I can't help you with Maria. Sorry, but there it is.' She didn't quite look him in the eye.

'*Help me* with *your* granddaughter?' His teeth felt as if they'd been welded together he gritted them so hard.

Vivvi's lip trembled. 'Tonight's my last with Redfern before his big op. I can't look after a two-year-old. What would I do with her while I'm visiting Red?'

'You're taking Loren with you. Can't you cover it between you?' Tension slithered around Nico's forehead and yanked itself tight.

'What exactly do you want me to do? Leave Loren here to overdose?' Vivvi flashed, illogically, as Nico hadn't mentioned anything of the kind. She dashed tears from her eyes. 'I'll ring her surgery for advice tomorrow but I don't know what else to do! Any good ideas in that chief executive head of yours? And don't say send Maria to her birth father because Loren doesn't even know how to contact him. I expect the authorities might but goodness knows how long that would take.'

It wasn't the time to point out that he was at least two management levels down from a CEO. He responded icily. 'Her birth father's a stranger to her anyway. I suppose I'll have to keep her for a few days.' Then, catching the sound of approaching voices, 'Here are the girls.'

Hostilities suspended, he managed a smile as he turned to see Josie, looking grown up next to Maria. 'Hello, Grandma!' said Josie.

'Ganma,' said Maria.

'Girls!' Vivvi, too, managed a smile. 'I've had a talk with Daddy and now I have to rush off because Grandpa isn't very well and I have to look after him. Mummy's coming with me for a few days, OK? So you both need to be very good for Daddy. I mean—' She faltered, obviously remembering that Nico wasn't Maria's daddy. She blew both girls a hurried kiss then headed for the door, Josie trotting alongside, obviously not understanding that she'd been dismissed, charging her grandma with messages about Grandpa feeling better and Mummy having a nice time.

Maria remained standing in the kitchen.

Nico looked at her. 'Unlucky, kid,' he murmured, heart twisting that she wasn't even surprised at getting short shrift. He thought of his own beginnings with two fantastic parents, even if they'd parted, and four fab grandparents.

He thought of Maria left alone to cry herself into dehydration. A mother and two grandparents too caught up in their own upheavals to spare her even basic attention. No father worth the name.

His resentments were bubbling over but they didn't lie

with the little girl. He crouched in front of her. 'Juice, Maria?'

A smile lit the hazel eyes that were not like Loren's and not like his. 'Yes, p'ease, Mydad.'

It wasn't hard to smile back.

Chapter Five

Hannah Anna Butik *mentioned you in a comment.*

Nico touched the notification on his phone screen and read Hannah's response to the comment he'd left on her page about how well her shop was dressed. *Genius indeed!* ☺

Hannah Anna Goodbody *has sent you a message.* As Maria was eating Frosties with *mmm-mmm-mmm*'s of enjoyment and Josie was upstairs cleaning her teeth, glum because it was Monday and she had to return to school, Nico opened that also.

Hannah Anna Goodbody *Didn't want to say it publicly but takings are up by over sixty per cent this week! Honestly, Nico, I owe you dinner. Thanks again and see you at the wedding.*

He spooned up the last of his granola. Hannah wrote exactly as she spoke and he could imagine her wide-eyed emphasis on 'Honestly, Nico!' He clicked reply. *Glad the customers are buying.* Then, after a moment's thought: *Dinner would be great but not expected.*

'Daddy,' said Josie in a small voice from the kitchen doorway. 'Can I stay and help you with Maria today?'

Nico's parent radar pinged into action. He put his phone away and gave his daughter a reassuring smile. 'It's a school day, sweetie. Maria and I will be fine till you come home.'

Josie looked down, blinking. 'I don't like school any more.'

He slipped an arm around her, seeing Emelie hovering in the hall, looking anxious. He said, 'This isn't like you. Mrs Calcashaw thinks you'll settle in.' He'd had several conversations with her on this subject.

The look Josie sent him was full of wounded betrayal.

The food he'd eaten turned to cold cement in his stomach. Did every parent feel like this when their kid was unhappy? 'How about Maria and I walk you to school today? It's a treat,' he added, when she brightened. 'I'd love to do it every day, but it's not possible.'

'OK.' Josie sighed.

Emelie said brightly, 'Shall we take Maria to the bathroom and help her wash her face and clean her teeth?'

'OK,' Josie repeated, not sounding comforted by this distraction.

Tilly arrived, blowing in through the back door, wiping her feet. 'Hey,' she said, briefly.

Nico glanced her way, suspecting from her economy of speech that he was on her shit list for asking her to do extra work. 'Hey.' He hesitated, revisiting his plan to have Tilly look after both girls after Josie finished school so he could get a few hours' work done each day. He was anxious about Josie. The bleak expression on her face. The depth of her back-to-school blues.

He'd told Anders that he'd try and get a bit done while he was at home this week but suddenly he rebelled. He was entitled to spend his annual leave how he pleased.

His companionship was what his daughter needed right now and he was going to give it to her.

Tilly was watching him from the corner of her eye and he had the feeling she was waiting for him to be conciliatory for what she obviously saw as asking too much of her. Instead, some of the resentment he'd been feeling found an outlet. 'About looking after both girls,' he began genially enough.

She cut in with the air of one who felt herself to have the high ground. 'It's just that our agreement is that you give me plenty of notice about extra work. Extra children are extra work, additional money or not.' She pulled off her coat.

'You're right.' Nettled, he started to collect up breakfast bowls. 'And I didn't appreciate that your gardening work's so important that you couldn't offer me even a few additional hours. But I need childcare for Maria so I've taken the week off.'

Tilly's expression became a little less victorious. She halted, one arm still in her coat. 'What does that mean for me?'

'I'll pay you for this morning, though you can go straight away as I'm going to take Josie to school, and then I won't need you for the rest of the week.' He swilled the bowls and stacked them in the dishwasher. Tilly had offered zero flexibility and there were consequences to that. He wasn't in the mood to butter her up with repeated apologies and greater offers of financial recompense. Recently, she'd started to try and score over him as if she was a diva girlfriend, not his paid nanny. He wiped down the breakfast bar. 'You'll be able to do lots of gardening.'

'But it's dark before four,' she said uncertainly. 'I said

I'd have both girls after school. You've given me no notice of this either.'

He hardened his heart and took a stand. The prospect of a week to spend as he wanted without much on the schedule felt great. He could hint to Emelie that she was welcome to spend a few days with her Italian boyfriend Bruno and he'd have his home to himself and Josie. And Maria. '*Our agreement*,' Nico reminded Tilly gently, 'is that your paid annual leave will sometimes have to fit in with that of your employer. As it happens, there's nothing about me giving you notice of that.'

Red-faced, Tilly struggled back into her coat and left without a word.

Nico went upstairs to tell Emelie. 'So you're free to take extra boyfriend time and a break from childcare.'

Her face lit up. 'Really? Glad you're giving yourself some real time off. How did Tilly take the news?'

He couldn't help a sheepish grin. 'Like a sore loser.'

Emelie tossed her hair as she began ramming things into a backpack. 'I don't know what's wrong with her lately. Surely she doesn't think a neglected hedge takes precedence over a neglected kid?'

'I agree but good nannies are hard to find,' he said diplomatically.

Emelie rolled her eyes and hugged him goodbye.

When it was time to leave for school, he wrangled a squirming Maria into the buggy, ignoring her protests of 'No! Walk!' and they made their way past Georgian sash-windowed three-storey houses like theirs with big rooms and narrow gardens. Josie paused to converse with a ginger cat on a garden wall, then they strolled around the corner to Barrack Road.

Josie's steps slowed. The wet-cement feeling in Nico's

stomach returned and though he kept up a flow of easy conversation to distract her, when the bell sounded he followed Josie to where Mrs Calcashaw waited at the door to see her class inside. 'I'm Josie's dad,' he reminded her pleasantly. 'I'd like another word about how Josie's settling down, please.'

Mrs Calcashaw was no ogre but she wasn't a smiley-smiley teacher either. Her face wore lines of resignation and her clothes were as tired as her eyes. 'Of course. We can set up a meeting.'

'The way the schools have been amalgamated hasn't worked for Josie,' Nico persisted as children began to stream past and Mrs Calcashaw kept most of her attention on them.

'If it's a matter of school policy, you could always see the head, Mrs Watts,' she suggested pleasantly.

He nodded, understanding that her job at that moment was to attend to an entire class full of eight-year-olds not one parent without an appointment. 'OK. I'll go round to reception. I'll pick you up later, Josie.'

Josie sighed, 'OK,' then kissed Nico and Maria goodbye and followed the others, Maria calling, 'Bah-bye, Yozee!'

Nico went to reception, through the double doors that opened automatically, easy to manoeuvre the buggy through. The young man on the front desk tried first to funnel him back in the teacher's direction with an appointment to meet Mrs Calcashaw but Nico had now decided Mrs Watts was his mark, and resisted. 'It's a matter of whole-school policy,' he said and the young man went off to consult Mrs Watts.

Maria passed the time by kicking until one of her red boots came off, then looking at Nico expectantly. He'd just restored the boot to her foot when the young man returned. 'Mrs Watts can see you in ten minutes if you don't mind waiting.'

'Great, thanks,' said Nico.

Maria kicked the other boot off.

Nico made a mock-scary face at her and laughter gurgled from deep inside her. It was impossible not to be enchanted so he passed the wait making Maria laugh. In Mrs Watts's room, Nico parked the buggy and took a chair. Mrs Watts, tall and thin with short black hair, smiled from behind her desk. 'How can I help you today, Mr Pettersson?'

Nico kept his tone genial, expressing his concerns about Josie being unhappy at school.

Mrs Watts smiled reassuringly. 'It's early days yet—'

'Two months,' Nico reminded her. 'Josie has never been unwilling to attend school before.'

'There's bound to be a little settling down when schools merge,' Mrs Watts said, comfortingly. 'Josie seems a happy little girl in school. We see nothing to concern us. And, of course, whenever things are unsettled in the family, children do make excuses to stay at home because they want to check everybody's still around.'

Nico realised he should also be making the school aware of Loren's troubles but felt it would only justify what the head had said, making it easy for her to further deflect him. Instead, he said, 'This is a direct request to put Josie back in Mrs Symonds's class.'

Mrs Watts tilted her head. 'The decision to put Josie in Mrs Calcashaw's class has been made, I'm afraid. Classes were decided with a view to what's best for the whole school, bearing in mind all the factors. It was considered that Josie's people skills would make her just the little girl to make a success of mixing with new children.'

Waning patience made Nico blunt. 'She's unhappy. The

children from both schools should have been mixed up in every class. Surely you can see that?'

'Out!' Maria demanded, from her buggy.

Mrs Watts's expression was sympathetic enough but she didn't budge. 'We're not under that obligation, Mr Pettersson. Once the building at St Kits became an issue we had to make prompt decisions with a view to the smooth running of the school. I'm afraid if I let one parent choose a class for his child then it would open the flood-gates of other parents wanting the same privilege, perhaps several times in each school year. Josie will soon be caught up in the whirl of Christmas,' she added bracingly.

He refused to be braced. 'She's unhappy as a result of your decisions. I'll put my concerns in writing to the governors.'

'Out buggy, Mydad!' Maria shouted.

Mrs Watts looked pained but repeated that the decision had been made and Josie would soon settle down.

Frustrated, but inwardly conceding that Mrs Watts had a point about parents choosing classes, Nico tickled Maria and said, 'OK, kid. We'll soon be home,' shook Mrs Watts's hand and went back to make the beds. Maria industriously patted duvets and shook pillows alongside him.

Then he lounged on the floor and listened to music while helping make towers out of Jenga bricks. Even when Maria bellowed, 'One, two!' and kicked each tower down it was easy work compared to his usual Monday morning madness and his applause made Maria's round face glow.

He didn't check his inbox or his team WhatsApp.

Instead, he set himself to returning the child latches he used to have for Josie to the lower kitchen cupboards. Maria crouched to watch, trying to grab his screwdriver. He gave her a plastic spoon to pretend with.

When she napped after lunch he continued to ignore his inbox and took a nap as well. It felt amazing. Then he wrote the promised letter to the chair of the governors without much hope of a positive response. Mrs Watts had deflected him effortlessly. It was obviously not her first rodeo.

He checked Facebook and saw Hannah had replied to his comment about dinner. *Then champagne at the wedding at least.* And an emoji of clinking champagne flutes.

He replied: *That's a cheat because it's a wedding. Champagne obligatory.* It was ages since he'd had time to do something as normal as exchange such inconsequential banter.

Before he knew it Maria was awake again and coming backwards downstairs, calling, 'Yozee? Mydad?' and it was time to fetch Josie from school. He began to think this week off, enforced or not, was what he needed.

Chapter Six

It was the Thursday before the wedding. Hannah looked at Albin in his slim-fit black, citified overcoat. 'So you haven't had a last-minute change of heart and decided to come to the wedding?' she joked. Half-joked.

Albin's eyes flickered. 'I'm going to work, *stumpan*. You take this trip to your lovely family alone.' Hannah found the Swedish term of endearment he used, 'little one', to be more condescending than endearing.

She got out her phone to summon an Uber to take her to catch the Arlanda Express to the airport, saddened by the smooth exterior she felt was contrived to keep her out. 'When I come back, we need to talk . . . even if work's still crazy.'

Albin laughed. Then stopped. 'Yes, let's do that,' he said softly before he left the apartment, leaving Hannah wondering at his odd manner.

Then she went outside to wait for the Uber. Julia was covering Hannah's five-day absence from the shop and she was determined to enjoy her trip home, whatever Albin's mood.

Coffee at the airport, a sandwich as she read on the plane, and a few hours later she was landing at Heathrow to a bright winter's day, clearing passport control then wheeling her bag down into the London Underground system to rattle along the Piccadilly line to King's Cross St Pancras and then take the mainline train to Peterborough. It was so relaxing that she read almost a complete book. Maybe Albin was right. It was better for her to make this trip alone.

Rob was waiting for her, lounging against a post on the station platform as the light began to fade. She stepped off the train, turning up her collar although England wasn't as cold as the Sweden she'd left behind this morning.

She gave her brother a big hug, examining his familiar grin and smart haircut. 'I thought Dad would fetch me. Aren't you busy being a bridegroom?'

He tugged her ponytail. 'Meeting you was an excuse to get away from the mayhem for an hour but don't tell Leesa I said so. The rehearsal's at six so I'm whisking you straight to the hotel.' His casual delivery belied the happiness and excitement in his eyes as they hurried to the car park. He stuck her bag in the back of his dark blue car and they battled the traffic up Bourges Boulevard onto Soke Parkway and out of the city. Familiar scenery whizzing past the car window, Hannah fairly buzzed at the realisation that it was finally here, this special weekend with her lovely, jolly family. 'What's been happening?' she demanded.

Rob groaned as he changed lanes. 'Han, you FaceTimed us yesterday! Do you think a Martian's turned up to take the service, or something?' Then his face altered. 'Actually, one thing's happened.' He took the road that headed north-east in the direction of Bettsbrough. 'Nico Pettersson's bringing two little girls to the wedding instead of one.'

Hannah stared at his profile. 'I presume one's his daughter. Where did he get the spare?'

'His ex's daughter, Maria. Loren's got problems and the little kid's got nowhere else to go. She's Josie's half-sister so he's stepped in.'

Hannah absorbed this information. 'Is he back with Loren?' Though she didn't know Nico's ex she felt a reconciliation might not be good for him. He'd given Hannah the distinct impression ending things had been his only choice.

Rob checked his mirrors then overtook a small red car. 'I don't think so. He rang yesterday and asked would it cause a shedload of problems if he brought little Maria along. He took her for a few days as an emergency measure but he's had her for nearly two weeks. He didn't go into details as to how that happened but we said bringing her would be fine. He'd booked a family room anyway and the meal's a buffet so it'll stretch to include an extra two-year-old.'

'Wow. Odd he should end up looking after the baby who wrecked his marriage.' But then they were sweeping up the drive to Port Manor Hotel and she bounced from the car and into the arms of her family, driving Nico's problems from her mind.

'Mum, you look lovely! Love the haircut, Dad.' She swapped hugs with her stocky mum and gangly dad then swooped on a tiny woman leaning on a walking stick. 'Nan! How lovely to see you.' Her grandmother possessed neither computer nor smartphone and though they were able to chat on the landline – what Nan referred to as 'the proper phone' – it wasn't the same as seeing her dear face.

'Well, don't squash me,' Nan joked from the depths of a hug. Her eyes twinkled through thick glasses, her face creased with ninety years of smiles. Her curls, newly set, looked as if they'd been cast in silver.

Hannah beamed at everyone and dealt breezily with the subject of her solo status. 'Albin sends his best wishes and hopes we enjoy the big day.'

Her mother, Mo, who'd worn the same pudding-basin bob ever since Hannah could remember, pressed her lips together.

It was left to Dad Jeremy to smile peaceably. 'That's nice, dear. Look, here comes Leesa's retinue.' They turned to greet the SUV lumbering up the drive. Leesa's parents were no longer around but her sister Jemima, nieces Saffi and Raya and bestie Amanda Louise were with her. As the doors flew open everyone began to speak.

'Hannah! Hellooo—'

'Hi, everyone—'

'The traffic was horrendous—'

'We're going to be bridesmaids and wear pretty dresses!'

They tumbled out, Leesa smiling blindingly at Rob as she stepped into his arms and the bubble of happiness they shared. Tears pricked Hannah's eyes. She was never sure about big weddings because of the costs but she suddenly understood Leesa and Rob wanting to invite half the world to witness the pledging of their lives to one another. It arose from pure joy.

Cool, blonde Amanda Louise brushed kisses on cheeks and said to the gathering at large, 'I'm worried sick something will go wrong.'

Hannah masked her irritation with a grin. 'You only have to get dressed and turn up, don't you? Leesa and Jemima have planned everything else.' Then the celebrants arrived for the rehearsal, two well-upholstered ladies in a well-upholstered car, and the events manager came to guide everybody inside Port Manor Hotel, a restored manor house with all the pomp and glory that implied. Hannah offered her arm to Nan to negotiate the steps up to the baronial polished wood doors. The party quietened as they formed a procession across the marble floor beneath crystal chandeliers, Rob and Leesa walking hand in hand at the head.

Hannah was very, very glad to be part of this wedding.

Friday passed in a blur of checking things that had been checked ten times already and welcoming family. Some were staying at Port Manor Hotel, others with Mo and Jeremy in Middledip. Rob was occupying his childhood room in time-honoured before-the-wedding tradition so Hannah was happy to bunk in Nan's narrow cottage in Rotten Row, a terrace of cottages edging one side of the three-legged junction named The Cross, hat-like dormer windows snuggled into tiled roofs.

'It's great to be back!' Hannah kept declaring, and was happy to be asked to run errands because it gave her an excuse to tour the village. When sent to buy extra pins because Mo was sure the florist wouldn't bring enough for the buttonhole flowers she took a long way round to the shop, Booze & News, marking off the familiar landmarks: Angel Café, the school, the playing fields and village hall, The Three Fishes pub – already lit up for Christmas and a sleigh and reindeer galloping over the roof. The red-brick terraces and stone cottages were comfortingly familiar with garden walls and picket fences. Roadside trees had shaken off their leaves as if to make room for the Christmas lights that would soon appear.

At the shop, she listened to Melanie behind the counter earning her nickname of Village Updates. When she finally got away, she collected Nan and they ambled arm in arm to Mo and Jeremy's detached pebbledash house up Main Road, opposite the Bankside Estate, for the gathering of the clan.

By evening the house was bursting with friends and relatives scoffing Mo's sandwiches and Jeremy's home-brewed beer. Hannah caught up with aunties, uncles, cousins and friends and everyone talked endlessly about the wedding.

Jeremy press-ganged people into the garage to admire 'The Bus', the 1957 split screen VW camper van that he'd finally finished restoring. 'She's going to take Mo and me all over Europe.' Proudly, he ran his fingertips over the paintwork in the original colours of palm green and sand green. Hannah thought it looked like strong pea soup and weak pea soup but didn't hurt his feelings by saying so.

It wasn't until late, when Hannah and Nan strolled back to Nan's little cottage that Hannah mentioned an absentee from the celebrations. 'Sorry to hear you and Brett have parted ways, Nan.' She gave a gentle squeeze to the shoulders of her tiny, shuffling grandmother. 'I thought you were an item.'

'Yes.' Nan sighed and tip-tapped her stick past a frosty hedge. 'He proposed.'

Hannah halted stock still. '*Proposed?*'

Nan pulled her collar closer against the chilly air. 'But he wanted me to sign a prenup.' Indignation rang in her voice.

'Oh.' Hannah turned this over as they crossed the fore-court of the village garage, MAR Motors. 'Because his family owns a farm? He'd have to be sure he was being fair to them.'

Nan snorted. 'How can you begin a marriage by acknowledging your husband-to-be doesn't trust you?' Stiffly, she rounded the final corner past the shop and unlocked the door on the side of her house. They stepped into the kitchen. Beyond lay the lounge, dining room and a tiny hall from which the stairs led.

Shutting the door and relishing the warmth, chilled by the slow walk, Hannah hunted for positives. 'But you and Brett liked each other. Couldn't you carry on without getting married?'

'Trust's gone. You need trust,' Nan said simply. 'Don't you trust Albin?'

Hannah hedged. 'I've never asked myself that question.' And now she did, she wasn't sure of the answer.

On Saturday, Mo was on the phone by eight a.m., checking Hannah would be ready when Jeremy called to run her to the hotel to get ready with the rest of the bridesmaids.

'Yes, Mum,' Hannah replied soothingly. 'And I'll have had breakfast, and I've got my wedding undies and overnight bag and I won't be snitty with Amanda Louise.'

Her mum laughed. 'Our Rob's nervous and it's spreading to us all.'

At the appointed hour, Hannah kissed Nan and got her coat. 'I'll see you there.'

Nan looked over her copy of *My Weekly*, blinking through her glasses. 'Yes, I'll go up in the wedding car with your mum later.' She returned to the latest serial.

The morning proved to be fun. Leesa's friends Zara and Francie, a hairdresser and beautician respectively, were doing bride and bridesmaids' hair and make-up in the bridal suite. Hannah stashed her overnight things in her room then joined the beautifying production line.

Even Amanda Louise was all smiles. 'There's this hot guy here. I overheard him talking about the wedding so he's probably a guest. If so, I saw him first, girls!'

Jemima's husband brought the smaller bridesmaids, Saffi and Raya, to have their hair woven into French plaits; the hotel delivered a brunch of fruit and pastries but Leesa and the little girls were too excited to eat and Amanda Louise too picky. Hannah and Jemima happily devoured *pains au chocolat* and nectarines.

When they were ready, Hannah thought they looked stunning. The little girls wore lace-trimmed dresses and Hannah, Amanda Louise and Jemima flowing satin. Amanda Louise and Hannah's long hair was plaited at the top, then flowed loose from headdresses of cream rosebuds and dusky green leaves. Although Hannah had protested against the jumpsuits she had to admit they looked amazing, clinging to waist and bum then flowing like a satin river to swirl about her calves above pale peach stilettos. She wasn't sure how she'd survive the ceremony, wedding breakfast and dancing in the suede stilts but it was what Leesa had chosen so she stepped into them.

The photographer arrived, a middle-aged man in a charcoal suit, and the bridesmaids gathered around the radiant Leesa whose cream dress shimmered, headdress glittered and veil floated like morning mist. Her bouquet of peach and cream rosebuds was a sweeping work of art.

Escorted by the sharply suited female event manager they formed a stately file down the sweeping stairs, the two little girls directly behind a Leesa now visibly vibrating with nerves, then Jemima. Hannah and Amanda Louise brought up the rear. Tinkling piano music wafted up to meet them over a hum of conversation from behind the function room doors. The events manager turned and beamed. 'Ready, Leesa? Ready, bridesmaids?' Then she opened the double doors and one of the celebrants raised her voice ceremoniously. 'Ladies and gentlemen, please rise.'

Music grew and swelled as they glided down an aisle formed by rows of blue and silver chairs. Hannah's eyes prickled as she saw Rob waiting with a beaming smile, shifting nervously on the balls of his feet. His best man was a guy called Eerich from Rob's work whom Hannah had barely met. He and the celebrants faded into the scenery. All Hannah could focus on was the love in Rob's eyes.

In fact, Hannah spent the entire service with a sob lodged in an aching throat. Rob and Leesa's wedding had been in the planning so long that she hadn't really understood the magnitude of pledging your life to someone in front of a crowd of people.

Imagine loving somebody so much that after decades, after children, after life's trials and tribulations, you'd still want more. She envisioned that in thirty years it would be Rob and Leesa with retirement adventure plans, like Hannah's parents, presently holding hands in the front row.

The service was beautiful. The guests sang, 'You raise me up' but Hannah was too choked to croak a word. Amanda Louise glared when she forgot to step aside during the vows and had to be nudged to the chairs reserved for the bridesmaids. A man's hand appeared over Hannah's shoulder and dropped two white tissues in her lap. All she saw apart from the hand was a snowy cuff and a dark sleeve but she gasped, 'Thank you!' and blew her nose.

93

It wasn't until the service was over and the register signed that Hannah, in control of herself now and hiding her damp tissue beneath her bouquet, rose to follow Mr and Mrs Goodbody Junior back down the aisle to a joyful march ringing out from the piano and saw the person who'd been seated directly behind her. The man with the snowy cuffs, dark suit and clean tissues was Nico Pettersson. His hair was neatly cut now and gleamed golden under the chandeliers. His closely shaved face looked lean rather than gaunt. A girl in a blue dress stood at his side, her plait over one shoulder, and a toddler wriggled in his arms. They must be Josie and Maria.

Hannah only had time to hiss, 'Thanks,' and flash a smile before Jemima urged her into her place in the bridal procession.

In the grand entrance hall Hannah hugged Rob and Leesa. 'Congratulations! Wow, that was so lovely.'

'Thanks, sis,' said Rob, beaming. He never stopped beaming, even through the interminable process of wedding photos as chattering guests looked on and wait staff circulated with trays of sherry and orange juice. The bridesmaids were needed as set dressing and Hannah's feet began to hurt.

Between photos, Amanda Louise hissed, 'Do you already know him?'

'Who?' Hannah waved at Nan, a vision in pale lemon with a matching feather in her white hat. Someone had fetched her a chair and she was watching with a fond smile and a sherry glass. Hannah could see her mum talking and her dad nodding along. Mo had clothed her cushiony body in a classic jade number and Jeremy wore a grey suit and a brocade waistcoat. Both parents looked pumped with pride.

'The hot guy,' Amanda Louise whispered. 'He gave you the tissues.'

'Oh. Friend of Rob's,' she said vaguely, feeling that Nico didn't deserve someone as annoying as Amanda Louise ferreting for information on him.

Then the photographer began to call for parents to join the photos and then aunts and uncles, cousins and friends. Eventually, the whole party was perched on the grand staircase behind the happy couple shouting, 'Hooray!'

Rob and Leesa shouted loudest of all.

Chapter Seven

Hannah was relieved when the wedding party was finally ushered to the top table, snowy white punctuated with peach napkins. She could glug down a glass of water and kick off her stilt-like shoes under the long tablecloth. She was still stuck with Amanda Louise. All the brides-maids were on Leesa's side of the table while Nan, Mo, Jeremy and Eerich the best man were lined up beside Rob.

Try as she might to remember that Amanda Louise, Leesa's best friend, had to be put up with, Hannah couldn't help but be irritated as her companion's gaze lit on Nico on a round table nearby and she began to gush ostenta-tiously about the hotel's gracious proportions.

The top table was being served by waiting staff but ordinary guests had to queue at a buffet and Nico, showing no sign of listening, went to juggle three plates of hot meats, quiches and side dishes. Hannah would have jumped up to offer a hand if he hadn't been managing so swiftly and efficiently. She watched Josie play a game with Maria, who was strapped firmly into a high chair. Josie was a slender child with a ready smile, Maria a cherub with curls at the ends of her hair.. Nico returned and set a plate before each girl.

As Amanda Louise expounded on the table wine Hannah ate hot beef, chickpeas and roasted tomatoes, still watching Nico's group. Nobody would guess Maria wasn't his. He divided his time equally between the two girls as Josie chattered and Maria ate with an approving, 'Mmm, mmm, mmm.'

When the feeding frenzy around the buffet had passed, the staff delivered cake stands to each table and shortly after came the tortuous business of the speeches. Eerich was funny and Jemima touching, wishing their parents were here to see Leesa married but still enjoying the chance to speak at a wedding. Rob thanked everyone for joining in their wonderful day and the toasts marked an end to formality.

The volume of noise rose and people began table hopping. Nico set Maria free and Josie got down to play with her. Other kids joined them and soon they were skidding around the polished floor in their socks. Nico arranged himself so he could watch them, stretched out his long legs, poured a huge glass of red wine and unfastened his top shirt button behind the knot of his tie.

Amanda Louise began lecturing again, this time on the subject of the bridesmaids' dresses. 'I tried to persuade Leesa we should have silk. Silk's so classy,' she said carryingly. 'I can't bear anything man-made.'

Hannah retorted before she considered her company. 'Not even orgasms?'

Nico snorted into his glass, then snatched up his napkin.

'Fun-nee!' sniped Amanda Louise and stalked off to talk to someone further down the room.

Nan shuffled up to take Amanda Louise's seat, bringing with her the remains of a chocolate eclair. 'That's Rob's friend, that Swedish boy, Nico, isn't it?' She licked cream from her fingers and nodded in Nico's direction. He glanced up and smiled, apparently hearing Nan when he hadn't acknowledged Amanda Louise's clarion accents.

'That's right.' Hannah gave him a wave.

Nico cast a glance at the playing children then got up and approached their table.

'Remember me, young man?' Nan demanded, her wrinkles refolding into a smile.

Nico's eyes warmed. 'Of course, Nan Heather. Rob brought me to your house and you gave us Battenberg cake. Hi, Hannah.'

Nan beamed at being remembered and was soon interrogating Nico about what he'd been doing since age eighteen and which of 'these lovely children' were his. Hannah tensed but Nico simply pointed his charges out. 'Josie's mine and Maria's staying with us.'

After a while, Hannah excused herself to visit the ladies', leaving Nico to listen to Nan talk about the children she fostered.

Hannah was still barefoot. She was waylaid several times on the way to the women's room and though it was exciting and fun to see so many relatives and people she knew, she was fairly bursting by the time she finally made it into the ladies' room – all flowered wallpaper and black basins – and shot into a cubicle. It wasn't until she tugged down the zip at her back that she realised two things. One: the zip had snagged at the level of her bra strap. Two: she was quite alone.

How could that be, with a hundred women at the wedding?

She stretched over her shoulder with one hand and up her back with the other, trying in vain to tug free. Swearing, she exited the cubicle and waited by the basins for a minute, sure that a helpful female would come in soon, then gave up and opened the door to the foyer.

Just as Nico Pettersson strolled by, heading towards the nearby men's room. 'Nan Heather's kindly watching the kids for a minute,' he called.

Hannah was so uncomfortable by now that she was nearly dancing on the spot. 'My zip's stuck,' she hissed. 'These bloody silly jumpsuits!'

Laughter jumped into his eyes. 'Turn around and I'll fix it.'

Hannah, face on fire, complied. It took him a tug or two, a touch of warm fingertips on her skin, then he shifted the zip a couple of inches down, murmuring, 'There you go.'

'Thank you.' Telling herself that the heat she felt was embarrassment, Hannah motored off into the loo.

Next time she saw him he'd returned to his table and been cornered by Amanda Louise who'd dragged up a seat and was leaning forward and talking intently, legs crossed and an elbow propped elegantly on one knee. She was an attractive woman, Hannah admitted to herself grudgingly as she checked on Nan, now happily occupied chatting to a cousin of Jeremy's. One of Rob's mates, a guy who owned the village garage, came up to shake Nico's hand and Amanda Louise looked miffed.

Hannah's attention was diverted when Maria scampered up with an adorable, pearly-toothed, wrinkle-nosed smile. 'It's our elephant,' she announced.

Hannah giggled. 'What is?'

Josie arrived breathlessly. 'She means "it's irrelevant".

She heard me say it and "it's our elephant" is her version. Now she keeps saying it because it makes people laugh. Is there cake left on your table?'

As the three half-full tiers were at Hannah's elbow Josie was obviously being polite but Hannah pretended surprise. 'Why yes! What do you fancy?'

'Elephant!' suggested Maria.

Josie giggled. 'There isn't any elephant, silly. I think you'll like this icing one. It looks like a mouse.'

'Mouse.' Maria nodded, clambering onto a chair in her white lacy tights.

Josie selected a custard tart and peeped at Hannah from the corner of her eye. 'You know my dad, don't you?'

'Mydad,' Maria pronounced, pointing a crumb-encrusted finger at Nico.

'From when we were teenagers,' Hannah agreed, selecting a chocolate brownie. 'Rob, the groom, is my brother. Your dad was his best mate and used to come to our house. And his dad, Lars, is your granddad, right? I knew him too. He was lovely.'

'What was Dad like?' Josie looked fascinated over this ancient history.

Hannah dropped her voice so Nico couldn't hear. 'He was an amazing ice hockey player. Fast and crazy. We thought he'd play professionally.'

Josie looked faintly surprised. 'Well, he doesn't. He's my dad.'

Their cakes disposed of, Josie lifted Maria off her chair, made an ineffectual attempt to clean her hands with the stiff wedding napkin then towed her across the polished floor, Maria squealing like a whistle.

Hannah glanced at Nico. Amanda Louise was still talking but Nico was watching the girls.

Then he looked over Amanda Louise's shoulder at Hannah and smiled.

Hannah's breath stopped in her throat.

Day had segued into evening and a function band on stage belted out popular tunes. Rob and Leesa were on their twentieth dance at least, faces alight, turning to talk to people but never quite breaking their embrace.

Hannah had danced with cousins, old school friends, with Nan and with Mum. She'd also drunk a lot of fizz. She was thinking about grabbing a seat when Nico appeared beside her. She hadn't seen him for a while, nor Amanda Louise either, a fact she knew shouldn't concern her. 'Nan Heather's a marvel,' he said.

She laughed. 'In so many ways! What's she done?'

'Got me a babysitter.' He'd shucked off his jacket and his white shirt lay open at the neck. 'Someone she knows is happy to sit in the room with the girls and knit and watch TV so I can rejoin the party. The girls met her before they went to sleep. With Nan Heather's recommendation and my phone in my pocket I feel at ease.'

Hannah could see his shoulders had relaxed. 'Nan still has lots of friends who are fosterers or childminders.'

The music slowed and Nico, as if it were a natural thing, offered her his hand. It felt just as natural to take it and follow his lead into a slow dance, her hands on the firm warmth of his shoulders. Coloured lights roved the room, switching his skin from rose to gold. 'Are you wondering about Maria?' he asked.

She gave a tiny shrug, saying, diplomatically, 'Rob said you weren't in the mood to talk about it.' Even through his shirt she was aware of his skin.

His face shadowed. 'Loren's having problems.' As they continued to move together, his hands on her waist, he went on to explain briefly that his ex had an alcohol and prescription drugs issue. 'Loren's mum's taken her home but her dad's had heart surgery and is quite ill. They can't look after Maria.'

Hannah tried to compute the situation. 'But . . .' She halted, not knowing how to say, 'How is this your problem?'

He sighed, his muscles flexing beneath her palms. 'But . . . what? Try and get her into care? Insist Loren takes her back before she's capable?' He blew out his cheeks. 'It's been a nightmare arranging the childcare – a mixture of annual leave, working from home, help from my cousin Emelie and Josie's nanny. It's nearly impossible to get day care at no notice and it would be yet another change for a small, confused kid. Unfortunately, my boss hasn't been sympathetic.'

'Wow,' she breathed. 'Nico, you are a seriously good man.'

He laughed, most of his body brushing hers as they segued into a new song, something by Taylor Swift. 'I guess I was brought up not to turn my back.'

She smiled up. Barefoot, she was short compared to him. 'Lars was always kind. You must take after him.' She added thoughtfully, 'Maria seems a sweet kid.'

He nodded sombrely. 'She wrings my heart. It's as if she knows she's reliant on my goodwill and hesitates inside doorways, wondering whether she's welcome.'

'That's so sad,' Hannah said, trying to imagine a two-year-old being that aware.

He changed the subject. 'Middledip still seems a great spot. Yesterday I drove into the village and took the girls for a walk. We stopped at a place called The Angel for cake.'

A vision of the coffee shop swam into her mind, resurrected from the shambles of a derelict Victorian pub and finished with a mish-mash of reclaimed features and restored furniture. 'I'll bet it was delicious. The Angel Community Café opened just before I left for Sweden. It's a great success.'

He was still looking at her, his blue eyes dark in the dim lighting. 'I'll be in Stockholm again on Thursday and Friday, the nineteenth and twentieth of November. Will you be free?'

Warmth spread through her. 'How about the nineteenth? Meet me at the shop and I'll take you for that dinner I owe you.'

'Great.' His eyes smiled. They danced on, talking about what Nico remembered of the village and those fun four years when he and Rob had played for the Peterborough Plunderers. Gradually, Hannah was aware of them heating each other's air space, their bodies brushing more often and more fully.

She watched his mouth and the light of laughter in his eyes. 'That looks good on you.'

'What?' His eyebrows rose.

'The smile.' He looked so abashed that she changed the subject. 'Don't you play ice hockey now?'

The laughter faded. 'Rarely. I gave up my athletic scholarship and went to Sweden for the final year of uni.' He drew her close enough that he could lower his voice and still be heard over the music. 'I had a friend in Minnesota, another Swede. Jan Frick. Our American friends called him "Freak" because he was so fast. Popular, talented, doing well in college games. Then he got involved in a

103

scuffle on the ice. Helmet came off and he took a hit to the head.'

'Oh, no!' Involuntarily, Hannah's arms tightened around his whipcord body.

He nodded. 'He's still with us but . . . head injury.' His eyes were full of pain. 'He can't live independently. I realised I'd never be hungry enough to get over things like that. It flattened my ambition.'

'I'm so sorry,' she breathed, wishing she could take away his distress. But even as she thought it she was more aware than ever of his height, his cheekbones and jawline, the small lines at the corners of his eyes. She wanted to comfort him, draw his head down to hers so she could kiss him softly, fitting her body to his.

Her heart kicked up a gear.

She had to lick suddenly dry lips.

Nico had stopped speaking and was staring into her eyes as if he were feeling it too. The air vibrated. His mouth hovered closer to hers and she half-closed her eyes, waiting, expecting . . .

Then Rob's voice broke over them, loud and jokey. 'What are you doing with my stupid sister, Pettersson?'

Hannah's eyes pinged open as she realised Rob and Leesa had paused beside them, beaming in each other's arms as they swayed to the music. She laughed shakily, knowing from Rob's red face and glittering eyes that a lot of the free-flowing fizz had flowed in his direction. 'Don't take any notice of my bonkers brother.'

'Such English terms of endearment,' Nico said drily. They all laughed and paused the dancing to chat, Leesa smiling as she listened, her arm hooked around her new husband.

Hannah soon took a back seat in the conversation too,

half her attention on the way Leesa looked at Rob and Rob stroked Leesa's bare arm. The other half was on Nico and how he was making her feel: heated, fizzy, breathless and excited. He'd asked to see her again. She wished things were already at an end with Albin. She'd have been free to . . .

She realised Nico was speaking, asking her, 'Are you OK?'

'Fine.' She smiled but her blood roared as she took in the fact that she'd just made the assumption that soon she'd be single. And, so far as she knew, Nico was too.

'Have you had too much to drink?' demanded Rob. 'You look weird.'

'Of course not.' But her voice seemed to come from far away as she acknowledged that if Nico had kissed her she would have responded. It opened a door and blinded her with a look at reality. Albin wasn't acting towards her as he used to, as if he cared. And she'd . . . what? Asked to talk about it as if their relationship were another business transaction between them? Been secretly relieved when he put off the confrontation? Shame settled over her. The jolt of electricity between her and Nico proved she was capable of so much more. *She'd wanted him to kiss her.* A kiss was intimate. A connection. You didn't want anyone to put his mouth on yours unless you knew it was going to feel like heaven.

Rob and Nico made a few jokey remarks and she smiled as if she were listening whereas actually practical problems about ending things with Albin were flying at her. The shop lease – Albin would be her landlord. Somewhere to live – Stockholm was cripplingly expensive. The room grew uncomfortably hot as she realised that she had a rocky road to travel . . . but that it had to be done.

Vaguely, she was aware of Nico taking a phone call. Saying, 'Babysitter. Josie's woken up. I'll check she's OK.' She watched his shoulders as he strode across the dance floor.

'Hannah, are you sure you're all right?' Rob asked insistently.

'Just tired, suddenly,' she said. It wasn't a lie because the confusion of feelings on top of the long day had hit her. 'I'll sit with Mum and Dad.' Her legs felt like noodles as she made her way to where Mo and Jeremy had set up camp in a corner. Nan was chatting to Nettie, a foster sister Mo had kept in touch with. Jeremy's sister, Hannah's Aunt Sally, was squealing with laughter. Jeremy was telling someone which European countries he and Mo wanted to visit in the camper van. Hannah smiled at her mum's cousins and Nan's village friends and took a seat on the edge of the group.

Although she assumed a listening expression, her mind scurried around like a mouse looking for a way out of a maze. Last night she'd seen her lovely grandmother upset that Brett had wanted to make legal provisions ahead of their marriage. But, putting herself on the other side of the fence, she wouldn't have minded the comfort of she and Albin having agreed up front what happened at the end of their relationship.

She might have thought herself ready to second-guess her decision . . . if she wasn't watching for Nico to come back.

Upstairs, Nico let himself into the hotel room, the TV flickering quietly in the corner, the babysitter seated comfortably in the bedroom armchair while she watched a cop drama. Her name was Jean and she had a round,

106

motherly face it was easy to trust. 'She's just about gone off again,' she whispered.

'Thanks.' He crouched by Josie, whose eyes fluttered open and then closed again. Her hair stuck out, crinkly from her earlier plait. He watched her even breathing, her hand curled on her pillow. Maria slept with her nose squashed and her bum in the air and didn't move a muscle.

'I'm fine for another hour or two if you want to go back,' Jean whispered, starting a new row of knitting.

'Thanks. Just ring again any time.' He jogged back down the red-carpeted main staircase, relishing the dizzy feeling of responsibility floating off his shoulders. He had a warm buzz on, too, after a typical wedding combination of sherry, wine and fizz . . . and dancing with a beautiful woman. It beat the hell out of feeling stressed and rushed. Maybe he ought to think about regular weekends in the country. Earlier, he'd been talking to one of Rob's mates he remembered from the old days – Ratty. He had some longer, very English-sounding name but everyone called him Ratty. Ratty owned several village cottages and Nico wished he could afford to rent one as a bolthole.

At the foot of the stairs he hesitated, seeing Amanda Louise lurking in apparent casualness at the door to the function room, tossing her head about as if inviting everyone to admire her blonde locks.

When she'd invited herself to talk to him earlier she hadn't made him laugh once – not like Hannah had with that outrageous comment about orgasms. He still had a few specks of red wine down his shirt as a result of over-hearing that.

Hannah. That's who he wanted to search out again. When he and Loren had married, the bridesmaids had been togged out in ruffled blue dresses that reminded him of Disney shepherdesses. He preferred the sleeker, shorter style Hannah wore. Particularly when the zip stuck. He'd enjoyed helping with that, though his fingers had fumbled as Hannah held her long hair aside, showing him her smooth back bisected by a lacy peach bra strap.

Nan Heather had told him Hannah's straight, glossy sheet of hair was 'tortoiseshell'. It wasn't an English word he was acquainted with so he'd looked on his phone and seen cats in a mixture of colours from dark to gingery brown. He could see what Nan Heather meant. The streaky hair went startlingly well with Hannah's knowing, intelligent eyes. 'Aquamarine' Nan Heather had said. He hadn't needed to look that up.

The blue-green eyes had been fixed on his face as he'd told her about poor Jan Frick and he'd read only horrified sympathy until . . . suddenly her gaze had contained something quite other. Something heated and intent, as if she were a cat herself and had spied something to hunt. Desire had rocketed through him. His life hadn't allowed him much freedom for sexual adventures since Loren. He'd hooked up a couple of times, of course, because what self-respecting man wouldn't when going through a divorce, but they'd been mechanical encounters.

This felt . . . different. Rich. Pulsing. Hot.

A voice in his ear disturbed his thoughts. 'Having a good time?' Rob demanded, lifting his voice over the music booming through the open doors.

Nico hadn't noticed that his and Rob's paths had converged as they crossed the hotel's grand lobby from different directions.

'Great,' he said truthfully.

They reached the doors to the reception room together,

which gave Nico hope he'd be able to get past Amanda Louise through being deep in conversation and pretending to be blinded by the strobing lights. Rob checked his progress. 'Remember when we were in the Peterborough Plunderers together? That rule we had against going out with each other's sisters or exes?'

Caught unawares, Nico stiffened. 'I'd forgotten till this moment.' A weight formed in his guts.

Rob went on, 'Well, aside from Hannah living with Albin—'

All the saliva in Nico's mouth dried as the words sank in. 'Hannah has a *sambo*?' The Swedish word for live-in partner came out in his shock. 'I mean, she lives with her boyfriend?'

Rob pulled a face. 'Yeah. A posh prick with a snooty apartment in Östermalm. Hannah's been trying to pretend work kept him away from the wedding but we know he thinks we're beneath him.'

Rob paused as an older woman bustled up and threw her arms around him, flushed and giggly. 'I haven't had a dance with my new nephew-in-law! Our Leesa's a lucky girl to have snagged you.'

Rob allowed himself to be pulled towards the dance floor with a good-natured grin, tossing back over his shoulder, 'We need to finish this conversation later.'

Nico watched him go, sobering up fast. Shit. Shit, shit, *shit*. Rob had warned him off Hannah. He could have negotiated past that juvenile old 'no sisters, no exes' team-mates rule but not that Hannah was living with someone, whether or not it was in the elegant district of Östermalm. Of course Rob was concerned if he thought Nico was poaching. Nico had been on the other end of that treatment and he remembered the misery of knowing he'd been cheated on. Anger rose up to throttle him. Hannah hadn't mentioned Albin! Being tipsy at a wedding didn't excuse the signals she'd been sending him or the fact he hadn't checked she was single. He had to stop it now.

His mood plunged.

Then a cooing voice called, 'Niiii-co! Let's dance!' and Amanda Louise swept towards him, tossing her hair. He didn't resist. At least dancing with her would keep him away from Hannah. And he was going to stop drinking right now.

Hannah's heart somersaulted as, beyond the shifting bodies on the dance floor, she saw Nico reappear in the doorway. But now his face had become a set, strained mask, completely at odds with the loose, smiling Nico who'd gone upstairs to his daughter ten minutes ago. Her stomach sank. Maybe he hadn't been able to settle Josie and was just popping down to tell Hannah goodnight?

But then a blonde head moved closer to his. Nico turned towards it with a perfunctory smile and he nodded. Hannah watched in dismay as the dance floor cleared sufficiently to give her a grandstand view of Amanda Louise leading him onto the polished floor, the swirling lights playing over her sinuous satin and his white shirt.

And Nico twirled her into a slow dance without looking Hannah's way.

She recoiled, shocked how much she minded. Stonily, she watched Amanda Louise entwine her arms about his neck and gaze into his face, her lips moving, her head tilting coquettishly, words swallowed up by the band and the hubbub of voices shouting over the thrumming music.

Hoping Nico was simply being polite because Amanda Louise had asked him to dance Hannah waited, hardly able to breathe. One dance became two, then three and four. Nico didn't look up from Amanda Louise once.

The rest of the evening felt like a five-mile slog through mud.

She talked to her family and danced with old friends but her insides seemed caked in ice. When she looked for Nico again both he and Amanda Louise had gone.

Hannah went to bed at two, carrying her shoes. In her room, her zip stuck again and she yanked at the fabric until, uncaring, she heard it rip. She was pretty certain she'd never wear the jumpsuit again.

Though exhausted, she tossed and turned. It felt unbelievable that a warm, smiling Nico had quit the room and a granite-faced Nico had returned, specifically to ignore Hannah, it seemed.

Eventually she slept fitfully, plagued by dreams of a stern-faced Albin helping her fit a bed in the shop and telling her she lived there now while Nico danced with Amanda Louise outside in the street. She was glad to rise at eight, having promised to meet Nan, who didn't want to broach the hotel dining room alone and said late breakfasts got on her nerves.

Other wedding guests were in the dining room, looking different without their glad rags, but no one from the family. Mo and Jeremy were probably still recovering and Rob and Leesa should already have been whisked off by limo for their honeymoon in Goa. Hannah sent a lightning glance around the dining room but there was no sign of Nico.

A waiter showed them to a table with cane-backed chairs and a white cloth then fetched hot tea while Nan slathered a thick slice of toast with double strawberry jam and Hannah helped herself to eggs and bacon. 'That boy

Nico,' said Nan, licking jam from her thumb. 'He's looking after his ex-wife's little girl.'

Hannah cut into her egg and watched yolk pooling on the plate with a waning appetite. 'I know.'

Nan sipped tea from the hotel's elegant white porcelain cup. 'Private fostering or kinship, it's called, when kids end up being looked after by uncles and aunts or family friends. Shame for the kiddie but she's fallen on her feet with that Nico. Compassionate man.'

Hannah nodded.

Amanda Louise arrived with a group of friends, smiling and nodding politely to Hannah and Nan.

'So,' challenged one of the friends as they settled at a nearby table. 'What happened? I saw you smooching with him. Snagged and shagged?'

Hannah's stomach lurched. She didn't want to know the answer but she could neither blame Amanda Louise for fixing her sights on Nico or Nico for taking advantage. Last night she'd dared to hope that a single life *might* lend itself to seeing Nico on his visits to Stockholm but if tall, striking Amanda Louise had given him the green light it would explain his suddenly turned cold shoulder.

But Amanda Louise said, 'He couldn't leave his kids,' and changed the subject. Relief surged through Hannah, even if Amanda Louise's tone implied the kids were the only reason Nico hadn't spent a wild night in her bed.

'I miss you living in England,' Nan said suddenly, her voice creaking.

It jerked Hannah out of her self-absorption. With horror, she saw a tear balanced on Nan's sparse eyelashes. 'I miss you too.' She gulped down the lump in her throat and slid a gentle arm around Nan's frail old shoulders. It dawned on her that with her parents on their travels and

Brett off the scene, Nan's Christmas might depend on Rob and Leesa. She hoped they'd welcome Nan with open arms because Hannah had no idea where she'd be living and, anyway, Nan could never make the trip to Sweden alone at ninety.

In fact . . . chances were Hannah's Christmas would be a lonely affair, with the shop shut on Christmas Eve and Christmas Day and not even Albin for company. Unable to think of words with which to comfort Nan, she just hugged her harder.

Chapter Eight

On the flight, Hannah tried to occupy her mind with Hannah Anna Butik's Christmas decorations. She'd already put up an illuminated star in the window and white lights around window and door. Perhaps she'd add icicle-shaped lights on boughs of spruce with baubles of gold and black.

No matter how hard she tried, her thoughts kept darting off. When would it be best to make Albin discuss their relationship? After the tetchiness as she'd left, her only contact had been a text to tell him she'd arrived and a WhatsApped picture of the bride and groom. She wouldn't land until ten-fifty p.m. She'd take the train from Arlanda airport and then an Uber to Östermalm, reaching Albin's apartment about one a.m. He'd probably be asleep. Tomorrow morning? Ridiculous to think of sliding it into the conversation before they left for work.

The butterflies that journeyed home with her fluttered wings of ice but when she finally let herself into the apartment she was surprised to discover Albin awake.

She greeted him warily, wheeling her baggage onto the

tiled hall floor. He smiled and put aside his book, rising slowly.

They faced each other.

Hannah searched his smooth face, her heartbeat jigging as she took a breath to speak.

Albin got in first, his voice soft. 'I waited up for you because it's time to talk.'

Relief broke over her. 'You're right.' The words 'This isn't working' rose to her tongue but suddenly it was Albin's mouth they were coming out of.

He added, 'We had great times together but they're in the past.' He smiled courteously, his voice dropping. 'Sorry I put off this conversation but I had things to arrange. I'm afraid I have to ask you to move out, Hannah.'

Thrown that he was speaking her lines she said the first thing that came into her head. 'What about Hannah Anna Butik?'

Sardonic amusement filled his eyes. 'Interesting that it's the shop that's your first concern. Not me. Not us.'

Blood raced to her face. 'Sorry – I . . .' She swallowed. 'I was going to raise the same subject but you took me by surprise. And,' she added, her eyes prickling, 'it's sad, after almost two years.'

'Let's sit down.' He didn't look sad as he took his customary armchair and she dropped down onto the sofa. Whatever she'd thought would happen when she faced Albin, it wasn't that he'd get in first. He leaned forward, holding her gaze. 'We moved from "fling" to "relationship" and, like letting you hang your red towels in my bathroom, by the time I acknowledged that it wasn't for me, I'd let it happen.'

Hannah was stung. 'I didn't know I was ever a "fling",' she said stiffly. 'But this is your family's apartment so, of

115

course, I'll move out. I'll just need time. I don't think I can live at the shop so I'll try and find someone who's looking to share.'

Albin's dark eyes narrowed. He sighed. 'Hannah,' he said politely. 'Your shop isn't working either.'

Instantly, she fired up. 'My takings are on a great trajectory!'

'A Christmas shopping spike, nothing else. Your shop was never in the right place. Köpmangatan is neither Stortorget nor Österlånggatan, but the road between the two.'

'I couldn't afford Stortorget or Österlånggatan, as you know, and Köpmangatan's fine. My upscale shop fits well with the antique shops and art galleries. It gets tourist footfall. It fits my economic landscape. If it's so crap, why did you sign the lease?'

He shrugged. 'It was what you wanted and – at the time – I wanted you. I was infatuated.' He sounded sheepish, as if he'd said, 'I was drunk.'

Hannah's hands hadn't warmed up from the journey from the airport and she clasped them between her knees. Albin was being implacable. Cold. Calculating. Reeling from the unexpectedness of finding her shop under attack, she was arguing from a position of weakness and had to fight to keep her voice from wobbling. 'I can live on the takings if I have time to organise myself.'

Calmly, he rose to pour them each a glass of malt whisky, glittering like liquid amber in the beam of his reading lamp as he sat down again. He said quietly, but inexorably, 'I'll be doing something else with the property.'

Hannah gaped. 'What?'

The ice in his glass clinked, as if he wasn't quite so

116

calm as he appeared. 'Confession time. I've never gone "hunting" in terms of taking a gun and killing creatures.'

'You haven't?' Hannah thought of the weekends he'd packed overnight things and given her to understand he'd be doing exactly that. Her repulsion. His intransigence.

'It was convenient to let you think that but our community, we're called "hunters".' He waited, as if expecting her to catch on.

She failed. 'What are you on about?'

A tiny smile played about his lips as if she was being incredibly thick. 'We're always "hunting" for the next sexual encounter. There are clubs. We like to live in the moment, shut the world out. Sex with strangers does that.'

Hannah felt dazed. 'Like swingers? Being polyamorous?'

He inclined his head. Then, when, stunned, she could do no more than gape, he added, 'It's an indulgence.'

Her hand had begun shaking. Very carefully, she put down her glass. 'I never satisfied you? Not even when things were good between us?' She felt sick. The conversation had spun far from the path she'd anticipated.

'No one woman could. That's the point. Hunters are always hungry.' He went on talking, calmly, graphically, about indulging his taste for group sex and stranger-sex.

Anger flooded through her as he calmly described the way he'd been fooling and humiliating her. 'So what's this polyamory stuff got to do with my shop?' she snapped.

He sipped before replying. 'From those premises—' he didn't call it her shop '—I'm going to run a discreet club "for the curious". Less tacky than arranging it via an app. People of like minds. Away from prying eyes.'

'In *Gamla Stan*?' She tried to picture a sex club amongst the tourists, the shops, the churches.

He shrugged. 'It's not illegal.'

'But it's my shop!' she all but wailed, misery sweeping away her anger.

He leaned in and patted her hand. 'I'm sorry, Hannah. It's not. It never was.' He was polite and civilised but inexorable. 'I drew up a plan while you were away. Whatever's in your business bank account is yours, obviously. In addition, you'll be owed the value of your stock. I've told Julia to perform a stocktake and give me the figure, then I'll dispose of it to a reseller. I'll also return the advance rent you've paid and—' he made a rocking gesture with his hand '—a little goodwill because you would obviously have anticipated a mark-up.'

Hannah could hardly believe her ears. 'But,' she stammered, 'you're keeping me away from my stock. That's stealing.'

He gave a short laugh. 'As I'm offering to pay you its full value, I don't think you'll get the police to arrest me. If you prefer, you can take your stock away – by arrangement, as I've already taken possession of your keys.'

'From my drawer?' she cried.

He inclined his head. 'My drawer, I think you'll find.'

Dazed, she stared at him, casting about for ammunition. She had no legal footing! Where would she put a shop full of belts and bags? Albin had allowed her to trade from premises on which he'd held the lease . . . and now he wasn't. There had never been a written agreement. If he'd taken the keys from the drawer by their bed then she couldn't open the shop. She managed, feebly, 'I employ Julia, not you.'

'But you've ceased trading,' he said slowly, gently, as if talking to a child coming down from a tantrum. 'There's nothing left for you in Stockholm. I'll pay Julia for performing the stocktake.' He rose, tossing back the last of his whisky. 'I've moved your things into the spare room . . . temporarily.'

She gazed at him, a hand to her throat as if her rage and shock would choke her, hurling her mind back over events to try to make sense of them. 'Why did we change?' she demanded huskily. 'It feels as if there should be a – a day, an incident, some *thing* that altered us.'

Something flickered in his eyes but he shrugged and said, 'Goodnight.'

For long hours, Hannah lay awake in the spare room, horror knotting her stomach as she entertained wild plans to take Albin to court and . . . and . . . do *something*. But Albin would swat such an attempt away like a bothersome fly. She'd been living rent-free in his family's apartment and she hadn't officially sublet the shop. Since leaving her job with IKEA in Kungens Kurva and her rented studio apartment in the southern Stockholm suburb of Farsta, Hannah's life in Sweden had been built upon Albin's goodwill.

She'd been crazy, now she looked back on it. Bonkers. She'd allowed herself to be carried along on the back of someone else's life. Albin could put her out the door like last year's coat. *There's nothing left for you in Stockholm.* He'd made sure of that.

As soon as it was light, Hannah hurried to Hannah Anna Butik, needing to see it with her own eyes. To rattle the door. The lights were off. She thought she glimpsed someone inside, maybe Julia, but her rapping on the glass was ignored. *There's nothing left for you in Stockholm . . .* She turned away, eyes stinging.

Wednesday saw Albin transferring Hannah's personal possessions to the apartment from the shop, even her mugs and tea and coffee. She stayed in the spare room and thought furiously. Early on Thursday morning she ventured into the kitchen when she heard Albin there.

His smile was that of a stranger. 'Shall we say you'll have made arrangements to vacate this apartment one week from today?' he asked. 'That will be the twenty-sixth of November.'

Hannah licked her lips. All she'd achieved since returning from England was to feel stunned by the magnitude of what had happened. She had no idea where she'd go but she stuck her nose in the air and said, 'I'll leave sooner, if I can manage it.' She stared at the alien who used to be her boyfriend. 'I'll need the money for my stock.'

His eyebrow lift was a masterclass in superciliousness. 'Payable when you're safely out of the apartment.'

'I have to have a deposit for accommodation. Stockholm's expensive.'

He sighed irritably. 'Why stay here?'

She didn't have an answer and the knowledge did nothing but fuel her anger and misery. Her life had been pulled out from under her. Most of her Stockholm friends were Albin's friends, except maybe Julia, and calls to her were going to voicemail. Probably she felt torn loyalties as Albin had been the one to get her the job as Hannah's assistant.

It was after he'd put on his coat and left for his office that a reminder flashed up on Hannah's phone. This evening she'd arranged to meet Nico Pettersson at the shop for dinner. Her fingers hovered. So much had happened since they'd made the arrangement as she'd danced in his arms. They'd both been full of alcohol. He'd blanked her afterwards. There had been zero contact between them since. But when she opened a text message to cancel, loneliness and isolation washed over her and she was overcome by the urge to see a face that reminded her of home. She found herself typing: *Are we still meeting this evening? Can it be the same bistro in Stora Nygatan rather than the shop? Will explain if I see you.* She kept her tone neutral, making it easy for him to back out.

An hour later she received, *I'm free. See you there.*

The day dragged. She forced herself to go accommodation hunting online but without an income it felt unfeasible. When the time came, she was glad to shove her laptop aside and put on a red sweater dress and flat black boots. The streets were freezing as she trekked from the broad residential thoroughfares of Östermalm, through chrome-and-glass shopping areas and the galaxy of Christmas lights that had just gone up until she could cross Vasabron to the colourful old buildings of Gamla Stan.

Nico awaited her at a table at the bistro Hörnan in a navy sweatshirt that made his eyes bluer. He smiled in greeting but neither of them initiated a hug. They ordered briskly and Hannah realised, with a dreary, sinking feeling that the Nico who'd turned up this evening was the same cool, remote one of Burger Town a few weeks ago. The man who'd gazed at her hungrily as they danced at her brother's wedding had vanished. Nico had evidently learned to thoroughly edit his feelings.

The conversation was light and impersonal. Nico asked if she'd had a pleasant flight home. She didn't ask him why he'd gone off with Amanda Louise. She felt as if her chest walls were made of stone and it took all her energy to inflate her lungs enough to make small talk, especially as a part of her wanted to climb into his lap and seek comfort.

Nico pushed his food around his plate more than he ate it and the several bites he took looked an effort.

Presently, feeling the need to take the conversation some-where other than the superficial, she asked, 'Did Maria go back to Loren OK?'

Nico didn't quite meet her eyes. 'Loren and I . . . are working on things.'

The words rippled through her as she absorbed them. His gentle emphasis on the final few words, the way he'd answered a different question to the one she'd asked, made it sound as if they were trying again. That was what Loren wanted, Nico had said before. Any notion she'd harboured of spilling her anxious outrage about Albin and having one week to find herself a home and way of supporting herself vanished into the bistro's herb-scented air.

'Fantastic,' she said hollowly. The following silence didn't invite further enquiry. From her bag, her phone buzzed.

'Feel free to answer.' With a polite smile he abandoned the remains of his fast-cooling meal and headed towards the men's room.

Hannah read *Mum* on the screen and opened the message: *Can we FaceTime?*

With a wriggle of alarm at both the brevity and lack of kisses she replied, *I'm in a restaurant. Can it wait an hour? Or should I find somewhere to call from? xx*

Mo came straight back. *Wait till you get home so we can talk properly. I'm in all evening. xx*

Nico returned and when she told him about the texts he called instantly for the bill, which he paid without looking at her or it.

'But I asked you to dinner for your help in setting Hannah Anna Butik on the right track,' she protested.

He shrugged.

122

Angry that he was so keen to brush her off, Hannah nevertheless thanked him politely, retrieved her coat from the rack and tamped down rising disappointment as he stood back politely to allow her before him up the stairs. At street level, the cold evening air pinched her ears.

They tramped together to Vasabron, passing through the massive arch of the graceful stone parliament buildings. Crossing the bridge, they huddled into their coats as the lights of the city danced on the icy black water below. He paused. 'I'm heading to Central Station. I hope everything's OK with your mum.'

'Thanks. And thanks for dinner.' She barely broke stride as she swung right onto her favourite route to Östermalm through Kungsträdgården without slowing to watch the ice skaters on the public rink and barely noticing the green illuminated NK sign revolving above the posh department store of the same name. The wind was icy and she felt as if she could taste snow on it as she trudged through the brightly lit, busy streets.

Albin's words echoed in her head, feeling truer by the stride. *There's nothing left for you in Stockholm.*

He was home when she got there, eating salad and watching the international news on the kitchen TV. He looked irritated to see her. She felt annoyed to see him. She went to the spare room without hanging up her coat. In moments she'd connected a FaceTime call to her mum and was looking at her round face, currently uncharacteristically crumpled and fed up. 'Is everything OK?'

Mo sighed. 'Sorry if I worried you. We've just got Nan home. She's fallen and broken her wrist. She's here with us for now. It's her right wrist, of course, so she's all of a do-dah trying to do things with her left hand.' She checked behind her, as if for eavesdroppers. 'She's upset.'

Hannah smoothed back her hair, feeling wobbly at the thought of poor Nan's plight. 'Because she's in pain?'

'No. Well, yes. But it's not that.' Mo's eyebrows tilted forlornly. 'It means we can't go off in The Bus on Saturday, as planned. Dad's so disappointed and he's trying not to show it. Nan's blaming herself and getting teary.'

'But she couldn't help falling,' Hannah protested.

Mo propped her head on her fist. 'Sort of, she could. Dad said he'd get her Christmas decorations down from her loft before we left but she tried it herself. Lucky she was only a few feet up! It could have been her neck.' She rubbed her nose drearily. 'Obviously, we can't leave her to fend for herself one-handed at her age, now Brett's not around. So we'll have to put off our trip till spring.' Threatening tears thickened her voice.

Hannah groaned, heart squeezing at her lovely mum's disappointment. 'Poor you and Dad!' Their retirement trip had been planned and saved for for so long. Hannah could imagine her dad trying nobly not to show what Nan's hastiness had cost him. Her mum feeling bad for both of them.

Mo was still talking. 'Rob and Leesa are on honeymoon for another two weeks, though I'm not sure what they could have done, with them both working during the day. We'll have to make the best of it and—'

There's nothing left for you in Stockholm . . .

'I'll come home,' Hannah blurted. Then, at Mo's open-mouthed stare, poured out everything about the break-up and how Albin had coated himself with Teflon from the start. 'He says there's nothing left for me in Stockholm and I'm beginning to think he's right,' she wound up.

'Oh, *Han*nah!' Mo wailed, tears for her daughter spilling easily when she hadn't allowed them to fall on her own account. 'How shitty of him, darling. How monstrously crap. But don't let him drive you away if you want to stay. Dad and me could lend you some money—'

'No,' Hannah heard herself declaring. 'Thank you but Middledip will be good for me. It's as if Albin's shaken my life like a snow globe and I'm one of the snowflakes, floating aimlessly. I can look after Nan while I decide what to do next.'

The making of the decision made her feel lighter. When the call ended she found Albin still in the kitchen watching TV. Wondering that they were apparently able to switch from partners to exes so swiftly and completely, she said, 'I'm going to the basement for my packing boxes. I'm moving out tomorrow and whatever I can't squeeze into my suitcases, I'll ship.'

Albin flipped his attention from the international markets, frowning. 'Where are you going?'

'What does it matter?'

He shrugged. 'I might need you.'

'You've made it plain you don't,' Hannah retorted. But added, 'I'm going home.'

He smiled as he turned back to the TV. 'I think that's best.'

Chapter Nine

Nico flew back to the UK on Friday, touching down at Heathrow at nine-twenty p.m.

Hannah was on his mind. Yesterday evening had been bloody. Her shining eyes when she'd first seen him had made him withdraw. If he'd responded, let her within his defences . . . he would have started something.

Instead, he'd deliberately let her think he was forging a new connection with Loren – far from true. When he'd delivered Maria home on Tuesday he'd felt so uneasy at Loren's bleak lassitude and Maria's lost expression that he'd said, 'You won't want Josie overnight for a while. A couple of short visits a week will be better.' Taking and fetching Josie would enable him to keep an eye on Maria and Loren too. There was no way he was leaving Josie on sleepovers unless he was certain Loren could cope and Josie wasn't scared of what her mum might do.

This definitely wasn't 'working on things' with Loren but it had felt preferable to saying he'd found out about Albin and why the *hell* had Hannah responded to Nico when she had a *sambo*? It was disrespectful to both of them and he hated wanting her despite his simmering anger. He could have fallen back on Rob's crap about not going out with a teammate's sister but he suspected she'd brush that away with a 'bonkers brother' remark.

So he'd put his ex-wife between them and the light had died from Hannah's eyes.

With only cabin baggage he cleared passport control and hurried down to take the tube to Holloway Road, using the time on his laptop. Then came the ten-minute walk from the station to his house. It was in darkness when he let himself quietly in. He went up to peep at Josie as she slept, letting the day's stresses melt away at the sight of her blonde locks swirling over the pillow as if blown there. Maria's bed being empty hit him unexpectedly below his breastbone and he hoped Loren was coping with her OK.

Emelie stuck her head out of her door to wave sleepily at him. He gave her a bar of Marabou chocolate he'd grabbed from the airport shop as she always appreciated a taste of home. She whispered her thanks gratefully. '*Tack!*' Ripping open the packet, she withdrew.

Nico went to his own room, undressed and let his tired body plummet onto his bed, groaning with pleasure at the clean smell of the duvet and its coolness on his skin. Then he made the mistake of glancing at his phone. Red notification dots had attached themselves to app icons like ticks. Three missed calls and eight texts with a couple of WhatsApp messages for good measure. He debated switching the bloody thing off but, with a sigh, checked the texts.

All six were from Loren's mum, though he felt less alarmed at the number when he saw she sent a message for every sentence. *Spoke to Loren. She sounded down.*

Are you likely to see her this weekend?

If so, could you ring me after?

Redfern's out of hospital and needs help but I could dash down tomorrow afternoon if I had to.

We mustn't let her get in a state again.

How's Josie?

He sent back: *Just home from biz trip to Stockholm but will telephone her tomorrow to see if I can take Josie to visit. Will contact you after. Josie seemed fine when we FaceTimed after school.* He added: *Is Maria OK?*

The missed calls were from Vivvi too so he disregarded them, glad there was no apparent emergency behind the blizzard of notifications.

The WhatsApp messages were from Tilly, his nanny. The first said, *Won't be able to take Josie to school Monday or Wednesday but will be able to pick her up as usual.*

The second contained an afterthought: *Sorry.* He was about to ask why she couldn't stick to her agreed hours but he lost patience and simply told her what the financial effect would be.

She replied instantly. *Thanks a lot.* It was no doubt meant to be ironic but though she'd helped with Maria as well as Josie after school for the second week of Maria's stay, it had been with a put-upon air, even when he'd been working from home and had shared the load. Their once-OK relationship was deteriorating by the day.

Wide awake now, he checked his work emails, glaring at his inbox in frustration because he'd got up to date at Arlanda airport but people worked from home on Fridays and wrote emails last thing about contract changes or tender requests to make it look as if they worked right up to the end of play.

In one email, Anders asked for a meeting early Monday about a concept rebranding and said the client wanted new promo material for all its thirteen leisure centres in four weeks. *SLS must grab this opportunity with both hands* meaning *Nico will have to shoehorn this into his crazy schedule even though he has annual leave booked in the affected period.*

He snapped shut his laptop and flopped back onto his pillows.

After an hour of lying sleepless, he got up to get the bloody emails out of the way so he could spend the weekend with Josie. At two a.m. he was about to close down when his eating plan and food diary on his desktop caught his eye. He hadn't filled it in for over a week. Then he realised he hadn't eaten since lunch. A gnawing stomach was so familiar he hadn't noticed it. He should have bought himself a big bar of Marabou chocolate too. His mouth watered. Then he caught himself. *No!* Binging on sugar was behaviour he'd left behind because it triggered the feeling that he ought to get rid of it again. He had orange and chocolate chip protein bars in his laptop bag and ate one to fill him up and assuage his sweet tooth. In a few hours he'd eat breakfast according to his plan – porridge. Josie liked porridge made the Swedish way with pudding rice, milk and cinnamon. They'd make it together.

Finally, he slept.

He woke to find Josie on the edge of his bed holding the cordless house phone and hissing, 'Daddy. *Dad.* DAD! It's Mummy.' Her narrow face was creased with worry, hair tousled from sleep.

He surfaced with an effort and took the handset. 'Thanks.' He winked at Josie and said, 'Loren?' into the phone.

'Can you take Maria today?' Loren sounded high and strained.

Nico rubbed an eye. He didn't recall any agreement about continuing to help with Maria and part of him wanted to ask Loren if she was getting him mixed up with Maria's actual father. Then a glance at the bedside clock told him it wasn't even six a.m. and this was odd behaviour. 'Is there a reason?' he asked neutrally.

After several seconds she admitted, 'I'm not feeling good.'

'Right,' he replied tentatively. 'I was going to call you to arrange to bring Josie for a visit so maybe we can discuss it further then.'

Loren's voice began to shake. 'I don't think it's a good idea for Josie to come today.'

Chilled, Nico put out a hand to stroke Josie's hair reassuringly, not sure how much she could hear. He phrased his next question carefully. 'Do you think it would be a good idea for me to fetch Maria soon?'

'Yes.' Loren's voice broke.

Quickly ending the call, Nico kissed Josie. 'Mum's not feeling well so we're going to have Maria home to play.' Josie trailing after him, looking as if she wasn't sure whether to be happy or worried, he woke Emelie to ask her to stay with Josie, dressed and drove to Loren's.

He found Loren sitting on the step of the street door to her apartment block, crying.

'Where's Maria?' he demanded, heart giving a giant leap that Loren should be out here on her own, hair greasy, tears trickling from her chin.

She wiped her face on her wrist. 'She's OK. Watching TV.'

Maria his immediate concern, Nico took the key Loren clutched, slipped past and ran upstairs. In the flat he found

Maria sitting on the floor of the lounge, watching *Peppa Pig* with tear-stained cheeks.

When she saw him she jumped up. 'Juice, Mydad?'

He swung her into his arms. 'Coming right up.' She drank two beakers full while he rocked her absently. She smelled stale and was fully dressed in grubby clothes so had probably slept in them. The thirst she was demonstrating, gulping and gasping as she drank, was that big red flag again, waving in his face, not to be ignored. When she was finally sated he wasted no time but went to her room. The bag he'd returned on Tuesday was on the end of her bed, still packed with most of the clean clothes he'd sent back, so he swung it over his shoulder and located her coat on the hall floor. As he threaded her into it, Maria beamed at him trustingly, making him ashamed of his earlier irritation at Loren's call. 'Shall we go see Josie?' he suggested.

Maria clapped her hands. 'Yes! Yozee.'

Loren came back into the flat, hovering, eyes red and swollen. The confines of the hall made it obvious that she once again smelled of alcohol. He paused. Here was someone else who needed help but he wasn't superman and he wasn't a saint. He could only help her indirectly. 'I'm going to call your mum, OK?' he said gently.

She managed a ghostly smile. 'I'll be OK. Just can't manage the parenting stuff right now.'

Not by any stretch of the imagination was Loren 'OK'. 'Grab some sleep,' he suggested. 'And how about a spare key?'

She found one in a drawer and he left, grappling with Maria, her buggy and her car seat. She barely looked at her mother.

At home, Emelie met him in the hall. 'Josie's in the

shower,' she said, 'Hiya, Maria!' Then, to Nico, 'What's going on?' Her eyes were soft with pity as she took Maria and helped her out of her coat, saying, 'I bet you want breakfast, hey?'

'Yes, beckfast,' Maria agreed, nodding hard.

'Thanks.' Nico whispered the bones of the situation to Emelie, adding, 'I have to call Vivvi.'

Emelie moved towards the kitchen, Maria trotting beside her. 'I'll make breakfast for the girls. And some for you for when you come off the phone,' she added, without looking at him.

Nico nodded, remembering his empty stomach and wondering if Emelie's comment meant he was looking too thin again. He retreated to the relative privacy of his bedroom to make the call.

'Why so early?' Vivvi demanded, when the phone had rung several times, her voice wavering between irritation and uncertainty.

'I've come from Loren's.' Economically, he tried to convey the gravity of the situation without inducing panic.

Vivvi groaned. 'Oh, no. She wouldn't speak on the phone yesterday but she texted to say she was OK.'

'Well, she's not,' Nico said bluntly.

Vivvi drew in an audible breath. 'I'll drive straight there. Be in touch with you later.'

Treading slowly downstairs, Nico entered the kitchen. The girls were absorbed with something on Josie's iPad, used cereal bowls abandoned. Emelie was emptying the dishwasher, her phone jammed between shoulder and ear. 'I haven't told Nico yet,' she was saying, ponytail swinging in time with her rhythmic movement between cupboards and dishwasher. 'It's *not* a good time. We've got an extra child again.' Pause to listen. 'I know, right?' Another pause.

'But it's not a good time!' Pause. 'Yes, you know I want to but I can't be a cow.' There was both longing and exasperation in her voice.

Nico, realising he was eavesdropping and suspecting he wasn't going to like knowing what was going on, said from the doorway. 'Finished breakfast girls?'

Josie flung herself off her stool and into his arms. 'Daddy! I've downloaded a free balloon game for Maria.'

Emelie swung round, blushing to the roots of her hair. 'Um,' she said into the phone, drawing out the syllable significantly, 'I'll call you back.'

Nico took the seat in front of a bowl of granola he assumed was for him and poured milk over it, listening to Josie chatter as if words had a shelf life if not delivered at top speed. Maria got the odd word in when Josie had to take a breath.

Emelie finished emptying the dishwasher in silence and then hovered. Nico felt better when he'd eaten and equal to hearing whatever she had to tell him. 'Josie, can you take Maria up and start running her a bath? I'll be a couple of minutes.' He waited till he could hear them clumping up the stairs, Josie making a lot of noise and Maria giggling.

'Something to tell me?' He smiled at Emelie. He loved his young cousin and hated to see her looking cornered and uncomfortable.

Emelie's fair skin went scarlet. 'Bruno wants me to move in with him,' she admitted. 'I've explained how things are here and that you rely on me and you've been great and everything . . .'

Heart sinking, Nico managed not to lose his smile. 'But you want to live with him?' How would the Josie rota survive without Emelie?

Emelie shuffled. 'Well . . . yeah.'

He fought to stay relaxed, noting the sparkle in Emelie's eyes despite her discomfiture. She was just twenty and her Italian boyfriend had asked her to share his life. If she wanted it, she should be free to grab it. 'What do your parents say?'

She shrugged. 'They're worried about me leaving you in the lurch. And,' she added honestly, 'they think Bruno and me are very young to settle down. I told them moving in doesn't have to mean settling down. We're students,' she added, as if that explained everything . . . which it probably did.

Crossing the kitchen, he gave her a hug. 'If you want to move in with Bruno then do it. I'm not your responsibility, sweetie.'

She looked torn. 'I could still help with some babysitting.' There was a slight emphasis on 'some'.

'That would be great,' he answered reassuringly. Then while she got jubilantly back on the phone to Bruno he went upstairs on leaden feet to check the bath water, though he reminded himself he could probably still ask Emelie if she could take Josie to school on Monday while he had his meeting with Anders. Damn Tilly for bailing on him. Though what would happen if he still had Maria by Monday morning . . .

Nico put his Dad face on as Maria slithered into the bath to play with the lid of the shampoo bottle, trying to avoid Josie's attempt to wash her hair. Between them they spilled at least half the shampoo, the sweet-shop smell of vanilla filling the room. Exchanging chitchat with them both, Nico hid the sinking dismay with which Emelie's news had filled him, answering cheerfully when, from downstairs, she shouted, 'Going out! See you!' before the front door slammed.

When he got the girls downstairs again he opened the post, including a letter from the chair of governors of Barrack Road Primary School acknowledging his concerns but backing up everything Mrs Watts had already said.

It was lunchtime before he remembered his eating plan and heated soup for all three of them. Maria liked squares of buttered bread sunk amongst the vegetables. She fished them out with a spoon and a finger, saying, 'Mmmm, mmmm, mmmm,' and conveyed each messily to her mouth. Josie, like Nico, just dunked the bread before spooning up the remaining soup.

The three of them sat around the breakfast bar, Josie providing a stream of questions. 'When can we have our Christmas lights up? And you know Mum's ill again, how long will Maria be staying?'

'I'm not sure.' Nico was aware he wasn't providing the positivity Josie searched for. She was too sensitive and intelligent to be fobbed off, but he added, 'What would you like to do after lunch?'

'Make charm bracelets,' Josie said promptly. She'd received a set as a birthday present. Unfortunately, but foreseeably, Maria loved the charms and the beads and tried to snatch them out of their compartments until Josie snapped at her. Maria began to cry.

'She's only acting her age,' Nico said gently, swinging Maria off her stool.

Josie acted her age, too, glaring red-faced at the glittering mess of charms. 'She doesn't have to be so stupid.'

That was when Nico's boss Anders chose to ring. When Nico saw his name on the screen of his mobile phone he switched it to silent and ignored it. But before he could get the girls into their coats to forget their spat with a walk on the common, Anders rang the home phone and Josie answered it.

'Yes, he's here,' she said. 'Dad, it's for you.'

'We need a meeting first thing Monday, Nico,' boomed Anders in his half-jovial, half-bossy manner when Nico had smothered a sigh and taken the handset.

'Yes, I replied to your email. It's on my calendar.' For now, Nico ignored the looming childcare issues.

Then Josie tried to help Maria into her coat and Maria protested, 'Mydad do it!' at a volume that made Nico realise he'd developed a headache.

'A new world war is breaking out,' he said lightly, over Maria's howls. 'I'd better go.'

A pause before Anders said, 'Sure.' He didn't sound any more understanding than he ever did as he ended the call but Nico didn't care. It was Saturday.

'Hey, hey, who's crying?' he exclaimed, wrapping Maria up in her coat and tickling her. 'The coat monster doesn't like crying!'

Maria began to laugh instead and as Josie was pouting Nico chased her around with Maria still parcelled in his arms groaning, 'The coat monster, the coat monster!' until Josie burst into giggles too.

As they were bundling the buggy into the boot of the car, Vivvi called. Nico answered, opening the car door for the girls to get in.

Vivvi muttered tearfully, 'Just quickly while Loren's in the bathroom. She's a bloody mess. I'm taking her home with me again. Red's not feeling so good so I've got to scoot. I don't know which way to turn but I'll call you later.'

He was left saying, 'Right, hope Red's OK,' to a dead phone.

They drove to the common beneath a sky of marching clouds. Exercise was his go-to so he kept Maria in her buggy for the first mile by shouting, 'Let's go-go-go!' and running up and down over frosty ruts and potholes to make her chortle with glee. Then they reached the climbing things and Maria yelled to get out to clamber on wooden animals and follow Josie up a cargo net. As nobody was around, Nico did twenty chin-ups on a horizontal bar, Josie counting aloud for him and Maria shouting, 'Hooray!'

Then they tramped on, Josie chattering about ice forming at the edges of puddles, Maria drowsing in the buggy. Part of Nico's mind was still occupied with what would happen on Monday. He tried to think positively. Maybe Vivvi and Loren could cope. If Maria went to join Loren at Vivvi and Red's, Loren would feel supported by other adults; Vivvi would only have to supervise.

He returned home to roast chicken breasts and root vegetables for dinner, his head clearer.

The girls watched TV, squashed together on the sofa as if it was National Cuddle Day. Nico could supervise them from the kitchen so he made time to call his mum Carina for the first time in weeks.

'*Hej, Mamma, det är jag*,' he said. *Hi Mum, it's me.* 'Any snow in Älgäng?'

'A flurry or two. Nothing that stayed,' she answered. 'How's life in England? Are you still coming for Lucia?'

One-handed, he got a bowl of frozen peas ready to put in the microwave. It was the only green vegetable Josie would eat without fuss, though she would happily have eaten iceberg lettuce with every meal, dipping it in gravy

137

as readily as in mayonnaise. 'Can't wait to be home.' They were used to him flitting in and out of Sweden without seeing his family. Stockholm was a four-hour drive from Älgäng.

They talked about work and then Carina said, with an edge to her voice, 'I saw Emelie's mother Ida in Nässjö, in Kvantum.'

Shit, thought Nico. Ida was married to his uncle on his father's side, and they ended up in the same supermarket in Nässjö at the same time, even though one lived in Älgäng and the other in Eksjö. 'Oh?' he said. He propped his backside on a stool, suddenly fatigued. 'I suppose she told you I'm giving a hand with Maria?' He hadn't bothered his parents with this news.

'My son certainly hadn't told me! I rang your father but he knew no more than I did.'

Nico's brows shot up. Carina must have really wanted to know about the situation to seek information from the man she'd divorced twenty-two years ago.

'She's two and being neglected,' he pointed out. 'You wouldn't have left her there either.'

Carina went quiet for several moments before, 'But, Nico, can you afford to be so magnanimous? You're already . . . busy.'

For 'busy' read 'overwhelmed', he thought as he answered calmly, 'So far, so good.'

When the call was over it still wasn't time to cook the peas so Nico hit Facebook, seeing a picture of his brother Mattias smooching with Felicia by the stream that splashed down the hillside outside Husqvarna Museum where Mattias worked. *Looking good,* Nico typed beneath.

Next on his newsfeed was a meme from Hannah. *Dear Life, before you hurl more shit my way, please give me a chance to get behind the fan.* People had posted laughing emojis or *Aw, what's up, Hannah?* Hannah hadn't enlightened them. With a dart of guilt he remembered Thursday evening and her getting a 'call home' text from her mum. Had it been something serious?

He stared at his phone meditatively. It provided several ways to get in touch with Hannah but that didn't mean he should. He put it away. He'd made a decision. He'd drawn boundaries. He shouldn't step over them.

It was ten that night when Nico flopped on his sofa and called Vivvi.

She didn't apologise that she hadn't rung as promised but answered with an enormous sigh. 'I think I'm getting to the bottom of things. The doctor prescribed antidepressants but Loren decided she liked the feelings from depressants – barbiturates – better and got supplies via a Snapchat contact.'

'Snapchat?' Nico echoed incredulously.

'A hotbed for illicit sales of prescription drugs, apparently,' confirmed Vivvi. 'She says she'll talk to a counsellor but goodness knows if she will. Her head's all over the place. Red's feeling drained and depressed and doesn't need this stress.'

Nico could empathise.

'Anyway,' Vivvi said with the air of one who knew it was her duty to tell the worst. 'I'm sorry. I can't cope with Maria.'

'Oh.' He digested that. 'Not even with Loren there?'

'Especially not with Loren here.' She took a big breath. 'We're hoping you can keep her until the situation's sorted out.'

Shock rippled through Nico, even though part of him

had expected this. 'Loren's her mother, you and Redfern are her grandparents and you're abdicating responsibility?'

Vivvi's voice wobbled. 'You have a nanny. Loren's in tears if I suggest she should make more effort with Maria. Or, for that matter, Josie.' Softly, she began to cry. 'I've been searching my heart. If you say no, I'll have to get her officially fostered. There are lovely families who look after children while their parents are ill.'

'Tilly isn't employed full-time.' But he knew Vivvi wasn't listening. He closed his eyes and let his head drop onto the back of the sofa, beaten up by problems.

'The child support would be sent on to you,' Vivvi added hopefully. 'Red and I might be able to weigh in with some money too, if that makes a difference.' He could almost hear the rustle of straws as she clutched at them.

Loren's family being prepared to help with expenses emphasised how much they wanted him to agree. How cornered he was. 'It's not the money,' he croaked, his throat feeling lined with sand. 'I can't—' he muttered. Then he cleared his throat. 'I can't commit myself tonight.'

'OK,' whispered Vivvi.

Too wired to sleep after the call ended, Nico lay on the sofa and, on his phone, pulled up a list of typical symptoms of substance abuse. His heart had been doing a lot of sinking but this weighed it down further. *Withdrawal from responsibility* was high on the list.

Yep. He was becoming excruciatingly aware.

Chapter Ten

On Sunday, Nico had a lot to think about. On automatic, he began the day with the porridge he'd neglected to make the day before while chatty Josie entertained her sister. Nico watched them play with pastel-coloured magnetic building blocks Josie had found in the back of a cupboard.

What the hell was he going to do? His mum was right: Maria wasn't his responsibility – but he didn't have the stomach for handing his daughter's sister over to the state.

Josie kept asking about Loren like a police officer trying to catch him out in an inconsistency. 'Where's Mum gone?'

'She's staying with Grandma and Grandpa till she's feeling better. Grandpa's recovering after his operation so we're helping out with Maria.' Yes, they all hoped Mum would get better. Same for Grandpa. Yes, Grandma did have a lot on her plate at the moment. But, yes, Mum would get better.

Maria listened, glancing between Josie and Nico as if checking they were still there.

After his thoughts going round in circles for most of

the morning, Nico realised he knew someone to talk to, someone with a wealth of experience. Nan Heather, Rob and Hannah's grandmother, had fostered many children. Correctly assuming an elderly lady would have a landline, he ascertained her number from thephonebook.bt.com and called her up while the girls played in the lounge.

He found he didn't have to remind her who he was. She wore her ninety years lightly.

'Can I help you?' Nan Heather's voice reminded him of a chesty mouse.

'Hope so.' He plunged into the story of how Maria had come to be staying with him again and what had been asked of him. 'I'm frying my brain, trying to decide what to do,' he ended ruefully.

'Hmm,' said Nan. 'You've talked of responsibility but you must also be pragmatic. Maria's birth dad isn't in the picture?'

Maria's dad. Loren's lover. To Nico he'd never had an actual name. 'Only financially. He's never met Maria and I'm told Loren doesn't have contact details.'

Nan Heather grunted. 'Social services will have! But let's assume it's not possible for him to help. Maria's mum and grandparents can't look after her. Do you care for her?'

His neck tightened. Was Nan Heather one of those who viewed single dads as second best when it came to child-care? 'Take care of her, do you mean? I think I do OK.'

'I'm sure. But, care. You know. Hold in affection,' she asked gently. 'The overriding need for any child is to be safe and well cared for.'

His stomach somersaulted as the various meanings of the English word 'care' dawned. When he'd read the phrase 'well cared for' he'd always assumed it related to food and shelter. Being safe from abuse. He had to sit down as he realised that he didn't just care for Maria . . . he cared *about* her. Not just if she was shut in her room, not just whether her stomach was empty but whether it was tied in knots of fear. The reason he couldn't bear to think of her going to strangers – including her birth dad – was that he cared whether she felt happy. He swallowed. 'It's hard not to. She's a cute, engaging little thing.'

The creaky voice on the other end of the phone softened. 'Then before you decide if you *should* look after her you need to establish: *can* you? You won't want to take her from one iffy, unsettled situation to another. If that were to be the case, you might have to consider letting her settle with experienced fosterers until it's established to what extent Loren will be in her life.'

'Right,' he murmured, shaken by quite this much pragmatism. 'You don't think her being with Josie is valuable?'

'Very,' she said promptly. 'And social services usually want to keep siblings together if possible, too. But it's only one consideration. Can you arrange your life to accommodate Maria?'

Nico deliberated. 'Childcare would be tricky. I'm already having trouble covering Josie's needs since Loren can't take her at all now, my cousin Emelie wants to move out and Tilly, the nanny Josie's had since she was tiny, has become less flexible. We'd need a 24/7 live-in nanny, which would part Josie from Tilly.'

'They're big changes.' Nan Heather's creaky, squeaky voice oozed sympathy. 'If you do offer Maria a home – especially on an open-ended basis – it's wise to inform social services. Don't be scared of them. They'll support a suitable friend or family member looking after a kiddie above trying to find them a home with strangers.'

'I hadn't thought of that,' said Nico quietly, a strange, squeezing sensation in his belly. Social services supported other people's families. Not his. He thanked Nan Heather for her insight and advice before ending the call.

Back in the sitting room, the girls were playing a game that involved Maria pushing Josie off the sofa with pudgy little hands and Josie falling with great, put-on wails. 'Nooooo! Nooo! Awwww, Maria, nooo!' Musical toddler chortles filled the air. Nico watched from the doorway, scenarios flashing through his mind like sweaty nightmares. Maria going to an unknown family. Nico taking Josie on visits. Trying to explain why Maria had to be left behind. Coping with Josie's emotions, her white, distressed face. Josie might raise her voice to Maria occasionally but she loved her violently.

His daughter's sister. It sounded like the title of one of those psychological thrillers.

Fucksake. Why him?

Awful tasks floating around him like demons in a horror movie, he phoned Emelie, reluctant to put on his big-hearted cousin who shouldn't have to be bothering her head with his issues. 'Is there any way you can do the early school run on Monday and have Maria until Tilly rocks up? I've got an unmissable meeting.'

Like Nan, Emelie was sympathetic but pragmatic. 'For that little time, yes. I'd love to offer to do more but I've got essays and stuff.'

His insides lurched guiltily. 'I realise I'm relying on your maturity to make up for Tilly's rigidity and that you have a degree to get. I'm going to try for unpaid leave from Tuesday.'

For the rest of the day Nico chewed over the Maria situation and decided it was Nan Heather's phrase 'open-ended' that was holding him back. He waited until the girls were asleep, then telephoned his ex-mother-in-law.

'If I took Maria it couldn't be an open-ended situation,' he said, hoping he was being compassionate but clear. 'At the outside, I could have her until Josie and I go to Sweden on December eleventh.'

Vivvi gave a strangled gasp of relief. 'Oh, that would be fantastic. It gives us nearly three weeks. I can't thank you enough.'

Decision made, Nico managed a reasonable night's sleep.

Josie once again had the Monday Morning School Blues. She stared down at her Weetabix as if wishing she could leap into it and vanish. Emelie had to coax her into her school coat and the image stuck to Nico like a burr as he hurried to the tube station through a raw wintry morning that nipped his ears.

He eventually reached the SLS offices in Holborn, using his pass to gain entry then hurrying up stairs tiled like a brown and cream chessboard.

Katya followed him into his office as he hung up his black wool coat. 'Meeting room two,' she said. 'Anders's PA just put it on the electronic calendar.'

'Thanks.' He swung his laptop bag back onto his shoulder, wishing he'd had more than five minutes' notice that the meeting was to take place two floors above.

Anders was there before him, hooking up his computer to the wall screen. Presumably the AV was the reason he'd decided on a meeting room as there was no sign of them being joined by other staff members. Anders rocked a mixed retro look with a Seventies moustache but a Sixties short-back-and-sides. His wide-lapelled suits teamed with busy floral ties were a fashion mystery.

As soon as Nico set foot on the dark carpet Anders snapped, 'We need to get this project going.'

The filter coffee machine was emitting an appetising fragrance and Nico headed for it. 'There's a lot to be said for scheduling it for January. What's the client's rush? Do you know?'

Anders pulled up a presentation on the screen. 'Here's what we sent them.'

'Yes,' Nico agreed drily, watching black coffee pouring from jug to cup. 'I put it together. But at no time did we discuss turning around the promo material in four weeks – especially when I have annual leave for one of them.'

A reproving frown creased Anders's forehead. 'It's an important new client, Nico.'

'We don't have contract approval. The acquisitions team hasn't—'

Anders took his eyes from the screen and fixed Nico with a glare. It was a technique he practised often. It was meant to make people back down.

Nico was not easily intimidated. He strolled to a seat at an angle to his boss's and returned a steady gaze. 'Is there a reason for the rush?'

'Is there a reason for us to underperform?' Anders returned coldly.

'Rushing when we don't need to might lead to our underperforming.' Irritation tightened Nico's shoulders. Anders's main leadership weakness was entrenching himself and refusing to budge. You could term it having the courage of his convictions or you could call it blind stubbornness. Sometimes it made his team step up; sometimes it made them flap about frantically and, to use his word, underperform.

Anders steepled his fingers and narrowed his eyes. 'The client and I have shaken hands on these dates.'

Nico felt his jaw drop. 'You've agreed an unrealistic delivery with my client on my project?' He was aware he wasn't speaking in the respectful manner Anders considered his due but the prospect of achieving such a target loomed over his head like an anvil with 'stress' painted on it. Anders clumsily sticking his fingers into Nico's carefully tended pies was disrespectful.

'The wrong' wasn't a place Anders occupied comfortably and his frown grew darker. 'We met socially. Happenstance. You have a problem with it?'

The air in the room was now so cold that Nico expected icicles. 'All those I've already mentioned,' he retorted. 'Especially as I need to request dependants' leave to take me up to my annual holiday.' He started to apprise Anders of the latest issues with Loren and Maria.

Anders interrupted. '*What?*'

Shocked that his boss wasn't even making a pretence of hearing him out, Nico tried a fact or two. 'It's lawful for me to request dependants' leave—'

'Twice in a few weeks?' Anders sliced in.

'I took the last lot as paid leave.' Nico felt the hairs on the back of his neck prickle. 'It's a reasonable request when I'm in difficult circumstances.'

White around his lips, Anders switched his gaze to his laptop. Very slowly, he closed it. 'I'll talk to HR and come back to you.' His contempt was plain, probably meant to elicit a stammering apology and retraction.

Nico felt something snap inside him. 'You have to go to HR? Management make decisions, not HR. You're beginning to make my position untenable.' He worked bloody hard and now Anders acted like an arsehole when asked for unpaid leave to deal with a tricky situation concerning the well-being of a toddler. Any reasonable employer would show compassion. Shaking with rage, he jumped to his feet, gaining satisfaction when Anders flinched. 'You've left me no alternative but to consider my position.' On those words he stalked from the room and worked furiously on conference calls before he left.

When he reached home he discarded his mood along with his coat, smiling his way through the evening, chatting with Josie, reading to Maria. Once Maria was sleeping and Josie listening drowsily to an audiobook in bed, he poured himself a glass of scotch and sat down calmly to work through his options with pen and paper. It didn't take long.

Stressed out

Poor work/life balance

Single dad with, presently, two kids to look after

Childcare for two-year-old different ballgame to childcare for eight-year-old

Tilly cannot/will not help with Maria

Emelie moving out – no longer able to help with either child except occasional babysitting

Anders being a twat, he added, unprofessionally. *Fundamental professional differences. Personally dislike one another but did expect a reasonable hearing.*

He took a gulp of scotch and wrote his conclusion:

I need to reassess lifestyle with a view to making myself happier and responsive to current childcare. He paused and studied the list for a few moments.

Then he wrote his resignation letter.

Chapter Eleven

It was *lovely* to be back amongst the cosy cottages and windswept lanes of Middledip. It was just that at first Hannah was too preoccupied to realise it.

Autumn seemed to have decided not to bother this year and winter had swept in as if from Narnia. Iron-hard frosts stripped the colour from the landscape, bleak but beautiful, but the ruthless removal of Hannah from her life in Sweden made her feel as if she were seeing it through a dirty window. Her two big suitcases were in the spare room, cramped by the jumble Nan collected between village hall sales. Mo and Jeremy had rumbled off in The Bus the day after Hannah arrived. They'd offered to put off their departure because Nan, sporting a plaster cast that looked too heavy for her twiggy arm, was grey with the shock of her injury.

'The Eurotunnel and your first two camping grounds in France are booked,' Hannah had argued. 'I'll take Nan to appointments and shopping. You two clear off on the retirement trip you've been planning for years.'

Mo had given her a cuddle. 'But you won't dwell on

Albin's cold treachery, will you? Keep busy, see your old mates. Visit The Three Fishes and The Angel Café.'

'I will.' Hannah gratefully accepted the use of Mo's old white Volvo and, finally, waved off the pea-soup-coloured bus.

Soon, Mo and Jeremy were travelling down the east side of France to a campground in Strasbourg's urban natural park, where the city of Strasbourg was almost on the doorstep. Rob and Leesa were halfway through their honeymoon in Goa. Excepting Nan, the family members who usually lived here were away while Hannah, who usually lived away, was here. She shopped, prepared meals and, late on Wednesday afternoon, took the jumble to village hall stalwart Carola so she had room to unpack.

When she hurried home through the yellow door into the warm kitchen she actually managed a smile because Nan exclaimed, 'Hello, honey bunny!' as if Hannah were still a child. Nan added, with a flash of her old self, 'How about we enjoy being single and go to the pub?'

Hannah giggled, enjoying this sign that her grandmother might be getting used to her injury as well as the loss of Brett. 'Let's. I'd love a big, fat pint of Ruddles County.'

Nan pulled a face. 'I'd be up peeing all night if I drank that. A nice glass of chardonnay will do for me. And maybe a salad.'

They huddled into their coats and, heads ducked into a bitter wind, staggered at Nan's stuttering, stick-step pace up Main Road to The Three Fishes. Last year, it had undergone a facelift after long-time landlord Harrison Tubb had retired with one-time barmaid Janice and passed the pub to Ferdy and Elvis. Hannah was still getting used to The Three Fishes without 'Tubb from the pub' behind the bar.

They stepped through a door edged with blinking fairy lights, greeted by blinding snakes of tinsel, a sparkly explosion of a Christmas tree and the easy-going hum of conversation from villagers enjoying a midweek drink. The curtains and carpet were a trendy grey that contrasted with colourful tiles in the dining area and the original, polished wood bar where more lights twinkled around the optics.

Nan chose a table distant from the big TV on the wall, near the wood-burning stove and featuring armchairs rather than stools. 'Look at Ben Bell and that lot gawping at the TV instead of talking to each other. They might as well stay home.' She nodded disparagingly at 'that lot', a group of men known as the blokey blokes: hair and beards shaved to stubble, big on beer, darts and TV sport. Nan had fostered Ben Bell when he was a ten-year-old needing shelter while his mother got away from his father, a couple of years before Hannah was born.

'Their five pints a night each probably keeps the pub afloat.' Hannah grinned, waving a greeting to the blokey blokes as she braved the massed fairy lights of the bar to buy drinks.

When Hannah returned with the Ruddles County she'd promised herself, Nan sniffed. 'In my day, women didn't drink pints.' She sipped her wine, holding the glass daintily by the stem.

Hannah took several unrepentant swallows of the rich bitterness that was English ale. 'It still is your day.'

Nan looked wistful. 'It doesn't feel like it. My day was when I was young and healthy. Middledip was smaller and everyone knew each other. People only left to go to war.'

'Blimey!' Hannah recoiled. 'That's a bit real, Nan. Wouldn't you rather they left to go on holiday?'

Nan laughed her creaking laugh. 'Yes, of course. I'm being nostalgic for when I was busy all day long with children. Memories glamorise even the terrible bits, I suppose.' She paused to wave at a couple who'd come into the pub. 'Look at that Arnott-Rattenbury boy and his wife. I never thought he'd settle down. My old friend Lucasta used to be great friends with his grandfather, if you get my drift.'

Everyone knew Ratty from the village garage and his wife Tess so Hannah, smothering a laugh at Nan's frankness, waved too. Ratty was quite swoony, though about eight years her senior. She remembered him talking to Nico at the wedding.

'Do you miss the foster kids?' Hannah asked, watching Ratty and Tess join another couple at a table. 'You must have stopped ages ago. I can barely remember it.'

'I gave up when I was sixty-five, a few years after Granddad died, so you'd have been seven. I miss the liveliness,' Nan said reflectively. Across the room, the blokey blokes groaned at something on TV and Ben Bell got up to play the gambling machine. He caught sight of Nan and grinned and winked.

When he'd finished with the machine, which, judging from its triumphant burp and jingle, was victorious in the encounter, he crossed to where they sat in the warmth of the wood burner. 'What have you been doing to yourself?' he demanded, indicating Nan's cast. 'Been in a fight?' Though he joked, concern clouded his eyes.

'Yes – you should see the other bloke.' Nan beamed. 'How are you, Ben?'

Hannah listened while they chatted. Bell, in his mid-forties now, was courteous with Nan though his usual persona was loud and brash. He'd once been known for the kind of 'jokes' that made women uncomfortable but he'd toned that down in the past few years. Presently, he replenished his pint at the bar and wandered back to rejoin the other blokey blokes before the TV.

Nan watched him go. 'Seeing Ben reminds me – that boy Nico phoned me on Sunday when you were at the supermarket. His ex's family want him to look after the little girl again, Maria, and he asked my advice.'

'Really? You didn't tell me.' A shiver tingled through Hannah at Nico's name, even prefaced with 'that boy', as Nan termed him.

Nan shrugged, settling her plastered wrist more comfortably. 'He's a good man and has a soft spot for the little tot. I told him to think whether he actually can take her in rather than whether he should. Two-year-olds don't look after themselves.'

Hannah digested this along with her next sips of ale, contrasting the hot, intense Nico she'd danced with at the wedding with the remote and chilly Nico that last time at Hörnan. 'Lots of men would have told their ex to get lost,' she observed neutrally, wondering how Nico having Maria fit in with him and Loren 'working on things'.

Nodding sagely, Nan polished off the rest of her wine. 'Lots. I'm not so much in the mood for salad now. I fancy chips. And they do a scrumptious chocolate tart.'

The evening slipped by. People came over to chat: first Ratty and Tess, who'd left their little boy with his grandparents while they enjoyed a date night. Next was the ever-present small, blonde Carola, who left her partner Owen chatting at the bar to come over. 'I hope you'll make the seniors village hall Christmas party?' she said to Nan.

Nan nodded. 'Hope so. Me and Hannah will come by

The Angel soon, too. I like your shortbread Christmas angels dipped in chocolate.'

Carola beamed. 'I hope we have another good year and that the new place won't affect us.'

A lovely, gentle man who lived on a smallholding with a menagerie of animals, Gabe, came up in time to hear her words. Nan still referred to him as 'new' because he'd only come to the village twenty years ago. He'd retired as a bank manager and now owned The Angel. 'We'll be fine,' he said soothingly. 'If Posh Nosh ever opens it'll be a three-mile drive from here.'

'Closer on foot,' Carola argued, pulling out a chair for him.

Gabe twinkled as he placed his pint on the table, tossed his thinning silver ponytail over his shoulder and sat down. 'Two and a half miles via the footpath through the Carlysle Estate,' he conceded.

Hannah was curious. 'What new place? Another coffee shop?'

Carola glowered. 'Simeon Carlysle took it into his head to convert the old stables on the estate into shops and a tea room called Posh Nosh. Supposed to be up and running for Christmas.' A line dug in between her eyes.

All the villagers knew the nearby Carlysle Estate. Some were employed there. Hannah knew Christopher and Cassie Carlysle by sight because they occasionally turned up at village events but their son, Simeon, was just a name to her. 'Whereabouts is it?' she asked.

Gabe explained. 'You have to drive right out of Middledip and nearly to Port-le-Bain village before you turn left.'

Hannah nodded. 'Oh, I know. When I managed Creative Lanes at Bettsbrough our coffee shop got business from our shops' customers. It wasn't the main draw.' Carola crossed her fingers, still looking doubtful.

Hannah was drawn into conversation with Kitty, mum of one of her old village friends Deanna and a fond grandmother to little Shelby, Deanna's three-year-old daughter. 'I'll tell Deanna I've seen you. She'll be stoked that you're back.'

'I'll call her so we can meet up,' Hannah promised. 'I'll be here at least as long as Nan has the cast on, I should think.'

Meanwhile, Nan was enjoying a chinwag with Melanie from the village shop. When Melanie eventually drifted off to another part of the warm and jolly pub, Nan whispered to Hannah, 'There's a job there, if you want it. Poor Melanie's got to have a hysterectomy. You run shops. You could temp.'

Hannah stared at Nan, whose cap of silvery white curls looked blue because of the Christmas lights. 'What about you?'

Nan drew herself up indignantly. 'I'm retired!'

Snorting with laughter, Hannah gave her grandmother a hug. 'I didn't mean what about you for the job,' she explained. 'I meant that I'm supposed to be looking after you.'

Nan glared at her plaster cast. 'It seems a shame for you to spend so much time cooped up with me.'

'It won't be forever,' Hannah consoled. She didn't say that the village shop was hardly what she wanted out of life. Her upscale luxury goods boutique in Stockholm's gorgeous, colourful Old Town had been only the start of what she'd planned. But bigger, better premises or even a chain of stylish shops selling beautiful things had definitely receded into the land of might-have-been for now.

Despite Nan's indomitable spirit, she couldn't cook or butter bread; she needed help with buttons, zips, her hair . . . dozens of things.

The situation would improve as Nan did but Hannah knew this limbo would continue for several weeks yet. Then Hannah could start again.

Albin had torched her dreams but she'd rise from the ashes.

Chapter Twelve

On Friday, Nan turned quiet and pensive when flowers arrived from Brett, red chrysanthemums with yellow centres. Hannah arranged them in a vase in the kitchen but Nan said she didn't want to discuss Brett and gazed out of the window at bare branches scratching at the winter sky. For the rest of the day she was abstracted, barely touching her evening meal.

After washing up, Hannah left her grandmother to watch *Coronation Street* and went upstairs to call Albin. She felt at home now in the little bedroom that smelled of lavender from the sachets Nan put in the drawers. From the bed she could see a black, starry night through the dormer window and gazed at its brilliance while she formulated a plan of attack.

It wouldn't have shocked her if Albin had declined her call but maybe curiosity got the better of him as he answered on the fifth ring with a brisk, 'Hannah.'

'I haven't received the value of my stock, returned rent and compensation payment yet,' she said steadily. 'I know you won't want to keep me waiting.' The stars were bright

157

tonight, like a million diamonds, like the lights glittering on the black water beneath Vasabron.

'I'll email a list of stock held and what you paid for it,' he said.

'OK,' she agreed, wondering when. 'I can cross-reference it to the paid invoices in my receipts bank. Then there's the display equipment I owned and the overpaid rent. I presume you've returned the till to the lease company?' Stars would be hanging over Stockholm, too, but the lights of big cities always dimmed the starry radiance.

Albin said, smoothly, 'Julia attended to it.'

Good for Julia. 'What about the compensation for lost income?' Hannah went on.

Albin assumed a terse, regretful tone. 'I've taken advice and there's no goodwill in the business because I'm not buying you out, as such. Goodwill is generally established by calculating the assets over the liabilities when taking over a going concern. I'm not buying a going concern. You merely ceased trading.' He went on talking about 'intangible assets' and 'external sources'.

Hannah looked away from the stars because they were too beautiful to be associated with this conversation. Maybe it was because he drawled the phrase 'merely ceased trading' when it had been the greatest disaster in her life and entirely at his instigation, but rage boiled up like molten lava. She halted his flow of business-speak. 'So you're breaking your word?'

He tutted. 'I'm trying to explain—'

'You offered, and I accepted, a *goodwill gesture* – which isn't the same as goodwill in a business – to compensate me for the mark-up I'd expected to make on that stock over Christmas. Now you're saying you're not going to pay that. Correct?' The scent of lavender became sickly.

158

Down the line, Albin sighed. 'I've taken advice, Hannah. I'm sure of my legal footing.'

Hannah could hardly hear him for her blood thundering in her ears. 'Don't think you have all the power. Do your parents want "The Lair" or "The Den" or whatever you "hunters" call the place you conduct your polyamorous activities associated with their name? Do the other traders in Köpmangatan know about the sleazy club you're going to open in their midst?'

A pause. Then Albin's voice sharpened. 'Threats aren't worthy of you.'

'Then don't go back on your offer,' Hannah returned, pretty sure her words were a tacit admission of threat-making but red-hot fury making it impossible to care. 'Stand by what we agreed: compensation for you taking my livelihood away.'

Abruptly, Albin's control snapped. 'I'll pay a small, reasonable sum to get you out of my hair and because of what was once between us.'

'You should pay because it's what you agreed and what's fair,' Hannah hissed.

'You're so provincial,' he shot back icily. 'I'm glad you're back in your unimportant little village. It's where you belong.'

Hannah felt a swell of triumph that she'd made Albin climb down from his lofty perch of smooth control to indulge in wild sniping. 'You're right. I belong with genuine, honest people who have integrity.' She put enough emphasis on the words 'honest' and 'integrity' to annoy him.

'I've learned from this,' Albin said slowly. 'I won't be led by my dick in future.'

It was an obvious attempt to diminish Hannah by

suggesting lust had led him into a relationship not worthy of him, just as he'd hinted before that he found her a bit downmarket. 'But isn't your new venture all about that part of your anatomy?' she drawled.

The call ended and it wasn't Hannah who pressed the button.

Her heart hammered and her palms sweated. She'd threatened Albin and wasn't sorry. In fact, she thought she'd discovered a hitherto unsuspected Achilles heel. In the past she'd heard his high-flying friends gleefully recounting cut-and-thrust business negotiations but had had no understanding of why they relished them. Now she knew. Putting him at a disadvantage had made her feel powerful.

Then she remembered that it hadn't got her any actual money and the feeling of power drained away. This tawdry bickering was all that was left between them. It was a sad end to what had been an exciting affair.

She trailed downstairs and found Nan opening the door to Carola who'd brought angel-shaped shortbreads dipped in chocolate, beaming from beneath her blonde fringe as she waved away their thanks. 'They're to make your wrist heal quicker, Heather.'

Tears pricked Hannah's eyes at the unsolicited kindness. It was a symbol of everything that was right about Middledip. Warmth. Kindness. Likeable people.

The spat with Albin woke Hannah from her post-relationship, post-repatriation daze. She spent Saturday, apart from helping Nan, mired in admin and bureaucracy at the little square dining table.

She began by emailing Albin with the suggestion of a compensatory twelve per cent mark-up on stock for being so abruptly tipped out of Hannah Anna Butik. *It's modest, to take account of being spared overheads,* she told him.

As a business transaction it was unsatisfactory and informal but going to a solicitor would be expensive and tricky as a non-Swedish national no longer living in Sweden. She turned her attention to change of address notifications and giving notice on her Swedish phone contract.

The phone in the kitchen rang and soon afterwards Nan poked her head around the door. 'Gabe's going into Bettsbrough so I'm going along for the ride.'

Hannah glanced up. 'You don't need me? Have a lovely time.' She helped Nan with her coat, scarf and mittens and waved her off in Gabe's small truck.

Next task on her list: tax authorities. She informed HMRC she was back in the UK but then stalled at knowing whether she should register as employed or self-employed, as she was currently neither. She left it for another day, along with completing a self-assessment to see if she could grab back some of the tax she'd paid in Sweden this year.

The website of Skatteverket or the Swedish Tax Authority walked her through the deregistration for 'F tax' and '*mervärdesskatt*', Sweden's VAT. *Bleurgh*, was the politest of her thoughts on the process. One thing about the lease being in Albin's name was that it made winding up the business relatively easy. A sole trader was simply ceasing to trade, and never mind her aching heart.

The afternoon wore on and it was dark by the time Hannah heard the sound of the back door opening. 'Thanks, Gabe,' she heard Nan say. 'Just put the bag in there.' Nan's rusty voice rose. 'Hannah, I've been Christmas shopping and you're not to look in the cupboard in the hall.'

Hannah felt her spirits lift at these homely, loving words. 'OK, Nan,' she called, as if she were a child. 'Can I come out now? I didn't realise the time. It's nearly seven and I've done nothing about dinner.' She shut her laptop and went into the old-fashioned kitchen to chat to kindly Gabe and invite him to stay for supper. 'I could do us a mixed grill because it will be quick,' she said, turning to take Nan's coat. 'New hat, Nan?'

The old lady beamed, the lenses in her glasses flashing under the kitchen light as she carefully lifted a plum-coloured fleece hat from her silvery white curls, giving a little pat to her new purchase. 'Closing-down sale. Honestly, half of Bettsbrough High Street's closing down and the other half's charity shops and coffee shops.'

'And we went in both,' Gabe supplied, eyes twinkling, silver eyebrows beetling. 'Supper would be wonderful, thank you.'

Hannah grilled sausages, bacon and tomatoes and scrambled eggs. Gabe stationed himself at the toaster and produced golden buttery toast.

'I should break my arm more often if it means a meal with lovely people and someone else to cook,' Nan said, as Gabe cut up her food. 'Bettsbrough looked beautifully Christmassy, Hannah. There's a huge tree at the edge of the square and lights strung over the main roads.' She munched on a piece of sausage before adding, 'Are you busy tomorrow, dear? Only it's the day to decorate the village hall ready for the old folks' party.'

Smothering a snort of laughter at ninety-year-old Nan referring to 'old folk', Hannah took the hint. 'I don't mind being an extra pair of hands. I'm not sure what you can do, though, with your arm.'

Nan beamed. 'I can enjoy the Christmasness.'

'Speaking of which,' Hannah said, 'shall we write your Christmas cards? I've made stickers to say "Written by Heather's granddaughter while Heather's arm is out of action". I printed them at Mum and Dad's when I went round to water the plants.'

'After supper,' Nan declared with relish. 'I like to get them done nice and early.'

When Sunday came around, Hannah had to admit that a dose of 'Christmasness' was welcome. They strolled through the village, waving at Melanie at Booze & News, passing the closed doors of Ratty's garage. Nan leaned on her stick while Hannah detoured up crazy paving paths to push jolly red envelopes through letterboxes.

Nan took a child-like joy in every cottage garden where frost rimed leaf and twig, twinkling in pale winter sunlight. 'Look how pretty those red berries are amongst the frosty spider webs. Everything feels quiet and peaceful.'

'It does.' Hannah was content to amble at Nan's pace, enjoying the still, spun-glass world of frozen fronds and icy bird baths.

The village hall was, in contrast, a hive of industry. Carola was in the middle of everything, directing people up stepladders or to the machine that blew up balloons. Children held paper chains, a small black dog clicked his claws excitedly on the wooden floor as if happy to be involved and the Christmas tree twinkled like a star shower. People called for scissors or tape and provided critical feedback: 'That angel's wonky!' or 'The holly leaves are the wrong green.'

Every single person wore a smile.

Hannah was back in the 'unimportant little village' where she belonged. She made cups of tea amidst the

163

banter and laughter and got all glittery from hanging decorations. The day sped by.

It was as they wandered home through the darkened village, past the pub festooned with lights, that Hannah realised Nan was subdued. 'Have you tired yourself out?' she asked, concerned.

Nan just grumbled, 'This wind that's got up is sharp enough to shave a gooseberry,' and huddled into her coat.

Hannah waited till they were home, warming up over a cuppa before she asked again. 'Tired after your busy day?' She got out the biscuits in the old Quality Street tin with the pictures that reminded her of the buildings of Stortorget, Gamla Stan, in the hope Nan would eat one or two. Age was shrinking her too quickly.

'Thinking,' said Nan, blowing her tea. 'Last year Brett helped with the decorating of the hall.'

Hannah twined her fingers with Nan's where they protruded from the cast. 'You miss him.'

'We were great friends.' The old lady turned her long-sighted gaze to the glowing bouquet of blood-red chrysanthemums and icy green eucalyptus. 'If I hadn't let him turn it into a romance then he'd never have wanted to marry me. He wouldn't have pushed that agreement at me and I'd still have my best friend.'

Gently, Hannah squeezed the papery fingers, cool despite the warmth of the room. 'Can't you go back to being friends?'

Nan's voice thickened. 'It wasn't enough for him, apparently. He said it was ridiculous not to share what time we had left, instead of being visitors in each other's homes.'

Hurting for this stalwart, elderly woman who deserved happiness after all the people she'd looked after in her life, Hannah murmured, 'There must be a solution. You miss him. He's sent you flowers.' She took a breath and prepared to get her head bitten off. 'Was the prenup idea so awful? You want what you own to go to Mum, I expect, not to pass to him and then his kids. He'll want the same on his side.'

'I haven't got much.' Nan's voice was small and tired. 'It was the not trusting.' But, for the first time, she didn't sound completely convinced. 'I think I'll have soup for supper then listen to the radio in bed. If your mum rings tell her I'll speak to her next time.'

Later, Hannah helped her to bed. Just before she left the room, Nan said, 'Try and find some time for yourself as well as looking after me, duck. You need to start thinking about what you're going to do next.'

Hannah nodded. 'I have been. I need to get my dosh out of Albin first, though.' Downstairs, she sipped a glass of wine before the fire. Nan was right. In January, when Nan didn't need her so much or Mo and Jeremy were back, she'd need to get her life going again, without Albin. The world, as the saying went, was her oyster. She could do anything. Go anywhere.

Then, without meaning to, she thought of Nico and where she might have gone if they'd met again when both were happily single.

Chapter Thirteen

On Monday evening, Hannah met her friend Deanna at The Three Fishes. Deanna's mum Kitty had agreed to babysit. Nan was watching a box set of *Call the Midwife* that had been delivered today, another olive branch from Brett with a note suggesting they talk.

Nan hadn't made up her mind about that, though Hannah had reminded her she didn't have to marry him. 'Everyone lives together these days.' Nan had given her an old-fashioned look.

It was 'Two meals for £15' night and the pub was busy. Ferdy's black-rimmed glasses reflected the colourful Christmas lights as he chatted a mile a minute with the customers. Elvis was quieter, neat in a shirt and tie and with a nervous habit of smoothing a hand over his bald head.

'Let's start as we mean to go on,' Deanna said as she ordered a bottle of cava. 'It's bliss to be child-free for the evening.' She sported four-inch heels that meant Hannah reached her shoulder and ripped jeans tight enough to look as if they'd ripped of their own accord. Her frizzy hair was caught up to cascade from one side and flipped people in the face when she turned her head.

In contrast, Hannah – because, hey, it was only the village pub – wore comfy jeans, flat boots and a slouchy blue top. The men from MAR Motors were lounging around a table. Two Hannah knew only by sight but Ratty, the one with dark curly hair and piercing blue eyes who'd been here with his wife last week, nodded hello.

'So why are you home?' Deanna demanded when they'd found a table. It was a bit near the dartboard for Hannah's tastes but only a few locals were playing rather than there being a raucous match against a visiting team.

So Hannah explained economically, 'Ex-boyfriend turned out to be a calculating shit at about the same time Nan needed help.'

Deanna murmured, 'Wow. It sounds a lot more exciting than nappies and clinic appointments.'

'A bit too exciting,' she said gloomily, pouring the wine, which fizzed and settled, reflecting the coloured lights all around the bar. 'I feel as if someone stuck me in a cannon and shot me home. Nothing's the same here. Nan's hurt, Mum and Dad are travelling and Rob's married.' Then, thinking Deanna might feel left out, added, 'And you're a mum.'

Deanna beamed. 'You haven't seen my Shelby since she was a baby, have you? You could have a job as my nanny.'

'But I'm not a nanny and I don't want to be one,' Hannah pointed out.

Deanna sighed. 'And I can't afford one. Fancy some crisps?'

While Deanna was at the bar, Hannah listened to the conversations around her. A couple discussed work. A group of youngsters laughed over their phones.

Ratty was talking about Simeon Carlysle. He spoke very Queen's English compared to most of the villagers and Hannah knew he'd attended a posh school, despite his tattoos and his business restoring old cars. 'Simeon was the same when we were at school. Spoilt boy,' he said. 'Carlysle Courtyard's almost ready and now he's vanished.'

One of his mates, a blond man Hannah suddenly remembered was called Pete, asked, 'Where's he gone?'

'Scotland. Met a woman and set off after her like a Jack Russell on heat. Refused to wait until he'd got Carlysle Courtyard open and safely trading. Cassie and Christopher Carlysle don't know what to do with a batch of unready shops and dissatisfied tenants moving into them.'

I could tell them, Hannah thought idly, remembering last week's conversation with Carola and Gabe about the old stable yard Simeon Carlysle had converted into cute country retail units. Retail start-ups were not new to her. She turned and stared at the men. She *could* tell them. She cleared her throat. 'Sorry to butt in but I used to help manage Creative Lanes in Bettsbrough and I ran a shop in Sweden,' she ventured. 'I might be able to help your friends if they need a project manager to get their shops trading. But I'm looking after my grandmother so wouldn't be able to do nine to five.'

Ratty looked at her with interest. 'No idea, to be honest. Would you like an intro?'

Hannah nodded. 'Yes, please.' She was ready to give him her email address but he whipped out his phone and in moments was saying into it, 'I'm at the pub and there's someone here who thinks she could sort out Carlysle Courtyard for you. Used to run a similar project. Are you interested or shall I tell her you're sorted?'

After a few moments, he handed the phone to Hannah. 'Christopher Carlysle.' He turned back to his own table as Deanna returned, bearing crisps and looking bemusedly from Hannah to Ratty.

Put on the spot, Hannah took the phone and introduced herself to a gruff-sounding man, repeating what she'd told Ratty and outlining her duties at Creative Lanes and her experience in starting up Hannah Anna Butik. 'Ratty thought you might need someone to get your project off the ground,' she ended, because 'I overheard Ratty talking about your business in a pub and butted in' probably wasn't professional.

'I'd love to think you're an answer to a prayer, dear,' said the gruff voice patronisingly, 'but can we afford you? That's the thing. This has cost us quite enough, frankly.'

Hannah bit back a sigh. Some people – like Albin – thought only they were entitled to make money. 'I understand,' she said coolly, knowing this guy Simeon wouldn't have been working for nothing. 'In-house management is your best option if there's no budget.'

She was about to end the conversation and return Ratty's phone when Christopher Carlysle muttered, 'Hang on.' The sound of muffled conversation followed.

Hannah waited while Deanna made 'What's going on?' faces. Then a woman came on the line. 'Hello, I'm Cassie Carlysle.' She acted as if Hannah's conversation with Christopher hadn't happened. 'Yes, we are looking for help in the final stages in opening Carlysle Courtyard – getting the shops spick and span for the tenants. Is that your thing?' Her voice held a hopeful note.

'It is.' In a few minutes Hannah had arranged to meet Cassie the next morning at ten. She handed the phone back to Ratty with a grin. 'Thanks!' Her heart lifted at having something, even a short-term project, to feed her ambitions.

He grinned back. 'Do you know where to find Carlysle Courtyard? We've a new tenant moving into one of our rentals in Little Lane tomorrow or I could show you.'

'I know, thanks,' she said. 'I owe you a drink.'

He glanced at his watch. 'Another time. I have to take the dog out before bed. Our little boy's teething so we're up half the night.'

Half an hour later, Deanna too began to yawn because Shelby had been up at the crack of dawn and Hannah left the pub at the same time as her, shivering and pulling up her hood as she realised something cold was falling, touching her face like icy fingertips.

'Snow?' Deanna gazed at the spicules dancing like moths in the halo around a street light.

'More like sleet,' Hannah decided, thinking of the big feathery flakes she'd grown used to in Sweden. 'Brr. Let's go.' After hugging goodbye, as Deanna lived on the Bankside Estate and Nan's cottage was in the opposite direction, she strode through the village, calling goodnight to other hurrying villagers huddled into thick coats.

She halted, captivated by a Christmas tree in a window of a red-brick terraced house, lights flickering green and red, tinsel glittering. Evidently, the little house's occupants were in a hurry to welcome Christmas.

Her heart warmed. She was going to be home in Middledip for Christmas after all with carol singers and festive meals, fairy lights glowing through winter mists. It would be the first of December tomorrow. A good day to make a new start.

Chapter Fourteen

Next morning, Hannah left fifteen minutes early for the meeting with Cassie, intrigued to see what was needed to get Carlysle Courtyard up and running.

Port Road took her out of the village past the performing arts college. A couple of miles later she turned left into Fen Drove. Hawthorn hedges edged the lane, a tracery of bare sticks and thorns in the pale winter light. The remnants of last night's sleet edged ruts and crevices like tentative white brushstrokes on a painting.

The turning into Carlysle Courtyard looked like a farm track, rutted and muddy. She swung her mum's car into the paved square that would once have been the stable yard and jumped out. Three small vans, two white and one yellow, stood on a gravel car park beyond the hedge.

All was quiet. The stone stables with slate roofs formed three sides of a square, hence the name 'courtyard', presumably. Given a new lease of life by their conversion into shops, their new, large windows were presently smeared with plaster and dotted with stickers. Signs above read:

Daintree Pottery, Posh Nosh, Paraphernalia, Fen Stones, Pix & Frames, Crafties and Mark's Models. Doors stood ajar and from somewhere came the whine of distant music. Everywhere was speckled and splashed with plaster like a Jackson Pollock painting. Empty sandbags huddled in corners, dirty and torn.

'You can't park there.' A middle-aged man wearing dusty overalls and a disgruntled expression emerged from Mark's Models. 'Deliveries can be made from the car park.'

Hannah met his dourness with a smile. 'I'm meeting Cassie Carlysle.'

'Good! I'd like a word with her.' He vanished back inside the dim interior.

Undaunted, allying herself naturally with retailers rather than landlords, Hannah followed, calling after him as she stepped over a spattered stone threshold into the acrid smell of new plaster. 'Are you the trader?' 'Trader' was generally better received than 'shopkeeper'.

He turned back. A scraper and broom at his feet suggested he'd been scraping clean the tiled floor. 'That's right. I'm Mark,' he acknowledged gruffly.

'I'm Hannah. Have any of the shops opened?'

'Ha!' He wiped his dusty forehead on his dusty sleeve. 'Not *quite.*' Dripping sarcasm plainly invited her to use her eyes and see the mess everywhere.

'Had you hoped to be, by now?' she asked sympathetically. 'I used to trade at Creative Lanes so I know what landlord issues are like.'

Mark's brown eyes showed a spark of interest as he snorted, 'We've been left properly in the cart. Simeon took himself off and the builders left this bloody shambles behind. When he was trying to get tenants for the place Simeon promised all kinds of opening hoopla but nothing's been done and he doesn't answer his phone. Mr and Mrs Carlysle fob us off.'

After they'd talked for a few minutes a small blue Mercedes swept into the square and a dainty woman in her fifties stepped out, well-cut hair blowing over the collar of her waxed jacket.

Hannah murmured to Mark, 'This is Cassie? How about you leave me to talk to her first?'

He agreed, picking up his scraper. 'I'm not going nowhere.'

Striding outside, Hannah pinned on her most confident smile and introduced herself.

Cassie, face pinched with worry, wasted no time on small talk. 'What do you think?'

Hannah glanced around the courtyard. 'What's needed to get the shops ready to open looks cosmetic. I've been talking to Mark at Mark's Models and his utilities are connected and he's signed a tenancy agreement. Everything ground to a halt in the final stages.'

Unsmiling, Cassie nodded. 'This was my son Simeon's project. Property development's all the thing, isn't it? Converting the old stables into a little country shopping area seemed a good business plan but he—' She hesitated. 'He can't be here right now.'

Hannah remembered Ratty's comment about Simeon setting off after a woman like a Jack Russell on heat. 'These things happen,' she said wisely.

Cassie's expression drooped. 'Simeon said Carlysle Courtyard's ready to go but it doesn't look like it.'

Hannah offered, diplomatically, 'I can look round and see what I think it would take to manage the project up to opening. I'm living with my grandmother because she needs help so I wouldn't be able to work regular hours but I'd pop backwards and forwards and work remotely from home.'

Cassie waved that aside. 'If you can get it done, how you accomplish it doesn't matter,' she proclaimed.

They spent the next two hours going over each shop unit. Hannah met Daintree from the pottery, who wore a headscarf tied at the front like a land girl, wisps of hair showing beneath the knot. 'Are we soon going to get sorted?' Daintree demanded of Cassie pugnaciously. 'I'm supposed to be open. I've got the kiln and the wheel in but that's about it. These units were meant to be handed over ready to move into. I'll stop my standing order for my rent if it's not done soon.'

Cassie shrank from Daintree so Hannah jumped in. 'I'm here to see if I can get things on track. Tell me about your unit.'

Daintree's shop was a large corner one, creating a pottery studio and sales area. Her potter's wheel stood idle. 'I'm spending hours scratching stickers off pigging windows!'

It was a similar story at Posh Nosh, where Hannah met Perla and Teo, who wanted their tea room and farm shop to reflect their Italian heritage as well as selling locally made treats like pies or mustard. Perla's dark ponytail swung as she showed Hannah stacks of chairs and tables in protective packaging. 'How can we open when the place is filthy?' she demanded.

Murmuring soothingly, Hannah took photos. Excitement and purpose filled her. Carlysle Courtyard wasn't the chain of shops or luxury emporium of her hopes and dreams but she could shake it free of its current dingy garb of cement dust and builders' detritus. Guiding the transformation to shining windows full of colourful stock to pull in non-high-street shoppers would be fun, as well as great experience.

Cassie, visibly stressed by the tenants' grumbles, said, 'I'll show you the office,' and ushered Hannah to a little building at the back of the others where a laptop computer lay on a desk.

'If that holds the records for the project, we're laughing,' Hannah observed. With Cassie's permission she began to rifle through a stack of paper. 'Tenancy agreements.' She read a file tag. 'And, thank goodness – there's planning permission for a sign on Fen Drove to show people where to turn in.'

Cassie began to cheer up. 'Simeon's had the sign made. Dark green with gold and white lettering.' She showed Hannah a pair of crossed fingers and a beseeching expression. 'Can you get Carlysle Courtyard ready for a nineteenth of December Christmas Opening? The conversion's cost a bomb and if the tenants start walking out . . .'

Hannah flipped through delivery notes for a multitude of building materials, wondering if everything had at least been paid up to date. 'Given the necessary budget and manpower,' she agreed absently.

Cassie bit her lip. 'Christopher's being tricky about the budget.'

Slowly, Hannah dropped the delivery notes. The exhilarated resolve that had carried her through the morning vanished like the mist that lay in hollows in the fields beyond the car park. She smiled ruefully at Cassie's anxious expression, making her voice reasonable. 'I'm afraid this isn't a charity project and I'm not a volunteer. If there's no budget I won't waste any more of your time.'

Panic flitted over Cassie's face. 'I'll talk to him.'

Hannah shrugged. This unwillingness to pay her worth

so hard on the heels of Albin making her wait for what she was owed prompted her to put in a reckless bid. 'I'd charge three thousand pounds to get Carlysle Courtyard open by December nineteenth. That would include getting the shops presentable, sorting out any snags, arranging the PR and the Christmas Opening itself. I'd support the traders through stocking and merchandising, place ads and have flyers and posters printed for Bettsbrough, Middledip and Port-le-Bain. Social media accounts are a must but you don't have time to develop a strong following for this year so I'd make use of community feeds wherever possible.' Adrenalin thundered around her body, her words pouring out in breathless sentences. 'I'd need additional funds for cleaning, hedge trimming and to get the roadside sign erected.'

Cassie's chin wobbled.

Hannah's heart sank. 'But if there's no budget then I'll just wish you well.' She shook Cassie's hand and left the office feeling colder than the icy breeze dictated. She almost reached her car in a murk of disappointment when Cassie called after her.

'Wait!' She caught up with Hannah, her jaw set in determination now. 'I accept.' She thrust out a business card. 'Send me images of posters and flyers and I'll get them printed because I've got a friend who'll shove them up the queue for me.' She held her hair back in the wind. 'OK?'

'I'll need the first one-third of my fee up front,' Hannah answered, examining the contact information on the card, trying not to feel suspicious.

Cassie nodded. 'Invoice me.'

'OK,' said Hannah cautiously. 'If you don't mind me saying so, that was quite a change of heart.'

Cassie drew in a huge breath, then blew it out on a shaky laugh. 'It was one of those "I am woman, hear me roar" moments. You see, Christopher inherited the estate and he's quite protective of it. But he asked me to sort this out so I'm going to do it my way.'

Hannah wondered how Christopher would take that but if Cassie was empowered to employ her then that was all she needed. 'Then I'll start in right away. Do you know why the builders left the site in such a state?'

'I'm afraid they got their final payment late. Just because of the general muddle,' Cassie added hastily.

Hannah could imagine. 'I think we should cut our losses there, as time's of the essence and we've lost their goodwill. I'll hustle hard to get a commercial cleaner here.'

Cassie looked enthusiastic. 'I'll bring estate workers in to do it. They can take care of the hedges too.'

Though she wondered why the hell Cassie or Christopher hadn't got on with these jobs, if they had the manpower at their beck and call, Hannah assumed a congratulatory expression. 'That's brilliant! I'll make arrangements with the traders.'

Another twenty minutes in the office and they'd phoned Simeon and demanded access to the laptop and necessary files. All had been emailed to Hannah.

'Gosh, I feel empowered.' Cassie looked a hundred per cent more relaxed. 'But I've got to rush because I've got reflexology with Liza at The Stables Holistic Centre at Port Manor Hotel at two.'

She drove away, still looking determined, and Hannah turned her attention to telling the traders on site about the clean-up starting tomorrow and that she'd be driving the Christmas Opening on the nineteenth. She thought Mark was going to cry. 'I can't believe it,' he kept saying.

'The relief! You've no idea. I ploughed my redundancy into this venture and I've been lying awake at night worrying.'

'Us too,' said Perla, whose ponytail was swishing happily now rather than like a cobra about to strike. 'The girl who's supposed to be supplying us with deli was quite nasty on the phone last night.'

'Can you hit a deadline of the nineteenth? It's only two and a half weeks away.' Daintree looked around dubiously at the messy buildings.

'It looks worse than it is,' Hannah assured her. 'People with the right tools and know-how will get rid of those splodges of plaster and paint in no time, and then they'll clear up the yard and the drive. In four or five days you'll be able to move your display stands in. Some of you might be trading ahead of the official opening.'

'You must have a magic wand,' said Teo. He gave Perla a big exuberant kiss.

'But I have to vanish now and get lunch for my nan.' Hannah checked her watch and leaped, energised, into her mum's Volvo.

At home, over lunch, she told Nan all about her morning. Nan gave her a one-armed hug. 'You're one of life's "doers", duck!'

The afternoon flashed by in a welter of telephone conversations and emails, Hannah organising information and identifying unpaid bills or vital tasks missed. Then, at just after four she received a call from Christopher Carlysle.

His voice was clipped. 'Before you get too carried away, I think we ought to talk.'

Hannah hesitated. It felt like a pivotal moment, one where she could definitely cause friction and offence. Or she could forge a better understanding.

'The Carlysle Estate has belonged to my family for years,' Christopher began icily.

Hannah took the opening. 'Mrs Carlysle explained that when she said you'd asked her to deal with Carlysle Courtyard and she engaged my services.'

It was Christopher's turn to pause, probably absorbing the fact that contradicting Cassie's instructions might rebound on him. 'Obviously, as my wife—' He halted again.

'I'd hate to upset her,' Hannah said, musingly, not exactly telling Christopher that it wasn't appropriate to talk to him without Cassie's say-so . . . but not exactly not saying it either.

Another silence. Then he said, grimly, 'I'll call in at the site tomorrow or the next day. See you then.'

'I look forward to it,' Hannah agreed, relieved to have hopped a hurdle without crashing into a dirty great ditch on the other side. She returned to work. And when she checked her bank account she saw that a thousand pounds had been deposited from Carlysle Estate. *Yesssss!*

By five, she took a break and realised they'd almost run out of teabags. Nan drank gallons of the stuff. 'I'll pop to Booze & News,' Hannah said, pulling on her coat. She skipped out, head full of Carlysle Courtyard's potential to provide a challenge – and income – with a mixture of on-site and remote working, exactly suited to the Nan situation.

At the shop she found not Melanie behind the counter but Jodie Jones, who'd been a year above Hannah at school. 'I'm only supposed to be covering a few hours,' Jodie grumbled, scanning the barcode on Nan's favourite PG Tips pyramid teabags. 'I'm supposed to be dropping an order at the garage before they close at five-thirty but Melanie isn't back.'

The mention of the garage made Hannah realise she owed Ratty a big thank you for introducing her to Cassie Carlysle and giving her something to do other than resent Albin and mourn Hannah Anna Butik. 'I can take it. I'd like a bottle of wine too, please. That Merlot with the black label looks good.'

When she'd paid, she cradled the box a grateful Jodie passed over the counter and, clutching the wine bottle by its neck, crossed Main Road to the garage, passing cars lined up on the forecourt in the light spilling through the open doors. Only one guy was still working, Pete, the blond one, hair hooked behind his ears as he curled over the engine of a vintage sports car. He grinned and took the box of coffee, sugar, milk, plastic bags and paper towels from her. 'Has Melanie got a new delivery girl?'

Hannah retrieved Nan's teabags off the top. 'She's off somewhere and Jodie's stuck in the shop. Is Ratty around?' She gestured with the wine. 'I got him a thank you because he helped me out.'

'He's at Honeybun Cottage sorting the water out for their new tenant. You could pop down or leave it with me.' Pete carried the shopping to the back of the garage where a kettle stood. 'Do you know Honeybun? First on the left down Ladies Lane.'

'I'll deliver it personally, thanks.' After saying bye to Pete, Hannah stepped back into the darkness of the late afternoon, swinging the bottle as she strolled past trimmed hedges towards Ladies Lane, which, further down, would touch the edge of the Carlysle Estate near the wood and lake.

Two men were putting up the tailgate of a removal van in the lane as she neared Honeybun Cottage. She looked up the drive and saw Ratty, hands in pockets, talking

180

through the open doorway to whoever was inside. 'The water should be OK now,' he said, 'but I'll get someone out if not.' He noticed Hannah hovering. 'Hi. Are you here to see me? Or to meet our new villagers?'

'I brought you something.' She ventured closer, stepping over cushions of thyme growing between paving slabs in the light from the windows. She handed him the bottle. 'Thanks for introducing me to Cassie.'

Ratty began to say something but then a man stepped into the lighted cottage doorway. 'Hannah? Are you back in England?'

Her heart somersaulted. 'Nico?'

The light shadowed his face. His hair was messy and he needed to shave but he looked a lot less bleak than when she'd seen him last at Hörnan in Gamla Stan.

Then Josie popped out beneath his arm, her face shining. 'Hello, Hannah! We met you at the wedding, didn't we? We've come to live here. It's called Middledip.'

Maria, not to be outdone, squirmed under Josie's arm, socks drooping off the ends of her toes. ''Ullo!' Her round face creased in a grin. The three of them looked like a picture entitled 'We are family!' Ratty glanced between them and Hannah with an expression of interest then thanked Hannah for the wine and melted away into the evening.

Nico's blue eyes held an unsettling expression. Was it consternation? Brain whirling, Hannah dropped her gaze to Josie. 'Wow, you've come to live here? I didn't know that was going to happen.'

'I've left my old school, Maria's staying with us and Mum's staying at Grandma's,' chattered Josie. 'Come and see our new room. Maria and I are sharing.'

'Well—' Hannah took a step back.

Josie patted Nico's arm. 'You were going to make coffee, weren't you, Dad?' Then, beckoning as if she could scoop Hannah into the house if she did it enthusiastically enough, 'We can show you upstairs while my dad boils the kettle.'

'Mydad kettle,' Maria echoed, puffing her lips and sticking out her belly.

With a small smile Nico stepped back. 'Come in. Apparently, I'm about to make coffee.'

Hannah didn't have the heart to disappoint the girls. 'I'll remember I have to rush home before you get to the coffee stage if you like,' she murmured, stepping past him into a kitchen where boxes littered the uneven flagged floor between plain wooden units.

'C'mon!' yelled Josie. Bare lightbulbs lit their way through a room where a sofa stood smothered by more boxes and into a miniature hall. Both girls took the staircase on all fours, Josie scurrying like a spider and Maria hopping like a frog.

It didn't take long to admire the new bedroom. Black bin bags stuffed full enough to pop were shoved against two bare single beds and wardrobes with matching drawers. 'Dad's going to get curtains. There are two windows,' Josie pointed out.

'One, two!' yodelled Maria and jumped onto a bin bag.

'I'm going to FaceTime with Mum later so she can see us in our new room.' Josie tugged Hannah out across the tiny landing to another door. 'This is Dad's room.' Another bare bed, this time a double, stood among the boxes and bags. 'And the bathroom.' Josie showed Hannah a room with just space enough for loo, basin and a bath with shower over.

Honeybun Cottage was even more compact than Nan's home. Still chattering a mile a minute, Maria scurrying in her wake and echoing the occasional word, Josie led the way back downstairs.

Though Hannah had opened her mouth to say, 'Must rush now!' in the kitchen she found the kettle boiling and Nico waiting to ask how she'd like her coffee. He smiled at the girls. 'Dinner's in the oven. Josie, maybe you could take Maria up and get your duvets and sheets out. You know which bags they're in, don't you?'

'Yeah! And the pillows!' shouted Josie, spinning around and racing back the way she'd come.

'Yeah!' echoed Maria, scurrying after her.

Hannah found herself alone with Nico, leaning on a worktop and drinking instant coffee made with powdered milk. Bumping and squealing came from immediately above their heads, marking the whereabouts of the girls' bedroom. 'Sorry there's nowhere to sit.' He gestured towards the space in the middle of the room. 'I need a kitchen table. We have a breakfast bar built in at home. In Islington, I mean.'

'Right,' Hannah murmured, trying to process events. 'You've actually moved to Middledip to live?'

Softly, he laughed. 'A lot's happened in the past couple of weeks. I've handed my laptop in and cleared my desk. Loren found she couldn't cope again. Her mum begged me to take Maria temporarily so I requested unpaid leave until we go to Sweden for Lucia.' He lowered his voice. 'We go on the eleventh so Vivvi and/or Loren should take Maria before then. I'm afraid Josie will miss her. Anyway,' he went on. 'My boss wasn't happy and we agreed a parting of the ways that gives me financial breathing space. I chatted to Ratty about his empty rental property at Rob's wedding, wishing I could afford it for weekends in the country. I loved the village when I was a teenager.' He

183

sipped his coffee, eyes becoming shadowed. 'Josie's been unsettled and unhappy at school. My cousin who was au pairing for us wanted to move in with her boyfriend and my nanny couldn't be flexible about childcare for Maria. I rang Ratty and asked if the cottage was still empty.'

'So it's a permanent move?' Hannah asked, trying to ignore a fresh tingle of curiosity over what had happened to Loren and him 'working on things'.

He shrugged. 'The tenancy agreement's six months. When I discovered I could let my Islington house for more than four times what the rent is here, it was a good opportunity to try village life and Christmas in the country. Hopefully, I can get Josie into the village school.'

'Rob and I went there. It's always been lovely.' As he'd been speaking Hannah had noticed how relaxed he was and the smoothing out of lines around his mouth. He wasn't gaunt now but he could still do with ten extra pounds, she thought critically.

'So what are you doing back in the village?' he said, watching her as she drained her coffee cup.

'Nan's broken her arm,' she said, placing her empty cup in the sink. 'I came to stay so Mum and Dad could go on their trip. It's hard to look after yourself one-handed at any age, let alone ninety.'

'I'm sorry to hear Nan Heather's hurt herself. Please give her my best wishes.' His expression of concern became a frown. 'You've left your assistant to run Hannah Anna Butik?'

Sudden heat seared her cheeks at the memory of Albin's amused contempt as he comprehensively manoeuvred her out of her own business. That last time in Stockholm she'd hoped to pour the story into Nico's ears but he'd been so remote compared to his heated attention at the wedding

– right before he'd snuggled up to Amanda Louise. In fact, he'd blown hot and cold from the first moment their paths had crossed again six weeks ago. The idea of exposing her naivety and hurt feelings to him now, just because he'd popped up in her home village with a smile, made her stomach shrink. Instead, she pasted on a grin and answered evasively. 'Julia's perfectly capable. Thanks for coffee. Welcome to Middledip. Say goodbye to the girls for me.'

She hurried off, pulling up her hood against the sleet as she crossed The Cross to Rotten Row, clutching Nan's teabags and telling herself it didn't matter that Nico was so unexpectedly living in Middledip. Nan's arm would heal in a few weeks. The Carlysle Courtyard Christmas Opening would have been achieved.

Hannah wouldn't be around to see what Nico did next.

Chapter Fifteen

Nico's first job on Wednesday morning was to visit Middledip Primary School, a one-storey brown-brick building up Port Road. He had fingers and toes crossed that there was a place in Josie's year group he could apply for. The alternative was to find a school in Bettsbrough but she needed friends who lived in the village.

They set off on the ten-minute walk from Honeybun Cottage with their breath hanging white in the freezing air. From the buggy Maria yelled, 'Walk! Walk! I wanna walk wiz Yozee!' face screwed up in frustration.

Other adult-and-child combinations were heading for school but Josie was acting as if she couldn't see them, which Nico knew to be a coping mechanism. Her nervousness was obvious because she didn't try and distract Maria with a game and her constant high-pitched chatter rang with faux confidence. 'I'm going to meet new friends, Dad, aren't I? I just don't know their names yet.'

Kids got you by the heart. Nico was so touched by her grimly positive attitude that he stopped to hug her. 'We're visiting today but new friends will come next.' He was desperate that she'd settle at this school and the white, trying-to-be-brave face he'd grown to loathe would be a thing of the past.

She frowned up at him from his encircling arms. 'When I'm at school, what will you do?' Getting her head around him not being at work was proving a task. Nico had always worked. Josie's care had always been shared. He wondered whether she thought he wasn't up to the task without Tilly, Emelie and Loren on board.

'I'll be fine,' he answered. 'But you won't stay at school today. After the visit we'll go shopping for a table. It was OK for you and me to eat on our laps last night but I think Maria pretty much rolled in her macaroni cheese.'

Josie giggled. 'And the curtains for our room. You'll let us help choose?'

'Yep. I promised.' They set off again and he steered the buggy through the black iron school gates. Josie's attention was taken by children waving goodbyes and filing into school with their teachers, doors to the outdoors from each classroom meaning each class could enter simultaneously.

Josie fell suddenly and ominously silent.

'Right,' said Nico brightly. 'There's the sign for reception. We're to report to Miss Anderton, take a tour and meet the year three teacher, Mr Hodge.' He hoped Josie wouldn't decide Hodge was a funny name as she'd decreed Calcashaw to be.

Josie halted.

Nico stopped, too. 'Let's go in then,' he said stroking her hair encouragingly.

The expression on her face was wooden. 'Is Maria coming in?'

Surprise made him frown. 'Of course.'

'When's she going back to Mum?'

'When we go to Sweden, I think,' he answered re-assuringly. 'And when we come back you'll carry on seeing her.' At least, there was no reason he knew of that she wouldn't.

She stared at him with a younger version of the eyes he saw in the mirror every day. He wished he could plug her into his computer and download whatever was going on behind those eyes to understand hidden worries. He'd assumed today's concerns would be about an unfamiliar school or life somewhere other than Islington but, of course, to Josie it was only one of the changes that had tossed her around lately. Gently he added, 'Don't worry.'

Josie nodded and they went together to reception, met Miss Anderton and then the head, Mrs Morrison. Josie smiled and chatted. Then Mrs Morrison escorted them along the corridors, peeping into the school hall and the central garden courtyard. They paused at Mr Hodge's classroom, where children were grouped around square tables, heads bent over workbooks, hands clutching pencils. On the walls, paintings and drawings were grouped around labels in the form of think bubbles. The classroom smelled of paint and pencil lead and the sound of young voices rippled like water in a brook.

A man of around Nico's age straightened and picked his way between the children, cautioning those who looked up, 'We don't stop work because visitors have entered the classroom, do we?' He pushed back brown hair and, as Mrs Morrison made the introductions, said, 'Hello! Nice to meet you.' He directed the comment first at Josie, as if she was the most important of the group. 'Over there you can see Miss Lewin, our teaching assistant.'

Miss Lewin lifted a closely cropped dark head and

smiled at them before returning her attention to a child beside her.

Maria, who'd quietened during the school tour, began shouting fiercely, 'Out! Out! Wanna get out!' A ripple of laughter ran through the class, the children seeing another excuse to look up from their books.

Josie laughed too and a girl on a nearby table said, 'Is she your sister?'

Smiling shyly, Josie nodded. 'She's Maria. Say "hello", Maria.'

''Ullo,' said Maria, wrinkling her nose.

'I'm Zelda,' said the girl. 'You're sweet.'

Maria shook her head emphatically. 'I'm Maria.'

The children laughed again and Nico felt himself relax. Mr Hodge chatted to Josie for a few minutes more, then Mrs Morrison showed them back to reception.

Nico thanked her. 'I'll apply for a place immediately.'

She beamed down at Josie. 'If the local authority sanctions it then the school has ten days to offer a place. We hope to see you in the new year.' Meanwhile, Josie was off school, into which time the trip to Sweden slotted neatly.

Soon they were outside in the winter sunshine. Josie was relaxed, considering she'd just met an entire class full of new children, and Nico suddenly realised that he was the one feeling odd and unsettled. The village street was quiet now the school run was over and unlit Christmas lights swung between leafless trees that were bent and gnarled like arthritic old men.

Then he realised what felt amiss – he wasn't in a hurry.

He wasn't rushing to the tube. He wasn't squeezing in emails between meetings. The only tasks he absolutely had to do today were shopping, caring for the girls and providing meals.

'Out, out!' shouted Maria, jerking forward against her harness.

'OK,' said Nico, obligingly. He unfastened the clip and lifted her onto her two feet. 'Hold my hand.'

Maria tucked hers into her armpits. 'Nooooo.'

He grabbed the hood of her coat to stop her charging off. 'Hand or buggy?'

Maria peeped at him to check he meant it then reluctantly gave him her miniature, chilly hand. He had to lean sideways to hold on to her so it wasn't a fast or comfortable walk home but Josie looked happy enough pushing the buggy while Maria paused to examine every stone or gate post and shouted, ''Ullo!' to a beagle looking out of a window.

He spent the saunter home, apart from answering Maria's stream of 'Look!' or 'What's dat?' musing on the speedy succession of events over the past week or so.

On November twenty-fourth, the day after his disastrous meeting with Anders, he'd emailed his resignation and phoned an agog Katya to explain. The HR manager had invited him in for a chat, which he attended in the late afternoon when Tilly could look after Maria alongside Josie.

The HR manager had talked about 'a potential solution that might be agreeable to all'. Nico imagined he'd already quoted SLS's policy on dependants' leave at Anders, which perhaps didn't entirely accord with the stance Anders had so far taken. Along with lots of legal jargon, the HR manager had broached a settlement agreement. Nico had been unsurprised: he'd held a senior role with access to client data and contacts and was about to resign owing to his boss's less than sympathetic behaviour.

He'd been wide open to a sum of money and an agreed

reference in exchange for waiving his right to take the company to tribunal. The settlement sum reflected holidays owed and the twelve-month non-compete clause in his contract and, in view of his circumstances and childcare difficulties, he wasn't expected to work his notice but would be paid until his official leaving date of the thirty-first of December. The relief had unstrung every one of his tense muscles.

He'd talked to Josie about changing schools. She had concerns, naturally, but had soon said she'd like to try living in the country if it meant no Mrs Calcashaw and no St Kits kids. The next day he'd picked up the phone to Ratty and agreed the six-month tenancy on Honeybun Cottage.

He'd also informed Cambridgeshire County Council of his temporary responsibility for Maria and had already chatted via telephone to a Gloria Russell from Children's Services, 'assigned to Maria's case'. He'd shrunk from the phrase. Maria, 'a case'? Gloria had also called Loren and Vivvi, presumably to check they were on a similar page to Nico, and said she'd visit Honeybun Cottage soon. Loren had passed along to Nico that Maria's birth father had been approached but indicated his inability to care for his daughter. Big surprise.

Emelie had moved into Bruno's flat in Highbury. It had been a wrench to hug her goodbye because she'd lived with them for more than two years. 'Don't tell anyone in Sweden yet,' he'd warned her. 'I don't want to tell my parents until I'm safely settled.'

'OK.' She'd beamed. 'Leave it to you. Maybe I can visit you after Christmas.'

Tilly had been stunned to learn Nico was moving the family to the country. 'Just like that?' she'd kept saying. 'Just like that?'

He'd heard regret in her voice as well as shock. 'I'm afraid so,' he'd answered. 'I'm downshifting. If I need a nanny in the future then it will be someone in Cambridgeshire, obviously.'

'But—' she'd begun twice, then her dark eyes had shone with sudden tears. 'Is it because I didn't go full-time while you had Maria?'

Considering their bumpy relationship recently, he'd felt unexpectedly sorry to sever ties. 'It's because I've left my job and I'm moving away.' Then honesty compelled him to add, 'But it's true that as you couldn't help me with one solution, I had to find another. I'm happy with choosing a new direction, though, so let's part as friends, eh? I'm sure Josie would like to stay in touch.'

He'd received the settlement offer on the twenty-sixth, agreed its terms, cleared things with Josie's old school and moved to the village five days later.

Now, he felt as if he'd been dumped into a reality TV programme without knowing the rules. However, logic dictated that as well as the tasks he'd shared with Emelie, Tilly and Loren now being all his, he could enjoy the novelty of strolling down a street of frosty cottages and fairy lights with two happy, healthy children.

At home, Nico made snacks then Maria accidentally closed herself in the sitting room and howled to be freed. Josie obliged while Nico googled furniture stores. Finding a promising warehouse of Italian furniture between Bettsbrough and Peterborough he took the girls to help him make a selection.

Maria approved his choice – a black metal base, round black shiny surface and four see-through chairs that she declared to be 'glass'. Josie said, 'Purple's better than black.'

Nico answered, faux regretfully. 'No purple option.' He

suspected the highly contemporary style wouldn't go with Honeybun's rustic kitchen but enjoyed buying something to his taste alone, remembering Loren's penchant for velvet love seats and spindle-back rocking chairs.

The girls behaved well, Maria accepting a queenly perch on his shoulders and tapping his head when she wanted him to look at something, so he took them to a nearby toy shop. Josie got a Christmas card craft set and a PVC tablecloth decorated with long-lashed dragons to protect the new table from glue, Maria a backpack with walking reins attached. Face shining, she chose a unicorn design with a silver horn. Josie grabbed the rein and became a princess with Maria as her pet magic unicorn. 'Hold on tightly,' Nico called. All he had to do was stroll behind as the princess and her unicorn trotted along the pavement. Who would have thought a pet magic unicorn moved so much faster than a two-year-old girl?

'Let's stop at this shop and buy a box of chocolates for Nan Heather because she's hurt her arm,' Nico called.

'That's the little old lady from the wedding, isn't it?' Josie demanded, slowing her unicorn to look round enquiringly.

'That's right. Hannah's come home from Sweden to look after her.' How hurt must Nan Heather be for Hannah to take weeks away from her boyfriend and business? Her blank surprise at seeing him yesterday had probably matched his blank surprise at seeing her . . . swiftly followed by a burst of heat he'd resolutely tamped down.

He drove home with Bastille playing and Maria lustily adding her own backing track of 'Neh, neh, noo, noo, noo,' as they purred into the village past a speed camera on which someone had painted a sad face, which Nico took as a warning that the camera was loaded and

193

dangerous. Not remembering the number of Nan Heather's house in The Cross, he paused at the garage to check with Ratty, whose oil stains stretched from his hands to the first tattoo on his forearm. Then he returned to Honeybun Cottage and put the table together, Maria 'helping' by poking her head between him and whatever he was trying to see and posting his spanner beneath the black range cooker so that he needed a coat hanger to hook it out.

After lunch, they pulled on their coats against a keen December wind and went out on foot, Nico happy to leave the buggy behind and let Josie be in charge of Maria's reins.

Josie tapped the chocolate box under Nico's arm. 'Do you think Nan Heather will share?'

'You've just had lunch,' Nico reminded her. Josie looked at him as if wondering what his point was.

Nan Heather opened the side door before they'd knocked. Her curls fluffed atop her head like a punk-rock sheep and her plaster cast stuck out from her sleeve. 'I saw you through the window. Hannah said you'd moved here, Nico. And the little girls, too! Hello, my ducks! Come in out of the cold. Would you like hot chocolate? Or orange juice?'

'Juice, p'ease.' Maria bustled happily over the threshold.

Josie followed. 'Hot chocolate, please.'

Nico followed on into Nan Heather's small yellow kitchen with white-painted cabinets and old-fashioned appliances. Cacti grew in a row on the windowsill like green hedgehogs marching from one rose-strewn curtain to the other and a row of Christmas cards glittered prettily from the dresser.

When he presented Nan with the chocolates, she

beamed, faded eyes looming through her glasses. 'You didn't have to do that!' Then, in the same breath, 'Let's get them open.' The girls clustered around her as she lowered herself carefully onto a kitchen chair.

Hannah appeared from the next room. 'This is a nice surprise.'

Nico had known he might see her this time so her smile didn't hit him in the groin so much as last night. Soon she was boiling milk for hot chocolate, pouring juice and making coffee. Through the doorway, he could see an open laptop and a notepad on the table.

'We've disturbed you,' he said apologetically, when she handed him a steaming mug.

'It's fine,' she said quickly. 'Nan's obviously delighted to see your kids.' She faltered as if wondering whether to revisit the term 'your kids' but he gave her an understanding smile and she went on. 'I've unexpectedly picked up a project. A local rich kid, Simeon, converted old stables into a courtyard of crafty, cutesy shops and a tea room. He's occupied elsewhere so I'm getting the traders into their units and doing the PR for the opening on the nineteenth. Simeon's mum, Cassie, employed me but his dad, Christopher . . . It's as if he suspects me of forcing Simeon to go so I can step into his shoes.' Her blue-green eyes were alight as she talked. Her hair was piled on top of her head and tendrils escaped as if shaken free by a busy day.

'Do you mind if I continue?' she went on. 'I'm creating a mammoth spreadsheet and I'm not quick at working out functions and sums.' She took her cup of coffee and disappeared into the other room. He was left to muse that she'd have missed most of the Christmas build-up in her own shop by the nineteenth.

Nan found things to interest Josie and Maria in the dresser drawers and Nico could see exactly why she'd made such a fantastic foster carer. Josie was soon cutting out ladies from magazines and Maria stirring a 'pudding' of pasta shapes in a bowl. He watched them absorbed in their activities.

From his seat he could see Hannah gazing at her laptop. Taking his coffee, he stole into the dining room to join her. 'I'm pretty handy with functions and sums,' he offered, making her jump.

She rolled her eyes. 'I can make the columns and rows add up but I need to separate out the VAT so we can reclaim conversion costs.'

He pulled out a chair. 'Just the VAT on the total? Wouldn't it be easier to analyse each sum ex-VAT and then total the VAT column?'

She tutted in exasperation. 'I've forgotten how to do the basics. With Hannah Anna Butik I had accounting software but I've cancelled the monthly fee.'

'I can help you with a template.' He paused to sip his cooling coffee thoughtfully. 'You're talking in the past tense about Hannah Anna Butik.'

Her hands froze over her keys. Then she sighed, letting them drop. 'I lost the shop.' Her smile was so bright it almost, but not quite, outshone the tears in her eyes. She had to swallow before adding, 'So when this project fell in my lap I thought I'd do it while I'm here with Nan.'

Nico nodded, the tears on her lashes hitting him beneath the breastbone. 'I'm sorry. That's . . . horrible.' He wanted to hug her. Was it financial trouble? She'd been delighted when he'd merchandised Hannah Anna Butik. Her takings were supposed to have shot up but maybe it had been too little too late. That would explain her scrabbling around for work in England while she cared for Nan Heather. But where did the rich boyfriend fit into that . . . ?

'It is what it is.' Her voice was rough with emotion but she transferred her gaze back to her computer screen, giving him the message that she didn't want to say more about the business she'd loved. 'I wish I had a magic wand. Simeon hasn't prepared a basic financial forecast – just listed bills with "monthly" or "annually" scribbled alongside.'

His heart squeezed at her obvious determination to battle through her problems. 'I love spreadsheets,' he heard himself saying. 'Why don't you bring your laptop round after the kids have gone to bed? You can tell me what you need and I'll do the magic.'

Her eyes widened. 'Really?' she croaked. The wintry dusk had fallen as they'd talked and her face was illuminated by her screen. 'I'd love help, thank—' Her words caught and she swallowed hard.

He patted her shoulder, pushing aside any concerns about whether spending time with a woman he should stay away from would be good for his emotional health. 'I'm a non-working man, remember. Happy to help.'

Hannah arrived at Honeybun's kitchen door at nine-thirty. Freezing fog had eerily blanketed the village and moisture beaded the coat she hung up. Along with a blast of chill winter air, she brought in her backpack, her laptop, paperwork, a bottle of white wine and a packet of Oreo biscuits. 'You bought a table,' she observed, straightening a soft blue jumper that clung. She glanced at the English farmhouse units and brass handles. 'It's not scrubbed pine or pippy oak but I like its clean lines.' She patted the black table top.

'My Swedishness came out. Try it for size.' He took down two wine glasses and a plate for the Oreos to keep his gaze from what her jumper clung to while she set out her things.

Though she accepted a glass of wine she plunged into her record-keeping needs, outlining what was being handed over to tenants and what remained the responsibility of the landlord. It was easy stuff. He created templates while she edged her chair nearer and watched him changing formats and introducing colour coding.

'You actually like doing this?' she asked, chin on hand.

He was creating the final sheet. The first glass of wine had gone down and he was almost used to her being so close he could smell whatever she'd used on her hair. 'I do.' His tapping fingers didn't pause on the keyboard. 'Though if I'm going to sit at a computer for fun I prefer to play with images.'

She sat up straighter. 'Like . . .' She drummed her fingers in an elaborate pantomime of thinking. 'Like graphics for ads?' She looked at him hopefully.

He grinned, saving the spreadsheet template. 'Like that. Give me a minute to check on the girls.' He ran upstairs, silently popped his head into the room, counted two kids sleeping peacefully in the street light shining in through the as-yet uncurtained windows and ran down again.

Hannah hadn't moved from her seat but had taken down her hair. He liked it down. At Rob's wedding it had brushed his hands as they'd danced.

'Here's the logo for Carlysle Courtyard.' It glowed from the laptop screen, golden-yellow lettering surrounded by green. She twisted her hair back up again, this time with fewer escaping tendrils. 'I need ads, flyers and posters. Do you want to do the creative stuff and I'll do the resizing for various social media channels?'

'Sure.' He freshened their glasses of wine and they worked together for another hour. Then Hannah closed her laptop. 'It's nearly eleven! I've kept you too long but it was great of you to give me your time. You can do this stuff twice as quickly as I can.' Her eyes sparkled, possibly because she'd drunk half a bottle of wine. She stretched, her body moving sinuously beneath her top and a lock of hair floating free again.

He found himself reluctant for the evening to end. 'I was sorry to hear you'd lost the shop.'

Her sparkle drained away. 'I thought I could keep it but I was outmanoeuvred.'

'Really?' He tried to make the word an invitation to confide. Curiosity was human. He'd left her in Stockholm two weeks ago apparently settled into Swedish life with a Swedish boyfriend and a business in the beating heart of the city.

She sighed. 'Albin—' Lines of grief puckered the skin above her eyes.

'Albin's your boyfriend?' She'd never officially told him she had a boyfriend. She'd left that little morsel to her brother.

She sucked in a wavering breath. 'He—'

Nico's phone began to ring where it lay on the table. *Loren* flashed up on the screen.

Hannah must have read it because she sprang to her feet. 'I'll leave you to answer,' she gabbled, scooping her possessions into her backpack.

It wasn't a call he could ignore anyway. 'Sorry,' he muttered, watching her hurry into her coat, looping a lilac scarf around her neck. She sent him a small smile and mouthed, 'Goodnight and thank you,' as he said, 'Hello, Loren,' into the phone.

'How are the girls?' Loren asked, sounding ineffably weary.

'Fine. Sleeping peacefully. We visited what we hope will be Josie's new school today and she liked it. The social worker, Gloria, is coming on Friday to visit Maria.'

The door clicked shut behind Hannah.

Nico turned his attention to being a dad.

Chapter Sixteen

It was the second day of what Hannah thought of as The Great Courtyard Clean-Up and Christopher Carlysle was striding about, huffing and puffing that he hadn't bargained for 'all these costs'. Estate workers backed a truck in to load up builders' debris and Cassie hovered around uncertainly. Her Hunter boots and waxed jacket looked as if they'd never seen mud.

Hannah, in contrast, wore here-to-work jeans, boots, an old coat and a woolly hat. She tried to soothe Christopher while remaining realistic. 'I know. The situation's not of your making. But these people—' she waved at the traders watching through doorways '—they've paid deposits and their first month's rent. They have agreements. They've given up other tenancies to come and be part of Carlysle Courtyard. They've paid for signage on their shops and they have their livings to earn.'

Christopher turned puce, frying her with a glare. 'Your fee is way out of order. Three thousand pounds? Pah!' With one last, scathing look around he stomped to his Land Rover and was soon roaring down the drive.

Hannah had approached the meeting prepared to re-negotiate the fee, which was, after all, a figure she'd plucked from the air in a moment of annoyance, but his snotty attitude reminded her of Albin and so she watched him leave, then turned back to Cassie. 'Do we still have a deal?'

'We do!' Cassie clutched Hannah with her manicured fingers as if prepared to keep her by force. The wind buffeted them and a disembodied voice from the Crafties unit swore about bloody dust in his eye as Cassie pulled up her coat collar and drew closer. 'I know Christopher was gruff. I'm afraid he's upset.' A groove dug itself in between her brows.

'I understand,' Hannah replied politely, though she didn't, not really. It was more than 'gruff' to be so overtly angry when Hannah was rescuing the project. Working on the adage of knowledge being power she added encouragingly, 'Is it something I've done that's upset him? Other than charged a fee?'

Cassie flicked back her hair, eyes wide and alarmed. 'You? No!' For an instant she looked as if she might cry. She sighed, as if seeing there was nothing for it but to explain. 'Simeon . . . he's not great at seeing things through. It was OK when he was younger, I suppose, but now he's over forty Christopher feels keenly that he should have achievements to show the world. He absolutely thought that Simeon had managed it with Carlysle Courtyard and Simeon did work jolly hard. But then he went off . . .' Her bottom lip trembled. 'Christopher feels Simeon's failed again. It's the disappointment making him tricky. Or maybe he's got some weird idea that you succeeding will make Simeon look worse in comparison and that's why he's barking at you. I am sorry.'

202

Sympathy now entering her heart, Hannah smiled. 'Thanks for explaining.' Poor Cassie was obviously doing her best and Christopher was probably a perfectly nice guy if you met him under the right circumstances. 'So,' she said brightly, thinking Albin had made her unnecessarily cynical about people with money. 'The cleaning and clearing of the units is underway and my goal's to have them all ready for traders to bring in their stock on Wednesday the ninth, six days away. They're free to open for business any time between that and the Christmas Opening on the nineteenth. That gives me two weeks and two days to get the outdoors perfect and blitz the publicity. I've emailed you the link to the Carlysle Courtyard blog along with the social media usernames and passwords.' She wasn't so sure she wouldn't earn every penny of that three thousand pounds. She'd worked long into last night, unable to sleep for spreadsheets dancing before her eyes and mulling over how sweet Nico had been. Hot/cold, Jekyll/Hyde Nico Pettersson.

When Cassie had approved Hannah's idea to buy planters of heather and ivy for the courtyard and swished off in her Merc, Hannah's attention was grabbed by an untidy woman in her fifties dashing out of Paraphernalia, beaming as if Hannah were her dearest friend. 'You're Hannah? I hear you've come to save us,' she cried. 'I'm Gina from Paraphernalia. I've put the kettle on. Come on in! Can't wait to meet you.'

As she was by now chilled through and Gina was a tenant she'd not yet met, Hannah was only too pleased.

Over steaming coffee cradled in chilly hands, Gina glared around the interior of what would be her shop. 'Look at all those splatters on the floor! And the emulsion's scratched. I've got boxes of dreamcatchers, crystals and ceramics all over my living room but I can't bring them into this mess.'

After her years at Creative Lanes, Hannah was well used to soothing traders' ruffled feathers. 'I can already imagine the scent of patchouli and the sound of wind chimes in here. People will love it!' She was pretty sure of that. Buying unnecessary things to decorate one's home was now a recognised British pastime. She rounded out with a dollop of reassurance. 'You won't recognise the place in a couple of days.'

Moving on, she found Posh Nosh now clear of builder rubble and stickers removed from windows. Perla and Teo were energetically washing down surfaces in the kitchen. Perla beamed at Hannah. 'Miracle! We think we can open at the end of next week.'

'Phew!' Laughing, Hannah pretended to mop sweat from her brow, enjoying the sense of community that was budding between herself and the tenants. Till she could start ideas-storming her own next move she loved the feeling she was making something happen here.

The morning passed quickly. The estate workers were a cheerful bunch in their dark green sweatshirts, scraping, sweeping, cleaning and carrying. One with his arms full of ripped plastic wrapping that had once packaged building materials said to Hannah, 'Lazy bleeders. I was a builder for years and I never left a site like this.'

Christopher would definitely not appreciate Hannah sharing the fact that the builders had marched off the site when payments got behind so she laughed it off, pretending to shiver. 'Not even a dusting of frost can make empty bags look better.'

On Monday, the sign could be erected. From the middle

of next week Hannah could pretty much leave the traders to stock their units, keeping an eye out for anyone who looked as if they might not be up and running by the nineteenth. She could turn her attention to the Christmas Opening.

It was after one when she managed to get away, whizzing along windswept Fen Drove, talking to the garden centre at Bettsbrough on her phone, getting their best price on six planted-up flower tubs and planning to add tinsel and lights.

She entered the village, enjoying the way lights and Christmas trees were decking the familiar stone cottages with festive bling. A large cotton-wool snowman had popped up to guard the school gates, his woolly hat and scarf in the school colours of plum and black. The school made her think of Josie, and Nico's family turning up in Middledip . . . without Loren. Was Loren about to join them? Hannah had waited for Nico to mention her. He hadn't, but then Loren had phoned him last night.

After parking the car she breezed into Nan's kitchen, rubbing her hands. 'Brr! That wind's arctic. I think my nose has frostbite. Fancy chicken soup for lunch? We've got some tiger bread left.' She halted. 'Ooh. Someone got a present?'

On the table, a gold-painted basket cradled a pyramid of fruit, elegantly decorated with Christmassy red silk poinsettia bracts and gold ribbon. Nan assumed an air of unconcern. 'Brett again.'

Hannah hung up her coat and took the soup from the cupboard, observing Nan from the corner of her eye. 'He's trying hard, isn't he?'

Nan shrugged one shoulder, the one on the opposite

side to the plaster cast. Hannah wished she'd thaw towards poor old Brett. They'd been good together and a ninety-year-old lady might not have masses of time in which to play hard to get, sad as it made Hannah feel to think it.

'Those grapes look lovely,' she tried tentatively.

'Probably full of pips,' Nan retorted. But then she grinned, her wrinkles making concertinas at the sides of her face, and blushed.

Cheered by that hint that Nan wasn't as unaffected by Brett's overtures as she'd been making out, Hannah chattered as she prepared lunch. 'Rob and Leesa get back from their honeymoon tomorrow. Rob's texted me that he wants to come and see you on Sunday.'

'I'll look forward to that.' Nan beamed.

'Me, too,' said Hannah . . . although she knew he'd want a full account of what was going on with Albin.

She still hadn't received the money Albin owed her. She'd email him later and ask what the hold-up was.

Nico felt more carefree than he had for years. It was amazing. Even though today, Friday, meant a ten a.m. visit from Gloria Russell from Children's Services, his step felt springy as he ran on the treadmill he'd shoehorned into his bedroom while the girls played with Josie's iPad on the bed. His feet made comforting rhythmic thumps but he wouldn't be human if he didn't wonder if he'd have to defend his motives for offering Maria a temporary home. He'd made up speeches in his head about Gloria being welcome to try and get her mother or grandparents to take Maria but the tot would go to strangers over his dead body – despite Nan Heather having assured him it wouldn't be like that.

When Gloria arrived, a smiling, middle-aged woman wearing comfortable trousers and a big coat, her first words were, 'Aren't the herbs growing through your paving lovely? Like little cushions.'

Disarmed, he stood back to welcome Gloria into the kitchen. 'Are they herbs? I'd noticed they smelled nice.' They introduced themselves and Josie and Maria came flying out of the sitting room to inspect the visitor. Josie wore a glittery Santa hat at a rakish angle. Maria's hair had been brushed ready for the important visitor but was now scrunched into a clasp at one side, probably courtesy of Josie, and one of her socks was missing.

Gloria greeted them with an easy smile. 'Hello! I'm Gloria. I've come for a quick visit.' She chatted to the children, admiring the Pokémon cards and unicorn with a rainbow matted mane brought for her inspection. She drank the cup of tea Nico made her, more interested in a comfortable gossip about family life than firing questions, watching the children play with a benign expression that Nico felt hid how to closely she was paying attention.

'Do you girls like drawing?' she asked, after a while.

'Yes!' Josie instantly scrabbled in the kitchen drawer for a pad and a blue pencil case and bossily told Maria to sit at the table. 'What shall we draw?'

Gloria assumed a considering air. 'How about a picture of how you feel today?'

'I draw,' said Maria, and took a yellow crayon and scribbled industriously on the paper.

'That's lovely! Can you draw me a face?' Gloria asked.

'No,' said Maria positively, changing to purple crayon.

Gloria grinned. 'If you did draw me a face, would it be a smiley face today or a sad face?'

Maria looked at her as if she were bananas and pointed

to the little unicorns dotting the pencil case and said, 'Horse.' Josie collapsed in fits of giggles, so Maria giggled too, screwing up her bobble nose and showing off all her pearly teeth.

It was when the girls had drifted back to the sitting room that Gloria moved into a slightly more businesslike mode. 'Loren tells me she's made a private arrangement with you. Children's Services just needs to make sure Maria is safe, healthy and happy during her mum's illness and that everyone gets the support they need.' She talked on about 'family and friends carers' and advised him that he may be eligible for fostering allowance or maintenance paid from the birth parents. Foster carers could get training and professional development, too.

He listened but said, 'It's only for one more week. The agreement is that Loren or her parents will take Maria before Josie and me leave to visit our family in Sweden on Friday.'

Gloria tilted her head and looked at him for a long moment. Then she smiled. 'You have my contact details anyway, if you need anything. I'll pop in again.' She went into a practised spiel about reports and the fostering panel and left him lots of information for him to consider. Nico thanked her, reasonably confident he was being put into the 'OK' category but with the knowledge that his days as a foster carer were numbered anyway.

In the afternoon he kept his appointment with the Bettsbrough solicitor who'd agreed to handle his settlement agreement from SLS. Josie entertained Maria with the iPad in a corner of the office while Mrs Ponderoy talked him through the document and he signed his part then he celebrated by taking the girls to McDonald's.

Fast food wasn't usually on his radar but he knew

occasional treats didn't hurt and he didn't want the kids to grow up with his hang-ups. Also, he felt optimistic and chilled. The urge to exert unnecessary control over his eating wasn't breathing on him as it did in times of stress.

Maria proved herself to be familiar with Macky D's by swivelling her head to look up at Nico and piping, 'Mydad, c'n I 'ave a 'Appy Meal?'

'You can.' He didn't remind her about saying 'please'. They were all going to have a guilt-free burger.

As they ate, Josie worked industriously on a colouring sheet from a dispenser on the wall, eating chicken with her other hand; Maria, in a high chair, ate nuggets and flung crayons around, luckily not getting the two mixed up. Then Josie concocted a game with the plush toys that had come in the Happy Meal boxes, Maria providing sound effects. Nico drank coffee and took the opportunity to telephone his dad.

'*Hej, Pappa*,' he said, when he heard his dad's voice. 'How are you?'

'Good! Fine!' boomed Lars jovially. 'I'll be working with the junior team at the rink this evening. Just been collecting my cones for the slalom.'

'Makes me nostalgic.' Nico imagined a bunch of eager schoolkids swapping from edge to edge on their skate blades as they weaved through the cones. He could almost smell the ice. 'Maybe I'll get some time at the rink next week.'

A staff member brought balloons attached to sticks, red for Maria and yellow for Josie and the girls began to bash the balloons together, Maria making up with enthusiasm for what she lacked in accuracy. Every time Josie bopped her on the top of her head she laughed a high baby chuckle. A woman on the next table whose kids were also in a balloon fight, sent Nico the smile of a fellow sufferer and . . . was that interest? She was pretty but not, he found himself thinking, as pretty as Hannah.

'You bet!' Lars answered in his ear. 'Come and meet the team. Show them a few things?'

'I'm rusty,' Nico protested. But, added, 'My skates are in your garage.'

'I'll dust them off,' Lars promised. He paused to cough. 'We'll find skates for Josie, too. And it's snowing. We could take her skiing.'

'That would be great,' Nico agreed. Then, because he'd already told his mother Carina, he told Lars about how he'd ended up looking after Maria.

'*Vad i helvete!*' Lars exclaimed. *What the hell!* 'That poor little girl. I know you have a nanny but it's a big responsibility. Loren's lucky you're a good man.'

Nico caught Maria's balloon as she flung it at some innocent passing lady. 'I don't have a nanny right now.' He spent the next half hour explaining his change of lifestyle.

'But anyway,' he rounded off, when Lars had finished exclaiming and worrying. 'I'm looking forward to seeing you next week in Sweden. Josie will have some Farfar and Farmor time and maybe I'll get a beer with my brother.' Or who knew? He was feeling so much better that he might ask a girl out and take his mind off Hannah Anna Goodbody, who had turned up so inconveniently in Middledip.

After signing off with his dad, he telephoned Carina, deciding he'd better get in quick with the leaving work news before it filtered back to her. She greeted his explanation with a pregnant pause. Then sighed. 'Nico.' She sighed again. 'You're all right, aren't you?'

'The best I've been for ages, Mamma. Honestly. Life had become pretty hectic.'

'I know.' She sounded close to tears. 'You had too much, with your job and Josie and what happened with Loren. Where is Maria?'

'Still with us.' He glanced at the girls. Josie was trying to write in wax crayon on Maria's hand and Maria was snatching her pudgy little digits away and giggling. 'Tickles, Yozee! Tickles!'

'Still? Her mother can't have her?' demanded Carina, sounding troubled.

'Should be this week,' he said. He was speaking in Swedish but somehow he didn't want to invite discussion of Maria going back to Loren in the noisy, public environs of McDonald's. He switched to English. 'Josie can't wait to bake with you next week.'

'Saffron buns,' Josie said, glancing up with a grin that showed the gaps where her grown-up teeth met her remaining baby ones. The last of her summer freckles spangled her nose and Nico's heart contracted with love.

'*Saffransbullar*,' he promised. 'Do you want to talk to Farmor?' He took over entertaining Maria by drawing around her hand with a crayon while Josie excitedly told Carina about their new bedroom and the purple satin curtains they'd bought from Dunelm at the weekend. 'Dad chose the kind with eyelets so he could just stick the curtain pole through them because he said he doesn't like all that pratting around with hooks.'

Once the call was over he took the girls home and spent the evening being a dad, watching Josie on TTRockstars, the online times-table resource Barrack Road didn't seem to have cut her off from yet, and playing counting games with Maria. One and two remained her favourite numbers. After a dinner of steamed chicken and vegetables – Nico couldn't help compensating for the burgers a *little* bit by preparing the healthiest meal he knew – Josie sighed, 'I wonder what Tilly's doing?'

Nico gave her a hug. 'Maybe she'd like to FaceTime. Why don't you message her and ask?'

'Yeah!' cried Josie. It transpired that Tilly was missing Josie so they were soon chatting, Josie carrying the tablet around to show Tilly the house and Maria trying to touch Tilly's on-screen image and breathing in astonishment, 'It Tilly! Look!' Then Josie FaceTimed Emelie and Maria got excited, trying to force her head in front of Josie's and shouting, 'Em'lie! Em'lie!'

When the girls had finally snuggled down in bed, Josie with a book and Maria with a toy unicorn, Nico went downstairs. The earlier conversations with his parents had made him conscious of the passing of time. He needed to gently remind Vivvi that soon he was going home to Sweden. This time, it wouldn't be for meetings in glass offices in Stockholm but a week with his family in Småland, the province of southern Sweden where he'd grown up. He could almost see the forests, fields and lakes.

Vivvi answered neither mobile nor landline. He tried Loren, with no better success, so texted Vivvi. *Can we arrange a time to talk, please? Need to touch base about Maria. I go to Sweden one week today.*

To Loren he sent: *Can we arrange to FaceTime? The girls would like it. Maybe tomorrow?* He added, *Hope you're feeling better.* He sent the message with a tug of sadness that, actually, neither girl had asked about Loren in the past few days. If they missed anyone it was Tilly and Emelie but most of the time they seemed content with just him.

Sunday morning arrived with a thick hoar frost that clothed every twig in a white fur jacket. Nico was coaxing Maria to walk to the village shop without stopping every time she saw a Christmas tree when he heard his name and, glancing along to Rotten Row, saw Rob and Leesa jumping from their car, bundled up in coats and scarves.

'You look unnaturally tanned for an English December,' he called as they hurried up to greet him and the girls. He felt envious. Since splitting up from Loren his summer travel had been restricted to taking Josie to Sweden . . . much like his winter travel.

'Honeymoon sunshine.' Rob beamed, slinging his arm around Leesa so enthusiastically that he nearly swept her feet from the icy pavement. 'What are you doing in Middledip? We've come to take Nan and Hannah to lunch. Nan's broken her arm and Hannah—'

Nico was already nodding. 'Hannah's come home to look after her. Our paths have already crossed.' He went on to explain his move to the village, while Josie talked to Leesa about her boots and Maria tried to spin her reins out of Nico's grasp.

Rob raised his eyebrows and whistled. 'So you've downshifted? It sounds fantastic. I'm dreading going back to the nine to five tomorrow. Nobody ever watches my projects while I'm away.' Rob worked for a company producing thermostats and heating systems.

'Same,' groaned Leesa, breaking off from boot talk with Josie. Nico was hazy about her career but thought it might involve the planning department.

213

'Come with us for lunch at the pub,' Rob urged Nico. 'We hardly had five minutes to chat at the wedding.'

'Awesome! The pub!' cried Josie, before Nico could reply.

Maria threw her arms up and echoed, 'Awesome! The plub!'

Leesa laughed and stroked the girls' heads. 'Looks like your kids are in favour.'

'But they're your family,' Nico protested. 'We didn't dress for—'

Rob brushed his objections away. 'You're a family friend and jeans are fine for a village pub. How about we meet there?'

With Josie and Maria shouting, 'Yeah!' Nico laughed and accepted. He liked Rob, Leesa and Nan Heather. And he liked Hannah . . . even if she had a boyfriend. He wondered whether she hoped to get back to Sweden to spend Christmas with him.

After visiting the shop, Nico and his princess with her magic pet unicorn made their way up Main Road to the swings outside the village hall so some energy could be expended prior to lunch. After fifteen minutes, they made their way to the pub.

Josie bounced in ahead of him. 'Look at the lights! Look at the tree! There's Nan Heather!' She pointed into the dining area where the Goodbody party had already claimed a table beneath a holly wreath.

By the time Nico got there, Josie was sitting next to Nan Heather excitedly displaying her Pokémon comic from the village shop. Nan Heather looked small and bowed, not much larger than Josie, but her smile was undimmed.

'Hi, everyone.' Nico tried to extricate an energetically

wriggling Maria from her coat while she yelled, 'Down, Mydad!' Someone had readied a high chair for her and Nico slotted her into it then fished in his pocket for her favourite small toy of the moment – a plastic cupcake that whizzed around on the spot when wound up. 'Har, har, har,' Maria chortled, trying to grab it and allowing herself to be strapped in. Nico pulled off his coat and took the last empty seat, which was between the high chair and . . . Hannah. Her long hair was plaited and swung over her left shoulder as she turned to smile.

Leesa, on the other side of Maria, cooed, 'Ooh, have you got a cake, Maria?'

'Cubcake,' Maria confirmed, generously letting Leesa take a look at her toy.

Rob sent Nico a wink. 'She's practising for when we have babies.'

Leesa blushed furiously and gave Rob a playful thump so Nico thought a family was probably in their future. A lovely couple, they'd make great parents. With Maria playing with the cupcake and Leesa and Josie chattering a mile a minute to Nan Heather, Nico was able to take a breath.

'How's the temporary job going?' he asked Hannah.

Her eyes shone. 'Good. Very engaging. Nan's grumbling about my phone "burping" with messages and emails, as she puts it. Your spreadsheets have been fantastic. I've got everything input onto them and I'm at the right place on the timeline. The premises should be sorted by midweek and I can concentrate on creating the most Christmassy Christmas Opening ever. If you hear of anyone selling a tonne of baubles and tinsel, let me know.'

'I will.' Nico copied her joking tone but was finding the way her plait dangled against her breast distracting.

In the crisp winter sunlight streaming through the window her hair was a hundred shades of gingery brown and her eyes bright enough to rival the Christmas lights twinkling along the beams above.

A member of bar staff appeared with crackers for Josie and Maria, small cardboard ones that barely made a noise when pulled but opened to reveal tubes of jelly beans. 'Yelly!' bellowed Maria, holding the clear tube out to Nico. 'Open yelly.'

'Please,' Nico added automatically, taking the tube.

'P'ease, tank you,' Maria added co-operatively, keeping her eyes on the prize.

Nico and Hannah both laughed. Then Nico noticed Rob watching them with a strange expression and his heart nosedived as he remembered Rob warning him off his sister.

Crap.

Hannah's shop might have gone down the pan but the rest of her life was back in Sweden. With her boyfriend.

Lunch arrived after a while. Nico cut up Maria's food and discouraged her from consigning cabbage to the floor. Conversation swirled around him and he mainly listened.

When the plates had been cleared away, Maria clamoured to be set free. She climbed onto Hannah's lap and curled up, eyes half-closing. 'She's going to go to sleep,' Nico warned her, recognising the way Maria was snuggling into her neck. 'Would you like me to take her?'

Colour touched Hannah's cheeks. She said softly, 'I don't think a child's ever fallen asleep in my arms. It's sweet.'

He smiled. 'It is. But she'll give you pins and needles and stop you getting up.'

Hannah smiled back. 'I'll chance it.' They made a

pretty picture as Maria yawned and tumbled into toddler sleep.

Rob looked about. 'The dining room staff have disappeared. I'll go to the bar for more drinks. Come help carry, Nico?'

'Sure.' Nico felt free to go with him as his charges seemed happy with their company. They waited their turn at the polished bar edged with glittering silver tinsel, Rob propping one foot on the brass foot rail. He winked. 'So, I didn't need your help after all.'

Nico mirrored his stance, so they were facing one another. 'Didn't you? With what?'

'Getting rid of Albin. Hannah managed it by herself. That guy was never right for her, looking down his nose at the rest of us.'

Nico's heart paused . . . then restarted with a thump. 'Hannah's not with Albin?'

His friend's smile was wide and satisfied. 'Nope. It's over. She emailed while we were on honeymoon. She was going to end things when she went back after the wedding but he beat her to it. And he's manoeuvred her out of her own shop as well. Told you he was a prick,' he added, with a scowl.

'Wow.' Nico let the news sink in. 'So that's why she was able to come and look after your grandmother.' He remembered how, that night he'd helped with her spreadsheets, she'd begun to say something about Albin. Then Loren had phoned and she'd made a hasty exit instead.

'That's right.' Rob broke off to give his drinks order to the barista, who looked to be about twenty, hair in two French plaits. He went on. 'When I saw you two smooching at the wedding I suspected she wasn't feeling everything for Albin she should have been. Bloody glad.'

217

Nico winced. 'You reminded me about not going after a teammate's sister but you also wanted me to know she had a boyfriend.' Was he meant to apologise?

Rob received a pint of beer from the barista and sucked off the froth, eyebrows flipping up. 'Remind you? I was trying to tell you *not* to worry about that old crap! I'd have *loved* you to get Hannah away from Albin. But Albin's history anyway, so no prob.'

What?

Mind spinning, Nico carried a tray of drinks through the crowd of drinkers, pausing whenever Rob greeted someone. Their conversation at the wedding had been interrupted but the mention of a boyfriend and the old 'teammate law' had made Nico withdraw from Hannah. And yet, immediately after the wedding, *her relationship had ended*?

Finally reaching the table through the throng of chattering customers, he distributed the drinks. Hannah, Maria still flaked out on her shoulder, sent him a fleeting smile as she listened to Leesa talk of the unbroken yellow sand of Calangute Beach in Goa.

The urge to try and get closer to Hannah burst into flame inside him but he forced himself to sit down and think the situation through. He was off to Sweden on Friday. Hannah was wrapped up in Carlysle Courtyard. She'd just come out of a long relationship and he hadn't discovered how she felt about that. Then there was his single-dad baggage . . .

As if that baggage wished to emphasise its presence, his phone began to ring.

Josie rolled her eyes. 'At least it can't be work, Dad.' It gave him an uncomfortable insight into how used she was to work intruding in their life. He saw *Vivvi* on the screen and said soothingly, 'It's Grandma.' Presumably she was responding to his calls and texts at long last. 'Hold on,' he said into the phone then, glancing round the table, 'OK to leave the girls for a minute while I take this?' Reassured by a round of good-natured agreement he moved to an empty table in the far corner.

'Sorry,' Nico said to Vivvi. 'Thanks for returning my call. We need to talk about Maria—'

Vivvi bulldozed over him. 'Loren's going into rehab for twenty-eight days.'

'Rehab?' Nico repeated stupidly. 'Rehab' was a word he associated with celebrities.

'She's been assessed and they've offered her a place on their drug addiction programme,' Vivvi ploughed on. She sounded weighed down with exhaustion. Something rustled and Nico imagined her reading from a piece of paper. 'Residential withdrawal detoxification then individual and group addiction therapy. She's been diagnosed with depression and addiction. Red's terribly down too, after his op, and not trying to help himself.' Vivvi's voice caught on a sob. 'I'm so worried. It feels like they're giving up and leaving me to deal with everything.'

Nico struggled for how to react. 'I'm sorry to hear it,' he said eventually but it echoed inadequately in his ears.

Vivvi sniffed. 'I'm at my wits' end. Loren's impossible. She's got no interest in herself, let alone what her dad and I are going through.' She blew her nose.

Nico closed his eyes, realising what was coming next. He could hear it before his ex-mother-in-law said the words. 'I'm afraid there's no way we can look after Maria at the moment.'

He let out his breath so slowly it made his head spin. 'You're assuming I'll keep her?'

219

Vivvi gave a strangled, angry laugh. '*In* the circs. *If* it's not too much trouble.'

A silence elapsed while Nico wondered quite where Vivvi got off with that bit of snark. But he didn't have time for hurt feelings. Nico had exactly the same decision to make as he'd made twice already. He could continue to look after Maria or ring Gloria Russell to try and get social services to arrange something.

He tried to imagine himself handing Maria over to some nameless, faceless authority and her wrinkling her nose as she quavered. 'Bye, Mydad!'

'I know we didn't quite get round to sending the child maintenance payments,' Vivvi said suddenly, perhaps realising that she could have sweetened her approach. 'But everything's so shitty we forgot. If it makes a difference, I'll do it now.'

'It's not my central concern.' He groaned, then sighed and collected himself. 'Josie and I are booked to fly to Sweden in five days. Cancelling and disappointing everyone's not an option so Loren's going to have to authorise me taking Maria.'

'Oh, Nico. You're a good man.' Vivvi was almost gushing now.

'So people keep telling me.' He let that sink in then said, 'I'll have to call you later because there's a lot to sort out and I'm not at home. I've never taken anyone else's kid on a trip before and don't know how it works.'

'Of course, of course.' Vivvi was all compliance now.

Nico shoved his phone back in his pocket and returned to the Goodbody table to stew silently, his pleasure in the gathering ruined. And Hannah? Vivvi's phone call had proved that he'd been right to hesitate. His baggage just grew by the day.

It was several hours later that he sat down at his new kitchen table with his laptop open and Vivvi on the phone. By the end of the session – interrupted three times by the girls – he'd discovered from the Home Office website how to travel with a child who didn't belong to him. He'd forwarded the template letter of parental permission and all Loren would have to do was fill in dates, destination, reason for the trip, Nico's relationship to Maria via Josie and sign it. Vivvi pledged to courier it to Nico along with Maria's passport. Nico emailed Gloria Russell, Maria's case worker, to apprise her too.

Booking a flight ticket for Maria proved easy enough and, by phoning the airline, he managed to get the two bookings under one reference. He requested that Vivvi meet the cost and, after a silence, she supplied the credit card details to allow that to happen.

They were both glad to hang up by the time they'd thrashed everything out and Vivvi didn't ask to speak to either of her granddaughters. Nico didn't suggest it. Vivvi couldn't see past her own problems and he'd had enough of listening to her.

When he got off the phone, though he knew he must call his parents, he chose to spend time with the girls first. Josie, he discovered, had decided to dive into her Christmas card kit and the bedroom looked as if it had been glitter-bombed. So did a giggling Maria.

Josie was blinking back angry tears because she hadn't done a good job on the cards she'd made. 'Maria was crawling all over them!'

Nico ruffled her hair. 'It probably would have been better to sit up at the kitchen table and let me help you but it was me who asked you to take care of Maria so I'll buy you a new set soon. How about we throw this

221

lot away and vacuum, then you two mucky kids can jump in the bath and wash the glitter away?'

'Yeah!' Josie, good spirits restored, grabbed a rubbish bag while Nico wielded the vacuum cleaner and accidentally hoovered one of Maria's socks off the end of her foot. She shrieked in delight so, refusing to tackle a filthy dust bag in pursuit of a sock, he hoovered the other off too, reducing both girls to tears of laughter.

When they'd bathed and the glitter had gurgled down the plughole, they returned to the girls' bedroom and Josie suddenly squealed, 'Snow!'

Nico squinted through the window to watch the occasional floating flake in the light from street lamps. 'Wow, yes, just about.'

They curled up on Maria's bed facing the window so they could see the tiny flakes dancing and floating on the air as he read them *One Snowy Night* and they enjoyed the kindness of Percy the Park Keeper. Maria fell asleep and Josie decided she'd get into her own bed with her Pokémon magazine rather than return downstairs.

Back in the kitchen alone, Nico got himself a beer and made the first phone call. '*Hej, Mamma.*'

Carina apparently read his voice. 'What's wrong?'

'Wrong's not the right word.' He laid out the Maria situation. 'As we're supposed to be staying with you I should have checked it was OK before I booked her flight but I couldn't risk all the seats being sold.' He didn't suggest he stay with Lars instead because she might take offence and Lars's house was no bigger than hers.

'It changes things,' Carina observed.

Nico wasn't fooled by her neutral tone. 'How much do you mind?'

222

She made a musing sound. 'Is "mind" the right word? I would say I'm wary.'

He considered. 'Wary I'm being taken for a mug?'

A pause. 'Not only that.'

His eyes were tired and dry. He rubbed them, gazing around Honeybun Cottage's sitting room. As it was so small and was the route between the kitchen and the foot of the stairs he'd stuck the sofa and TV in there and that was all. He tended to divide his time between kitchen and his bedroom. It was surprisingly restful to live in a compact house and here he didn't need room for Emelie and sometimes Tilly. His place in Islington was more than twice the size and much more than twice the hassle.

Swivelling to lie down with his feet on the sofa arm, he asked, 'So what are you wary of?'

She sighed. 'Is she a nice little girl?'

'Yes,' he assured her. 'You needn't worry that I'll bring some awful imp into your house. She's as little trouble as a two-year-old can be. She's cute.' His mother loved small children.

After a short silence, Carina said, 'If you're OK with the situation then I am too.' Nico couldn't get her to say more and finally ended the call, still wondering.

He got another beer before he telephoned his dad. Lars wouldn't be difficult but Nico felt he needed the pick-me-up. He was tired. Strained. His mind kept straying to Hannah but he had to make sure everything was OK surrounding Maria.

Poor little Maria. His heart shifted uncomfortably. She'd come into the world by accident and nobody had made adequate provision for her care. Many kids resulting from contraception failure were born to parents who forgot the

223

pregnancy had been a shock in the joy of the child's arrival. But some . . .

Some kids were never welcome.

He rubbed his eyes. Difficult days made him want to eat a huge bar of chocolate to feel better. He wouldn't, because he didn't have a huge bar of chocolate in the house – no coincidence, that – and because he knew the urge to purge would hit him within thirty minutes of eating it. He was having nothing to do with that cycle. He'd dumped it in a place labelled 'the past'.

He picked up his phone again. His dad's warm, rolling tones would be comforting.

Chapter Seventeen

The sky was inky black over Carlysle Courtyard. Hannah parked the car and jogged into the courtyard, gazing in satisfaction at the black tubs of purple heather and crinkly white brassicas. Christmas lights surrounded the doors and windows of Posh Nosh, Daintree Pottery and Mark's Models. Paraphernalia's front window was half-stocked with its highly ornamental stock.

With a rattle like gravel, a shower of hailstones flung themselves into the courtyard, pinging off windows and bouncing on the ground. Hannah hurried into Posh Nosh for her meeting with Perla and Teo, Mark, Daintree, Gina and the others. They were already there when she jogged in brushing hail from her shoulders.

'Hi. Wintry weather we're having! Wow, doesn't it look amazing in here?' She had to lift her voice over the clatter of hail on windowpanes, gazing at Posh Nosh's interior in satisfaction. The kitchen gleamed and Wedgwood blue chairs and tables awaited customers. Green swags and red berries hung between so many tiny white lights they looked like fairy dust. 'Won't keep you but I want to go over the plans for the Christmas Opening.' She began to pass out printouts, the hands accepting them matching their owners. Daintree's nails were rimed with grey clay, Mark's fingers smeared with glue, Perla and Teo's hands the kind of clean that came from constant encasement in nitrile gloves and Gina sporting salon-worthy purple talons.

Hannah raised her voice above the ratta-tat of hailstones. 'We have ten days. Anyone going to struggle? My notes say Fen Stones and Pix & Frames hope to be up and running this weekend and Teo and Perla on Friday.'

'Yes.'

'That's right.'

'Fantastic.' Hannah beamed. 'And the rest of you are already open, though visitors are still building. The Christmas Opening should drag the punters in.' She felt bright and buoyant. 'Here's the opening-day running order. At eight a.m. the yellow and green balloon arch will be erected at the end of the drive and a Christmas gazebo in the centre of the courtyard. Hopefully we won't have hailstones at the time!'

Laughter rippled through those gathered around the rectangular table as the hail increased in volume, crossing the roof in waves.

Hannah continued. 'Each shop will have a big jar of sweets to offer to customers and I've lined up a couple of students to wander about giving out mince pies. Half the gazebo will form Santa's grotto – Santa and an elf already booked – and I'll be around to encourage people into shops, also dressed as an elf.' She paused for laughter before going on. 'Demos will take place beneath the gazebo. Mark's constructing a balsawood sleigh at eleven, Teo making chocolate truffles at noon, Daintree—'

'Ah. Here you are. Good morning,' boomed a voice.

Hannah swung round to see Christopher and Cassie Carlysle striding down the large room towards them, Christopher beaming, Cassie pinched and apprehensive. Behind trailed a dreamy-looking man with untidy dark hair, reminding Hannah of a taller, better-looking Mr Bean. Beside her Mark muttered, 'Oh, shit.'

Daintree groaned. 'Just what we didn't need.'

Hannah looked sharply from dismayed face to dismayed face. 'What?'

Before anyone could enlighten her, Christopher drew the dark man forward. 'Look who's here!'

A couple of the traders muttered, 'Hello, Simeon.'

Shock flaring, Hannah stared. 'Simeon?'

'Of course! You probably haven't met our son, have you, Hannah?' Christopher rubbed his hands together as people did when trying not to betray how uncomfortable they were.

'No,' Hannah agreed hollowly. She should get up and shake hands, not sit here thinking someone had swapped her legs for cooked spaghetti.

'Christopher,' Cassie said tentatively. 'I really feel—'

But Christopher ploughed on with the air of someone intending to get a difficult job over with. 'Simeon's back now,' he pointed out. Then he smiled apologetically at Hannah as if waiting for her to join up the dots.

Feeling sick, Hannah looked at a pale Cassie. 'What does this mean?'

Christopher answered. 'It means Simeon can manage Carlysle Courtyard again.' He didn't add 'of course' but his blustery tone implied it.

Hannah ignored him. 'Cassie?' Cassie looked as if she might cry. Simeon, as crimson as his father but less leathery, stared over everybody's heads.

Christopher snapped, 'If you need it spelling out, Miss Goodbody, Simeon's returned to take this project back. I'd like you to hand over to him this morning.'

Hannah's heart thundered in her ears. 'Cassie employed me so I'm afraid you can't sack me.'

Christopher sucked in a huge, indignant breath. 'Cassie, tell her!' he barked. Then, before she could, 'Miss Goodbody, I hold the purse strings here.'

Under the gazes of everybody in the room Hannah rose, forcing her knees not to buckle. 'Cassie?'

Cassie swallowed audibly. 'You've got every right to be upset, Hannah. Every right.' Her eyes pleaded for understanding. 'But Simeon's our son.'

'I see.' Hannah wondered why, at times of shock, your mouth went dry. Squaring her shoulders, she said, 'If you make the second payment, which is due today, I'll hand over everything to Simeon—'

'What?' Christopher went from scarlet to puce. 'I was expecting a partial refund. How on earth do you justify that?'

Hannah gave up her attempt to deal professionally with the person who had engaged her and rounded on Christopher with a hiss. 'Because I've worked my arse off – eighteen hours a day, sometimes – to rescue this mess. I have emails agreeing to pay me a sum and I've only had one-third of it. Nowhere in those emails is there a proviso for the project being snatched away from me with no notice and no courtesy but I've accomplished everything except executing the social media plan for the final ten days and putting up the posters and delivering the flyers for the official opening. I've done well over two-thirds of the agreed work.'

Christopher actually took a step back. 'Those emails were a gentleman's agreement at most,' he rumbled.

Hannah snapped, 'They constitute a contract. Gentlemen's agreements only work when you deal with gentlemen.' Christopher had the grace to look discomfited. Unable to meet the eyes of the traders, though she felt both alarm and sympathy coming off them in waves, she steamed on. 'And to be blunt, if the second payment isn't forthcoming then neither is a handover. You'll be in as big a mess as you were when I got here because the information's not yours until you've paid for it.'

Christopher opened his mouth again but Hannah addressed Cassie, saying, bitterly, 'I accepted this work in good faith and I expect to hear from you.'

The silence she left behind was colder than the wintry scene she found outside, where the last of the hail was plinking down like the final words in a gigantic icy argument.

'Hannah!' Daintree hurried after her, hugging herself against the winter wind. 'Are you OK? I'm so sorry this has happened. But you wouldn't really go without handing over?'

She looked so agonised that Hannah halted. In her fury and humiliation she hadn't considered the innocent traders. A glance told her that a couple of the others were watching from the Posh Nosh doorway – Teo in a white apron and Mark in a brown smock. She'd begun to view the Carlysle Courtyard folk as her friends. She knew Mark lived with a cousin because his wife asked him to leave the family home, that Daintree wore head-scarves because she'd developed alopecia during a past, abusive relationship. Perla and Teo had borrowed family money to start their business.

'Sorry,' she muttered, giving Daintree a hug. 'But it's like there's a conspiracy to take away anything I earn.' Albin considered it OK to hold back what he owed her for stock indefinitely and Christopher sodding Carlysle had so obviously expected her to roll over and accept a loss that it made her want to yowl like an angry cat. Trembling, she ran to the car and drove numbly along Fen Drove, as cold as if she'd stood naked in the courtyard for the entirety of the storm.

Knowing she'd burst into tears if she went straight in to Nan she parked at The Cross and stomped round the corner into The Angel to order a large cappuccino and a chocolate brownie. Carola, blonde hair tucked under a fetching cap, gave her an old-fashioned look from behind the counter. 'Thought you'd be at Posh Nosh,' she said pointedly. 'My info is you're running things up at Carlysle Courtyard.'

'Your info's out of date!' Hannah gritted out as she paid for her order. She waited in silence for the coffee machine to spit and hiss and Carola to add sprinkles to the froth and press a holly leaf shape into it.

'Not having a good day?' Carola asked more mildly as she slid cappuccino and brownie onto a tray.

Unable to speak for tears, Hannah shook her head and grabbed the tray, choosing a table in the furthest corner of the room. She'd drunk half the cappuccino when Cassie phoned, voice trembling.

'That was handled quite dreadfully,' Cassie said. 'I can only apologise. You must think Christopher's an utter pig.'

Hannah swallowed. 'What I think is best left unsaid.' But she kept her voice calm, understanding that Cassie was caught in the middle.

'I hadn't realised Christopher would go at things like a bull in a china shop,' Cassie went on. 'I *do* apologise. It was nothing personal. Honestly!' she added, when Hannah made an indignant noise. 'He was just jubilant

230

that Simeon had finally faced his responsibilities and wanted to clear away all obstacles to returning him to Carlysle Courtyard.'

Hannah managed not to snort that Christopher hadn't so much cleared away obstacles as galloped roughshod over everyone else's rights and feelings. Making this call couldn't have been easy and if Hannah were to have any chance of that second payment it would be through Cassie. She eased her throat with a swig of cappuccino. 'So where do we go from here?'

Cassie sounded grateful for the opening. 'I'd like to take you up on your offer. I'll pay the second one thousand pounds into your account and you do a proper handover to Simeon.' Then, in a small voice, 'Please.'

'OK,' Hannah agreed heavily. All her beautiful plans and hard work were to be handed over to someone else and her fun, glittery opening would go ahead without her. 'Can Simeon meet me this afternoon? I need to go home, get Nan a meal and put stuff together.'

They agreed on two-thirty and after Hannah ended the call she emitted a loud, 'Bleurgh.'

Carola looked startled. Then she turned to the coffee machine. Hannah, slumped dismally on one elbow, suddenly saw a fresh, steaming cappuccino slide onto her table. She looked up.

'You let the last one get cold,' Carola whispered. 'But if you tell them at Posh Nosh I give away free cappuccinos I'll deny it.'

Half-laughing, Hannah thanked the older woman by clasping her hand, ashamed she'd stalked in here in a snit. 'I'll carry the secret to my grave.' It was one more example of the kindness of the villagers.

Once she'd drained the second cappuccino she trudged

off back to Nan's and let herself into the warm, worn kitchen. There she discovered her grandmother playing snap with Josie – quietly, because Maria was asleep in her buggy.

'Snap!' whispered Josie, slapping down a two of spades on a two of hearts. 'Hey, Hannah!' She jumped up and gave Hannah a hug.

Holding the warm little body in her arms, Hannah thought how nice hugs were when you felt like crap. 'Hello, Josie. Have you come to play with Nan?'

Josie slid back onto her chair. 'Daddy brought us. He needs to take a 'portant phone call.'

Nan's magnified eyes fixed on Hannah. 'Nico has something to sort out.' Her tone suggested she knew more but couldn't air it in front of the children.

'Right.' Hannah nodded. 'I'll make sandwiches for lunch soon.' Intending to go up to her room first, she opened the door into the dining room, which led, cottage style, to the sitting room, and then the stairs. She was in the sitting room before she spotted Nico in one of Nan's beige armchairs, his phone beside him.

Her heart jumped and she jumped with it. 'Sorry! I didn't know you were in here. Josie said you were on the phone but I assumed you'd gone home for the call.'

The small twitch at the corner of his mouth might have been a smile but he was deathly pale. 'I've imposed on your grandmother. I don't know many people in the village.' His hair was on end.

She advanced further, sinking onto the edge of the sofa. 'Are you OK?'

'Not really.' Even his lips were white. 'My brother Mattias called. Dad's had a heart attack. I didn't want to scare Josie by letting her hear my end of the conversation. Nan Heather

232

said she'd keep the girls in the kitchen. She's a kind soul.' His voice cracked and he covered it with a cough.

Forgetting her own worries, Hannah fell on her knees beside his chair. 'Oh, no! Poor Lars!'

Nico wiped his eyes on his sleeve. 'It was such a shock. His neighbour found him collapsed in the garden so he was very cold. She covered him with blankets until the ambulance could take him to hospital in Jönköping. The one in Eksjö is closer but didn't have the right bed available. Nässjö doesn't have its own A and E.' Twin tears oozed from the corners of his eyes and he wiped them away. 'When Mattias said . . . I thought the worst.' His voice broke again.

She grasped his cold, hard hand. 'Do you know how Lars is now?'

'Conscious. Exhausted. Confused.' He gave a half-laugh half-sob. 'Mattias says he's grey, but trying to joke about an elephant sitting on his chest. Luckily, everything's booked for me to fly to Sweden in two days anyway. Vivvi and Loren can't take Maria after all so I've got the documentation sorted for her to come with us – including clearing it with social services. This morning Maria's case worker visited and said she might be able to arrange respite instead but I'm still not having Maria go off to strangers. I'll manage somehow.'

Hannah held his hand tighter. 'Josie's very good with her and maybe your mum will have the girls while you visit Lars?'

He managed a smile. 'Apparently she's rushed to the hospital. Who would have thought it? She told Mattias that they've been "sort of seeing each other again". I'm not sure how that will go down within the family considering they split when I was fourteen.'

From the kitchen came a wail. 'Maria's awake,' he said, wiping his eyes more rapidly.

'I'll go to her while you get yourself together,' Hannah offered. 'Nan can't get her out of the buggy with her arm in a cast.' She gave his hand a last squeeze then slipped back into the kitchen. Josie was undoing Maria's straps while Nan clucked, 'There, there, my duck.'

Maria's face was red and crumpled. 'Mydad?' she whimpered.

'He'll be here in a minute,' Hannah said soothingly. Cautiously, because she hadn't had much to do with children, she lifted the little girl up and cuddled her.

'Mydad,' Maria whimpered again.

Instinctively, Hannah held her closer, finding it poignant that Maria didn't call for her mum. 'Two minutes and he'll be here,' she crooned, rocking Maria while Nan found a plastic beaker and poured apple juice and water into it. 'Here's a drink. That's lovely isn't it?'

'Juice,' Maria said more happily and took several gulps.

'Is Dad coming?' Josie glanced at the dining room door.

'He's finishing his call,' Hannah said soothingly. 'Who won at snap?' If Nico hadn't yet dried his tears he wouldn't want Josie to see them.

Josie allowed herself to be distracted. 'One game each. This one's the decider.'

'You play and Maria can watch. I'll make drinks,' Hannah suggested brightly, popping Maria onto a chair now she'd cheered up. She made Josie a glass of juice and tea for her and Nan, putting it on the dresser where Nan could reach it but Maria wouldn't knock it over. Then she carried a cup to Nico, closing the door behind her.

He looked more his normal self now, on his feet and eyes dry, if a bit pink. 'Sorry,' he muttered, thanking her

234

as he took the mug she proffered. 'It was the shock. I knew as soon as I saw Mattias's name that there was something wrong because I'm always the one to ring or email.' He drew in a long breath through his nose as if fighting emotion again. 'It's as if being separated during our teen years has all but severed our fraternal tie.' He stopped. 'I'm babbling. Still in shock.' He sat down again suddenly. 'I'm a mess. Loren's gone into rehab.'

'I didn't know that about Loren,' Hannah said softly, feeling sorry for Nico and the way everything was landing on him at once. 'That's why you agreed to take Maria to Sweden with you?'

He nodded, cradling his teacup. 'I got the call when we were in the pub on Sunday but I couldn't say anything with Josie listening.' He looked directly at Hannah and added, 'All there is between Loren and me is Josie and, via kinship link, Maria.'

'Oh,' she said. That wasn't how he'd made it sound over that last uneasy meal in Stockholm but now didn't seem the time to ask for clarification.

He returned to the immediate issue. 'I was wondering about bringing our flights forward to tomorrow but I haven't begun packing yet.' He swallowed hard. 'Dad doesn't seem in immediate danger.'

'I thought I was having a shitty day but you've put it in perspective,' she said. And remembering how much better she'd felt when Josie had thrown her arms about Hannah, she leaned in and gave him a good hard hug. 'Why don't I make soup and sandwiches for us all? Nan loves having kids around. I don't have to go out again until after two.'

Nico didn't even pretend to fight this plan. 'Thank you.' He followed Hannah into the kitchen, smiling and telling

Josie calmly that Farfar wasn't well so it was a good job they were going to Sweden anyway.

Josie agreed, 'Good job!' and turned to Maria with an exaggerated gasp of excitement. 'We're going on an aeroplane in two more sleeps!'

Maria made the same noise, beaming, too young to get what was going on but happy at whatever made her sister happy.

Hannah began heating soup while Nan gave Nico and the girls directions on setting the dining table. 'The one in the kitchen doesn't have room for us all.' She observed the obvious warmth and love between Nico and the girls. Happily child-free till now, for the first time she wondered if she'd been missing out.

After a jolly meal, Hannah checked her bank account and saw the second thousand pounds had arrived from Cassie Carlysle – bloody Albin's money still hadn't arrived – so she said, regretfully, 'I have to go up to Carlysle Courtyard.' She grabbed her laptop and paperwork, eager to get the handover done now she'd been unceremoniously dumped.

Soon she was driving past the cheerful yellow and green Carlysle Courtyard sign with a pang. She parked and found Simeon awaiting her in the office. 'Right,' she said crisply, glad she didn't have to deal with Christopher again or even Cassie. 'I haven't had time to prepare this handover so we'll have to wing it.'

'Of course. I'm very sorry about this, you know.' Courteously, Simeon pulled out a seat for her.

It was an empty apology because he could have refused to comply with Christopher reinstating him. 'Thanks,' she said, briefly. 'Bullet points: by the weekend, all the shops will be trading; the Christmas Opening is on the nineteenth.'

She worked through everything she'd slaved over, sharing contact details and her and Nico's beautiful spreadsheets, then the extensive scheduled social media posts. 'That's it,' she wound up an hour later. 'You have the log-in details. Posters and flyers need to be distributed. If you have any questions you can text me.' She scribbled down her phone number.

Then she realised Simeon was gazing at her, a small smile playing around his mouth. 'Anything else?' she queried, poised to drag on her coat and shake the dust of Carlysle Courtyard from her boots.

'Fancy dinner this evening?' he asked.

She gaped. 'With you?'

'There's a lovely old mill bistro opened near Bettsbrough. Shall we give it a try?' He smiled boyishly.

It was a perfectly pleasant invitation but it rankled that he didn't bother to thank her for her hard work and making the handover so easy for him or acknowledge the impact on her income of his return. 'Thanks, but I'm busy,' she said, snapping shut her laptop.

He edged closer. 'Choose your evening.' He didn't make it a question.

He reminded her overwhelmingly of Albin – born in comfortable circumstances and regarding ordinary girls as playthings. 'Good luck with Carlysle Courtyard,' she said. And left.

Chapter Eighteen

Back in Middledip, she found Nan watching TV and flopped down beside her on the sofa to catch her up on the disheartening events at Carlysle Courtyard. 'So I won't be working there any more,' she concluded with a sigh.

The old lady massaged the fingers of her injured arm and frowned thoughtfully. 'Christopher isn't usually so bullish. That boy of theirs, he's disappointed them so often it's made him touchy.'

Hannah took over massaging Nan's fingers, gentle with the loose papery skin and dainty bones. 'Cassie said something similar,' she admitted.

They watched the TV together for a while. It was a documentary about World War II. Nan had been a teenager for most of the war, had known gas masks and evacuees and how people had helped each other.

'I chatted with Nico after you'd left,' she said suddenly. 'He was so looking forward to his trip home. But now he's worried about his dad and managing Maria. You can't expect as much of a two-year-old as you can an eight-year-old if there's a lot of hanging about in hospitals.'

Hannah considered what she knew of Nico's circumstances. 'I know he left their old nanny behind in London and his cousin has uni. Maybe he has relatives in Sweden who'll help.'

Stiffly, Nan edged round to face Hannah. Her age showed in the sad drooping of her wrinkles. 'I asked him. No grandparents left alive and no aunts, uncles or cousins who aren't busy working. He says he'll try and get a temporary nanny from an agency when he gets there, if he has to. Cost a packet, I bet.'

'Poor Nico. He's stepped up to have Maria and been left to cope with the extra hassle.' Hannah thought of the sunny toddler and her chatty big sister. Lovely kids, but lively.

'You speak Swedish,' Nan said.

Hannah swung her gaze on her grandmother. 'And . . .?'

'Those little girls know you.' Nan pursed her lips and her wrinkles reassembled in a new pattern.

'Barely!' Hannah protested instinctively. 'I'm not a nanny. I know nothing about kids. Nan, you're not suggesting I save the day by volunteering to go with them, are you? It would be like one of those non-empowering chick flicks when a woman offers herself as a support act to a man.' Especially when she'd just heard he wasn't trying again with his ex-wife after all.

The lines of Nan's face deepened. 'You're not going to be working at Carlysle Courtyard. You could track down that Albin and get your money back while you were there.'

'I'm not here to work at Carlysle Courtyard. I'm here to help you. I can't leave while your arm's in a cast. I know Rob and Leesa are back but they have full-time jobs.' Hannah patted her grandmother's soft, crepe hand. She thought about being back in Sweden, with Nico, and

239

a wistful note crept in. 'It's a point about Albin but you need someone to get your meals and help with zips and things.'

A few minutes later Hannah popped out to Booze & News to buy Oxo cubes for the supper casserole, glancing down Little Lane in the direction of Honeybun Cottage and hoping Lars was OK and Nico would cope. She hadn't missed that he'd been too upset to eat properly at lunch-time, though he'd put on a show for the kids. She rarely heard Nico complain. He set his jaw and tackled every obstacle. She felt guilty about her waspish remark to Nan about women supporting men. It hadn't been Nico who'd made her position untenable, like her ex-boyfriend Luke; or taken her business from her, like Albin; or viewed her as a potential date instead of taking her seriously as a person, like Simeon. But she couldn't abandon Nan, even if Nan was the one to suggest it.

The shop door gave a *ting* and clattered shut behind her. She chatted to Melanie, whose op had been postponed because of pressure on beds, then hurried home again, a box of beef Oxo in her pocket but thinking more about Nico than casserole.

She found her grandmother replacing the phone in its wall cradle. 'Right,' Nan said briskly. 'I've telephoned Brett to settle our differences.'

'Blimey, that's an about-face.' Hannah halted, wrong-footed.

Nan grimaced. 'I suddenly saw how self-centred I've been. My refusal to speak to Brett tied you to me and the village. You're a wonderful granddaughter to have given up so much time but Brett's invited me to stay with him. So that frees you up.' Nan gave Hannah a very direct look.

'Frees me up to act as Nico's nanny?' she asked slowly, trying to keep up with this dizzying change in circumstances and examine how she felt about it.

Nan grasped Hannah's hand with her one good one. 'It wouldn't be about being Nico's nanny. It would be about being his friend. He needs one.' As an afterthought she added, 'And just don't think about you being a woman and him being a man.'

Yeah, right.

Nico was exhausted. The girls, driven by Josie's over-excitement about flying to Sweden, had run up and down stairs yelling until Maria's cheek collided with Josie's elbow, making Nico end the game and Josie grouse at her howling little sister for spoiling everything. It had taken cuddles, bath time and an extra special Mydad-created bedtime story about a unicorn called Maria before she'd go to bed. Nico had sent Josie up a scant hour later, saying gently but inflexibly, 'Read quietly until you feel sleepy.'

Josie had given him a sulky look but complied.

He suffered the look nobly. The sitting room looked as if there had been a bombing raid. If the girls were going to continue to be batshit crazy until he got them to Sweden his frustrations would be off the scale. He felt sick whenever he thought about his big, gentle dad in a hospital bed, hooked up to machines. Mattias would be doing everything needed, Nico knew, but he wanted to jump on a plane, be with his family now, not the day after tomorrow. The two little girls upstairs prevented him acting on the urge.

Righting a red plastic toy crate in the sitting room he scooped Barbie-sized clothes and accessories into it one-handed as he called his brother. They'd already arranged that if he was at the hospital Mattias would have his phone set to vibrate so it wouldn't disturb others. He answered, 'Do you want to talk to Dad? He's brighter this evening.'

Relief flooded through Nico. 'That would be fantastic.' He could hear the background noise of the ward as the phone was passed over.

Lars sounded tired but very much himself. 'Don't think this means you're excused a trip to the rink next week.'

Nico laughed. 'I wouldn't dare. Have you been having chest pain?'

'A little,' admitted Lars. He broke off to cough. 'I didn't want to tell you. I don't have time to be ill.'

'Looks like you've had to make time,' Nico broke in, caught in his anxiety for his father.

'Looking forward to seeing you on Friday,' Lars said, obviously not wanting to pursue that. 'Here's your brother.'

Mattias came back on the line and the noises of the ward receded. 'I've come out into the corridor. He's exhausted,' he told Nico, sounding uneasy.

Queasiness swept Nico and he got to his feet. 'I'm sorry not to be able to get there tomorrow—'

'There would be no point,' Mattias interrupted. 'That's when he'll have his angiogram. He's almost bound to need intervention – either stents or bypass surgery.' He blew out a sigh. 'They've suggested short visits in the evening. Mum's here all the time! You wouldn't think they'd been divorced twenty-two years. She's cornering doctors and giving nurses instructions like the most anxious of relatives.'

Nico digested this. He realised his hand was full of Barbie shoes and let them clatter into the toy crate. 'Wow. How's Dad reacting?'

Mattias half-laughed. 'They were holding hands when I got here tonight. Ironic, really. When we needed them together, they split up. Although you took up Dad's time anyway.' He switched subjects. 'Do you need fetching from the airport on Friday?'

'I'll have a rental car,' Nico answered automatically, still working on Mattias's words. 'I spent a lot of time with Dad because of the ice hockey.'

'Yeah. Well, I'd better get back to the ward,' said Mattias. 'See you soon.'

Nico was left holding a silent phone and frowning.

His uneasy thoughts were interrupted by a knock at the kitchen door. When he answered, he found Hannah, holding a padded bag.

'Hope I'm not imposing.' Her coat hood framed her face. 'I made this casserole for Nan and now she's made things up with her boyfriend and he's swept her off to a restaurant and as I need to talk to you anyway I thought we might share it. Unless you've eaten already.'

He stood back to let her in. 'Thank you! Eating together would be great. The girls wanted cheese on toast for supper, which I didn't fancy.' Now here was Hannah with something that smelled delicious and suddenly he discovered an appetite.

She stepped inside, roses in her cheeks from the chill evening. 'It's in an insulated thingy so it'll still be hot.'

'I'll warm plates,' he said, unexpectedly soothed by the domestic feel to these arrangements. 'Fancy a glass of wine?'

Hannah did and before long they were each sitting down steaming casserole and chilled chablis. Nico raised his glass to clink it with hers. 'I'm never sure where British casserole ends and stew begins.'

'Me neither,' she admitted cheerfully, lifting her glass of gleaming white wine too. 'Casserole sounds posher.'

'Whatever you call it, it's delicious,' he said, tasting succulent beef that fell apart on his fork. It was nice to feel a normal kind of hungry.

She entertained him as they ate by telling him that her project at Carlysle Courtyard was her project no more. Though she was light and amusing, he was sure being publicly and shockingly shoved aside must have been distinctly unfunny.

'That stinks!' he complained, frowning.

The remnants of pain flashed in her eyes. 'Cassie explained that Christopher was insensitive because he was so focused on the bloody son, Simeon – who waited till I'd handed over then asked me out to dinner.'

That Nico had more sympathy with. He was enjoying Hannah's company himself, after all. 'You refused?'

Her eyes twinkled. 'Important date with a casserole.' She indicated her plate with her fork and changed the subject to Nan Heather and how she hadn't been speaking to her boyfriend until today.

He grinned. 'If any ninety-year-old lady would be giving her boyfriend the run-around, it would be her.'

'I'm afraid she felt he'd messed up. But he's been sending gifts and today she suddenly phoned him. He's invited her to stay at his house.'

'Any idea why the change of heart?' He wasn't worried about the details of Nan Heather's love life but he enjoyed watching Hannah as she talked.

'I know exactly.' Sighing, she laid her cutlery neatly on her empty plate. 'It's so I don't have to stay with her. I've called my parents – they're in southern Belgium – and they agree that if Nan's going to stay with Brett there's no need for me to be here.'

'Oh.' He hadn't quite finished his meal but his appetite switched off. 'Will you stay in the village?'

'Not sure.' She fidgeted. Expressions he couldn't read flitted across her face. Then she screwed up her face and blurted, 'Nico, if you want help with the children now your dad's in hospital, would you like me to go to Sweden with you?'

His heart hopped like a frog in a frying pan. 'Oh, jeez, yes,' he managed huskily.

Hannah barged on, her cheeks glowing with colour. 'Nan's convinced you'll leap at it because I speak Swedish reasonably well and the kids know me, so you could leave them with me and know I could take them around OK. But the more I think about it the more I think inviting myself along is crazy! Your family won't necessarily be able to put me up and I expect you can cope with one hand tied behind your back. Offering feels intrusive and cheesy. Although it would also be convenient for me if I could make a dash to Stockholm to sort out a business matter while I'm in Sweden.'

'It would be perfect,' he got in more loudly.

She stopped. Her gaze flew to his. 'What would?'

'It would be incredibly kind and appreciated if you'd come,' he said simply. 'Apart from speaking Swedish, you're dependable and independent. It would be a weight off my shoulders to know that whatever happens with Dad there's someone there to take care of the girls.' To hide the fact that his throat was tightening – and he'd already shed tears in front of this woman – he reached for his laptop. 'Let's see if I can get you on our flight.' Then he stopped, conscious of silence from the other side of the table and big, aquamarine eyes fixed on him. 'Or am I moving too fast?'

She laughed uncertainly. 'No. Maybe. I thought you'd hum and haw and talk things over with your family.'

A grin took charge of his face and he opened the British Airways site with fingers metaphorically crossed that there would still be an available seat. The screen flickered and flashed and offered ticket availability. 'In or out?' he asked, finger hovering over the buy button.

She gave an incredulous giggle. 'In!'

He took out his credit card, waving away her offer to contribute. 'You don't do someone a huge favour and then pay your own way. Leave me to talk to my mum about accommodation.' Neither of his parents nor his brother had large homes but he was sure they could stick a camp bed in his mum's study or something.

He was going to spend a week with Hannah.

And, though she hadn't yet told him herself, she was no longer coupled up with Albin.

While Hannah put the dishes in the dishwasher and made coffee, Nico called Carina, raising an eyebrow to discover she was still at the hospital with his dad but not commenting. He outlined Hannah's offer.

To his surprise, Carina didn't, as he'd expected, leap in with queries and questions. 'Let me talk to your father,' she said. The line became muffled for a while, then she returned. 'Lars says you should take over his house. It makes perfect sense. Hannah can have a room and you can share with the girls. If you came to my house it would be more cramped.'

'But Dad might come out of hospital while we're there,' Nico pointed out.

'Wait a moment.' Another muffled conversation. Then: 'If that happens, he will come to my spare room for a few days because it's tricky coming out of hospital when you

246

live alone. Now he's falling asleep so I'll say goodnight. *Lycklig resa.*' She added the wish for a fortuitous journey quickly, as if to forestall further questions.

Well, now. Nico had no idea how to take that little development. It gave him a warm feeling to picture his parents together on some basis but all he said to Hannah as he came off the phone was: 'Looks like we've got ourselves somewhere to stay.'

Chapter Nineteen

As the aircraft circled Gothenburg airport, passengers craned to see the grey shapes of cleared runways and curving wheel tracks cut into dazzling white snow. A rank of snow blowers and ploughs stood in readiness for the next snowfall.

Josie was in the window seat and, tingling, Hannah gazed at the view over her shoulder. She hadn't realised she'd missed Sweden until this moment.

Last night she'd phoned her parents to update them just as they'd been snuggling down in The Bus with their books and bedtime Bovril, prompting a perfect hail of anxious questions about whether she and Nan were doing the right thing. Hannah had been as soothing as she could without reversing her decision.

Next, Rob had rung, no doubt tipped off by Mo. Hannah had half-joked, 'Mum clears off on the big adventure then wants a say in what happens at home! I suppose you don't think I should go either?'

'I think you should,' Rob corrected her, comfortingly. 'Leesa and I will call on Nan and Brett at the weekend and check all's OK. You go drink snaps, eat that Christmas smörgåsbord thing – what is it? *Julbord*? And tell Pettersson he's lucky to have help from my stupid sister.'

'I will.' Hannah, whose mind had whirled with a mix of excitement and doubts all day, had relaxed, though she wasn't sure she'd follow the advice about snaps. The fiery Swedish liquor was meant to help you digest but she generally preferred a nice glass of wine.

Now her ears popped as the aircraft throttled back for its final descent. She glanced across the aisle to see Nico giving Maria a drink. He was a thoughtful dad. Probably because Sweden was a few hundred metres below her, Albin flashed into her mind. What kind of father would he have made? She could barely imagine. He'd had such a strangely distant relationship with his own parents he'd have no warm and loving example to follow. Would he have thought to give a toddler a drink so her swallowing would equalise the pressure in her ears?

She couldn't imagine that either.

Turning back to the window to watch the airport rushing closer, snowy pine trees ranged behind its white-roofed buildings, she wondered again if she'd be able to grab time to whiz up to Stockholm and track Albin down. The funds he owed her still hadn't arrived and now he wasn't answering her phone calls except with brief texts like, *Incredibly busy*. It was as if he was enjoying playing telephone tag, awarding himself points for not responding adequately to messages or calls. The train took two and a half hours from Älgäng to Stockholm and she'd need another half hour to get from Stockholm Centralstation to Frihamnen where his office was. Building security was high but a hullaballoo in reception should force a reaction from him.

She'd probably avoid Gamla Stan. It would upset her to see her lovely shop in its new guise as a sleazy 'private club'. She shuddered.

Then they were landing, bumping onto the runway, the engines roaring into reverse thrust. Josie turned and grinned, blue eyes dancing. 'I feel as if Mr Invisible's pulling me out of my seat.' She called across the aisle. 'Maria! Did that feel funny?'

Maria laughed and dropped her cup to clap her hands. 'Yeah! Funny, Yozee. Funny, Mydad.'

Nico deftly caught the cup and grinned at Josie and Hannah. '*Välkommen till Sverige*.'

'*Tack, det är härligt att vara här igen*,' Hannah replied. Then she translated 'Welcome to Sweden' and 'Thanks, it's good to be back' for Josie. 'Now you can say, "*Tack, Pappa*," for "Thanks, Dad."'

'Dad taught me that,' Josie cried. '*Tack, Pappa*. And if Farmor gives me a meal I say, *Tack för maten*.'

Hannah congratulated her and they collected their things for the boring business of disembarkation. Clearing passports was slowed by the processing of Nico's permission to travel with Maria. He answered questions easily and politely and Maria, clinging round his neck, demonstrated the warmth of their relationship by giving his cheek a big kiss with a loudly enthusiastic, 'Mmmmwah!'

The passport control officer almost smiled as she waved them through.

Baggage reclaimed, Hannah entertained the girls by blowing white clouds into the bitingly cold air, pretending they were dragons while Nico picked up their rental car, trying to tune in to the rhythms of the Swedish being spoken around her. Eventually they were on the road to Älgäng. It looked as if Sweden was enjoying a really wintry winter. Snow made the roadside banks into marshmallow mounds and rivulets had frozen into icicles on vertical rock faces. The road cut through the whitened forest and the miles of fencing prevented elk from straying into the paths of cars.

Although Lars's house was in Nässjö, Nico drove first to the A6 shopping mall and bought the girls snowsuits. Maria's was splashed with purple daisies to go with her purple boots. She giggled at the process of sliding her legs into it and looked at Nico questioningly. 'Coat?'

'Snowsuit,' Nico said.

Maria erupted in *har, har, hars* and did a little dance, as if to check her padded legs still worked OK. 'Snowsuit, Yozee!'

Josie rolled her eyes. 'Mum got you one last winter, Maria. You grew out of it.' But last winter was, obviously, almost half a lifetime ago to a two-year-old.

They arrived at Nico's mum's small house in nearby Älgäng for a late lunch. Carina's was a traditional Swedish house, rust-red and white, the changing pitch of its roof sitting on the building like a bonnet, its corner plot sheltered by towering pines. White lights and illuminated stars glowed from every window and along the verandah. A *tomte* with a grey hat and long white beard, the house gnome of Swedish folklore, guarded the door.

Carina appeared as the car pulled into the drive between rough mounds of cleared snow. She was tall and her short hair was much darker than Nico's. Her eyes were dark, too, sparkling as she bombarded her son and granddaughter with cuddles. Her English was more accented than Nico's but still quick and idiomatic as she greeted Hannah warmly, welcoming her to Småland with a hug. Then she crouched down to Maria's level. '*Hej, stumpan.*'

251

Josie said, 'Farmor, this is Maria. Maria, say hello to Farmor.' She obviously didn't see anything tricky about whether Maria was entitled to claim Carina as a grandma or, literally, 'father mother'.

Maria smiled shyly. ''Ullo, Farmor.'

Indoors, Hannah helped Maria out of her coat while Nico asked for an update on Lars. Carina said, 'I rang earlier and he'd passed a comfortable night so he's fit for his tests this afternoon. You can see him tonight.' She looked anxious and Hannah caught an interested look in Nico's eyes at the slightly possessive way his mum talked about his dad.

Then Nico's brother Mattias arrived with his girlfriend Felicia. Maria looked unsure of yet more new people and grabbed Nico's hand in both of hers as if staking a claim.

Mattias was dark and slender, like his mother, Felicia smaller and still darker. She presented Nico with an almond caramel cake or *toscakaka* and Mattias assured Nico, 'She's generous and kind to everyone,' as if making sure Nico knew he wasn't getting special treatment.

Nico merely hugged Felicia with a good-humoured: 'You're lucky she's such a wonderful woman, Mattias. I'm glad to see you happy.' Mattias returned a small smile.

Hannah noticed that Nico asked Mattias about his work as assistant curator at the Husqvarna Museum and about their apartment in Huskvarna, which he hadn't seen. Mattias didn't respond with an invitation to visit but instead told Hannah about 'Husqvarna' being the brand and 'Huskvarna' the town. He was a dull old penny next to Nico's golden sovereign glow.

After their late lunch of open sandwiches and *pepparkakor* straight from the oven Josie gazed longingly

252

outside. 'We haven't played in the snow yet and it's almost dark.'

It was three p.m. 'Swedish winter days are short,' Hannah explained. 'I'll take you out in the garden, if that's OK with Farmor.'

'Yes, please!' Josie ran to find the new snowsuits and Maria trundled after with her usual cheerful willingness. Hannah made sure they had boots and gloves and then they stepped out into the garden where the snow was undisturbed but for the footprints of birds and animals. Light streamed through the house windows, suffusing the white, glistening garden in a magical glow.

Josie sniffed in a huge breath and released it in a white cloud. 'Mmm, it smells snowy.'

Hannah sniffed too. 'You're right. Isn't Farmor's place pretty? It looks like a gingerbread house.' Then she caught sight of Maria trying to eat snow with a mittened hand. Her snorts of laughter bubbled into the air as the two-year-old smeared the icy white crystals across her face.

'Snowman!' cried Josie, heaping snow against Maria's back.

Maria glared at Josie. 'Nooo!'

'Maybe not a snowsister,' suggested Hannah, hastily. 'Let's make a proper snowman. It's good squeaky snow so it should hold together.' She began to roll up a ball of snow, which Maria immediately tried to kick.

Then the back door opened and Nico jumped out, a plume of gleaming white flying into the air around him. 'We're making a snowman, Dad,' Josie cried and Hannah let Josie and Nico take on the serious construction work while she made mounds of snow for Maria to kick.

Eventually the snowman stood smartly to attention in

a black furry hat Carina passed out through the door, with pebbles for eyes and a potato for a nose. Maria began to yawn and yank her mittens off, then cry because her hands were cold. 'I think it's time to get settled at Dad's house,' Nico said, swooping Maria into a warming cuddle.

Carina and Mattias wrapped up well and came out to wave them off. While Nico was making arrangements with Mattias about seeing Lars that evening Hannah thanked Carina politely for lunch.

Carina smiled but her eyes were on Nico. 'He looks a little . . . thin,' she said carefully.

Hannah was whizzed back to when she'd seen Nico in Stockholm almost seven weeks ago and had suspected he was living on the streets. He'd improved since then but she didn't think it would comfort his mother to share that thought. She answered, equally carefully. 'I think he's conscious of the need to eat properly and set a good example to the girls.'

Carina flicked a glance at her as if wondering how much she knew. 'He's becoming attached to Maria.'

Unexpectedly, Hannah felt herself bristling. 'I think he's done something worthwhile in earning her trust and affection when she seriously needs stability.'

'Yes. But even a big heart can be broken.' Carina sighed as she pulled a knitted hat out of her coat pocket and crammed it on against the frigid air. 'Don't you think he'll be unhappy when Loren takes her back?'

Hannah stared at the older woman. 'You're worried about that? I suppose I've looked at it from Maria's point of view. I hadn't thought about Nico getting hurt.' She'd seen him as put-upon and kind . . . but not vulnerable.

Carina smiled wistfully. 'He's my son. I know him well

so of course I worry.' Then she changed the subject. 'Yesterday, I visited Lars's house and changed the beds. It's a small house but you'll have a room of your own. I've made airbeds up for the girls in Nico's room.'

'That's very kind. Thank you,' Hannah answered mechanically, her thoughts still occupied with Nico's feelings. Then he was gathering them up and ushering them out to the grey bulk of the rental car for the ten-minute journey to his dad's house in Nässjö, deftly performing the routine fatherhood things like wrangling Maria into her car seat, answering Josie's constant stream of questions at the same time as ensuring hats, mittens and scarves weren't left behind.

Maria took against her left boot and tried to lever it off, tiny eyebrows becoming curls of indignation. 'No boot!' she hollered, kicking violently.

Nico screwed round from the driver's seat and tickled her tummy through her snowsuit. 'Yes boot! Or the snow monster will gobble up your toes.'

As suddenly as the tantrum arrived, it vanished. Maria wrinkled her bobble nose to show him her white baby teeth and laughed.

He'd been born with parenting superpowers, Hannah decided as Nico waved through the windscreen at his family and started the ignition. It was the only explanation.

The road out of Älgäng to Lars's house threaded through the pines. Posts with reflective discs denoted the road's edges where snow had been ploughed into berms. As they drove into a town bedecked with tasteful white Christmas lights they passed a lake and Nico told them his childhood family home had been on the other shore. The lake was icy at the edges. 'We used to skate on it,' Nico reminisced.

Then he swung the car uphill into an area of older homes and into a small drive. 'Here's Farfar's house. Nice of him to let us stay here while he's in hospital.'

The house was slate grey and white with a rounded turret under a hat-like roof and, the way the snow had clad one side, looked slightly askew, drunk and beautiful like a bride on her hen night. A lady emerged from the next house, bundled in woollens and enormous boots, to talk earnest Swedish over the hedge to Nico. Hannah, letting Josie out and then scooping Maria from her car seat, caught most of what was being said. The neighbour had found Lars lying in the snow when she'd come out to her car. He couldn't have been there long or he would surely not have survived. Nico clasped the woman's hand and thanked her.

The neighbour beamed at Hannah, Josie and Maria. 'Such a lovely family!'

Nico didn't try and explain who was who but thanked her again before she scurried back to the warmth of her house. He jumped up on the white-painted porch, fishing a key from his pocket and letting them in. They left their boots in the alcove inside the door rather than track snow onto Lars's parquet floors while Nico went back for the luggage.

Hannah looked around. There were two big rooms downstairs: a sitting room and an L-shaped kitchen-diner that led to a snowy back verandah and a garden with a birdhouse. Nico reappeared, stacking up their bags, wind-blown and out of breath.

They climbed the uncarpeted wooden stairs to examine the two bedrooms and bathroom. Hannah's room was a typical spare, home to a collection of cardboard boxes and an ironing board as well as a bed with a white and yellow quilt. Lars's room, where Nico and the girls would sleep, ran across the back of the house and sported a king-sized bed and two airbeds, neatly made. As soon as the girls saw the airbeds they flung themselves down, considerably reducing the neatness.

Nico groaned theatrically as he deposited the suitcases on the floor. 'I don't think I'll get to sleep late with this pair so close.' Then they stood at the window while he pointed out landmarks above the rooftops – his high school, the church where his parents had married. Farmland and forest out of town. He looked happy and relaxed to be back where he'd come from.

They'd unpacked and the girls had eaten a little of Felicia's cake when Mattias arrived to pick Nico up for the drive to the hospital in Jönköping.

Nico dragged on his coat. 'I'm going to see Farfar.' He hugged Josie and then Maria. 'Be good for Hannah. When I come back we'll go back to Farmor's house for *julbord*. It was arranged before Farfar was ill and Farmor still wants to do it.' He hugged Hannah, too, warm, firm. Brief.

After he'd hurried back into the snow, Hannah decided to take the girls food shopping. Google told her there was a Kvantum supermarket in Bandygatan, a few minutes' drive away and soon she was pushing Maria in a trolley while Josie darted back and forth, asking if she could buy tinsel for Farfar's sitting room and falling on Marabou chocolate with a delighted cry of, 'This is *the best*.'

'Wan' chocyut,' Maria decided, trying to crane backwards to scoop it out of the trolley.

Hannah beat her to it, replacing the enormous bar Josie had selected with two much smaller ones. 'We'll put them in the fridge and ask Dad when you can have them.'

'Awww,' groaned Josie, folding her arms.

'Awww,' groaned Maria, folding hers too, though not as neatly.

'Poor you,' Hannah joked. 'Let's get cereal bars and fruit, juice, milk, tea and coffee.' Not certain what shape the week would take, she added bread, ham, cheese, salad and soup. It felt very domesticated to be shopping with two children in tow. At the checkout she stepped back to let a very pregnant lady go ahead of her and helped load the till belt to save her having to bend over her considerable bump. Must be funny to be pregnant, she found herself thinking. All that waiting. Wondering. Then, at the end of the waiting, suddenly there was a Josie or a Maria. Her mind strayed to Loren, who'd given birth to these bright, lovely girls. If she ever had children she'd fight through anything to keep them with her, she decided. Then she brought herself up sharply, realising that she'd never experienced what Loren was going through so had no right to judge.

They'd been home half an hour when Nico returned, subdued, though he smiled for the children. 'I saw Dad for twenty minutes,' he reported to Hannah in a low voice. 'He gets his angiogram results tomorrow. He's pretty tired and looks—' he paused to select the right word '—colourless.' He sighed. 'Do you mind if we get straight off to Mum's? It sounds as if she's gone to a lot of trouble and my great-aunts, Astrid and Ellen, will be there, along with Ida, my cousin Emelie's mum, and a couple of male cousins of Mum's who go wherever there's free nosh. Mattias and Felicia have gone straight there.'

'Sure.' Hannah gave him an impulsive hug. 'Try not to worry about your dad. He's in good hands.' When she saw an answering gleam in his eye she blushed, realising a comforting hug was different to a hug hello or goodbye.

Maybe she was getting too deeply into this family role. It was as if she thought she was a wife.

In the event, they didn't stay late at Carina's. Mattias proved prickly and moody, Felicia casting him anxious looks. Nico was quiet too. His great-aunts Astrid and Ellen had identical grey wavy hair and called Nico 'Nicke' explaining to Hannah with evident delight that 'Nico' was a German name. Nicke was Swedish. Nico just smiled but Carina retorted that she was entitled to give her sons any names she pleased, Germanic or not. It appeared to be a family discussion of long standing. Carina's male cousins ate and drank stolidly, and though Ida, who was Lars's brother's ex-wife, was a chatty, homely lady, Hannah concluded it was a gathering to get all the hospitality owed to peripheral family over with at one time.

The adults sharpened their appetites with a small glass of *glögg*: mulled wine. The girls loved the drink Julmust, which always tasted to Hannah like flat cola, with their Prinskorv sausage, spare rib and meatballs. They dipped happily into the gravlax and the beetroot salad but weren't sold on herring or *Janssons frestelse* of potato, anchovy and onion.

The cheesecake and *ischoklad* – 'ice chocolate' – found great favour. Even Nico ate three of the little sweets. She ate eight, herself.

Finally, Nico said it was time to get the girls to bed and they said their goodnights and drove in silence through the forest between Älgäng and Nässjö, moonlight turning the snow and trees to a landscape of black and white.

Maria had fallen asleep as soon as the car wheels turned and stayed more or less that way through being changed into pyjamas, taken to the loo and slipped beneath her quilt.

'You're tired too,' Nico murmured to Josie. 'You can read in bed for a while.' She yawned and fished unicorn-strewn pyjamas out of a suitcase.

Hannah went down to the sitting room, switched on a couple of lamps and built a fire in the corner of the open fireplace in the Swedish way, enjoying the crackle as the flames took hold.

A soft tread on the stair. Nico appeared and passed through the corner of the room headed for the kitchen, reappearing in a few moments with a bottle of red wine. 'It's Dad's but I'll replenish his stock.'

'That looks great.' She added another log to the fire and returned to her place on the sofa. Nico handed her a brimming glass of the jewel-red liquid and stood the bottle on a small table. He dropped down beside her and helped himself to a share of her footstool so that their feet, in thick woolly socks, were not far apart.

He drank half his wine and sighed, letting his head loll back against the sofa. 'I need this. Dad looks grey and Mattias has an ant up his arse about something. He was morose when he drove me to Jönköping, as if I'd offended him.'

Hannah thought of Mattias's earlier terseness and Felicia's wary expression. 'Is he usually happier to see you when you come to Sweden?'

He shrugged. 'No, but he's not so obviously . . . distant.' He shifted slightly, his shoulder settling lightly against hers. She didn't break the contact but examined the pleasure the innocent touch gave her and the way her heart began to hurry the blood around her veins. His touch felt deliberate. A signal. A tentative approach.

'Yours and Mattias's relationship is different to mine and Rob's. I often didn't see him for weeks, even when we live in the same country, but we always find time for messages or calls, even if it's just to exchange friendly insults. Maybe we're lucky that we like each other as well as love each other.' When they met they hugged. They were siblings. She couldn't imagine any other way.

'It's different,' he agreed with a sigh. 'That "bonkers brother" and "stupid sister" stuff is filled with love.' Nico laughed, his blue eyes darker than usual in the low light. 'You look out for each other, too. He used to warn his friends off you when we were teenagers.'

Hannah snorted. 'No self-respecting sixteen-year-old would pursue someone of twelve, anyway. And you guys were sophisticated and glamorous. Your names appeared in the *Evening Telegraph* in the ice hockey reports. I was overawed by your fame.' Although she made her voice mocking, truth lay beneath her words.

His eyes crinkled to slits. Then he sobered. 'We used to have a rule about going out with teammates' sisters and exes so you'd be out of bounds on that score too.' His gaze remained firmly fixed on her. 'Rob reminded me of that at his wedding . . . after he'd seen us dancing so close together.'

Her breathing hitched at the memory of his body moving against hers, his hands on her bare back above her jump-suit, his lips hovering as if offering a kiss. But then . . . 'After? Ah.' That explained why Nico had abruptly cooled on her and danced with Amanda Louise. She finished her wine, irritation prickling beneath her skin. She'd still been with Albin then but she'd known the end was near and without Rob warning Nico off she could have left things on a more promising note.

Men were weird. They had their codes about not sleeping with a mate's sister but saw nothing wrong in slow-dancing with a woman, gazing at her hungrily . . . then ignoring her.

'I'm tired. I think I'll go up,' she said abruptly, not feeling quite so kindly disposed towards Rob now. 'I'll see you tomorrow.'

'OK,' he answered, sounding surprised at the suddenness of her exit. 'Goodnight, Hannah.'

She awoke on Saturday feeling sheepish at last night's prickliness. Nico had been discussing sibling relationships and she'd somehow made it about her. So Rob had made some blokey remark about a teammates rule? Nico and Rob were adults, now, and not teammates. Nico could have told Rob what to do with his warning. He'd probably simply fancied tall, sexy, beautiful, smug, spoiled Amanda Louise more than Hannah. That was his prerogative.

Once dressed, she ran downstairs, hearing Josie's high piping and Maria's insistent cooing long before she caught Nico's reassuring rumble. He looked up when she appeared and smiled. 'Best breakfast. Porridge and milk? Or pastries and juice?'

'Pastries and juice,' she answered promptly.

'Yay!' shouted Josie.

Nico shook his head. 'You people have no idea.' But he put out pastries and poured juice.

Hannah fathomed out Lars's coffee machine and made herself white and Nico black then picked up Maria, who could barely see over the table, and sat down with her on her lap. Maria slapped the table top and chortled as she tried to snag the biggest pastry for herself.

Nico sat down, plated the smallest pastry for the toddler and passed it across. 'My plan's to light my candles this morning while Dad sees the consultant. I'm hoping to visit him this afternoon.'

Hannah pushed her coffee aside so Maria couldn't touch the steaming mug. 'Light your candles?'

He wiped butter from Josie's plate so it couldn't transfer itself to her sleeve. 'At the cemetery, for my grandparents and an assortment of relatives. Do you want to come? Josie always does so I'll take Maria too.'

Josie backed him up, pastry flakes sticking to her cheeks. 'It's snowing again! Come with us, Hannah. It'll be awesome.' Her ponytail jiggled as if in emphasis.

Hannah smiled at her excited face. 'Then I will.'

They finished breakfast while, beyond the window, the snow swirled like white bees swarming and banking in the wind. Josie was shouty with the thrill of it and Maria shouty because if her big sister shouted then shouting was obviously in.

Nico whizzed out to Kvantum supermarket to buy candles while Hannah got the girls to clean their teeth, visit the loo and wrap up in snowsuits, boots, gloves and hats. Maria was easily bored by the dressing process and tended to shed gloves and hat with a soft, 'Noo.'

When Nico returned they set out, the snow squeaking beneath their boots on the pavements while cars sailed past with a muffled swish and the snow tried to immediately paint over the tracks. Snow made cotton wool of twiggy hedges or lay along tree branches like white snakes. Hannah lowered the flaps of her hat to cover her ears from the stinging flakes that flung themselves at her and the freezing air bit the back of her throat.

'Cold!' Maria kept squeaking, eyes dancing and cheeks pink. 'Snow cold.' Luckily, her mittens were waterproof because she plunged them into the white mounds at every opportunity. Hannah made a snowball and gave it to her to hurl at Nico. Maria managed to fling it behind herself and stamped on it instead. Nico threw his head back and laughed, his black woollen hat low over sparkling eyes.

Fairy lights twinkled and lighted stars glowed from windows beneath roofs like white witches' hats as they trekked along the quiet residential streets past traditional wooden houses and brick-built modern apartment blocks. Then Nico turned through a gateway to the cemetery where dwarf conifers and heather poked through the snow.

It looked unexpectedly beautiful. A man sweeping the path between the hedges said, '*Hej*,' as they crunched past. Pine trees towered like giant pointed figures holding up spiky dresses to catch the snow. The headstones were small rectangles, set out in rows with lanterns beside them. Hannah was struck by the dignity and simplicity of the plain memorials rather than the larger, ornate kind she'd seen in English graveyards. It felt very Swedish.

Josie was obviously familiar with events. When Nico stopped at a pair of stones and brushed them off she said, 'Can I light the candles?' Hannah watched them crouch together, prising the top off the glass lanterns and carefully positioning inside stubby ivory-coloured candles from Nico's backpack. Then he took out an igniter and Josie pressed the trigger. Its flame leaped to the candlewicks. Hannah kept Maria's mittened hand in hers. With the lantern lids replaced, the flames flickered prettily.

Nico rose, brushing snow from his knees. 'My grand-parents.' He gestured at the stones. 'Mormor and Morfar. They used to take me hiking and skiing when I was young.' From '*mor*' at the beginning of each word Hannah didn't have to be told these were his mother Carina's parents.

264

Wandering deeper into the cemetery they repeated the action with Nico's Farmor and Farfar and then a cousin and a great-uncle. 'We did this with Mum when we were little. It's a peaceful thing to do,' he said, hooking the now empty backpack over a shoulder.

They retraced their footsteps, the girls scurrying ahead, hand in hand, their chatter floating on the icy air. 'Feeling peaceful's important to you?' Hannah asked as he held a branch so she could squeeze through a gap in the hedge. Snow whispered down around them.

'I prefer it to stress,' he answered. 'Peace makes me a better dad. I don't mess with my eating to try and get a feeling of control. If I look after myself better, I look after others better.'

The wind was behind them now and it was easier to walk without the snow flying in their faces. She said, 'It's like when you're in a failing aircraft and the masks drop down. You have to get your own oxygen flowing before you can help others.'

His blue eyes glowed. 'Yes, it's exactly like that! That's a great analogy.'

'Do you feel at peace in Middledip too?' she ventured, watching the snow fly and bank around them, muffling the noise from the nearby road. 'Or do you think you should be back in Sweden?'

He didn't hesitate. 'Our lives are in England and I wouldn't separate Josie and Maria by such a distance. I like Middledip and soon I hope to hear that Josie will have a place at the village school. All the stretched feeling of juggling work and childcare has faded away. I'll find something to do in a while – maybe some way of working from home – but there's time for that. I'd like to integrate with the village more. Get involved in fun stuff.'

'There's an old folks' party at the village hall on the twentieth,' Hannah teased. 'You could take Nan.'

He shrugged. 'Happy to. She's an interesting lady and I wouldn't mind helping out on the tea urn or ferrying plates about. My life's been so structured, my working life so make-or-break, I've barely had time to get involved in a community. I could be the pain in the arse who organises everything and is always trying to rope people in.'

'We've already got one of those. She's called Carola and works in The Angel,' Hannah said, with a gurgle of laughter.

His eyes crinkled at the corners. 'In that case I'll be assistant pain in the arse.'

Then Maria began to cry because she'd face-planted in the snow and he hurried to swoop her up and brush her down, drying her tears with his gloved fingers and then putting her on his shoulders for the journey home.

Josie dropped back to walk with Hannah. 'You know what would be really, really good? If we filled the whole garden with snowmen. Then when Farfar comes out of hospital they'll still be there even though we've gone home.'

'What a lovely idea!' Hannah laid her arm on Josie's shoulder. 'How about this afternoon while Dad's visiting Farfar in hospital? We could keep it as a surprise.'

'Yeah!' Josie tried to skip but skipping in snow was like skipping in glue. She raised her voice. 'Dad! We've got a secret and we're not going to tell you!'

Nico turned, a tall figure wearing Maria on his shoulders like a fashion accessory. 'Is it about my Christmas present?'

'No!' Josie laughed. Then she looked up at Hannah and whispered worriedly, 'I haven't got him anything because we usually make presents for our parents at school.'

266

'We'll think of something.' Hannah realised there was now no wife/nanny/cousin in Josie's life to check Josie made her dad a gift. As if her offer promoted Hannah to a new level in Josie's mind, she chattered all the way back. First she talked about Loren. She didn't seem to Hannah to regard her as a child normally regarded her mother, with love and a recognition of maternal authority, but more as someone for whom allowances must be made, someone who couldn't completely be trusted. How must it have felt for Josie to find Maria hungry and thirsty, crying hopelessly in her room? Nothing like it had happened in Hannah's childhood and she could only imagine how scary it would be. No wonder Josie clung to the safety of Nico.

When Josie talked about her dad her tone was different. No confusion, no wariness. 'Dad says he'll . . .' or 'Dad says we'll . . .' littered her sentences.

And every time delivered with no doubt that whatever Dad said, it could be relied upon.

Chapter Twenty

The hospital smelled of chemicals and people, with the occasional whiff of bowel.

Nico had driven the hire car to Jönköping. Mattias was working in the museum until two and would go home to Huskvarna after visiting Lars. He, Nico and Carina converged on the ward as it opened. Carina hugged her sons, Mattias gave Nico a wintry smile and turned to his dad, lying in bed with an impressive number of wires emerging from his gown to create bleeps and graphs on various machines.

'The doctors have told me off,' Lars said. His hair stuck up and his face looked rumpled. His smile was marginally less tired than yesterday. 'I have coronary heart disease and a bad diet. Once I stopped coaching professionally I let myself have all the pizzas and chocolate I once preached against.'

Not thinking it was for him to comment on someone else's relationship with food, Nico patted his dad's hand, noticing the age spots. 'So, what next?'

'Angioplasty, where they put a balloon in your arteries

to widen them, and possibly stents. I'll be here a few more days.'

'When will these procedures happen?' Mattias, this time.

'Tomorrow.' Lars pulled a comical face. 'They're in a hurry to fix me.'

'And get rid of you, I expect,' Carina joked back. But tears stood in her eyes. Nico felt torn. It was good to see his parents close again but it made him wish they'd never parted. Maybe then Mattias wouldn't treat him like a stranger. On the other hand, if they'd stuck together then maybe he'd never have lived in England. He couldn't imagine that, much as he loved Sweden.

He listened as his family chatted, smiling at Lars's jokes or when Carina termed him and Mattias 'the boys' as if they were still children in primary school – *småskola*. Lars asked Nico to go to the rink at Jönköping at six to take the ice hockey under sixteens skills training.

Wondering at the flash of anger he caught in Mattias's eyes, Nico groaned, but agreed. He kept hockey gear at Lars's house and his dad knew that.

'And I have four tickets for the HV71 home match on Monday,' Lars sighed, referring to Jönköping's Swedish Hockey League team. 'I planned for you to come, Nico, with Mattias, Felicia and me.'

Mattias interrupted, 'Now you're in hospital, let Nico take his family.'

'But—' Nico protested but Mattias was grabbing his coat and muttering about how busy he was.

Later, Nico strolled back to the car park with Carina. 'Do you know what's bugging my little brother?'

Carina gave an elaborate shrug. '*Ingen aning.*' *No clue.* She didn't deny Mattias's remoteness, though.

Nico sighed as he saw Carina back to her car and hugged her goodbye. 'I'll try and talk to him.'

The journey back to his dad's place was slow. The snow lay six inches thick now and when he eventually swung into his dad's driveway he was cautious of the snow that had accrued since he left.

The sound of laughter from behind the house drew him to the back garden where he found Josie, Maria and Hannah, bright-eyed and rosy from the cold.

'Look, Dad!' Josie squealed as soon as she saw him. 'We've made snowmen to remind Farfar of us when we've gone.'

He moved closer, pausing to absorb the rugby tackle Maria sometimes bestowed as a hug. She shouted, 'Look men, Mydad!' The lying snow was scraped and trampled now and from the centre of the welter rose four snowmen – or snow persons – beneath the snowy pines. One tall; one a little smaller with what looked like a swollen chest; and two smaller still, one Josie-sized and one the height of Maria. He grinned, realising the snowy figures were, indeed, them, with pebble eyes and carrot noses. The one with the swollen chest must be Hannah and he could imagine Josie's literal mind at work there.

'Fantastic,' he pronounced. 'I'll take photos and send them to Farfar.'

'It was my idea!' Josie boasted, bouncing gleefully. 'Take our photo with them.'

He obliged, and they all crouched down for a selfie, ears and noses stinging in the cold. Then he said, 'I've let Farfar persuade me to take under sixteens' hockey skills training at six. Do you guys want to watch? Or stay here?'

'Watch,' said Hannah and Josie simultaneously, Josie adding, 'Can we have supper out afterwards?'

270

'Supper?' repeated Maria expectantly.

'Deal,' said Nico. It was already after five so he went to his dad's garage to take down his skates from the wall, unsurprised to find them sharpened and ready. In a box was his practice gear and he brought it indoors to warm up. It smelled musty but that proved you were a hockey player.

It was weird driving to the rink or *ishall* in Nässjö because butterflies fluttered in his stomach. He'd assisted his dad a few times when he was home for his winter visit but he hadn't taken a group himself since college in the US when he'd helped coach a junior team, those far-off days of trying to keep up his training and his grade point average simultaneously.

Lars had got someone at Nässjö rink to inform the parents of the change of coach but some would have encountered Nico when he'd helped Lars before. A couple he knew from school.

Hannah ushered Josie and Maria to the seating area behind the boards and a few parents stayed to help with gearing up. One, Henrik, acted as assistant coach and Nico shook his hand. The level of teenage chatter, mostly in Swedish, was enough to pop an eardrum. Nico answered questions about Lars or about college hockey in the States. As he talked he pulled on protective undershorts then strapped on his shin pads and huge hockey oversocks that attached to the undershorts. Stepping into hockey pants, he pulled them up and with familiar, automatic movements, secured lacing and belt. Skates next, snug but not cutting circulation, then the shoulder pads secured at chest and bicep. Elbow pads, checking the slash guard was on the outside, then emerald green jersey. Helmet with face cage but no mouth guard as he'd be talking to the kids. Gloves and stick – it had taken so much energy to dress he almost needed a nap now – and for the first time in a year he was ready to hit the ice.

A check of the kids' equipment, removal of blade guards, then he slid through the gap in the boards under bright rink lights, the kids spilling onto the ice after him, sticks in hands. Henrik was the last, juggling a tower of cones and closing the boards behind him.

For an instant, Nico was super-conscious of Hannah, Maria bouncing on her lap and Josie waving. Then he snapped into focus and sent the kids for a couple of warm-up laps while he and Henrik set out cones at the corners, the pitch lines showing colourfully through the ice.

'OK,' he shouted, and the kids slowed and joined him in the centre, the showier ones being sure to visibly shave the ice as they halted. 'Speed around the rink. I'm looking for a smooth, galloping stride and you need to pass outside the cones. Number one, go!'

Everyone did an individual lap, Henrik on the stop-watch, Nico skating in a smaller oval shouting, 'Weight forward! Really push against that ice,' over the sound of panting breath and swishing skates. As each kid started their second circuit he dropped a puck and flicked it into their path shouting, 'Pass it back!' It was an old trick of Lars's so the team members took it pretty much in stride. Then he set up a slalom with uneven spacing culminating with a slapshot at goal, the two goalkeepers on the squad taking turns at guarding the short, squat net. He did a couple of runs himself, flipping the puck into the back of the goal then feeling guilty that he'd once hoped to play National Hockey League or Swedish Hockey League so it wasn't a fair contest against the Nässjö under sixteens. But, hey. He was so rusty he creaked. The red, sweaty, smiling faces told him that everyone was enjoying themselves, which was the most important thing.

Hannah and the girls met him in the foyer when practice was finally over and he got away from the stream of questions about why he'd never turned pro. 'You've been ages!' Josie said accusingly. 'We're starving. Can we have burgers?'

His instinct was to go for a healthier choice and he saw Hannah's eyebrows twitch as if anticipating a negative answer but he could cause problems in the kids by over-forbidding and instead of saying, 'But you went to McDonald's in Bettsbrough less than two weeks ago,' said, 'OK, for a treat.'

Instantly, Josie moved on to her next request. 'Can we go skating this week?'

He nodded. 'If we can fit it in.'

'Can we hire skates?' Hannah asked doubtfully. 'Everyone in Sweden seems to have their own and mine are in England.' She swung a lagging Maria up into her arms.

Nico took Josie's hand as they walked through the sliding doors to the car park. 'Dad runs a skate exchange for the kids he coaches because growing teens sometimes need to change twice a year. I expect we'll find something for everyone in his collection.'

The burger bar visit was brief as Maria was almost too tired for food. Nico ate a modest-sized burger and enjoyed it without experiencing a knee-jerk reaction to get rid of it after. He drove home, Maria drowsing in her car seat. Indoors, he pulled her out of her snowsuit, which made her giggle sleepily, ready for an abbreviated bedtime routine. He was pretty sure she was asleep by the time he switched out the light.

Downstairs Josie had found *Daddy Day Care* on an English-language channel and they vegged out in front of it, Hannah drinking coffee and he and Josie drinking milk as they laughed at Eddie Murphy. He was very conscious of Hannah. The three of them were squeezed together on the sofa. Josie was in the middle but Hannah was close enough to touch. Her hair was messy from wearing a hat but glossy as it tumbled down her back. Last night he'd made the most tentative of tentative overtures towards her and she'd jumped up and run like a frightened cat. He'd learn from that and wait to see if she became comfortable being alone with him.

He would have thought she wasn't interested if it hadn't been for those slow dances in November, when, her body plastered excitingly against his, her silky hair flirting with his skin, interest had pulsed off her. He cursed Rob for jolting him out of that heat haze. He wanted it back.

Sunday was the thirteenth of December, St Lucia's Day. Carina was busy readying the church and helping the children of the procession. Lars had his angioplasty and two stents put in place in the morning and called Nico to say he needed a nap but wanted to see Nico and co later in the afternoon.

'We'll come,' Hannah listened to Nico assure him. 'See you at four.'

Hannah felt doubtful. 'I'll wait outside. He'll be exhausted.'

Nico tucked his phone away, golden stubble accentuating the determined shape of his jaw. 'Dad will want to see you too,' he declared firmly. 'He says he'll be fine after a rest.'

'It would be lovely to see him again so maybe for a

274

few minutes,' she agreed cautiously. The UK ice hockey leagues had restructured at around the time Nico left for the US so Lars had returned to Sweden, leaving the ice rink to a new team and a new coach.

The girls behaved well at the hospital, though Nico had to act swiftly to prevent Maria grabbing the drip of a patient being wheeled down a corridor. He apologised profusely but when he turned away made an 'OMG!' face at Hannah that made her smother giggles.

Lars occupied a room with three other men. Hannah let Nico go first, stooping to give Lars a gentle hug. '*Hej, Pappa,*' then switching into English so the girls could understand, 'How are you?'

'Rubbish earlier, sluggish from the anaesthetic but good otherwise,' Lars said. His hair was wispier and he was pale and lined but Hannah had no trouble recognising his kindly eyes and round face.

Josie, who talked to her grandfather frequently on Skype bounced into the conversation to tell him about their visit to the rink last night. 'And Daddy kept skating backwards. He's going to teach me. And he scored two goals.'

'I wish I'd seen it, Josie.' Lars gave Josie's name the Swedish pronunciation, very like Maria's 'Yozee'.

Hannah watched Nico blush. 'I hope the under sixteens didn't mind me trying a couple of shots,' he said apologetically, making Lars's face crease into a smile.

Hannah, seeing Lars's wires and tubes and mindful of the near-miss with the drip was happy to stay back with Maria hanging around her neck.

But Lars spotted her. 'Hannah Goodbody? You've grown up beautiful.'

Hannah's cheeks heated. She laughed. 'It's good to see you again. Rob sent his best regards.'

His gaze fell to Maria. 'Who is this little pixie?'

'I Maria,' Maria cooed, and waved at Lars when Hannah asked her to.

Despite Lars's protestations of being 'fine, now,' after fifteen minutes Hannah took the girls to the cafeteria for a drink so they didn't tire Lars out.

Nico joined them after a while. He had a smile for the kids but murmured to Hannah, 'He's tired. He needs time to heal and maybe return to the healthy eating he used to preach about. It's good that he's always been active.' He paused. 'Mattias turned up. I felt he wanted one-on-one time with Dad, so I came away.'

Although he spoke lightly enough, Hannah saw his shadowed expression. She covered his hand with hers and he returned the pressure. Then they headed home for a snack before driving to Älgäng church for Lucia.

Hannah had never attended St Lucia Day service. She found it beautiful. The church was elegantly vaulted and though ornamented with touches of plaster and gilt, not weighed down by acres of it as she'd seen in churches in Italy and Switzerland. Carina flitted around the hand-maidens and star boys, checking clothes and angles of hats. They processed up the aisle, their beautiful young voices lifted in the chorus of the famous song, 'Sa-anta-a Lu-ci-yah, Santa Lucia,' candles in their hands and in the crown of the young woman selected to play Lucia to bring in the light at the darkest time of the year. Carina slipped into the pew next to Mattias and Felicia, behind Hannah, Nico and the girls.

Hannah, serenity sinking into her, stopped thinking about the hardness of the pew or the chilliness of the church as song followed song. Josie and Maria, seated between her and Nico, were so enraptured by the sweet young voices

276

that Hannah found a tear trickling down her cheek. Nico slid his arm around the girls until his hand came to rest on Hannah's shoulder. It squeezed, then remained, gently comforting through the thickness of her parka.

After the service, they gathered at Carina's for cake. Maria and Josie cuddled up together while Josie played a game on Nico's phone. Nico tried to start a conversation with Mattias and Felicia, though Mattias didn't seem to have much to say. Hannah went into the kitchen with Carina to make drinks.

As she took down cups and saucers Carina said thoughtfully, 'I'd love to see Nico really happy.'

Hannah nodded, though she wasn't sure why Carina was sharing. 'He seems relieved to have left his job.'

Carina shrugged. 'Happiness is more linked to people.' She arranged tarts and a cake on a rectangular platter and Hannah carried it into the other room. Josie and Maria instantly revived and tucked into bruin-brown *Körsbärschokladtårta* or chocolate cherry cake.

Carina addressed Nico as she passed around napkins. 'I have something to say to you.'

Nico lifted an enquiring eyebrow. Hannah fielded a half-chewed cherry Maria was trying to drop beneath the table as if feeding an invisible dog.

After a moment to take one of the hazelnut tarts called *Kejsarkronor*, Carina went on. 'Before I knew Maria and Hannah would be with us this week and Lars fell ill, I'd arranged a surprise – to take Nico and Josie to Stockholm on Tuesday and Wednesday. Mattias and Felicia will be at work, of course.' She smiled at Josie's sudden indrawn breath. 'I promised you a visit to Skansen to learn more about Sweden, Josie, didn't I?'

Hannah instantly perceived herself and Maria to be the

flies in this plan's ointment. 'Don't cancel it unless you think you need to be near Lars. I'll stay with Maria.'

Carina smiled comfortably. 'But I've talked to the hotel and they can add another room to the booking for you so we have one family room and two singles. *Finns det hjärterum så finns det stjärterum.*'

Hannah giggled because that translated to *if there's room in the heart there's room for the bottom*. Then she sobered. 'Actually, I'd hoped to make contact with my ex while here and he does live in Stockholm.'

Carina looked taken aback, the smile fading from her dark eyes. 'Ah. There's someone in your life.'

Hannah snorted. 'He's only "in my life" in that he owes me money. I'd like to encourage him to settle up.' Briefly, she outlined the story of Hannah Anna Butik. 'The ratbag's declining my calls. Tracking him down in person might make him realise I'm not going to be meek.'

Carina's smile returned full force. 'We'll make time for you to "encourage" Albin.'

Josie was bouncing in her seat, obviously awaiting her turn in the conversation. 'Is Skansen the place with the animals, Farmor?'

'All the Swedish animals like elk and wolves, lynx and bears,' Carina agreed, gently staying Josie's movements in case it joggled her plate from her lap.

Not quite able to believe this opportunity to chase Albin down Hannah said, 'But will it be OK to leave Lars?'

'We'll only miss Tuesday because we'll be back in time for Wednesday-evening visiting and then Lars will come out of hospital on Thursday,' Carina said. 'Mattias will see his father on Tuesday, I'm sure.'

'Of course,' said Mattias, woodenly. 'But we have to leave now. Work tomorrow.'

Carina looked surprised. 'It's not even nine o'clock—'

But Mattias was already fetching their coats and bidding everyone goodnight without offering hugs or giving Felicia time to do so.

Nico jumped up and followed them to the door but soon returned wearing a baffled expression. Carina, too, looked surprised. 'Have I offended him?' Nico asked her in Swedish, presumably so Josie didn't ask a load of questions.

Carina shrugged. 'He's been tense lately. Probably it's a reaction to your father's illness.'

They spent Monday morning helping Carina and her choir clear up after the Lucia service. White and gold festive flower arrangements remained in place but a couple of hundred people dropped a surprising amount of tissues and sweet papers. In the afternoon they drove into the snowy forest, which had the happy consequence of sending Maria to sleep, making her fresh for the evening ice hockey.

It was Hannah's first live match, sitting up on the tiered rows by the halfway line. 'These are great seats!' Nico enthused, eyes darting about as if trying to absorb every detail of the brightly lit and colourful rink. HV71 was the local team and Nico was a lifelong fan. Josie was happy because there would be hotdogs and Maria was happy because the stiff programme, folded like a fan and banged on her leg with gusto, made a sound like loud applause.

Josie, however, forgot hotdogs the moment the players burst out of the tunnel in a shower of fireworks and was literally on the edge of her seat. 'Goal!' she yelled, arms aloft. 'No, no goal. Nearly a goal, eh, Dad? Oooooooooh, that man banged into the other man!'

'Enthusiastic defence,' Nico explained economically, craning to watch a forward flying up the rink as opposing defence men swarmed to block him.

'Owwwww!' protested Josie, as a back smashed the forward into the boards. 'You didn't used to smoosh people against the side like that when you played, did you, Dad?'

'Wellllll . . .' Nico coloured.

The 'smooshed' player shoved the enthusiastic defender, who shoved back and added a few short jabs of his stick for emphasis and the referee blew a foul. 'You didn't get in *fights*, did you Dad? You didn't bang into people or sorry-not-sorry trip them up? You never got put in the penalty box, Dad? It's like a naughty seat!'

Nico was fire engine red by now. 'Wellllllllll . . .' He rubbed a hand over his jaw. 'Darling, it's a physical game.'

Hannah smothered a grin as his daughter turned an astonished face his way. 'Dad! You *did*,' Josie breathed. 'You were a naughty hockey player.'

'I was a back. Had to protect my goalie,' Nico defended himself. 'Watch the game.'

By the time they went home, full of hotdogs, Maria was half asleep but Josie still wired and clamouring to know when they could watch another game. Nico got her to bed by letting her watch a past Sweden versus Switzerland match on her iPad. When he came downstairs he disappeared into the kitchen, returning with two glasses and a bottle of white wine.

Hannah put aside her e-reader. 'Josie's been bitten by the ice hockey bug.'

He passed her a glass and dropped down to join her on the sofa, swinging his legs up on the footstool. As before, his shoulder settled warmly against hers. 'I'm still stinging from being branded a naughty hockey player.'

She gurgled at the memory of his heated cheeks. 'You were squirming.' The wine was cold and slid down her throat like nectar. Or what she assumed nectar might taste like.

'At least she said "naughty" rather than "dirty",' he observed.

'It's better to be naughty than dirty?' Hannah felt herself settle against him, as if their bodies knew each other. Funny how she could be both super-aware of him yet totally relaxed in his company.

He regarded her through slitted eyes. 'I'm pretty sure I could be either.'

Then, as if he hadn't made a remark loaded with innuendo he asked her what she'd thought of the match while heat spread from her cheeks to every other part of her.

Chapter Twenty-One

After taking the early train through a snowscape that could have been made from blinding white icing they arrived in Stockholm on Tuesday in time to dump their overnight bags at their hotel and set off on a blue tram through the wintry city. Soft feather snowflakes floated down, forming giant eyebrows over windows and making all the statues look as if they wore barrister's wigs. Hannah was excited to be back but apprehensive about confronting Albin.

'Train!' Maria kept declaring, apparently unconvinced that 'tram' was the correct name for their smooth, swooshing mode of transport.

Josie said, 'I don't see a tram's much different to a train either, except it runs through the traffic.'

'Then that's the difference,' observed Carina, adjusting Josie's fleece hat.

They alighted near the Swedish History Museum because Josie wanted to visit the Gold Room and make a wish. 'There's loads and loads of gold down there!' she cried, with a skipping shuffle of her snow boots.

Hannah had visited but pretended to be a Gold Room virgin to give Josie the pleasure of showing her down the stairs past the enormous vault doors. They took photos of each other with towering rune stones then wandered around glass cabinets that glowed with enough treasure for a thousand pirates.

'See those big gold necklace collar thingies?' Josie tugged Hannah's sleeve. 'They look like seven plain strands but if we take a photo and zoom in – look!'

'Wow!' breathed Hannah, impressed by the on-screen image. 'Teeny tiny patterns all over. How on earth did they do that?'

'They were Swedish,' Josie said, as if that explained the unearthly skill required. Poring over the magnified image they could make out not only minute circles and scrolls gracing each strand but tiny figures, both human and other, carved into the solder joining the strands together. It prickled Hannah's skin to think that fifteen or sixteen centuries ago this stunning piece of jewellery graced the neck of a Scandinavian chief.

Maria's interest in gold waning, they approached the circular pool at the centre of the vault, leaning over the thick railings to gaze at coins shimmering like a gilded carpet of autumn leaves beneath the water. Sifting through the kronor in their pockets for coins, everyone made a wish. Josie was very secretive about hers, screwing up her entire face with the effort of wishing. Carina was pensive as she threw her coin, eyebrows knitting. Nico's expression was hard to read, though the planes of his face were captured perfectly in the golden light, and he flipped his coin so that it spun high in the air before hitting the water with a tiny splash.

When it came to Hannah's turn she found herself making

one of those wishes that are half-formed in the back of your mind, a yearning you've hardly admitted to yourself. It concerned Nico.

Maria, unfamiliar with the concept of wishing, was happy to hurl coins into the water, clapping at the tinkling splash as they hit the surface. 'More money, Mydad!' she urged, and cleared the adults of their small change while they laughed at her beaming smile.

'Let's head for Skansen while it's still light,' Nico suggested. Skansen was on the island of Djurgården, which meant, literally, animal garden. A bus carried them to the main gate. As they bought tickets the snow stopped falling, though it still clung to every twig and rolled a white carpet over the paths that wound up through a rocky slope. Hannah had come to the vast open-air museum of Skansen for musical events but the rest hadn't been sophisticated enough for Albin. However, Nico and Carina knew Skansen well enough to select a route without consulting the map.

The clouds cleared, bouncing the winter sun blindingly from the snow and turning shadows blue as they explored old dwellings that had been gathered from all over Sweden to form exhibits. Hannah was particularly struck by a home for two families that, although basic and old-fashioned to her, had still been occupied recently enough for a photograph of the final occupants to stand on the mantel. Josie liked the old school house because its ceiling-scraping Christmas tree was hung with handmade ornaments of coloured paper and oranges studded with cloves. Ladies in traditional dress gave them delicious warm *pepparkakor* to munch.

They meandered onward to the animal enclosures, gazing down at a lean, thickly pelted wolf pack playing in the snow like puppies. One wolf lifted its long snout

284

and howled, its ruff sticking out like a lion's mane. 'Woooooooooo,' Maria crooned back.

They saw lynx, wolverines – or 'funny badgers' as Josie declared them – and a huge, lugubrious elk who lay comfortably chewing, gazing back at them through rustic wooden rails. A couple of his buddies stalked up on their long legs to snuffle through oversized noses, making Josie laugh. 'It's awesome here,' she said. 'It's like Narnia. Magically snowy, the little houses are from the olden days and the animals are weird.'

'They're not weird,' Carina reproved her. 'They're Swedish.'

Josie's eyes danced as if she could comment but Nico lifted an eyebrow so she returned her gaze to the elk instead. Hannah wondered if she'd ever have an eyebrow that could discourage a cheeky comment like that.

They paused at the cafeteria to eat then carried on, Nico teasing Josie when she mistook lights in the shape of icicles as the real thing, popping Maria on his shoulders when she tired, catching Carina's elbow when she slipped on an icy patch. Smiling at Hannah as if checking she was there.

They waited until nearly three to see the sunset, gorgeous over the water, making silhouettes of the buildings and spires of the other shore and turning the snow a breathtaking pastiche of pink and apricot.

Fairy lights shone out as dusk darkened the sky to lavender blue and they made their way to the exit to begin the trek back to the hotel. Maria became whiney and overtired so they stopped for hot chocolate and cookies. 'Hey, hey,' Nico said, drawing her onto his knee. 'Cheer up, kid. These cookies have chocolate chips.' Maria took the cookie but was almost too worn out to eat.

Josie leaned her head on Carina's shoulder and yawned. 'I'm tired too. We walked about a hundred miles.'

'Or maybe two,' Hannah joked. 'It was so beautiful at Skansen. I could go on exploring for ages.'

'Don't take me with you,' groused Josie, munching a cookie with her eyes shut.

Their hotel was in the heart of the city at Vasaplan. The girls were so exhausted that Hannah ordered a seven-seater Uber on her app and occupied the middle row with Josie and Carina while Nico and Maria took the back. They edged through the traffic past massive reindeer made of a constellation of tiny lights and people hunching into their coats and tramping paths in the snow.

Maria fell asleep and descended into red-faced, kicking revolt when lifted from the car. In the hotel's reception, Nico tried to calm her with cuddles and Hannah distracted Josie from what she termed her 'dead feet' by counting the glass balls suspended from the lofty ceiling. Carina, as she'd made the booking, went to check in.

By the time she returned, Maria had wound down into moaning wails and Josie had snapped at her to shut up. 'Well, well!' Carina clasped Josie's hands and pulled her to her feet. 'Two tired, grouchy girls. But, good news! In the family room is a whirlpool bath. Just the thing to cheer you up. And then we'll have supper here in the hotel and watch TV together. It will be fun.'

It didn't sound like a fun way to spend an evening in Stockholm to Hannah but Josie brightened and Maria wiped her nose on Nico's coat and sat up.

Carina gave key cards to Hannah and Nico. 'I'll take the family room with the girls. I don't spend enough time with Josie and I'd like to know little Maria better.'

Nico halted in his tracks. 'Surely I'm taking the family room with the girls?'

Carina pulled off his black knitted hat and tousled his hair as if he was about ten. 'Nico, I have paid for the rooms, so I decide. Take advantage of a night off and relax. You need it.' She sounded as if she were telling him off. 'Maria and Josie, you want to play in Farmor's whirlpool bath and eat nice things in front of the TV, don't you?'

Both girls answered, 'Yes!' and grabbed Carina's hands. The overnight bags were collected from the luggage room and they took the lift. At the third floor, Carina and the girls wished Nico and Hannah a cheery goodbye and turned up the green-carpeted corridor as the doors swished shut. The lift slid smoothly onwards up to Floor Six.

Nico contemplated his empty hands. 'I hardly know what to do.' He grinned but Hannah wondered how often in the past few years he'd found himself without anyone to look after outside work hours. When the lift doors reopened they stepped out into another corridor, this one carpeted in beige, and found their rooms were opposite one another.

Nico glanced from one door to the other and smiled. 'Would you have dinner with me? Or are you deserting me for a whirlpool bath too?'

She smiled back, her heart kicking at the walls of her chest. 'Dinner would be great.'

He glanced at his watch. 'About an hour?'

'Perfect.'

They turned to opening their respective doors, Hannah taking two goes to insert her card the right way around.

Inside her room, which held two four-foot beds rubbing shoulders in snowy bedlinen, she dropped her bag and pulled off her hat. Was *Would you have dinner with me?* different to *Fancy dinner?* or *Looks like it's just us?* Was it . . . a date?

If so, she was for it. The longer she spent with Nico the more he occupied her thoughts. Anyway, date or not, she had no worries over what to wear. She'd brought only jeans and a couple of tops.

She showered and, choosing the more evening-y of the tops, a cold-shoulder turquoise velvet, dried her hair while checking the family WhatsApp. Rob had posted: *Saw Nan and Brett. Both fine.*

Hannah replied: *I'll ring Nan myself tomorrow. Gave Lars your good wishes. He hopes to be out of hospital in a couple of days.*

Mo jumped in. *Where are all the lovely pix of Sweden? Here!* Hannah quickly uploaded views of Christmas-card-perfect Stockholm, the sunset turning the snow pink and apricot and the snowman family in Lars's garden.

When her hair was dry and glossy she left it down so she could pull her hat over the top and scrabbled for a mascara wand in the bottom of her handbag. No matter how informal Swedes were, an evening in Stockholm felt wrong with an entirely naked face.

Then Nico tapped at her door and she answered, feeling tingly. He'd shaved and his hair was as neat as his tumbled ripples got, his skin a healthy pink from the day in the open air. 'It's snowing again,' he said.

She grabbed her coat before he could suggest anything boring like eating in the hotel. 'Stockholm's magical on dark snowy nights.'

His face lit up. 'Then I'll take you to one of my favourite haunts.'

They went down in the lift, dragging on hats and scarves

288

as they exited the automatic doors to the street, the whistling wind driving the falling snow diagonally. Hannah pulled down her hat as her ears began to burn. 'Whoo! It's turned wild.' Snowflakes stung her skin like Jack Frost's kisses.

'A storm's forecast.' He helped pull her hood over her hat then they set off along gritted pavements that crunched beneath their feet, turning off when they reached Mäster Samuelsgatan then off again to cut through Sergels Torg, its geometric paving disguised by grit and slush. Fairy lights flickered and writhed through bare trees like snakes at a rave and the fragrance from a kiosk selling Halv special hot dogs stoked Hannah's hunger.

'Where are we going?' She clasped her hood close to shield her face from the snow.

Nico didn't seem to hear, so she tugged his gloved hand. His fingers curled around hers as he answered. 'Near Kungsan.'

'Kungsan' was the pet name for Kungsträdgården or 'King's Garden', a popular spot in Stockholm and one Hannah knew well from her daily walks between Gamla Stan and Östermalm. It was hard to think of that though as she absorbed the seamless way they'd ended up holding hands. It felt warm and promising and . . . well, nice.

They tried to talk as they passed beneath dangling Christmas lights, gold against the night sky, but the driving snow stole their breath and the wind made their words swirl around them. Nico laughed, blinking snow from his eyes. 'To think we could have stayed safely indoors.'

The streets were half-empty in the deluge and they soon reached the restaurant, falling in through the door, gasping at the warm air replacing the cold in their lungs. Cutlery gleamed on royal blue cloths and a cream and gold tiled wood stove stood in the corner of the room. They were able to get a table by the window with a view over the water to Stockholm Palace and the bridges to Gamla Stan.

'Beautiful,' Hannah breathed, admiring the lights of the city playing over the glassy night-time sea, enjoying the lazy hum of conversation and clink of cutlery from the other diners.

'How about fizz?' Nico suggested, reading the wine menu. He took her hand, switching her attention from the view to him.

'Fizz sounds fantastic,' she murmured, feeling as if several glasses were already dancing through her veins when his leg came to rest against hers. It was hard to concentrate on the leather-bound food menu so she chose the local speciality. 'Meatballs. I can't come back to Sweden without eating meatballs.'

'Fizz and meatballs, a meal fit for the king.' Nico ordered and the smiling woman who served them brought a silver ice bucket containing a bottle with Hatt et Söner grande cuvée on the crest-like label. Actual champagne, not just a bottle of cava. Hannah's skin prickled with the feeling that something special was happening.

Nico's gaze was warm when it rested upon her. 'I telephoned Dad before we came out.' He still held her hand.

Hannah was distracted by the feel of his skin, warm and soft yet slightly rough, like a cat's tongue. She had to force herself to concentrate on his words. 'How is he?'

'Much more his old self,' Nico answered drily, the flickering flame from the candle on their table reflecting in his eyes. 'He told me how lucky I was to be out this evening with a beautiful, warm, kind, intelligent woman.' A smile made his eyes bluer. 'As if I hadn't noticed.'

'Oh,' she breathed, her heart launching into a gallop.

'Tell me something,' he went on, but paused to lift his wine glass to his lips. Was it her imagination or was there a sheen on his skin as if from nerves? 'Is Albin in your thoughts much?'

She swallowed, feeling as if her reply was important and wanting to be honest. 'He's crossed my mind a couple of times. It would be odd if being a mile as the crow flies from Hannah Anna Butik didn't remind me but, apart from the little matter of the several thousand pounds he owes me, he doesn't mean anything to me. Not now. He killed my feelings when he showed me his unpleasant side.' She didn't add that the man who filled her thoughts was Nico.

He nodded as if satisfied and released her hand as their meal arrived, the sauce from the meatballs pooling around boiled potatoes and dark red lingonberry jam. He ate well, with hardly any of the playing with his food that Hannah had observed in the past, and she wondered if it was a sign he was feeling better about life. The level of champagne sank until all that remained in the bottle was air.

'More champagne?' Nico asked, laying his cutlery neatly on his empty plate.

'Not for me, thanks.' She was already floating on a cloud of bubbles. 'But I'd love coffee.'

He ordered then leaned closer once again, voice low, eyes bright, so close she could see tiny flecks of green and gold among the blue. 'What did you wish for in the Gold Room today?'

She flushed as she remembered that half-formed but fully felt wish. 'You can't share wishes. They don't come true.' Not even superstition was going to make her jeopardise whatever magic was trembling just within her grasp this evening.

291

'Was it X-rated?' he murmured. Then, deliberately, 'Like mine?'

She swallowed, mind flying to exactly what X-rated thoughts his wish could have involved.

He lifted her hand to his mouth and kissed her fingers. 'I've been wishing since your brother's wedding that we could have those slow dances back.'

Her skin tingled from the brush of his lips but she couldn't let his comment go unchallenged. 'It wasn't me who went off and danced with Amanda Louise.'

He propped his chin on his fist. 'It wasn't me who didn't own up to having a boyfriend.' His tone was as challenging as hers.

Wrong-footed, Hannah frowned, trying to remember events. 'I don't think I deliberately didn't tell you. I knew there was something wrong with the relationship and actually made the decision to end things on that evening. I'd already tried to talk to Albin about why he'd changed towards me but he claimed to be under too much stress to deal with it. Turned out it was so he could sort everything out in his own favour while I was away. I was trying not to sour the wedding by thinking about him,' she admitted. 'Sorry.' Then, because she wanted to know, she said, 'I think Amanda Louise might have been hoping for more from you.' She told him about the 'snagged and shagged' conversation she'd overheard at breakfast the next day.

Surprise flitted over his face. 'I went to my room alone to relieve the babysitter . . . and think about you.'

'Oh,' she breathed, both intrigued and charmed at his frankness. 'Well. We can't dance here. No music.' She shrugged in mock despair, glancing around the beautifully dressed tables as if an orchestra might be hiding behind a white napkin.

A grin quirked his lips. 'There must be a killer chat-up line about you and me making beautiful music together but I'm not enough of a lizard to carry it off.'

She smothered a laugh. 'I'm not sure anyone is.' Then her amusement faded and this time she was the one to take his hand as she looked him in the eye. 'The only feelings I have left for Albin are disappointment and irritation. The nicer emotions vanished like a snowman in the rain.'

He kissed her fingers again then smoothed back her hair. 'I'd very much like to go somewhere where there's no table between us.'

Heat rushed up from the soles of her feet. 'I want that too.'

They paid their bill and zipped their coats. They stepped outside and the snowstorm swallowed them up. 'Whoo!' shouted Hannah, trying to shield her face from the driving, stinging snow.

'Come on!' Nico threw his arm around her and they were blown back to the hotel by the storm's wintry breath, staggering on slushy pavements.

Finally, they burst into the hotel foyer, faces pink and burning. They shoved back hoods and stripped off icy gloves and scarves and Nico kissed her all the way up in the lift, lips cold and tongue hot.

In the corridor between their rooms he halted, kissing her more gently, lips soft against her chilly cheeks and the corner of her mouth. 'I don't want to take anything for granted,' he breathed, more a question than a statement.

'My room has twin beds,' she said against his mouth.

'One of the things I like most about you is that you're so refreshingly direct,' he murmured. 'You've no idea how relaxing it is not to be permanently guessing or playing games. My room has a king.' In a second they were through his door, kissing while he fumbled one-handedly with the lights. He dragged her out of her coat. She pulled off her hat.

He caught his breath as her hair fell around her shoulders. 'You're so beautiful.'

Then he fast-forwarded himself out of his coat and sweatshirt. Used to him in winter clothes, she let her gaze travel pleasurably across his torso, lean but full of muscle. The cords of his arms shifted as he reached for her, stroking, caressing, rumbling with pleasure in the back of his throat. He kissed her shoulders where they showed through the cut-outs in her top. 'I've wanted to do that all evening. There's something so sexy about that small amount of naked flesh.' It didn't deter him from sliding the top up and over her head. When he unfastened her jeans a thrill rushed through her as she felt the air on the sensitive skin of her belly. Her legs lost their bones.

'My jeans won't come off over my boots,' she murmured.

He steered her gently towards the bed. 'Leave them to me.' He laid her back on the cool cotton covers. A couple of flicks as he dealt with her laces then two tugs and the boots were gone, then her jeans. Nico rose, eyes glittering, and managed to hook her into his arms and up the bed. He paused to kiss her, then pulled back, kicking off his boots and shucking his jeans, his eyes roaming over what heated skin wasn't covered by her black panties and yellow-flowered bra. Dropping onto the bed beside her, he nuzzled the tops of her breasts. 'Mmm, Hannah.' It curled her toes.

Pressing against his erection, she ran her palms over the firm heat of his shoulders and chest. His breath caught as her hand travelled down, relishing the smooth, taut abdomen and snaky hips.

His unfocused gaze met hers. 'The refreshing directness gets better and better. Jeez.' His gasp as she slid her fingers inside the elastic of his boxers was muffled by her breasts, his breath hot on her skin.

He reached around for the clasp of her bra and as he pulled it slowly off she forgot how to breathe, almost levitating from the bed at the pure pleasure of his skin sliding over hers. He eased aside her underwear and touched her and she felt a jolt of excitement so fierce she wanted to shove against him till he filled her up. Her whole body was consumed with the intimacy of making love, the give and take, the electricity that set fire to her nerve endings and fried her brain.

She kissed the hot skin of his neck and shoulders. 'I hope you have condoms. I want nothing more in the world than you inside me.'

She didn't have long to wait.

Chapter Twenty-Two

His phone ringing was as unwelcome as a drunk bellowing in the street as you drifted off to sleep. Nico took a moment to orientate himself, the night rushing back to him as he saw Hannah blinking sleepily on the pillow beside him, silky, tawny hair tumbling. He dropped a kiss on her temple then leaned out of the bed to extricate the phone from his jeans pocket. Its screen told him it was exactly eight a.m. The name that flashed up was his mother's, but it was his daughter's voice he heard.

'Hi, Josie,' he mumbled, voice gravelly from sleep, examining the unfamiliar feeling of being in bed with someone other than Josie's mother while he talked to Josie. 'OK, sweetheart?'

Josie's young excited voice burst in his ear. 'Dad! It's snowed and snowed! And Farmor says are you ready for breakfast? You are, aren't you? Farmor says some of the snow will go from the roads but it'll stay in the parks.'

Nico smiled at the joyful young voice. 'I need to shower. How about in an hour?' He gazed down at Hannah and slid the duvet away from her beautiful breasts. His hand slid down to cup her and Hannah slipped her own hand beneath the covers and, judging from her, 'Mmm,' was happy to find morning glory in full bloom. He hadn't thrilled to the sexy, life-affirming experience of waking to a hot, naked woman in his bed since the early days with Loren. Making love to Hannah had been amazing.

In his ear, Josie's voice became muffled before returning full strength. 'Farmor says half an hour should be ample. We're hungry.'

He smothered a sigh but was too caring a dad to insist on an hour because he wanted sex again. 'OK. See you downstairs.' He ended the call and dropped his phone in favour of scooping Hannah's soft, curvy body against his own. 'Bloody kids.'

Hannah laughed, then her own phone began to shrill. Groaning, she rolled out from beneath the warmth of the quilt, casting around until she tracked the sound to the bag she'd abandoned by the door last night. Unselfconscious about her nudity – which suited him *perfectly* – she skipped back to the warmth of the bed. 'Hi, Josie,' she said into the handset, grinning at Nico.

Josie's strident little voice reached Nico without needing to be put on speaker. 'Oh, good, you're not asleep. We're meeting in half an hour for breakfast, OK? And have you seen how much it's snowed? Farmor says Daddy'll have to carry Maria or a snow plough will cover her up.'

Hannah managed an authentic-sounding yawn. 'OK, see you soon.' She managed to end the call before bursting into laughter. 'I feel as guilty as a teenager up to no good,' she murmured, kissing his neck.

He eased her closer, knocked out by the combination of soft skin and firm flesh. 'One of the perils of being a

297

parent is finding ways to have sex without scarring your offspring for life.'

She rolled her eyes. 'This parental responsibility thing is tougher than I thought.' She sobered. 'I understand that you don't shove your sex life in your kids' faces. I'll go back to my room to shower.'

'Shame,' he sighed. But she was right. He was getting so much enjoyment out of watching her hunt naked for her clothes that they'd never get downstairs on time if he got her soapy body in his hands.

Breakfast was leisurely, though Maria was outraged to discover the hotel had no 'Beetabix', as she called it. He diverted a tantrum by telling her she could have sponge cake instead. Her scream-face miraculously transformed into contentment and she munched cake between slugs of apple juice, pointing out of the window and saying, 'Snow!'

'It is.' Nico hadn't anticipated how hyper-aware of Hannah he'd feel and had trouble concentrating on even that level of conversation. It was obviously not appropriate to advertise to the assembled company how he and Hannah had spent the night and, judging by the way she focused on her breakfast, she was all too aware.

'Do we have a plan for today, before we go home?' Carina asked, stirring cream into her porridge.

Hannah reminded her, 'I need to go off and track down my ex. He doesn't know I'm in Stockholm so I hope to surprise him. I've been thinking and, although I don't altogether want to, I should see what my old shop's been turned into before heading for Albin's office. I doubt I'll get past the front desk but at least I can go public and loud there. People employed by the financial industry aren't meant to be financially iffy.'

And he probably wouldn't want details of his sex life

298

bandying about either, Nico thought, even as he recoiled from the scenario Hannah described. 'Why don't I go with you?'

'Because it's not your problem,' she said reasonably, turning her beautiful eyes on him, more green than blue in the winter light streaming through the windows. 'You don't want the kids around. Imagine if some security guy ejects me.' She smiled, but with a steely glitter that told him she considered herself capable of dealing with this.

Her solicitude for the kids ignited an unexpected flame of happiness inside him but he searched for a way to prevent her from bearding Albin alone.

Unexpectedly, Carina came to his rescue. 'It's always better to have a witness to a dispute. I love to visit Gamla Stan so let's go there together. Then Nico can go with you and I'll take the children to my favourite tea shop.'

After a moment's deliberation, Hannah nodded. 'Good point about a witness. Thank you.'

They checked out after breakfast, stowing their bags once more in the luggage room, then crunched along gritted, slushy pavements to the nearby open area of Rosenbadsparken where the tree trunks were painted green with lichen. The kids wanted to run – or, in the case of Maria, stagger – over the fresh white snow until their tracks criss-crossed a hundred times. Nico helped them make a giant snowball but it was difficult to encourage Maria to keep her gloves on and when she began to cry at her reddened hands Hannah picked her up and wrapped her own scarf around the frozen digits. For reasons best known to a two-year-old, this proved more acceptable than gloves and she remained on Hannah's hip shouting, 'Yo-zee, My-dad, Far-mor . . . snow!' and going off into a musical 'har har har har *har*' when Josie slipped and landed on her face.

Eventually, Nico called a halt. 'Time to go to Gamla Stan.' He took Maria on his shoulders for the ten-minute walk, a mode of transport they both favoured over the buggy, which he'd left in Nässjö in any case.

They ambled across Vasabron gazing at the rushing water and the boats, the network of bridges connecting various parts of the city filled with cars or trains. Under the arches of the soaring parliamentary buildings Maria demanded to be returned to ground level to inspect the concrete lions placed in the streets as barriers to a repeat of the Stockholm truck attack. 'RAAAAAH!' she roared in her tiny voice, curling her fingers into claws as the lion gazed peaceably out from under his snow blanket. Nico was glad the innocence of children associated the lions with play, rather than the mowing down of innocent people who'd done nothing worse than be in the wrong place at the wrong time.

They turned uphill, passing shops and restaurants with blackboards offering hot chocolate, skirting the Nobel Museum, the old Stock Exchange, to browse the colourful Christmas market of Stortorget nestled between the buildings painted sage green, amber, blood red, pink or shades of honey, grey cobbles gleaming wet through trodden snow. The pretty red wooden stalls selling toys, ornaments, gifts and scarves were webbed with tinsel and coloured lights, the air heavy with the toffee-smell of street food.

Hannah was silent, though Josie's chatter and Maria's exclamations filled the air as she gazed around, her hair tumbling between hat and scarf, her gorgeous eyes wistful and apprehensive.

'You OK?' he murmured.

'It's odd to be back,' she returned quietly. *Odd*, not *good*, he noticed. They were now yards from the shop she'd worked so hard to make a success and had such plans for, the shop that was inextricably bound up in her last relationship. He may have made love to her three times last night but, in comparison, he'd so far made it only to the fringes of her life.

He linked their gloved hands and she managed a smile but she clutched her stomach too. 'I'm dreading seeing Hannah Anna Butik erased by some tawdry club with black curtains and a sinister sign above the door,' she confessed.

He squeezed her fingers. His mum had taken the girls to look at a stall of wooden carvings painted green and red. 'You don't have to see it. We could head straight for Albin's office in Frihamnen. Or I'll pop round the corner and check it out and tell you.'

For a moment she looked tempted. Then she lifted her chin. 'That feels too much like letting Albin win. It'll be like the dentist – I'll feel better once it's over.'

Carina came back from the stall and agreed to take the children to the tea shop in Västerlånggatan, swinging Maria up into her arms. Nico dropped kisses on the girls' heads and, after much waving goodbye, watched the little party depart, Josie trying to skate on the slushy snow.

Then, gripping Hannah's hand, aware of her taking a deep breath, strode beside her out of the square and into Köpmangatan, more muted than Stortorget both in colour and noise level. As their feet carried them over the cobbles and around the corner onto less trampled snow, her stride faltered.

Nico halted.

The facade of Hannah Anna Butik didn't look to have changed.

Fairy lights edged a window display of red hats and white scarves punctuated by the dull sheen of leather

301

goods. As they watched, a woman emerged from the shop with a green paper carrier bearing the legend *Hannah Anna Butik* in gold.

Hannah dropped his hand, gasping, 'What the hell?'

'I don't know. Let's find out what's going on.' Nico had a nasty feeling Hannah wasn't going to like it.

With a convulsive movement she marched up and blew through the front door like a storm. Nico followed a few casual paces behind, thinking it might prove useful not to make it obvious to whoever Hannah was about to confront that she had back-up. He closed the door, which was still trembling from the force of her entrance. A sweeping glance told him a man and a woman were standing behind the counter gaping at Hannah. He turned a browsing shopper's stare on a stand of leather belts.

Hannah's voice, though harsh, shook. 'I didn't expect to find you two here. Or that Hannah Anna Butik is still Hannah Anna Butik.'

The man recovered first. 'Hannah,' he said in a tone so silky that Nico's skin crept. 'Why don't you come through and we'll talk?' His dark hair was smooth and his business suit well cut. His voice was educated and his English an immaculate drawl.

'Because, Albin, I prefer to hear your explanation right here.' Hannah's voice gained a splash of acid. 'Let's talk about why you stated this shop was unprofitable and that you were going to obliterate it in favour of some sleazy club. Instead, here you are . . .' her voice dropped to a velvety hiss '. . . selling stock you haven't paid for.'

Nico kept moving closer, studying a stand of scarves. They'd been folded and wound with precision but he would have paid a lot more attention to colour. Angling so he could see the man posed haughtily behind the counter, the woman pale and silent at his side, he unwound first a black scarf then a red one and left them out untidily. He might not have existed as far as Albin and Julia were concerned. They were totally focused on Hannah.

'You are by nature impatient,' Albin began condescendingly.

'Bullshit,' Hannah snapped. '*Why is the shop still open and why are you selling my stock?*'

Suddenly, Albin's attitude changed. He tilted his head and shrank like a puppy who knows he's done wrong but also knows he's cute. 'I fell on hard times—'

'BullSHIT!' Hannah howled, slapping her hands on the glass counter with a force that shook a display of purses. 'All you ever fell in was a pile of money! What is going on?'

Albin dropped the act, tilting his nose up in a way that looked much more his natural style. 'To acknowledge that we meant something to each other once I'll tell you this much. The club was a fabrication designed to encourage you to leave and I never thought it would work so well. I suppose it wouldn't have if you hadn't been needed back in the UK but, believe me, Hannah, I was always going to get you out. You built your business on what I provided.' He gave an elaborate shrug.

'And . . . and your sex life?' Hannah stammered. 'Was all that sex-with-strangers stuff fabricated to make me want to get away from you?'

Nico winced at the shock and distress in her voice. Albin gave another shrug but amusement flickered over his face.

'You've been playing a game with me over the money you owe me, too, haven't you?' Hannah breathed, as if everything was so obvious to her now that she was cursing herself for a fool. Nico could imagine the hurt on her face. She seemed physically to be caving in, head and shoulders drooping. 'I see your point about building my business while I lived with you,' she muttered in a tiny voice, though it was a damned sight more than Nico saw. He messed up more scarves in irritation. Hannah went on, her voice filled with uncertainty. 'But why are you running the shop? Why not just sell the lease?'

Albin scoffed, the way people did when they were stating the obvious and waiting for the other party to catch on. 'Erm . . . Julia *wanted* the shop? It's a profitable business. I . . . call in on my lunch hour sometimes. We were about to put up the closed sign for half an hour when you arrived.' He smirked meaningfully and Julia smiled up at him like a spaniel: pretty, glossy and adoring. They couldn't have said, 'We're having an affair and Albin comes here for lunchtime quickies' more clearly if they'd posted a notice in the window.

Hannah's head turned towards Julia. Julia's smile fell away as if whatever she saw in Hannah's expression killed her amusement stone dead. 'I see.' Contempt filtered into Hannah's voice. 'Julia's taken my place. Don't give up your own apartment, Julia, because it leaves you with nothing when he turns on you. Read your future in my past.'

When Julia looked up at Albin this time her expression was less certain.

Hannah turned back to her ex. 'You're still working as a fund manager, Albin?' she asked slowly, as if yet to make sense of everything.

Nico saw Albin roll his eyes. 'Obviously.' He seemed to feel no remorse for the manner in which he'd switched from one of the women before him to the other. He might even be pleased that he'd come out of it so well.

Hannah took a step away from the counter. 'You're not going to pay me out until you're good and ready, are you? Even if it's unfair and I need the money? Even though it's what you agreed?'

'I'll probably get round to it,' Albin said carelessly.

Hannah finally turned away and Nico saw her eyes were diamond hard. She joined him at the scarf stand saying to him sweetly, 'So it will have to be your lawyer friend.'

It didn't take a genius to play along. 'Sure, we'll go to his office now.' Nico essayed a sharky smile. 'A trader in such a sensitive area as stocks, bonds and securities is excruciatingly vulnerable to legal action. My friend loves the opportunity to bring down arseholes who think themselves above the law and he owes me a favour.' He didn't look Albin's way, pleased by the make-believe scenario he was spinning as fast as he could talk. It was more fun than creating bedtime tales of unicorns and princesses for Josie.

Julia gave a horrified gasp at the same time as Hannah said, 'You're brilliant.'

'Not as brilliant as him.' Nico was enjoying the frozen, incredulous silence from Albin. 'He's savage. Made his name trashing the reputation of others.' He held out his hand and Hannah took it as they turned for the door.

Albin unfroze. 'Who is this? Who are you?' he demanded furiously. 'What are you talking about?'

Nico turned back and gazed at him. 'I think you heard.'

He opened the shop door unhurriedly, stepping back to allow Hannah through first. 'Hungry yet?' he asked, as if they'd already forgotten about Albin and his manipulative, unpleasant games.

Hannah answered, 'Maybe,' just as Albin yelled, 'Wait!'

305

They paused and looked back.

Ugly anger rang in his voice. 'You fucking piece of shit,' he seethed at Hannah. 'Have your fucking money and get out of my life.' He worked at his phone screen with bad-tempered swipes. 'Done!' he snapped.

Hannah turned away, smiling into the wintry air as she fibbed happily. 'We're around a while so visiting Nico's friend in a few days will be no hardship if the international transfer doesn't come through. Merry Christmas.'

Albin called a word after her that made Nico drop Hannah's hand and spin around but she snatched at his arm. 'Don't. That's what he wants. It's his last roll of the dice to see if he can get you on an assault charge. Leaving him to stew impotently on loser status is much the sweetest revenge.'

Nico could do no more than seethe silently as he let Hannah draw him up the street.

It wasn't until they got around the corner that she let herself pause, white in comparison with the colourful buildings of Stortorget. 'Phew. That was horrible. He's an ugly customer when he doesn't get his own way.'

Nico enveloped her in his arms, aware of her curves through the down-filled layers of their coats. 'He's a shit.'

'I don't care so much about that.' She laid her head on his shoulder. 'But my beautiful shop! It's been taken from me and forever tainted.' Then she added fiercely, 'Whatever life holds for me next, it will be something that's completely under my control.'

They joined the others in the tea shop, though the encounter with Albin had left Nico with a bad taste rather than an appetite. Then it was time to retrieve their bags and take the train home. The girls both slept on the journey. As the snow-coated scenery flashed past the window, Nico linked fingers with Hannah beneath the table. He thought he'd been discreet until Carina hugged him in the station car park before getting into her own car, whispering, 'She's a good girl. I hope she makes you happy.'

Nico hugged her back and murmured, 'So far, so good.' Then he took a refreshed Josie to visit his dad in hospital as Hannah professed herself happy to be dropped off to put Maria to bed.

Lars was beginning to look more of a normal colour now. He beamed, hair sticking out untidily. 'Out of hospital tomorrow. Then I'll have to behave myself, under your mother's nose again.'

Nico laughed. 'One of these days, Dad, you'll have to explain your relationship to me.'

Lars beamed harder. 'When I understand it myself.'

Eventually, Nico drove Josie home and she got into her unicorn onesie to cuddle up on the sofa between him and Hannah and play a game on her iPad. He was far too early to tell Josie about the change between him and Hannah but he watched the warmth of their interaction with pleasure. 'Come on,' he murmured when Josie's eyelids began to close, sliding her slight body into his arms. 'I'll carry you to bed.'

Josie giggled. 'I'm not a baby!' But she snuggled into him as if she were Maria. 'Stockholm was awesome,' she told him sleepily as he kissed her goodnight.

'It really was,' he agreed.

Later, he carried Hannah to bed, too.

The rest of the Swedish trip passed in a blur.

Nico turned up at the hospital to fetch Lars and was surprised to find Mattias already there. '*Hej*,' he said. 'I thought I was moving Dad into Mum's spare room.'

Mattias shrugged a shoulder. 'I got a couple of hours off work.'

Nico had little to do but watch medical staff swishing around and listen to the noises of the ward while Mattias packed Lars's things. Then Lars drew the curtains around his bed to dress. 'Dad staying with Mum,' Nico tried, rather than stand in silence. 'Makes you wonder what the divorce was about.'

Mattias suddenly swung on him, eyes blazing, voice a hoarse whisper. 'It was about your ice hockey career, which came to nothing anyway! Dad got the offer and you, golden balls, had to go off with him to the UK.'

Nico was hurt but it was definitely time he had things out with his little brother. 'You think he wouldn't have accepted the UK job if I'd stayed here with you? I might as well accuse you of keeping Mum from me because you were so ridiculously good at school she wouldn't move you.'

Mattias reared back in shock. 'Everything goes right for you,' he snapped, but with less conviction.

Nico laughed harshly, just about holding on to his temper. 'Like not making it in ice hockey because I didn't have a strong enough stomach? Like my wife cheating on me and getting pregnant so my marriage ended and I became a single parent? Like Loren using Maria as a weapon to jerk my chain?'

Mattias hissed furiously, 'A weapon? You already had a beautiful daughter and then you got a spare child arrive on your doorstep! And now you're having an extended holiday in the country.'

A slow, deep breath. Nico murmured, 'I'm attached to Maria now but I was pissed off to start with. She's a tiny kid with big issues and it was made hard for me to refuse her a home. As it happens, downshifting has been good but it was a surrender to the shit life threw at me, not a chance to take a long holiday. I was frantic. I had to give up a good job and moving to the country made it financially possible.'

Voices rose and fell around the ward, curious glances telling Nico that the furiously muttered argument wasn't going unnoticed. Beneath the curtain he saw Lars place his shoes on the floor and step into them. Mattias frowned. 'You've moved? It's not a holiday? But when Loren's better won't it be tricky with her living in Islington and you in Cambridgeshire?'

The clatter of a trolley and a nurse saying something bracing to a patient receded in Nico's ears. Sweat popped on his brow. 'Shit,' he muttered. 'How has this not occurred to me?' Had he made a terrible mistake uprooting Josie? Term ended tomorrow and he hadn't heard that she had a place at Middledip Primary. What if she had to go to school in Bettsbrough and be the odd one out again? People were always praising him for his parenting but at that moment he felt as if he shouldn't be in charge of a garden gnome. 'Shit,' he repeated bleakly.

Awkwardly, hesitantly, Mattias patted his shoulder. 'I didn't mean to bring up something bad. Felicia and I are upset at the moment.' He swallowed before adding, 'We can't have children. We've just found out we're sort of allergic to each other. I suppose I thought Maria had gone your way, as everything does. I'm sorry,' he added belatedly, his voice as bleak as Nico's.

Nico stared at Mattias, his mind refusing to supply the comforting words that he wanted to offer. So he put his arms around the brother he sometimes hardly knew and gave him a long, long hug.

'Don't tell Mum and Dad,' Mattias choked against Nico's shoulder.

It was a phrase siblings said to each other all the time but it was so long since Nico had heard it that he had to swallow a lump in his throat. 'No, I won't. It's up to you and Felicia how and when you tell people. I'm incredibly sorry.'

Then Lars began to draw the curtain back and they broke apart. Mattias said, 'You might as well take Dad. I'll go back to work.' He stuck out his hand to Nico. 'Have a good trip home tomorrow.' It made Nico hope that they'd reached a better understanding.

While Lars rested after lunch the girls baked with Carina, Maria spending a lot of time squidging one piece of dough but Josie lapping up all the stirring and rolling. Nico watched, heart aching. The sisters were getting closer and closer. He'd been so wrapped up in solving the immediate problem he hadn't thought of the long game. He couldn't believe he'd been so stupid.

He mooched out of the kitchen and collapsed on the sofa in the next room, mind whirling.

Hannah followed him out. 'Are you ill?' she whispered, her face creased with concern.

He shook his head, holding out his arms. 'Just realised that when Loren gets well, the girls won't be living a ten-minute walk away from each other. They're going to be wrenched apart.'

'Oh.' Her arms tightened around him. 'I hadn't thought of it.'

Josie burst in wearing an apron that wrapped right around her like a dress. 'When we go to the rink, Farmor's going to stay with Farfar and cook pork with mushrooms for dinner. It's our Swedish Christmas tonight, isn't it?'

310

'You're right,' said Nico, summoning a smile that Josie was taking no notice that he was hugging Hannah. Each night they'd spent together they'd been careful to be back in their own beds well before the children woke up because there were certain scenarios you eased kids into carefully. Josie might not ask after Loren very often but was bound to be unsettled by the realisation that Nico had found somebody new. 'After Farmor's special dinner we're going to exchange our Swedish family gifts. We'll go soon so Farfar can rest. Your saffron buns will have baked ready for when he wakes.'

They had fun at the rink, of course they did, though Nico's heart felt like a rock in his chest as he watched the girls together. Maria wore double-blade trainers over her snow boots because she was too small for proper skates. Josie had had enough practice to stay upright and cross over at corners but Nico resolved to enrol her for a course of lessons at home so she could have more fun on these winter holidays in Sweden. Hannah skated well, after learning as a teen and then living in Sweden. She took Maria, holding on to a push-along reindeer, while he taught Josie to pick up speed and confidence. Then it was time to go to Carina's, his heart still heavy as he fetched his gaily wrapped family gifts from the case for Josie and Maria to give out – though they were much more interested in ripping the shiny wrapping paper from the pretty clothes and dolls their grandparents gifted to them with scant respect for the lovely ribbons that had no doubt been tied with care. Carina had found time to buy for Maria and Nico felt a stab of love for the mother who wasn't differentiating between the two children.

At least he received an email from Middledip Primary School offering Josie a place when school reopened in

311

January and directing him to where he could buy school polo shirts, sweatshirts and a PE top. Josie just grinned when he told her and he supposed that she hadn't thought there would be any other result.

Carina took him aside before they left for their temporary home in Lars's house. 'Maria's a lovely little girl,' she said, patting his arm through his thick fleece top.

He gave her a hug. 'I told you I wouldn't bring an imp into your house. Thanks for treating her so well. I know you were worried about me bringing her.'

Carina smiled painfully. 'Not for my sake, Nico. For yours. I could see you making a place for her in your heart as well as in your family. I grieve for your heartache when she goes back.'

A lump rose to his throat. 'I know. I worry about how Josie's going to take it too. But how could we guard our hearts against her?'

Carina laughed. 'Impossible. She's adorable.'

Nico got one more night sleeping with Hannah before they rose early and drove back to the airport. They returned the rental car and moved on to the airport building, where festive decorations were decidedly low-key. Josie and Maria began a game with the toys they had in their backpacks.

Nico was turning his mind back to mundane matters like the Christmas presents he'd ordered ready to pick up from Argos on Monday and the Tesco groceries that should arrive first thing tomorrow, the nineteenth, and thinking unenthusiastically of Christmas lunch. Cooking a roast dinner was a trial for him. Thank goodness for ready-made Yorkshire puddings. A pleasant thought struck him and he turned to look at Hannah. Her hair was pulled up on top of her head and he wanted to nuzzle the downy hairs in the nape of her neck. 'What are you and Nan doing for Christmas lunch? Maybe we can join forces?'

She gave him a dazzling smile. 'All being together would be great . . . unless Nan has plans with Brett, of course.'

Then her phone rang and she regarded the screen with one eyebrow up in her hairline. 'Christopher Carlysle?' She couldn't have sounded more astonished if Santa himself had rung.

'I won't beat about the bush,' Nico heard the clipped voice say because Hannah leaned in so he could listen. 'I'm ringing to ask you to oversee the Christmas Opening. I'm afraid my son's vanished again. Tenants are up in arms and Cassie's hardly speaking to me. Says I was bloody awful to you and you should tell me to get knotted. But I'm hoping you won't,' he added humbly.

Hannah closed her eyes. 'You were incredibly rude.'

'I was.'

'You were a bulldozer.'

'Under pressure,' Christopher acknowledged unhappily. 'I admit it and apologise, Miss Goodbody, but the traders are crying out for you and I'll make it worth your while.'

'Actual money?'

'How about three hundred pounds for the day?' he suggested.

Hannah frowned, following Josie and Maria's game with her eyes though her thoughts were obviously else-where. Then she sighed. 'For the sake of the traders who have sunk so much into Carlysle Courtyard,' she agreed at length. 'But I'm flying home from Sweden today so I can't be there any earlier than seven-thirty tomorrow.' For the next ten minutes she talked and Christopher thanked. She came off the phone half-smiling and half-aggravated.

'Men!' she joked. 'Always ready to take advantage.'

313

He took her words semi-seriously. 'Like me? Accepting your help on this trip?'

She put her phone away and twinkled naughtily. 'I got a lot out of it. A trip to Sweden and Albin sorted. And . . . some lovely, *lovely* other things.'

Nico didn't let her joke it away. He checked the girls were still busy with little fat dolls and ran his fingertips over her neck. 'This time with you has made me happier than I've been for years.' They hadn't talked about the future but it suddenly felt very important that she know that.

Pleasure blooming in her fine eyes, she blew him a tiny kiss. 'Same here,' she whispered.

Chapter Twenty-Three

Middledip sparkled with evening frost, Christmas trees twinkled from windows and the pub was lit up like a float in a Christmas carnival. It would have been scrumptious to follow Nico and the kids into the welcoming warmth of Honeybun Cottage but Hannah knew hers and Nico's feelings were as new and delicate as spiders' webs, so she hugged them all goodbye and towed her rolling luggage to Nan's.

Nan was still staying with Brett and the house felt empty without her. Hannah had called her on the drive from the airport and told her she'd be managing the Christmas Opening tomorrow after all. Nan had exclaimed in her creaky voice, 'Me and Brett will call in. Can't wait to see you, duck.'

'Nico and the girls plan to visit too,' Hannah had answered, hoping her happiness didn't filter into her voice and prompt Nan to ask searching questions. She was still getting used to the way he made her heart beat and didn't want even one sceptical word to disturb the precious beginning of something she felt would be deeper and more grounded than anything she'd ever felt for Albin.

A small heap of unopened Christmas cards lay on Nan's doormat along with a key to the Carlysle Courtyard office. The note inside the envelope read, *You're a lifesaver. Think Christopher and I would have divorced if we'd had to run the opening. Cassie x*

More than half wishing she hadn't agreed to undertake the mammoth day's work Hannah set her alarm for six-thirty and plummeted into bed, glittering dreams of the promised Christmas with Nico swimming through her mind.

In the morning, with no opportunity to get hold of a proper Christmas costume, she pulled on thermal under-wear then thick black leggings and a green overshirt cinched in with a yellow belt, hoping it was the kind of outfit Santa's helpers might wear. She stapled a ball of silver tinsel to the point of a bright red woolly hat and it stood upright and looked quite elfish once she'd stuffed it with her hair. With fingerless mittens and knee-high black boots she hoped she'd be able to put up with the cold.

In her mum's little car she bowled beneath the lights hanging gaily between the trees lining Main Road and took the lane to Fen Drove, headlights picking out the icy skeletons of hedges, mind fixed on the day ahead. 'It is what it is,' she philosophised aloud. 'Even Christopher Carlysle can't expect Christmas Opening perfection. I'll settle for avoiding chaos.'

She arrived at Carlysle Courtyard to see every shop brightly lit. Mark from the model shop emerged dressed as a beaming Santa, lengths of tinsel floating from his hands. 'You're a sight for sore eyes,' he cried. 'That idiot

Simeon's locked the gazebo in the office. How are we supposed to get it up and decorated?'

'I have the key.' Hannah brandished it, buoyed by a fizz of excitement at temporarily returning to the Courtyard team.

Gina hurried out of Paraphernalia, her denim-clad legs and sweater-covered arms emerging from a Christmas pudding outfit. 'Hannah – hoorah, you've come to save us!' just as Perla and Teo trotted out of Posh Nosh in reindeer costumes and painted-on red noses.

From that instant, Hannah felt completely steeped in Christmas. Mark and Teo helped erect the gazebo. It wanted to lurch like a drunk on the uneven pavers but Mark, talented at assembly, made it submit. Soon it shone with red, blue and green lights. A small pick-up arrived with the balloon arch for the entrance and Hannah pulled off her coat and sprinted up the drive in her elf costume to supervise its placement.

Cars began to arrive, including Christopher Carlysle's. 'Oh, good,' Hannah panted when she saw his bulky figure, her hands busily twisting tinsel around the gazebo uprights. 'Can you do the car park marshalling? There are no lines on gravel. If you see Santa, send him straight to the grotto. He's late.'

Christopher put on a high-vis vest and meekly went to do as bid. Hannah blew on her chilly fingers and surveyed the courtyard. Every illuminated shop window glowed and twinkled, tinsel glimmered and a rainbow of baubles reflected the magical scene. She snapped her fingers. 'Presents for the grotto!' They were in the office, wrapped already and piled in a hessian sack with rope handles – Simeon had at least followed her plans and kept everything bubbling.

Now all they needed was Santa. He arrived five minutes late, red coat flying, puffing apologies. 'Had to go back for my beard!' The people milling in the courtyard waiting for the shops to open clapped and Santa – real name Ivan – began ho-ho-hoing as beaming kids lined up, craning to admire his corpulent red figure and luxuriant white beard.

Then it was ten o'clock and the shop doors were thrown open with gleeful shouts of, 'Merry Christmas! Welcome to—' And each trader tried to shout the name of their shop louder than the others.

Nan and Brett were among the early birds, Brett wearing a Cossack hat over his thin hair, Nan's eyes watering behind her glasses. She gave Hannah a huge hug. 'Isn't it lovely? There must be a thousand lights blazing. Have you had a wonderful time in Sweden? Was it even more wintry than here?'

'Awesome,' Hannah replied honestly, hugging her grandmother's tiny figure. She felt as small and slight as Josie. 'Have you had a lovely time with Brett?'

'He's looked after me beautifully,' Nan declared. Brett smiled bashfully. He was a quiet man. Unless directly addressed, his conversation usually amounted to 'Hello, there!' and, later, 'Cheerio!' Nan's voice dropped to a whisper. 'I'll be glad to get back home though. We've decided we're too set in our ways for marriage. I think I'm Brett's girlfriend.'

Hannah couldn't resist whispering back, 'And I think I'm Nico's girlfriend.'

'Oh, Hannah! He's such a nice boy.' Nan gave her another squeeze. 'I'm too tired for shopping so we'll just tootle off to Posh Nosh for stollen and mince pies.'

'I won't mind if you want to go straight home,' Hannah said, concerned.

But Nan smiled. 'No, I'll hang around. Maybe something exciting will happen.'

'Mark's doing a demo of making a model sleigh at eleven if that's what you mean,' Hannah joked. 'If Nico arrives, Nan, no teasing him about me, OK? We haven't talked about when or if to tell the girls.' Flushing that she sounded vaguely proprietorial about 'the girls' she pulled her phone from her shirt pocket as Nan and Brett headed for the warmth and delicious smells emanating from the tea room. She'd known Nico and co wouldn't arrive early because of his scheduled supermarket delivery but it was nearly eleven. She tried calling but was directed straight to voicemail so she texted instead. *You all OK? Christmas Opening going well. xxx*

Then it was time to transform herself into a human PA system, cruising the courtyard calling, 'Mark's fantastic model making demo is about to begin under the gazebo! Free demo!' and an expectant crowd began to gather.

Half an hour later, when the demo was over, Nan appeared again, wearing mince pie crumbs on the front of her coat.

Hannah paused in handing out lollipops to children. 'Are you going?'

Nan craned to look over Hannah's shoulder. 'Not yet.' Then she waved energetically, grinning. Brett, who'd followed Nan, waved and grinned too.

Hannah swung around in time to see The Bus turning into the car park, its pea-soup colours cheered by tinsel streaming from the door handles and her parents' faces beaming through the windscreen. 'Mum! Dad!' she shouted in astonished delight.

The Bus paused for Mo to manoeuvre her body through

the passenger door, pulling on a purple coat. 'Hannah, darling! Are we a nice surprise?'

Jeremy drove on because Christopher was gesticulating violently that he was holding the traffic up and Mo and Hannah raced towards one another.

Hannah's heart soared as her small, round mother cannoned into her arms. 'I thought you were spending Christmas in Switzerland!' Mo smelled of buttered toast and her hug felt like love.

'We missed you all too much. Christmas isn't Christmas without your loved ones, is it? Nan's known we were coming for the past few days but we thought we'd surprise you.' Mo extricated herself to hug Nan and Brett, too.

The Bus safely parked, Jeremy hurried up for another round of cuddles and the family ignored the jostling of the shoppers around them as they caught up on all the news.

Teo's plaintive voice broke in. He looked decidedly chilly in his chef whites. 'Hannah, are we going to get my demonstration going?'

'Sorry!' she called back hastily. She beamed around her family. 'This morning's crazy.'

'We're ready to see Middledip again so we won't linger,' Mo declared, hugging her again. 'You're in your element amongst all these pretty shops, aren't you? I'm proud of you, Hannah.'

The afternoon whizzed by in a flood of people flowing in and out of festively twinkling shops as if they had only this one day to accomplish all their Christmas shopping. Christopher Carlysle sought Hannah out. 'Bloody amazing,' he boomed. 'Can't thank you enough. The traders should finally be happy we've kept to our agreements.'

It was as if he'd never been rude or unfair. Hannah

smiled sweetly, her mind more on the continued non-appearance of Nico and family than Christopher finally dismounting his high horse. She heard her name called for the hundredth time that day and hoped six p.m. would hurry up so she could call at Honeybun Cottage and check everything was OK.

Nico's day began badly.

The girls had jumped in the bath together and he'd been sorting out clean towels when he'd heard Josie give a horrified squawk. 'That's my dad's phone!'

Nico whipped around but was too late to stop Maria scrubbing his phone industriously with a yellow, duck-shaped sponge.

'I jus' washing it!' Maria protested indignantly, hiding the phone . . . underwater.

Nico swallowed back the swear word on his lips. He'd left the phone on top of the cistern while he'd daydreamed about how much he missed Hannah after spending this last week with her and wondering when to reveal their altered status to Josie. 'We don't wash phones, sweetheart. It breaks them,' he told Maria ruefully, retrieving his property and regarding the unresponsive screen. He knew the trick to drying out phones by sticking them in a packet of dry rice but he had to wait until the girls were dressed and the Tesco delivery – without rice – had arrived before they could buy some at the village shop, Josie in one of her talk-a-mile-a-minute moods and Maria yanking on her walking rein like a disobedient puppy. By the time they reached home again it was lunchtime. He sealed the phone in the rice without a great deal of hope it would fix it then made scrambled eggs, trying to be calm and cheerful as parents are meant to be.

Without a working phone he couldn't check how Lars was doing. Neither could he contact Hannah to say he'd decided to give the girls lunch at home rather than undergo Posh Nosh with the girls clamouring for sugary treats that would make them hyper, a stress he didn't need even if accompanied by piped Christmas carols.

He'd just finished washing up when a crescendo of bumps followed by howls sent him racing into the hall to find Maria at the foot of the stairs, nose pouring scarlet blood. Heart banging, he swooped her up and she clung to him. 'Oh, baby girl, your poor little nose,' he crooned, hurrying to soak kitchen towel in cold water to staunch the bleeding. At ice hockey they'd always pressed the cold towel to the bridge but Maria's was such a button nose that he could only aim for the whole thing.

'Nooooooo, noooooooo,' she wailed, snatching her head from side to side and smearing his cream sweatshirt with blood. It took a long time for her to calm down while he soothed her against his shoulder, Josie saying, 'Aw, poor Maria,' and stroking her sister's leg. He was wondering whether he should try and rock the toddler into a catnap, a well-known antidote to a biffed nose, when Josie gave a strangled gasp.

'Uh, uh—' Then, in a shriek, 'MUMMEE!'

Stomach dropping, Nico swung around still wearing Maria around his neck.

Josie had run to the window and was waving, dancing, beaming and laughing.

And through the glass he saw Vivvi and Loren coming up the short drive, clutching their coats close around them, Vivvi's car parked in the lane across the gateway as if to prevent him escaping.

322

'Well, well,' he said aloud. *Oh, shit,* he thought. 'This is a nice surprise, Josie, isn't it?' *Why the hell isn't Loren in rehab as she's supposed to be?* 'Let Mum and Grandma in.' *Because I see no alternative.*

Loren stepped into his cosy, flagged kitchen bringing in the chill of the outside world. Vivvi followed, shutting the door without turning the handle so it banged like a prison door.

Josie jigged before them, words flying from her mouth. 'Mum, I didn't know you were coming! We've just come back from Sweden. We baked with Farmor and Farfar was in hospital and Dad ice skated and we went to Skansen and there was snow!'

Maria clung silently to Nico, gazing at the new arrivals, occasional hiccupping with the remains of her tear storm.

Loren gazed at Nico. She was pinched, her eyes haunted, but her hair was clean and she wore make-up. So far as Nico could tell from where he stood, she didn't smell of alcohol. 'Hi,' she said.

'Hi.' He looked past her. 'Hello, Vivvi. Josie, how about you step back and give Mum space, sweetheart. Then she'll have a chance to say hello to you.'

Thus prompted, Loren turned her smile on Josie. 'Hello, darling! Wow, I think you've grown. You're so pretty.' She swept Josie into a hug, curling around her with her cheek on the top of Josie's head, making fond, 'Mmm, mmm, mmm,' noises.

Vivvi hugged Josie in turn. 'Mum's right – you've grown.'

When Loren said, 'Maria! Darling!' and held out her arms, Maria buried her face in Nico's neck. 'Noooooo.'

Loren's face went slack with shock.

Nico soothed Maria's back. 'She's banged her nose and

she's shaken up. Give her a minute.' He slid an arm around Josie's shoulders. 'Shall we get drinks for Mum and Grandma? You could put biscuits out.'

'Yeah!' Josie hopped and skipped to the cupboard and took down a big plate.

Nico attempted to put Maria down but she scrunched her arms and legs around him. 'Noooooo!'

So, employing the one-handed skills of a practised parent, he filled the kettle and took down coffee and mugs, beakers and juice.

'One sugar for me, please,' said Vivvi brightly, not lifting a finger.

He halted. 'Ah. Sorry. I don't have any.' He wasn't sure why he was apologising. He didn't take sugar and his guests had arrived unannounced.

Vivvi smiled. 'Never mind. I have sweeteners in my bag.' She wandered into the sitting room uninvited and Loren followed while he poured juice for Josie and juice with water for Maria.

He couldn't slosh boiling water about with Maria hanging on him like a misplaced backpack so he sat her on a chair. 'Just while I do the hot water, OK?' She nodded but put her arms out to him again the second he completed the task, just as Loren and Vivvi reappeared.

'Bijou house,' Loren commented.

'Yep.' He added milk to their coffee and set it on the table, gesturing to his guests to sit on the 'glass' chairs, some slobber-marked because Maria enjoyed squashing her face against them to peer through. He took Maria on his knee. Josie chose the seat next to his. She'd quietened now, drinking her juice and sending Nico questioning glances. He smiled reassuringly and patted her shoulder.

'Redfern's cheering up,' Vivvi volunteered, as if Nico had asked after the health of his ex-father-in-law.

'It's good you feel comfortable to leave him,' Nico commented.

'Only because he's gone to his brother's house for the day.' Vivvi answered so hastily she almost ran the entire sentence into one word.

Nico nodded.

Loren added her mite about how worried they'd been after her dad's heart operation then Josie interrupted. 'I'm starting a new school after Christmas. The sweatshirt's burgundy.'

'What was wrong with the old school?' Loren asked in the tone she might have used if Josie had spent her pocket money on a new pen when she already had twenty in her pencil case.

Josie frowned, glancing at Nico uncertainly. He said gently, 'It's OK to tell Mum how you feel.'

The explanation Josie poured out about Mrs Calcashaw, the 'wrong' class and playground politics was rushed but no less than heartfelt.

Nico slid his arm around her but looked at Loren. 'You'll remember we discussed this. Part of the reason I moved to Middledip was its small and friendly village school. I've sent you updates on visiting the school and that Josie liked it. I also forwarded the email offering Josie a place.' Nico knew she'd only had access to her phone at certain times in rehab – but she wasn't in rehab. She was here, after only twelve days of the projected twenty-eight.

'Of course.' Loren smiled vaguely.

Josie's smiles had completely vanished and her voice might even have held a note of challenge when she said,

'We're going to have Christmas here with Hannah and Nan Heather. Dad's ordered lots of nice food from Tesco.'

'Who are Hannah and Nan Heather?' Vivvi asked. 'New friends?'

Josie nodded emphatically. 'Nan Heather's very, very old. Dad knew her when he was young here with his friend Rob. And Farfar used to work near here, didn't he, Dad?'

He smiled at her. 'That's right.' He had a bad feeling. It wasn't that Hannah's name had come up – he and Loren were divorced and the evidence as to why was currently sitting on his lap and slurping juice. But Loren's unscheduled visit must have an agenda and it was tricky dealing with someone who had a different view of reality to yourself, especially when they were in stealth mode.

'Hannah's Rob's sister, and me and Maria like her a lot,' Josie added. Then, picking perhaps not the best moment for a candid question, she peeped at him. 'Is Hannah your girlfriend now, Dad? I saw you cuddling at Farmor's house.'

'Yes,' he said gently. Ideally, he would have checked with Josie that his relationship was OK with her and he hadn't agreed terms of reference with Hannah either but at least the casual question indicated a willingness for Josie to absorb Hannah's presence in her life.

Both Loren and Vivvi greeted the news in silence.

Josie had never met a silence she couldn't fill. 'Hannah went to Sweden with us and she can whoosh along on ice skates, like Dad does! And we made a snowman family of us in Farfar's garden.'

Nico could have changed the slant by explaining that Hannah joined their winter trip to help with the girls after Lars was rushed into hospital with a heart attack. He didn't. Everything had changed last week and Loren was entitled to know who was playing a part in Josie's life and how better than from Josie's own lips?

It was another half hour before coffee was drunk and Maria had got over her shyness sufficiently to accept a hug from her mother. Nico wanted to get to the bottom of Loren's visit. 'I bet Grandma would love to see yours and Maria's bedroom,' he said to Josie.

Vivvi must have been in accord with his wish to speak to Loren alone because she jumped at his plan. 'That would be great!'

'Yeah!' Josie leaped to her feet. Maria, her faithful shadow, cooed, 'Yeah!' too and leaped to hers. Their voices travelled through the sitting room and faded up the stairs.

When footfall told him they had reached the room over his head, Nico propped his elbows on the table. 'You're still scheduled to be in rehab, aren't you? Or are you out for Christmas holidays, like at school?'

Loren looked away and sighed. 'When you're trying to give something up, the desire has to come from inside. Rehab's an intolerable regime. And therapy feels like punishment.' She continued irritably, explaining, excusing, making the system sound the next thing to abuse.

'So you've left? What's your next step?' he asked, his stomach shifting uneasily. Her artificiality with the girls and the surprise element left him in no doubt the visit wasn't simply the result of maternal yearnings.

She uttered a manufactured laugh. 'I'm going to sort myself out. No one knows me better than me, after all – my body and mind, my strengths and weaknesses. I know where to get support rather than having "changes" and "choices" forced down my throat.'

With a sinking feeling, Nico recognised this Loren. Unwilling or unable to give up prescription meds under rehabilitation's professional and properly resourced support she was kidding herself she felt strong enough to beat addiction, although she'd never exhibited that strength before. This was Loren not dealing with real life in exactly the same way she'd refused to accept her pregnancy with Maria until she was more than four months gone or refused to accept Nico was ending their marriage until the fifth communication from his solicitor. This was the Loren who used to use alcohol as a crutch and snapped at him for intimating it might be a problem. Only weeks ago he'd found her in drugs and alcohol-induced insensibility and she'd begged him to look after Maria . . . yet she was weaving a picture in which she felt safe and justified in her actions.

She embarked on a repetition of her intention to coach herself out of her addiction but he interrupted her. 'How?'

She stopped. 'What?'

'How? What's your plan? What will you put in place to make recovery possible?' He left the question wide open but the specific subjects he saw as top of the list were childcare and income. Upstairs, footsteps clunked across the floor and Maria giggled, apparently restored to her usual sunny self.

Loren finally met his gaze, eyes shimmering with tears. Instead of answering his question she said, 'I'm sorry I was unfaithful, Nico. It was a mistake.'

Shock tingled through him that she'd try and construct her false reality from that far back. 'A mistake? You didn't trip up and land on the guy,' he pointed out. He didn't actually say alcohol had played its part in her hook-up. Loren knew it. He knew it.

The tears welled over the rim of her eyes and trickled down her cheeks. The short December day was darkening outside the window. She lunged suddenly, taking him by surprise, clasping his arms and digging her fingers in. 'Nico,' she implored, face crumpling. 'It's your help I need. Everything in my life comes back to you.'

'What on earth do you mean?' He jerked his arms free, breath tripping in his chest. He wanted to jump up, get away from her, even if it was only to put on the light, but it was too important that he understand what was happening for him to risk interrupting her. 'Be straight-forward,' he said crisply.

Loren pulled herself upright and fixed him with huge, beseeching eyes. 'OK. I've come to ask for us to be one family. You, me, Josie and Maria. It's the obvious thing to do. Maria loves you! I'll get clean, with your support.' Her words shot out in emphatic bursts. 'You're so stable, Nico. You cope with everything. Like, like—' Her eyes flickered around the room as if the words she needed to convince him might be hiding in the cupboards. 'Like, it's too much for me to be a single mum but look how strong you are as a single dad.'

Astonishment stole Nico's voice. Dimly, he could hear yells upstairs; Vivvi was trying to persuade Maria to do something and the chirruping little voice was rising obstinately. 'Want Mydad! Want Myyyydaaad!'

'Let's make a family home,' Loren pleaded. 'We can go back to Islington and—'

'Josie's got a place at school here,' he said automatically.

'She can go back to her old school.'

'She's off the roll there and she hated it,' he snapped, furious at the way Loren was dismissing Josie's feelings.

Loren looked around herself, bewildered. 'You can't live

329

here. It's the back of beyond. There are no shops. Nothing to do.'

'We love it here. OK, there's only one shop but there's a town and a city nearby.'

She rose, getting in his space, stubbornly trying to stop his plans standing in the way of hers. 'There's nothing for Maria.'

Not enjoying being loomed over, he rose too. 'There's bound to be preschool. I haven't enquired because I believed Maria would be going to you or your mum before I went to Sweden.' His heart gave a great pang. Remembering the great time they'd had in Sweden, Maria laughing at the snow, wrinkling her nose, riding on his shoulders. He halted, newly aware of the trauma lying in wait for the girls if they were split up again. Right in front of him was an opportunity to make a proper family for both girls.

Loren gazed at him with her eyes full of fear and longing. Pity rose up as if to choke him.

The sound of arguing voices came rapidly nearer and Maria burst in, eyes like saucers. She flew across the room as if she were being hunted. 'Mydad, Mydad,' she sobbed.

'See,' whispered Loren, as if this proved everything she'd been saying.

His heart was breaking. A trap was closing. A police siren sounded in the distance, speeding off to deal with somebody's crisis. He wished you could do something as simple as calling the police when you were being put in an emotional stranglehold.

Automatically, he hugged Maria, patting her shuddering back.

Josie skipped into the room, Vivvi close behind. 'Maria

didn't want to stay upstairs with me and Grandma, Dad. She wanted you.'

Vivvi's gaze flicked from Loren to Nico speculatively.

Nico glanced between his ex-wife and ex-mother-in-law. 'Vivvi, maybe you could take the girls out?' he said wearily. 'Loren and I need to talk.'

Chapter Twenty-Four

Hannah couldn't turn into the drive of Honeybun because a car was parked across it. She pulled up behind and, catching her breath at the icy air as she jumped from the car, scampered towards the gate.

'Hannah!' shouted an excited young voice, making her swing around. 'We've been to The Angel with Grandma for cake. Why have you got tinsel on your hat?' Josie bounded towards her, hood up and cheeks pink. A middle-aged woman in a stylish coat of grey wool hurried to catch up, Maria in the buggy slapping her hands on the sides and shouting, 'Out!'

'Oof!' Hannah gasped as Josie cannoned into her midriff. 'Is everything OK? I've been working at the Christmas Opening of Carlysle Courtyard today. I thought you were coming along. Hello, Maria!' She waved, which made Maria stop slapping long enough to wave back. Hannah smiled at the woman guardedly. 'Hello.'

The woman didn't alter her pinched expression but asked Josie, 'Is this Daddy's friend Hannah?'

Josie beamed. 'Yes! Hannah, Grandma let us have cake for supper. I had two bits. Dad'll go mad.'

The woman's lips tightened at the implied criticism and Hannah decided, diplomatically, not to comment. Parent–grandparent politics weren't her field.

'Hello,' she tried again in an effort not to be dismissed. 'I'm Hannah Goodbody.'

'Vivvi Myot,' the woman replied briefly. Maria was still shouting so, tutting, Vivvi unfastened her straps and swung the little girl brusquely to the ground. 'Here you are then, miss.'

Hannah put out her arms. 'Hello, Maria! How are you?'

'Hat!' Maria demanded, trying to snatch Hannah's red woolly hat.

'Maria fell downstairs and got a nose bleed,' Josie gabbled. 'Then Mum and Grandma came and—'

'Chatterbox!' Vivvi interposed sharply. 'Please hold your sister's hand and take her indoors to Mummy and Daddy before she gets cold. I'll be there in a minute when I've folded up the buggy.'

'But—' Josie began rebelliously.

'Do as you're told.' Vivvi raised admonishing eyebrows.

'OK,' Josie sighed, leading Maria away.

Hannah started after them but then halted, suddenly conscious of the uncertainty of her role here. Loren was visiting. She was Josie and Maria's mother so no surprise . . . except she was supposed to be in rehab. That might explain Nico's odd silence today.

Vivvi collapsed the buggy with a couple of snaps. 'Just a moment.'

Neck prickling, Hannah turned back.

'Nico and Loren are *talking*,' Vivvi said in a pointed, curt way. She looked Hannah up and down as Hannah's

333

coat blew open, no doubt taking in the leggings and shirt, the tinsel she'd wrapped around her belt. Feeling foolishly like a kid playing dress-up, she yanked off her hat and let her hair fall down.

'I'm aware of Nico's liaison with you,' Vivvi went on coldly. 'It's not to be wondered at if he looked elsewhere for "entertainment"—' she said the word as if she didn't want it in her mouth '—while he and Loren went through a difficult time. But they have these two little girls. It's time for them to try again.'

Offence at words like 'liaison' and 'entertainment' was completely subsumed by a wash of horror as Hannah took in Vivvi's final words. Shame followed as she realised the horror was for herself. Nico had not given her any form of commitment. 'They've been divorced for ages,' she said through numb lips.

Vivvi bristled. 'These challenging chapters happen in adult relationships,' she said in a way that somehow implied Hannah wouldn't know. 'It's hard when Loren suffers a bout of depression but Nico never gives up on her. Taking Maria was his way of showing Loren he could accept her so they could create a stable home together. Loren's my daughter and it pains me to say this, but she needs that man and he finds being a single dad lonely – hence you, I suppose. But even you must see that those lovely kiddies need both their parents.' Vivvi sniffed. 'Sleeping with you a few times doesn't compare to years of marriage. He's a man – why wouldn't he sleep with you, if you were on offer? But if there's one thing Nico Pettersson is all about, it's facing up to his responsibilities. It was him who asked me to take the girls out while he and Loren talked. Josie and Maria are going to be so happy when they're all one little family again!'

This last was delivered with a caring sympathy Hannah didn't buy.

But that was irrelevant – or 'our elephant' as Maria had once said. Every word the woman said was shrivelling her heart with guilt and humiliation.

She tried to think, remembering Nico not answering a single text or call today. Not turning up as promised. All the times he'd blown hot and cold . . . she'd forgotten them once he'd turned his brilliant blue eyes on her in Sweden. Been blinded by his lovemaking and the easy way he'd brought her into his family. They'd laughed over Carina's matchmaking but maybe Hannah *had* been so conveniently 'on offer' that he'd taken advantage of it?

Mortification colder than the wind that blew between the cosily lit cottages swept her as she remembered his words on the aircraft. *I didn't even have to ask you to help me on this trip*. He'd followed up by saying she'd made him the happiest he'd been for years but if he'd been unhappy as a single parent, that wasn't saying much. And he'd been getting sex.

Gagged by tears, Hannah blanked whatever else Vivvi was saying and fumbled for her keys. She'd go to Nan's and leave Nico to contact her. If Vivvi was horribly and completely wrong then he'd just tell her, wouldn't he?

She had to perform an ignominious twenty-point turn in the lane under Vivvi's watchful gaze and drove shakily home – her temporary home, anyway – in a haze of pain. Nan's house was cold and empty but she was glad. Right this minute, she didn't want to see her lovely family because the sympathy she knew would pour out of them would rip out what was left of her heart. She dragged herself upstairs for a hot bath that didn't cure her shivers, her phone within reach.

The hours ticked by and it didn't ring.

She crept off to bed to lie awake, gazing into the darkness.

Hopelessly, she faced facts. Nico was a wonderful parent. He'd been upset at the idea of the girls being split up again. Making the family one unit would make sense. And if Vivvi hadn't been telling her the truth he would have called her by now.

And still the phone didn't ring.

Suddenly she was angry.

Bloody men. How many more would think it was OK to bugger things up for her? To live his own life and if she became disruptive, winkle her out of it? It filled her with impotent rage.

When the clock beside her bed said two a.m. she got up. If Nico hadn't sent so much as a text by now he wasn't going to. He could even be in bed with Loren.

Grief-stricken, she took down the presents she'd stored atop the wardrobe. Two new nighties for Nan and a book about the stately homes of England. A super-duper car care kit for her dad and a box of chocolate liqueurs. Champagne for Mo, who dearly loved it but would never consider buying it for herself. Clinique mascara and eye liner for Leesa, who appreciated brands, and a North Face sweatshirt for Rob.

Neatly, methodically, she wrapped up and labelled each gift. Then she packed them in Mo's little car along with a backpack and a medium-sized case. When she judged her parents would have finished breakfast she drove to their house and was surprised to find Nan there.

'Brett and I need a break from each other,' she confessed. 'Your mum fetched me last night because I didn't want to butt in on your evening but today I thought—' Then,

336

slowly, her wrinkles sagged as she gazed into Hannah's face. 'What's the matter?'

Hannah slumped onto the sofa that her parents bought when she was about sixteen and closed her eyes. 'I thought something was happening with Nico. But it's gone wrong.'

'Oh, Hannah! Nan whispered to me that there was something between you.' Mo dropped on the sofa beside her. 'Get her a strong brew, Jeremy.'

Slowly, between sniffs, sobs and sips, Hannah unravelled the whole story. 'So it looks as if his wife's back and we won't spend Christmas together,' she finished dolefully.

'You spend it with us,' Mo urged. 'Dad's got the tree out of the loft and we've begun decorating it. We'll bake mince pies and have a cosy village Christmas.'

Hannah was already shaking her head. 'Thanks, Mum, but it's too . . . raw.' She blew her nose, then looked at her dad. 'Can I ask a really, really big favour?'

Instantly, Jeremy proclaimed, 'Nothing's too big for you, Han.'

'Can I borrow The Bus?'

'Borrow The Bus?' he repeated faintly. Then, as if it weren't his pride and joy, 'Of course.'

'I'll treat it beautifully,' she said, too desperate to escape to have qualms about borrowing something she knew he wouldn't normally lend. 'I want to be on my own for a few days and not be . . . bothered. The girls are too important not to be given the chance of two parents. I know that. I just need time to come to terms with it.' She gulped. 'I don't want to hang around for explanations, even if he thought it was a holiday fling.' That might even be too polite a term for what he'd thought. His damned mother-in-law had certainly made her feel like a little tart. She blotted her tears with her sleeve.

Nan shook her head. 'A holiday fling? Nico's too mature to sow his seeds in a garden he didn't wish to tend.'

Hannah gasped a shocked laugh. 'Nan! Is that as rude as it sounds?'

Nan stuck out her chin. 'It's euphemistic.' She scratched beneath her cast, which was grubby at the edges now. 'Don't you think you ought to talk to him, duck? You never know—'

'I want to go away, if you can spare me,' Hannah interrupted firmly.

Mo put both her soft, comforting arms around Hannah. 'I can help Nan now. Don't worry about that. But you will come home for Christmas?'

'Maybe.' Hannah laid her cheek on her mum's shoulder. 'I've brought my gifts to leave here, in case I don't. If – if you see Nico and the girls, will you give them theirs, please?' She rushed on. 'You'll have Rob and Leesa and Nan. Everyone at The Three Fishes and The Angel you've known your whole life long. They're here for you.'

Jeremy chirped up. 'And for you, Hannah. Don't forget that. And for you.'

Hannah nodded, then arranged her Christmas gifts beneath their half-decorated tree and spent an hour driving The Bus under Jeremy's instruction. 'Such an old gal has her little ways,' he explained, as they sailed sedately up Main Road and past the cotton-wool snowman outside the school. 'I've fitted a quick shifter so she won't shake you to bits when you change gear. Go gentle with her. Fifty's top speed or you'll blow her up.'

'I'll take it steady,' she promised, wondering whether she'd blow up if the engine did and if she'd care.

In freezing rain that matched Hannah's mood they filled up with fuel and checked tyre pressures. Jeremy showed her how to transform the seat into a bed. 'And, see,' he said. 'The radio looks retro but it's repro and has iPhone connectivity and DAB.'

'Wow,' said Hannah, mechanically.

She hugged everyone goodbye, battling guilty tears at white, anxious faces, then drove carefully back to Nan's, feeling strange and high up compared to her normal driving position. The engine was at the back and clattered like a giant sewing machine. At the cottage, she flung in her bags and bedclothes and didn't bother connecting her phone to her dad's smart radio. She got in as stiffly as if her heart was pumping slush through her veins, and drove.

Anywhere that wasn't here.

Nico stayed up late in case Hannah came, thinking about her warm lips and hot mouth. Waiting, tied to the cottage by sleeping girls upstairs, he opened the Christmas box of Roses chocolates and ate about twenty. For the seconds the sugar was in his mouth he felt better.

When the comfort swung to guilt he drank black coffee to drown the taste of the chocolate and resisted the urge to purge. It was strong but he was stronger, he told himself. Everyone got urges and you had to challenge those suckers. That's what he'd told Loren this evening.

Why hadn't Hannah come to discover why he and the girls hadn't attended the Christmas Opening of Carlysle Courtyard? He was glad she hadn't walked into Loren and Vivvi's visit, though. They'd upset the girls, disturbing the happy, calm atmosphere with their false smiles and supposedly disguised conversation that Josie had kept catching on to. 'What do you mean "if things change"? What responsibilities?' With them there, it had taken all his powers of persuasion to get the girls to bed, Josie still questioning, Maria clinging.

Then Loren had grabbed his hands. 'Nico, you're my only hope.'

He'd pulled away. 'No, I'm not. I'm the fucking easy answer.'

Vivvi had lost her temper. 'I should just leave Loren here!'

Nico had replied through gritted teeth. 'Don't try to manipulate me. How would abandoning your daughter affect her mental health?'

Vivvi burst into tears. 'Everything's been left to me. Nobody worries about my mental health, living with an invalid and a flake.'

'No one worries about mine but I'd never use such insensitive language,' Nico had been stung into lashing back.

She'd flashed triumphantly, 'See! You do still care!'

Eventually, reluctantly, the two women had returned to Reading to let Nico think things over. Maybe it'd been a blessing Hannah hadn't shown up but he couldn't sleep for wanting to know she was OK. He wished like hell Maria hadn't washed his phone or that he had a handset to plug into the landline. The messaging app on his laptop wouldn't work without the mobile phone to sync to. He'd never had a use for Hannah's email address so didn't have it. He jumped on Facebook but there was nothing more recent from her than a picture of the snowman family in Lars's garden. He didn't bother trying Rob because it was late . . . and surely he'd find Hannah at Nan Heather's tomorrow.

Then Maria woke screaming, pointing to a shadow on the floor and yelling, 'Witch! Witch!'

Nico dredged up the strength to chuckle. 'It's not a witch. It's your shadow, sweetheart. The shelf behind you is giving it a pointed head, that's all.'

Josie complained sleepily, 'No one's afraid of their own shadow, Maria.'

Nico lay down to cuddle Maria back to sleep. Next thing he knew, it was Sunday morning and she was shaking him awake by his nose.

Whether it was sleeping late or tension from the evening before, the girls greeted the day in difficult moods.

'Has Mum gone? Is she back at Grandma's? Are we still going to be with Hannah for Christmas?' Josie demanded, her small face pinched.

He tried to distract her. 'Shall we go for a walk through the village to count Christmas trees after breakfast?'

But she refused to be distracted. 'Is Mum taking Maria back? I don't want her to.' She threw herself at him and clung, sobbing. Maria screwed up her face and joined in, seeking comfort. 'Mydad! Mydad!' It was impossible to do anything but gather them up and say soothing things – not that he had a huge stock of those.

Loren was entitled to take Maria back. The child's welfare was paramount – Gloria Russell, the case worker, had told him that – but what was best for Maria was not clear-cut. Loren could probably do an OK job if she remained with her parents but if she took Maria back to Islington alone Nico would never have a quiet minute, unless he took Josie back to Islington too, ready to step in, even though he assumed social services were watching the situation too.

He could see *exactly* why Loren had come up with her plan. Forming the four of them into a family unit would give her someone to lean on, Maria a reliable parent and

Josie both her parents in one place. It would change all their lives.

After a beautiful frosty day yesterday, rain now beat at the windows. Hoping it would ease, he put up their Christmas tree, tested the lights then let the girls loose on the decorations, all of which were unbreakable. Usually he would have been entranced by their joy, watching Maria pull faces at her own fish-like reflection in the curve of a bauble and be charmed by Josie combing the hair of the tree-top angel. The magic of Christmas touched him via the children but it didn't make him forget that Hannah still didn't come.

Mid-morning, regardless of the downpour, he got the girls into coats and boots and set out for Nan Heather's, his heart trotting uncomfortably as they neared the red-brick cottage with its cute dormers. His heart fell when he noticed the lights were out on the small Christmas tree at the window. The car Hannah had been using wasn't outside and, when he knocked on the door, nobody answered.

'Urgh, this weather's yuck,' moaned Josie, while Maria looked doleful under her dripping hood.

'Yeah. Let's go home.' Nico felt as miserable as the weather. Then inspiration struck. 'No! Let's jump in the car and go out for lunch.' There was a tea room at Carlysle Courtyard and maybe Hannah was working there again today.

'Yay!' shouted the girls.

They cheered again to see the balloons and lights and he had to put Maria on his shoulders to keep track of her. At Santa's grotto he asked an elf if she'd seen Hannah. Santa looked up from his sack of presents to observe, 'She put together a cracking opening for us yesterday but I haven't seen her today.'

They queued for sandwiches at Posh Nosh but the dark-haired woman behind the counter shook her head when he asked after Hannah. 'Don't think we're expecting her.' Nico decided he wasn't going to wait a week for his phone to dry out. Where the hell was Hannah? And how was his dad? They drove to Bettsbrough and the kids bickered over colouring things at a play table in a phone shop while he sorted himself out with a new model – at huge cost; he'd have to check out his insurance policy – then returned to Honeybun to wait for it to activate while the girls snuggled up with him to watch Disney.

The phone came to life on his original number and he rang Carina first. 'Dad's taking things easily and drowsing in front of the TV,' she reported, which left him free to ring Hannah. He knew with deep, gut-clenching certainty that the Loren nightmare wouldn't seem so bad if he could talk it over with her, even see her smile and feel her arms around him. It wasn't like him to be the one in need of a cheerleader but her acerbic good sense would banish the spectres that danced around him.

There were a few messages from her from yesterday and also some missed calls, but nothing since. He called her and got voicemail. He left: 'Hannah, are you OK? Can you get back to me?' He texted, too, in case she was somewhere she couldn't take a call. After an hour he called again. And again.

No response.

Late in the afternoon, though it was still raining, he got the girls back into their outdoor things and they splashed through the puddles to Nan Heather's. His heart lifted to see the windows lit from within and the jolly mixture of coloured lights on the tree. Impatiently, he rapped at the kitchen door.

After a short wait, Nan answered, holding her arm awkwardly in its cast. 'Wondered if I'd see you,' she said, her slippers squeaking on the quarry tiled floor. 'I'm at sixes and sevens because I've only just come back but my daughter's brought me a lovely basket of French goodies from her travels. Would you like to help me unpack them, girls?'

'Yes, please!' cried Josie. 'Where's Hannah?' She looked around expectantly.

'Not here, I'm afraid.' Nan shot a sidelong glance at Nico and his senses went on alert.

Something was wrong. His heart heaved. 'Is she OK?' he asked quickly.

'Far as I know, duck.' Nan led the children to the adjacent dining room and pointed at a basket on the floor, circular with an enormous hoop handle, decorated profusely with red, white and blue pompoms. 'Pretty, isn't it? But I can't undo the cellophane.'

Nico recognised unpacking it as a job invented to keep kids busy but Josie happily unhooked the cellophane, trying to preserve the silver ribbon and began lifting the packets of biscuits and jars of preserves and passing them to her tiny sister to 'carefully, carefully, *carefully*, Maria!' stand them on a tray Nan brought in.

Nan slid the arm without the cast through Nico's and kept him in the doorway to watch the girls. 'She didn't say "don't tell Nico",' she said in her hoarse voice. 'I think you ought to know what your ex-mother-in-law's done. She's a piece of work, by the sounds of it.'

His head whipped round. 'What? Yes, she is.' Every muscle tensed.

The wizened skin around Nan's lips quivered. 'She's got our Hannah thinking she's a tart who's been leading you astray.' She blotted her eyes with her sleeve. 'She called her your "entertainment".'

Nico swore viciously – in Swedish, so he didn't have to hold back.

Nan's voice creaked more than usual. 'She's gone away!'

'Where?' he demanded.

Nan's lip quivered. 'She wouldn't say.'

On Monday, Nico spent a lot of time thinking. He rang Maria's case worker, Gloria, who said she was in the area and would like to call in and see how the girls had enjoyed Sweden. The girls were happy to tell her all about it – Josie in entire sentences and Maria in exclamations. 'Snowman! Wolf!' Then Nico took Gloria in the kitchen while the girls watched TV in the tiny sitting room and he told her quietly about Loren's pleas. It was good to open up to someone unbiased yet experienced. Not as good as a heart-to-heart with Hannah, but useful.

She talked through the situation and said, 'I'll offer what support I can to promote the best outcome for everybody concerned.'

On Tuesday morning, Loren and Vikki returned to Honeybun.

Loren's coat looked too big as they trudged up the drive. Vivvi was firing words at her, forehead corrugated by a frown.

Nico had learned from the last unannounced visit and, as the girls were watching *Frozen II* in the sitting room, he said to them, 'I'm going to shut this door so if I make a noise in the kitchen it won't spoil the movie.'

''K,' Josie murmured, evidently on a level of entrancement way beyond removing her gaze from the screen on

345

which Anna and snowman Olaf danced along a railway track while Anna sang about things never changing.

He closed the door before letting his visitors in. 'I was going to call you,' he said. 'I've given it a lot of thought and I agree that something has to change.'

A wide smile of satisfaction slid over Vivvi's face but Loren's expression barely altered. She looked dull and ill and her hair was stringy. 'What's that mean?' she asked.

He gazed at the woman he used to love, the woman he shared a child with. 'A few days ago somebody told me something that affected me on a fundamental level. I had no inkling at the time, but it's the key to the future.' He took her hand. 'When you're in a plane crash you have to get your own oxygen flowing before you can help others.'

Chapter Twenty-Five

Hannah put her phone on Do Not Disturb, ignored the little red circles that denoted calls and messages racking up, switched off notifications and refused to let herself turn tail for cosy old Middledip.

Instead, all Sunday she drove slowly, numbly, south through England until it was dark and she found herself near the coast of Kent, spent and needing to stop. Wanting people nearby, not to mention loos and showers, she accessed the internet and found a site a few miles away open over Christmas. They kindly squeezed in her small camper by moving flower tubs aside. As it wasn't a designated pitch there was no electrical hook-up and Hannah, Jeremy's warnings ringing in her ears, was frightened of flattening the battery. It wasn't the one that fired the engine but she was terrified of being left without light. Wearily, she made up the bed and switched on the gas for the heating and the tiny hob.

Red, green and blue lights made the campground twinkle like a grotto and campers wore beaming smiles along with their gumboots and coats as they strode to the shower block but all Hannah saw was icy puddles between iron-hard wheel ruts and Jack Frost breathing on her windows. Morning in The Bus was like waking up inside an ice cube, nothing like gazing out on magical snowy Stockholm from the sanctuary of a warm hotel.

It might have been different if she'd shared the space with Nico. The cramped quarters could have been intimate and even the dread of having to hurry across the dark campground for a wee in the night laughed off.

How was he doing? And Josie and Maria? Maybe he was moving back to London so the Pettersson Family Unit Mark II could spend Christmas together. Or – her heart squeezed so hard she gasped – had Loren moved into the warmth of sweet little Honeybun Cottage?

Monday and Tuesday dragged. She walked to a local pub and drank two large glasses of wine but they didn't make her feel better. It was hard to concentrate on reading or watching something on her phone. She hadn't switched off banking transaction notifications and so saw the international transfer finally arriving from Albin but felt none of the triumph she'd anticipated. Thousands in the bank but emptiness in her heart.

On Wednesday she toyed with checking messages but wasn't sure she could bear to face any Nico might have left. She posted a daily *don't worry, I'm fine* on the family WhatsApp and felt guilty that her hiding out in The Bus was worrying them all. But the thought of going home and perhaps seeing Nico if he hadn't left the village flattened her. She and The Bus *could* spend Christmas together. It was just another day. And there would be people here on the site. They came every year and had a riotous time, someone in the shower block had told her.

Thursday was Christmas Eve. Fellow campers wished her 'Merry Christmas!' every time she ventured outside.

Trying to outdistance her misery, Hannah got The Bus ready to roll and paid her fees then drove towards Folkestone with a vague idea of crossing to France. But the mere idea of trying to get on a ferry or a Eurotunnel train, let alone locating a French camping ground open for the festive season, made her stop short on an isolated clifftop where she could switch off the chattering engine and watch the grey, corrugated sea. Here, it was possible to ignore Christmas. Not a single gaily decorated tree or glowing white star reminded her that there would be jolly parties in Middledip, that Carola would be leading sing-songs in The Three Fishes, Mo and Jeremy would have friends round with Nan joining in, wrinkles lifting as she laughed.

But she didn't need the sound of party poppers to remind her that her family would be missing her. Dark clouds flew like ragged flags above white horses racing on the waves. Seagulls soared and swooped like fighting kites. Grass and gorse topped chalk cliffs curving in either direction. She could not see a single other human being.

Stiffly, she pulled on her outdoor things and got out. The wind met her with an unfriendly shove and tried to snatch her hat before slamming the camper door with a bang that would have made Jeremy faint. Hardly caring whether the gale spat her over the cliff into the booming sea Hannah coiled her hair under her hat and staggered along a path frozen to iron, almost enjoying the fight.

A smiling woman appeared suddenly beside her, well kitted out in hiking gear. 'Blowy, isn't it? Are you one of the Turkey and Tinsel crowd?'

Not having been aware of anyone coming from behind, Hannah jumped. 'Turkey and Tinsel?'

The woman fell in step, pulling up her hood. 'I thought you might be at the Fernleigh Hotel along the cliff. Their Christmas breaks are called Turkey and Tinsel. If you're one of the solo folk we can walk back together.'

'Oh. I'm not, sorry.' Hannah tried not to appear terse, to adjust from solitude to company. 'Is Turkey and Tinsel fun?'

The woman laughed. 'Well. Needs must. A lot of people on their own. The hotel staff make a big effort. This is my third year, since my husband and I split up.'

Not everyone had people with whom to share Christmas but Hannah wasn't sure how you reacted to it. Sympathy? Patronising. Questions? Rude. 'Have a wonderful time,' she said, eventually.

The woman's smile wavered. 'It'll be OK. Merry Christmas! Must get on. Don't want to be late for lunch.'

'Merry Christmas,' Hannah echoed, as the woman hurried off.

She watched her grow smaller and smaller until she disappeared around the curve of the path, her words to her parents echoing in her head: '. . . you'll have Rob and Leesa and Nan. Everyone at The Three Fishes and The Angel, everyone you've known your whole life long. They're here for you.'

Jeremy's response rang loud in her imagination: 'And for you, Hannah. Don't forget that. And for you.' Years of family Christmases flew at her. Mince pies, Christmas lunch, crackers, silly hats, wine that made Nan sleepy, carefully selected gifts. Mum cooking, Dad carving, Rob supplying drinks. Villagers dropping in. There would be turkey and tinsel in Middledip too – but a hell of a lot more. Warmth. Laughter. Love. Caring. Her people. Her place.

It was too much to give up to avoid Nico and the painful truth.

She about-faced. Instead of fighting her, now the wind supported her and made retracing her steps easy. When she reached the right spot, she turned onto the scrubby grass and saw the pea-soup green bulk of The Bus.

Just waiting.

Hannah and The Bus rumbled into Middledip at eight that evening and parked outside her parents' house where fairy lights glowed all around the garden like a swarm of fireflies. All the windows were illuminated. Her parents were at home.

Everything about Hannah ached, from her heart, which seemed to know it might be near Nico, to her bum, on which she'd sat in endless strings of traffic as everyone headed home for Christmas. Her stomach rumbled as if it scented home cooking, then the door opened and Mo was there in fluffy slippers and an apron depicting lugubrious reindeer. Hannah clambered stiffly from The Bus.

'We'd just about given you up.' The tremor in Mo's voice didn't come from the arctic wind blasting up the garden path.

Eyes burning, Hannah dived into her mother's arms to be hugged and hugged like nothing else mattered. Mo murmured, 'Let's get you upstairs. We've got the neighbours in.'

Hannah stumbled into the hall as Jeremy emerged from the sitting room, shutting the door on laughter and conversation, and hugged her every bit as tightly as Mo had. 'I'll bring your stuff in. You go with your mum.'

She was home.

Upstairs, Mo didn't ask a single question. 'We've got a

buffet going but if you don't want to see anyone ping me a text and I'll bring you a plate up.'

Hannah sniffed. 'Nico's not downstairs, is he?'

Mo looked surprised. 'No, pet.'

Jeremy puffed up with Hannah's case and a glass of red wine. 'Here you are, my darling.'

Hannah was wordlessly, pathetically grateful. She even, after an hour to shower and dry her windswept hair, went down and joined the neighbours she'd known for years in scoffing pork pies and mini quiches and another glass of wine. After days of self-imposed exile it was bliss to hold hands with Nan, who had two weeks till her cast came off, and bathe in the light of a Christmas tree that, amongst elegant shop-bought baubles, sported decorations she'd made at school.

If she left the chat to others, nobody minded.

Chapter Twenty-Six

Christmas morning. Hannah could hear Mo and Jeremy chatting cheerfully downstairs against the background of 'Silent Night' on the radio. The choir's exquisite voices reminded her of Lucia in Älgäng church but she refused to let tears fill her eyes. In her childhood room she may be but she was an adult. Her wobble was over. Christmas was a good time for new beginnings.

Her phone lay in her hand like a ticking time bomb. Should she read her messages? There would probably be words from Nico like 'explain' and 'sorry' and 'goodbye'.

Not today, she decided. Today her smile was going to be as bright as Christmas lights. She refused to spoil anybody's day.

Dumping her phone on the dressing table she showered, dressed in a turquoise top and black trousers that would survive the odd splash of gravy and whisked her hair up into a glittery slide. She ran downstairs. 'Merry Christmas!' she cried, giving each of her parents a hug.

'Merry Christmas!' Their arms were strong and warm and they beamed with love and joy.

Mo said, 'Just go get Nan, will you, dear? She can't walk with her parcels and her arm. She's coming for breakfast so we can do presents after.'

'No problem,' Hannah breezed. She checked the parcels she'd left beneath their tree last weekend, flinching to see Mo had apparently not found time to pass on those for Nico and the girls.

She didn't glance in the direction of Little Lane as she bowled her mum's car down to Rotten Row but bounced into Nan's house calling, 'Merry Christmas!'

'Merry Christmas, duck.' Nan was dressed in her posh frock and just needed to be zipped up, then they drove straight back to her parents' house, Hannah lugging in Nan's black bin liner of gifts.

The morning passed in a welter of preparing food, eating food and exchanging gifts to the accompaniment of a carol concert on TV. Rob and Leesa arrived with their gifts wrapped in red and gold, looking happy and relaxed. Hannah received jumpers and boots, make-up and perfume, vouchers and wine. Mo tripped as she carried a box of chocolates as 'breakfast afters' and showered everyone with Milk Tray, making them all howl with laughter.

It was a wonderful, jolly, family Christmas Day, peeling sprouts or wrapping pigs in their blankets, laughing and chattering. Jeremy and Rob set the dining table, their voices the only male ones as Brett was with his daughters and not seeing Nan till evening. Leesa, who was artistic, folded dark green paper napkins into Christmas trees. 'You look as if you've made loads,' Hannah commented, unfastening the cellophane on the box of crackers.

Leesa cocked an eyebrow. Marriage seemed to have enhanced her sweet prettiness. 'Mo said nine.'

'She probably looked at her notes upside down,' Hannah giggled. 'You know how she writes herself a schedule of what to do and when to do it. I only count six people.'

The only tense moment was when Hannah came upon her parents in the kitchen and heard her dad hiss, 'Mo, I think we ought to tell Hannah about Nico.'

'No, don't!' Hannah said quickly, before Mo could reply. 'It's no accident that I haven't asked about him. Let's not spoil today. Please.'

Mo looked at Jeremy smugly through a cloud of steam as she drained the parboiled potatoes ready to throw them in the oil to roast. 'See.'

Jeremy rolled his eyes. 'She doesn't know—'

Mo gave her husband a hug. 'She *said* she doesn't want to be told. Let's respect her wishes.'

Wishes, Hannah thought with a pang, remembering the half-formed wish she'd made in the Gold Room. If she'd got her wish, today would have been spent with Nico, Josie and Maria, glorying in the bonds they'd formed in snowy Sweden – or bonds she'd thought they'd formed. The snowman family in Lars's back garden was all that was left of that, unless a thaw had already turned it to puddles.

Jeremy hesitated, then seemed to resign himself. 'Whatever you want, love.'

It was an hour later and Hannah was feeling overheated, stirring gravy with one hand and bread sauce with the other, when she heard someone go to the front door and open it. Rob's voice said, 'Oh! Hello!'

Then Hannah froze as a familiar, high, excited voice called, 'Merry Christmas!' and a shriller, younger one echoed, 'Many Nissmass!'

The third voice was deep and male. 'Merry Christmas, Rob. Here's some wine – stop jumping about, Josie – and chocolate mints. Maria, wipe your feet, please.'

Hannah's knees turned to butter. 'Whoops,' said Mo, taking the gravy pan off the heat. 'Let's try not to boil it over.'

Slowly, Hannah turned accusing eyes on her mother, whose round face was redder than her Christmas jumper. Mo took the bread sauce off Hannah as well, her eyes huge and apprehensive. 'We invited them for Christmas lunch. There's a good reason and you did say—'

Hannah didn't hear the rest of the sentence. Panic boiled the blood in her ears. The room receded and rushed back. Nine Christmas-tree napkins had been the correct number. Nico was here and she'd have to face him. Every drop of comfort she'd been soaking up from Christmas alone with her lovely family evaporated. 'MUM! How *could* you—?' she began.

'HANNAH!' Josie flew down the short hall. 'Hannah, where've you been? I thought we were going to make decorations and you'd help me wrap our present for Dad. Never mind,' she ended consolingly, winding her arms around Hannah's waist and gazing up at her with starry eyes. 'We're having Christmas dinner together.'

Then Maria's short legs caught up and she hurled herself on Hannah too, demanding, 'Up, 'Annah, up!' and holding out her arms.

Josie, with big-sister pragmatism, scooped Maria up to join the cuddle. Hannah's eyes burned as she clutched the children to her. She hadn't let herself think about how much she'd missed them in the past few days. They – and Nico – were not hers to love.

Then awareness danced across her skin and he was in

the room, his eyes blue and watchful. '*God Jul*,' he said softly.

'*God Jul*.' She couldn't read his expression because he was a tear-drenched blur. She put Maria down and freed herself from Josie. 'Why don't you run and see Nan Heather in the sitting room? I'm helping my mum with the meal,' she suggested brightly.

Mo began, 'I'm sure—'

'I'm helping in here,' Hannah muttered fiercely, turning her back on Nico. After a few moments, she heard his voice in the next room, telling Rob he'd fetch Maria's high chair from the car.

It took her several minutes of straining veg and slapping it into serving dishes before she could trust herself to look at Mo, who'd been working in uncharacteristic silence. Awash with every emotion from misery to horror to anger that seeing Nico had threatened to reduce her to tears, she was tempted to strop out like a teenager. 'You deliberately misinterpreted my wishes when I said I didn't want to know anything about Nico,' she muttered.

Then she saw the tears trembling on her mother's lashes. 'Sorry,' Mo whispered. 'I came over romantic when I invited him. He was so pleased. I thought he might rush in and sweep you off your feet. It seemed like a good reason. But he didn't. Oh, the look on your face! Hannah, lovey, I'm sorry.'

Hannah's heart melted. 'Do you know where Loren is?' Now she'd been flung into Nico's presence she might as well face the worst.

Mo shook her head, wiping her eyes on her apron. 'He said you deserved to hear about her directly from him.'

'Right.' Hannah's heavy heart felt as if it was pressing on her lungs. 'That's what I've been trying to avoid. But things can't be avoided, can they? Let's eat Christmas dinner while the food's hot and delicious. I'll pin on my happy face and quietly make an arrangement to talk to Nico later.'

Mo heaved a deep sigh. 'OK.' Then she sailed into the dining room with a cheery, 'We're about to bring out the food. Rob, will you be able to help Nan cutting hers up? Jeremy, wine needs putting on the table, dear.'

'Oh, the napkins are Christmas trees!' Josie cried. 'Come on, Maria. I'll help you in your high chair because we're going to have a lovely lunch.'

'Lunch!' yodelled Maria, lifting her foot into Josie's cupped hands to be thrown up into her high chair as if she were mounting a horse.

'That's their latest trick,' Nico told Hannah drily.

'Clever girls!' Hannah ferried plates and dishes from the kitchen. As promised, she kept her smile pinned in place, though Rob raised his eyebrows at her in a silent question as to what the hell was going on. Hannah just smiled through Josie's account of FaceTiming Tilly and Emelie this morning. She ate, though the food might as well have been cardboard. She pulled a cracker with Josie and wore a cerise paper hat that clashed with her top. She laughed at jokes and thanked Mo for the wonderful meal.

'*Tack för maten*,' Josie added, looking enormously pleased to be able to thank Mo for the food in Swedish. Then she screwed up her face and said to Nico, 'Should me and Maria call Hannah's mum Mormor?'

Hannah couldn't look at Nico but every square inch of her skin burned scarlet. Josie surely hadn't understood that 'Mormor' literally meant 'mother's mother'. She must think it was a courtesy title like 'Nan Heather'.

358

Nico's voice was husky. 'I think we should be a little quieter before our food goes cold.'

Josie subsided and Jeremy covered the moment by lifting his glass and crying, 'Let's drink to Rob and Leesa's first married Christmas!'

Hannah lifted her glass to her brother and his wife but her mind whirled. How long would Nico stay after lunch? Could they get the explanations quickly over with? Or maybe she could slip round later, when the girls had gone to bed . . . if Nico didn't have other plans with Loren. Her heart really, truly hurt.

The first course cleared, Jeremy made brandy sauce for the Christmas pudding because he had a lovely touch with it.

'I'm full.' Nan beamed. 'I've got room for Mo's pudding though. I think she began making it in July.' She took Hannah's hand. 'I missed you while you were away.'

Warmth crept through Hannah. 'I missed you, too. I could stay with you till you get your cast off instead of here, if you want,' she offered.

Nan regarded her gravely through her thick glasses. 'Then what?'

Hannah felt as if everyone at the table had ceased their conversation to listen to her answer. She pulled an exaggeratedly thoughtful face as she tried to summon up some of her old dreams. 'Start a new business, probably. I've learned a lot between Creative Lanes, Hannah Anna Butik and Carlysle Courtyard and the new business will be all my own.'

Josie frowned. 'But not back in Sweden? Because then we'd only see you twice a year, when we visited.'

A ball of tears lodged itself in Hannah's throat. 'Maybe not in Sweden,' she managed.

Then in came her parents, Mo bearing the shiny mahogany dome of Christmas pudding and Jeremy two jugs of brandy sauce. Mo explained the pudding rules for those who were unfamiliar with them. 'There's a lucky silver sixpence somewhere in the pudding. Whoever finds it makes a wish . . . but then gives me the sixpence back because it's the old money we used to have when I was tiny so I reuse it each year.' Mo turned to Nico. 'Check the kids' portions before they eat so they don't choke on it.'

Nico grinned as he agreed. His grey shirt made his eyes look particularly blue but he'd been quieter than usual. Hannah was so achingly aware of him that she'd noticed.

Mo set the pudding down and cut it into steaming portions as speculation began about who would get the lucky sixpence.

Hannah joined in mechanically. Maybe if she got the coin she could wish for Christmas to be over and, *shazam*, it would be gone.

But, presently, it was Nico's voice that dragged Hannah back to reality. 'I have the sixpence.'

'Awwww,' Josie sighed, apparently disappointed even though Nico had checked her portion for sixpences already. 'Make a wish, Dad.'

Nico's glance flickered Hannah's way. 'My wish is to go for a walk with Hannah.'

Sudden silence. Hannah's face flamed. What?

Josie frowned reprovingly. 'Dad, that's not how it works. You wish quietly and don't tell anyone or it won't come true.'

'I misunderstood,' Nico apologised gravely.

Mo glanced from Nico to Hannah then whispered

conspiratorially to Josie. 'If Dad didn't understand properly then I think we should let him off, don't you? Would you and Maria stay here and help me? Dad and Hannah can stretch their legs while there's still daylight. Then . . .' she paused thrillingly '. . . as soon as they come back we can have presents.'

Josie cried, 'Yay!' and Maria chirped, 'P'esents for me, too?'

Face stiff from so much fake smiling, Hannah said, 'OK. We won't be long,' and marched off for her outdoor things. Getting the conversation with Nico over with would at least get her out of the washing up. Nico fetched his coat and soon they were stepping out into the eerily quiet Christmas Day village with cheery trees shedding their light from almost every window.

'I'm sure if the man in the moon came down and saw everyone indoors and coloured lights everywhere he'd wonder what the humans were up to,' Hannah said as they turned left out of the house down Main Road, not wanting to get into anything heavy while in sight of her parents' house.

The moment they'd passed the pub, which looked as if it had been caught in a fishing net made entirely of fairy lights, she cut to the chase. 'You're not spending Christmas Day with Loren.'

'I'm taking the girls to Reading to see their mother and grandparents tomorrow,' he answered neutrally.

Hannah's throat began to ache. So he wasn't spending today with Loren but it sounded as if he was leaving tomorrow.

After a couple of minutes they turned into Little Lane and Hannah hesitated. As if he'd been expecting it, Nico caught her hand and towed her in through the gate to

Honeybun Cottage. With quick movements he thrust open the door and ushered her inside, shrugging off his coat and hanging it up.

When she just stood there, thinking unhappily that he must be expecting her to burst into tears to have given her such privacy, he unzipped her coat and slid it down her arms as if she were Maria, and hung that up too.

She looked at him.

His face was set in hard, uncompromising lines. 'Nan Heather gave me some idea of what my dear ex-mother-in-law saw fit to tell you,' he said grimly. 'Was that why you went off on your own?'

She swallowed, rubbing her arms, although the kitchen was warm and cosy. 'I wanted to make it easy for you and the girls,' she said.

'Bullshit,' he snapped. He thrust his fingers through his hair. 'You disappeared and ignored every call and text.'

'My phone's on Do Not Disturb,' Hannah admitted. 'I thought I'd leave my messages until after the family Christmas.'

Nico took her hand and towed her to the sofa in the sitting room, pulling her down and fixing her with a level gaze. 'Hannah,' he said with quiet emphasis. 'Vivvi had no right to say what she did. But you had no right to refuse me a hearing. Nor, when we arrived at your parents' house today, look as if you'd like to cut my heart out and spit on it.'

Ruffled, Hannah interrupted. 'But I understand your responsibilities. I don't blame you for getting back with Loren—'

'So you get to listen now.' He talked over her, as if his

362

patience hung by a thread. When she didn't try to interrupt again, he uncoiled. 'So Vivvi spun you an emotional story about Loren asking me to get together again for the sake of the girls?'

Miserably, she nodded. 'And I can see why you'd—'

He placed his finger to her lips. 'Well, I said no.'

Chapter Twenty-Seven

Nico saw astonishment make an O of Hannah's lovely mouth.

He angled himself to face her. 'Sorry if I'm snappy but I've had several long, anxious days. The relief of receiving a text from Rob last night to say you were back dissolved my bones. It's like when one of the kids runs across the road without looking. Once you know they're safe, relief turns to anger.' The frank amazement in her eyes didn't do anything to dampen his negative emotions. It had been a hideous time knowing Hannah had unquestioningly given up on him.

He strove for his usual calm. 'I've been so scared, Hannah.' Her expression softened, even if it was still wary. He continued, 'Loren and Vivvi completely blindsided me by suggesting we should get back together. It sounded so plausible. I felt trapped. Horrified. Maria clung to me. It was like being buried in emotions and responsibilities and I was scrambling round for rational arguments. Rational thought, even.'

Hannah sat still and pale. He remembered how beautiful

she'd looked when the snappy cold of Sweden had painted roses in her cheeks. She said, 'You couldn't call or text? Give me a clue?'

His smile flickered briefly. 'Maria washed my phone. It died without a fight.'

Her mouth made a smaller O this time. He wanted to lean forward and kiss it. But it was too soon. She'd built up a wall of doubt and hurt and he didn't want to put rejection between them too. 'I bought a new phone on Sunday and I've been trying to make contact ever since. Nan told me about your . . . absence.' He'd been going to say 'crazy trip' but that would put her on the defensive.

'On Saturday night I asked Loren and Vivvi for time. I said it was so I could think but actually I just had to get them the hell out while I got my ducks in a row. I wanted to talk to you about my intentions.' A dart of pain hit his chest. 'But you removed that possibility. I was able to talk my plan through with my parents and Maria's social worker but it was you I wanted.'

She moistened her lips. 'What plan?'

Her hand lay on the sofa between them and he picked it up. Instead of replying, he sighed. 'Talking to an addict's difficult. They try and draw you into their world view. They're plausible and persuasive. They get you questioning things you never ought to. Loren found rehab too hard and saw me looking after her as easy. She thought I'd enable her to avoid the professional help she needs. It's tough to make someone like her accountable when she acts as if I've made her promises I'm trying to go back on.' He remembered the agonised conversation that had taken place in the kitchen while the girls sat in the sitting room, mercifully entranced by *Frozen II*.

Hannah's eyes were huge with remembered pain. 'Her mother told me you'd agreed that you all belonged together.' Her voice shook.

He kissed her hand, furious with Vivvi all over again. 'Loren and Vivvi share some traits, I guess. Vivvi's under stress and her instinct was to try and unload it. It's a human frailty. But I agreed to nothing. I told Loren I wouldn't be emotionally blackmailed into taking her over like another dependant.' He was calming now at having Hannah near him again and listening. 'I had to keep repeating I didn't cause the situation and it wasn't up to me to fix it. Refusing to be manipulated by an addict isn't always easy but sometimes it's for the best.'

'Then she's not going to accept your decision easily.' Worry rang in her voice, though she shifted closer.

He slid an arm around her, his heart quivering at feeling her against him. 'I'm afraid that's a possibility. It's a bit like me and bulimia. By purging, I could eat what I wanted and not get fat. Loren thinks that sharing my life would mean she could do what she wanted and I'd see she was OK.' He withdrew enough to look into her face. 'I told her what you said about being in a troubled aircraft and having to get your own oxygen flowing before you could help others. And I told them, "I can help others. But Hannah's my oxygen. I can't do it without her."'

A tear eased from her eye. 'But where does that leave Maria?'

His heart flipped. 'That's the plan I wanted to talk over. I've offered to take Maria permanently. Initially, it'll be considered long-term foster care. After a year I may be able to make it more official and assume parental responsibility. It means Josie and Maria won't be separated. They'll be able to see their mum but live with me.'

A frown puckered her forehead. 'So in the first year Loren could change her mind?'

'Yes,' he admitted baldly.

'In which case, what?' Her aqua eyes were like sea glass.

'A huge amount of hassle and upset, I suspect.' Despite his earlier resolve, he dipped down and pressed a small kiss to her mouth. It felt warm. Tender. Right. 'When I took Josie at the end of the marriage it wasn't spite and it wasn't financial. It was because Loren finds it hard to be a good parent. Maybe I put too much down to post-natal depression after Josie was born but she relied on alcohol and, who knows? She may have been misusing other stuff even then. The woman I divorced was not the woman I married. She's lost the ability to put others first and will continue to abuse the support of others till she gets proper help. That might include another attempt to use Maria as a weapon.'

He paused to ease Hannah onto his lap so he could bury his face in her neck and breathe her in. 'You're probably thinking there might be a rocky road ahead. You're right. You're probably thinking I'm offering you a situation where I've already got two people to put ahead of you, and that's a crap bargain. I'll be unhappy if you say no but being unhappy is acceptable. It's being unhappy and not trying to find a way out that's not.'

Hannah sat unresponsive in his embrace. He leaned his forehead on her shoulder. 'Sorry,' he said miserably.

She stirred, tilting his face up so she could look at him. 'Nico,' she said slowly. 'You haven't said what you're offering.' But there was a glimmer of light in her eyes that hadn't been there before. It looked like something good, like hope. Or love.

'Oh!' He laughed shakily. 'Me. My heart. My two kids.

My crazy, shit-filled life. Everything I have. Everything I want. Every Christmas until I die. You're my oxygen and I love you. When you shut me out . . .' He closed his eyes for an instant and shuddered, dreading that she might shut him out again, but permanently. He wouldn't blame her but it would be hell.

Then a tiny kiss landed on his cheek. Another on his temple. His eyes sprang open, relief flooding through him. He'd thought he might never feel her mouth on him again.

'I love you, too. I'm sorry I didn't stick around to hear your side of the story.' Tears slid down her cheeks even while she smiled. 'Because I love your two kids and your crazy, shit-filled life.'

'Are you quite sure about the kids?' he said resignedly, spotting something over her shoulder. 'Because Josie's peeping in the window.'

Hannah broke away, laughing, crying, wiping her eyes. 'I guess we shouldn't have let Mum promise her she could have presents when we got back.'

'They're here, Rob!' Josie hollered. 'But they're cuddling again.' She made it sound as if she'd caught them shoplifting.

Nico caught the sound of Leesa's laugh and Rob saying, 'Josie! You should know better than to run off. We're supposed to be going to Nan's for her blood pressure pills, not taking a diversion to spy on people.'

'I wanted to know where Dad was,' Josie complained, but her voice began to recede.

'I must teach my daughter that glass isn't soundproof.' Nico slid his hand off Hannah's behind, 'and remind myself that glass is transparent.' He groaned, feeling the need to be honest even though his arms had fastened around her

368

as if they'd never let her go. 'An adult relationship conducted with children around is tricky. You get ready for a date night and they throw up over you. You're cuddling and they join in. You're in the middle of the hottest sex of your life and they wake up with a screaming nightmare.'

Hannah's eyes had grown enormous as she digested this litany. Then she smoothed her hair and twitched her top straight with an air of determination. 'I have a lot to learn then, don't I?'

When they strolled back through the sleepy Christmas village, Hannah felt as if she were floating at least two inches above a pavement beginning to twinkle with frost. Nico's hand was hot around hers and her nerves were jumping, her blood dancing in her veins.

She giggled. 'I feel like I've stepped through a magic portal to happiness yet my family are probably having an after-lunch nap.'

His eyes glowed into hers. 'I can say with certainty that no one in the household will be sleeping until the girls get their presents.'

They reached the door to the house she'd known all her life and Hannah opened it.

'They're here!' an eight-year-old squealed.

'Dey here!' squeaked her two-year-old echo.

The girls galumphed into the hall, Josie going into reverse to let them in and nearly flattening Maria. 'Dad! You've been ages and—' She paused and flushed, probably deciding not to remonstrate with him about the kissing in case Rob had been right and she shouldn't have been peeping. 'And everyone's dying to open their presents.'

'Everyone?' he queried mildly.

'P'esents, Mydad. P'esents, 'Annah,' Maria affirmed, jumping on the spot, wearing one pink slipper and one drunken sock.

Nico relented. 'OK. I'll get ours from our car boot and you can help give them out.'

'P'esents!' Maria squealed.

Hannah watched the girls run off as she took off her coat and boots. Voices drifted to her: Jeremy asking about whisky, Mo telling him she'd put it on a high shelf because there were children in the house. Nan saying she'd sooner have sherry. Her ordinary family's normal Christmas she'd depended on to cheer her up, rumbling gently on.

Joining them, she found Josie and Maria sitting on the carpet near the Christmas tree. 'Your mum said we'd get our presents if we waited nicely,' Josie said guilelessly.

'My mum's always right,' Hannah assured her, as Nico walked in, hair tousled as if the wind had run its hands through it.

Taking pity on the two excited girls, Hannah gave them her gifts: matching jumpers with unicorns on, books and DVDs about princesses. They grabbed and unwrapped with seamless efficiency, Josie yelling thanks, Maria yelling because Josie did. The rest of the family, used to absorbing whoever Mo invited at Christmas, even at what had to have been short notice, had managed small gifts – colouring things, stickers, puzzles and games for the girls, beer and shower gel for Nico.

Hannah's gift to him was an experience day he could build up out of various sporting activities from swinging through trees on ropes to hill biking. To facilitate it, she'd created a voucher for *One babysitting day from Hannah*.

'Wow,' he breathed, flicking through the brochure of

what looked to her to be brutal activities with glowing eyes.

'What? Without us?' Josie demanded indignantly.

Hannah hugged her. 'You, me and Maria will do something fun of our own.' Josie looked mollified and Hannah congratulated herself on developing her child management skills.

Then Nico pressed a small, rectangular parcel on her. '*God jul*,' he murmured. 'Something from Stockholm.'

'What is it?' demanded Josie, crawling closer to investigate.

The gift was wrapped in gold paper with a red ribbon rosette. A red box lay inside and when Hannah opened it she found a necklace with two hearts in amber, secured together by two tiny golden clasped hands. She looked at him with glowing eyes, seeing past the prettiness to a message of two hearts secured by two small children.

Josie, however, dismissed it with small-girl scorn. 'Soppy, Dad.' Then, brightening, 'But it definitely means Hannah's your girlfriend if you bought her hearts, so yay!'

Hannah's face heated to the tips of her ears. 'Apparently, I needn't make any announcement so long as Josie's around so – yay!' She looked at her parents, hoping they didn't mind.

Mo beamed. 'Your face made the announcement for you when you walked in, lovey. You look like one big happy.'

Her dad lifted his whisky glass to her in a toast and repeated, 'Yay!'

Nan did the same with her sherry glass and soon the whole family was showering Hannah with their laughter and approval.

Nico waded through the discarded Christmas wrapping

371

to scoop her up and settle her in his lap. He fastened the necklace behind her neck then opened his arms so Josie and Maria could scramble into the hug too. 'I have everything I could wish for.'

Josie nodded wisely. 'Good job it was you who got the Christmas pudding sixpence.'

It was nearly midnight.

In Nico's bedroom at Honeybun Cottage a bottle of champagne rested in a cooler. One of Hannah's gifts had been scented candles and their sinuously moving flames added a glow to the room and a sultry fragrance to the air. A chair had been wedged under the doorknob in case of intruding children.

Hannah lay in Nico's arms, boneless after the last hour of lovemaking. He traced the shape of her new amber necklace, which was all she wore.

She snuggled into his rangy body. 'This has been the best Christmas.'

He murmured an agreement, his breath hot on her skin. 'I was scared it was going to be the worst. But every Christmas from now on is going to be just as special. The anniversary of when you told me you loved me.'

She kissed the corner of his mouth. 'It's our love-iver-sary.'

'Tomorrow we get a taste of the future,' he said seriously, the planes of his face gilded by the candlelight. 'The girls are going to Loren at Vivvi and Redfern's house for Boxing Day. Josie and Maria might be worried I'm not coming back for them or want to stay longer than arranged. Loren might be having a bad day. Vivvi might boss everyone about. But it's also an opportunity. You and I can find somewhere open for lunch or walk by the canal. It's not the most exciting Boxing Day date but at least we'll spend time alone.' His voice became apologetic. 'I can't leave the girls two or three hours away in Reading and come flying back here to spend the day in bed, much as I'd love to.'

An idea hit Hannah with a tingle. 'We could borrow The Bus!'

He snorted a laugh. 'Seriously?' Then: 'Hell, yes, let's borrow The Bus. It's a mobile bedroom, for goodness' sake. The best Boxing Day date venue ever. We can take a picnic.'

He rolled onto his back, snuggling her half on top of him so her hair spread over them both and they fitted together all the way down. 'Hannah Anna Goodbody, we're going to be great together.'

And, as she watched him slide gently into sleep, she felt her ideas of going it alone fade away. Her old relationships had just been her trying to find the real thing and not a warning never to rely on a man. With *this* man, she'd never find 'together' a bad place to be.

Loved

Christmas Wishes?

Then why not try one of Sue's
other cosy Christmas stories
or sizzling summer reads?

The perfect way to escape
the every day.

This Christmas, the villagers
of Middledip are off on a
very Swiss adventure . . .

Escape to a winter wonderland
in this heartwarming romance from
the *Sunday Times* bestseller.

One Christmas can change everything . . .

Curl up with this feel-good festive romance, perfect for fans of Carole Matthews and Trisha Ashley.

It's time to
deck the halls . . .

'I love all of Sue Moorcroft's books!' *Katie Fforde*

The
Little Village
Christmas

Sue Moorcroft

Return to the little village of
Middledip with this *Sunday Times*
bestselling Christmas read.

For Ava Blissham,
it's going to be a
Christmas to remember . . .

'I love all of Sue Moorcroft's books!' Katie Fforde

The Christmas Promise

Sue Moorcroft

Countdown to Christmas as you step into
the wonderful world of Sue Moorcroft.

Sparks are flying on the island of Malta

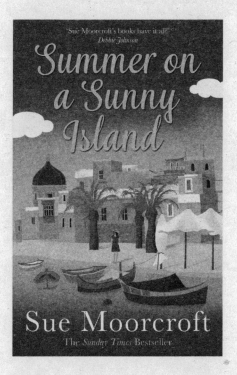

An uplifting summer read that will raise your spirits and warm your heart.

Come and spend summer by the sea!

Make this a summer to remember
with blue skies, beachside walks
and the man of your dreams...

What could be better than
a summer spent basking
in the French sunshine?

Grab your sun hat, a cool glass of wine,
and escape to France with this
gloriously escapist summer read!

In a sleepy village in Italy, Sophia is about to discover a host of family secrets . . .

Lose yourself in this uplifting
summer romance from the
Sunday Times bestseller.